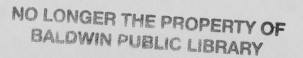

Also by José Saramago in English translation

Raised *from* *the* Ground

José Saramago

Translated from the Portuguese by Margaret Jull Costa

HOUGHTON MIFFLIN HARCOURT

BOSTON ◆ NEW YORK

2012

First U.S. edition

www.hmhbooks.com

First published with the title *Levantado do Chão* in 1980
by Editorial Caminho, SA, Lisbon

Library of Congress Cataloging-in-Publication Data
Saramago, José. [Levantado do chão. English] Raised from the ground /
José Saramago ; translated from the Portuguese by Margaret Jull Costa. — 1st U.S. ed.
p. cm.
"First published with the title Levantado do chão in 1980 by Editorial Caminho,
SA, Lisbon" — T.p. verso.
ISBN 978-0-15-101325-8 (hardback)
I. Title. PQ9281.A66L4813 2012
869.3'42 — dc23   2012017326

Book design by Melissa Lotfy

Printed in the United States of America
DOC 10 9 8 7 6 5 4 3 2 1

This publication was assisted by a grant from the Direcção-Geral do Livro
e das Bibliotecas / Portugal

To the memory of Germáno Vidigal
and José Adelino dos Santos,
both of whom were murdered

I ask the political economists and the moralists if they have ever calculated the number of individuals who must be condemned to misery, overwork, demoralization, degradation, rank ignorance, overwhelming misfortune and utter penury in order to produce one rich man.

— ALMEIDA GARRETT

Raised from the Ground

HERE, IT'S MOSTLY countryside, land. Whatever else may be lacking, land has never been in short supply, indeed its sheer abundance can only be explained by some tireless miracle, because the land clearly predates man, and despite its long, long existence, it has still not expired. That's probably because it's constantly changing: at certain times of the year, the land is green, at others, yellow or brown or black. And in certain places it is red, the color of clay or spilled blood. This, however, depends on what has been planted or what has not yet been planted, or what has sprung up unaided and died simply because it reached its natural end. This is not the case with wheat, which still has some life left in it when it is cut. Nor with the cork oak, which, despite its solemn air, is full of life and cries out when its skin is ripped from it.

There is no shortage of color in this landscape, but it isn't simply a matter of color. There are days as harsh as they are cold, and others when you can scarcely breathe for the heat: the world is never content, the day it is will be the day it dies. The world does not lack for smells either, not even here, which is, of course, part of the world and well provided with land. Were some insignificant creature to die in the undergrowth, it would smell of death and putrefaction. Not that anyone would notice if there were no wind, even if they were to pass close by. The bones would be either washed clean by the rain or baked dry by the sun, or not even that if the creature were very small, because the worms and the grave-digger beetles would have come and buried it.

This, relatively speaking, is a fair-sized piece of land, and while it begins as undulating hills and a little stream-water, because the water that falls from the skies is just as likely to be feast as fam-ine, farther on it flattens out as smooth as the palm of your hand, although many a hand, by life's decree, tends, with time, to close around the handle of a hoe, sickle or scythe. The land. And like the palm of a hand, it is crisscrossed by lines and paths, its royal or, later, national roads, or those owned by the gentlemen at the town hall, three such roads lie before us now, because three is a poeti-cal, magical, spiritual number, but all the other paths arise from re-peated comings and goings, from trails formed by bare or ill-shod feet walking over clods of earth or through undergrowth, stubble or wild flowers, between wall and wasteland. So much land. A man could spend his whole life wandering about here and never find himself, especially if he was born lost. And he won't mind dy-ing when his time comes. He is no rabbit or genet to lie and rot in the sun, but if hunger, cold or heat were to lay him low in some secluded spot, or one of those illnesses that don't even give you time to think, still less cry out for help, sooner or later he would be found.

Many have died of war and other plagues, both here and in other parts, and yet the people we see are still alive: some perceive this as an unfathomable mystery, but the real reasons lie in the land, in this vast estate, this latifundio, that rolls from high hills down to the plain below, as far as the eye can see. And if not this land, then some other piece of land, it really doesn't matter as long as we've sorted out what's mine and thine: everything was recorded in the census at the proper time, with boundaries to the north and

south and to the east and west, as if this were how it had been or-
dained since the world began, when everything was simply land,
with only a few large beasts and the occasional human being, all
of them frightened. It was around that time, and later too, that the
future shape of this present land was decided, and by very crooked
means indeed, a shape carved out by those who owned the largest and sharpest knives and according to size of knife and quality
of blade. For example, those of a king or a duke, or of a duke who
then became his royal highness, a bishop or the master of an order,
a legitimate son or the delicious fruit of bastardy or concubinage, a
stain washed clean and made honorable, or the godfather of a mistress's daughter, and then there's that other high officer of the court
with half a kingdom in his grasp, and sometimes it was more a case
of, this, dear friends, is my land, take it and populate it to serve
me and your offspring, and keep it safe from infidels and other
such embarrassments. A magnificent book-of-hours-cum-sacred-
accounts-ledger presented at both palace and monastery, prayed to
in earthly mansions or in watchtowers, each coin an Our Father,
ten coins a Hail Mary, one hundred a Hail Holy Queen, Mary is
King. Deep coffers, bottomless silos, granaries the size of ships,
vats and casks, coffers, my lady, and all measured in cubits, rods
and bushels, in quarts, pottles and tuns, each piece of land according to its use.

Thus flowed the rivers and the four seasons of the year, on
those one can rely, even when they vary. The vast patience of time
and the equally vast patience of money, which, with the exception
of man, is the most constant of all measurements, although, like
the seasons, it varies. We know, however, that men were bought
and sold. Each century had its money, each kingdom its man to
buy and sell for maravedis, or for gold and silver marks, reals, dou-
bloons, cruzados, sovereigns or florins from abroad. Fickle, various
metal, as airy as the bouquet of a flower or of wine: money rises,
that's why it has wings, not in order to fall. Money's rightful place

is in a kind of heaven, a lofty place where the saints change their names when they have to, but not the latifundio.

A mother with full breasts, fit for large, greedy mouths, a womb, the land shared out between the largest and the large, or, more likely, joining large with larger, through purchase or perhaps through some alliance, or through sly theft, pure crime, the legacy of my grandparents and my good father, God rest their souls. It took centuries to get this far, who can doubt that it will always remain the same?

But who are these other people, small and disparate, who came with the land, although their names do not appear in the deeds, dead souls perhaps, or are they still alive? God's wisdom, beloved children, is infinite: there is the land and those who will work it, go forth and multiply. Go forth and multiply me, says the latifundio. But there is another way to speak of all this.

T HE RAIN CAUGHT UP with them toward the end of the afternoon, when the sun was barely a half-span above the low hills, to the right, however, the witches were already combing their hair, for this is their favorite weather. The man reined in the donkey and, to relieve the animal's load on the slight incline, used his foot to shove a stone under one wheel of the cart. This rain is most unseasonable, whatever can have got into the ruler of the celestial waters. That's why there's so much dust on the roads as well as the occasional dried cow pat or lump of horse dung, which no one has bothered to pick up, this being too far removed from any inhabited place. No young lad, basket over his arm, has ventured this far out in search of some natural manure, tentatively picking up the crumbling sphere, which is sometimes cracked like a ripe fruit. In the rain, the hot, pale earth became spattered with sudden dark stars, falling dully onto the soft dust, and then a torrent flooded everything. The woman, however, still had time to lift the child down from the cart, out of the concave nest formed by the striped mattress squeezed in between two large chests. She held him to her breast, covered his face with the loose end of her shawl, and said, Good, he's still asleep. This was her first concern, the second was,

Everything's going to get drenched. The man was looking up at the high clouds, wrinkling his nose, and then, in his male wisdom, he declared, It'll pass, it's only a shower, but just in case, he unrolled one of the blankets and draped it over the furniture, Why did it have to rain today of all days, damn it.

A flurry of wind sent the now sparse drops flying. When the man gave the donkey a slap on the back, it shook its ears vigorously and tugged at the shafts and the man helped by pushing against the wheel. They set off again up the slope. The woman followed behind, her child in her arms, and, pleased to see him sleeping so soundly, she peered down at him, murmuring, There's a good boy. The ground to either side of the cart track was thick with undergrowth, in which a few lost, choked holm oaks stood, trunk-deep, abandoned or perhaps born there. The wheels of the cart gouged and squelched a path through the sodden earth, and now and then gave a sudden violent jolt whenever a stone raised a shoulder above the surface. The furniture creaked beneath the blanket. The man, walking beside the donkey, his right hand resting on the reins, was silent. And so they reached the top of the hill.

A great mass of dense, towering clouds was heading toward them from the south over the straw-colored plain. The path plunged downward, barely distinguishable between the crumbling ditches planed almost flat by the winds sweeping in across the empty expanse. At the bottom, the path would join a wide road, a rather ambitious word to use in a place so ill served by roads. To the left, almost hugging the low horizon, a small settlement turned its white walls to face the west. As we said before, the plain was vast and smooth, interrupted only by a few holm oaks, alone or in pairs, and little else. From that modest vantage point, it was not difficult to believe that the world had no known end. And seen from there, in the yellowish light and beneath the great leaden sheet of the clouds, the settlement, their destination, seemed unreachable. São Cristóvão, said the man. And the woman, who had never traveled so far south, said, Monte Lavre is bigger, which, while apparently a merely comparative statement, hinted perhaps at homesickness.

They were halfway down the hill when the rain returned, at first in the form of a few plump drops threatening a downpour, so much for it being a passing shower. Then the wind swept across the plain, pushing everything before it like a broom, scooping up straw and dust, and the rain advanced from the horizon, a grayish curtain that soon obscured the distant landscape. It was a steady rain, of the sort that looks set in for many hours, one that arrives and is reluctant to leave, and when, finally, the earth can't cope with all that water, it's hard to know then if it's the sky or the earth doing the drenching. The man again said, Damn it, the kind of thing people say if they have learned no grander expressions. Shelter is far away, and with no coats to put on, they have no alternative but to receive on their backs whatever rain may fall. From there to the village, given the speed at which this weary and somewhat reluctant donkey is traveling, it will be at least another hour's journey, and by then it will be dark. The blanket, which barely protects the furniture, is soaked and dripping, the water falling in drops from the white threads, what hope for the clothes in the chests, the few migratory possessions of this family who, for reasons of their own, are making this cross-country trek. The woman looks up at the sky, an ancient, country way of reading the great blank page above our head, this time in order to see if the sky is clearing, which it isn't, looking, rather, as if it were heavy with dark ink, the weather won't change this evening. The cart travels onward, it's a boat plunging into the deluge, it'll go under at any moment, that seems to be why the man is driving the donkey forward, but it's only so that they can reach that holm oak, which will shelter them from the worst of the storm. Man, cart and donkey have arrived, and the woman is nearly there, sliding about in the mud, she can't run, she would wake her child, that's how the world is, we never notice other people's problems, not even when the people involved are as close as mother and son.

Underneath the oak tree, the man was gesticulating impatiently, he obviously doesn't know what it's like to carry a child in his arms, he'd be better employed checking that the ropes on the cart haven't slackened, because traveling at that speed, the knots are sure to have slipped or the furniture shifted, and the last thing we need now is for the little furniture we have to fall and break. Under the tree, the rain is lighter, but large drops still fall from the leaves, this is no dense orange tree, standing beneath these enormous, widespread arms is like standing beneath a porch full of holes, indeed, it's hard to know where to stand, but just then the child began to cry, prompting the mother to perform a more urgent task, unbuttoning her blouse and giving him her breast, almost empty of milk now, barely enough to stave off hunger. His crying stopped at once, and mother and child were at peace, wrapped about by the steady murmur of the rain, while the father walked around the cart, untying and retying knots, bracing his knee on the side of the cart to pull the ropes tight, while the donkey, abstracted, shook his ears hard and gazed out at the puddles and the flooded path. Then the man said, We were so near, and then all this rain, these were words spoken in mild anger, uttered almost unthinkingly and hopelessly, as if to say, the rain won't stop just because I'm angry, well, that's the narrator speaking, which we can quite do without. We would be better off watching the father, who asks at last, How's the child, and goes over and peers under the shawl, he is her husband after all, but so quickly and modestly does his wife cover herself up that he can't be sure now whether it was his son he wanted to see or her bare breast. He just had time to make out, in the tepid darkness, in the scented warmth of crumpled clothes, his son's intensely blue eyes watching him from that private interior, with that strange pale light that usually stared out at him from the cradle, transparent and stern, an exile among the dark brown eyes of the family he was born into.

The heavy clouds had thinned a little, the first torrent of rain had slowed. The man stepped out onto the path, looked up questioningly at the sky, turning to the four cardinal points, and said to his wife, We'd better go, we can't stay here until it's dark. And his wife said, Let's go then. She withdrew her nipple from the baby's mouth, the child sucked air for a moment, seemed about to cry, then stopped, rubbed his face against the now withdrawn breast and, sighing, fell asleep. He's a quiet child, good-humored, and a friend to his mother.

They were walking along together now, wrapped about by the rain, so wet that not even a cozy barn would tempt them, they'll stop only when they reach their new home. The night was coming on fast. In the west, there was only a last faint glow that grew gradually red, then was gone, and the earth was a dumb, black well, full of echoes, how large the world seems at nightfall. The squeaking of the wheels seemed louder, the stuttering breath of the donkey as unexpected as a secret suddenly spoken out loud, and the whisper of their wet clothes was like a continuous murmured conversation between friends, with no awkward silences. For leagues around, not a light was to be seen. The woman crossed herself, then made the sign of the cross over her son's face. At this hour of night, it's best to defend the body and protect the soul, because ghosts begin to appear on the roads, either passing in a whirlwind or sitting down on a rock to await the traveler, of whom they will ask three questions to which there is no answer, who are you, where do you come from and where are you going. The man walking alongside the cart would like to sing, but he can't, all his energy is going into pretending that the night doesn't frighten him. Not much farther, he said when they reached the road, we just keep going straight now and this is a better road too.

Ahead, far away, a flash lit up the clouds, no one could have guessed they were so low. Then a pause and, finally, the low rumble of thunder. That's all we need. The woman said, Holy Saint Barbara save us, but the thunder, if it wasn't a remnant of some distant storm, seemed to be taking a different route, either that or Saint Barbara had shooed it away to places of lesser faith. They were on the road now, they could tell because it was wider, although any other differences could only be found with great patience and by the light of day, they had come through mud and potholes, and through mud and potholes they continued, and now it was so dark that they couldn't see where they were putting their feet. The donkey advanced by instinct, walking alongside the ditch. The man and the woman skidded along behind. Now and then, if the road curved, the man ran blindly ahead to see if he could catch a glimpse of São Cristóvão. And when they saw, amid the darkness, the first white walls, the rain suddenly stopped, so abruptly that they barely noticed. One moment it was raining, the next it wasn't. It was as if a great roof had stretched out over the road.

It's hardly surprising that the woman should ask, Where's our house, a perfectly understandable question in someone who needs to take care of her child and, if possible, put the furniture in its proper place before laying her weary body down in bed. And the man answers, On the other side. All doors are closed, only a few faint chinks of light betray the presence of the other inhabitants. In a yard somewhere, a dog barks. There's always a dog barking when someone walks past, and the other dogs, caught unawares, pick up the first sentinel's word and fulfill their canine duty. A gate was opened, then closed. And now that the rain had stopped and the house was near, husband and wife were more aware of the cold wind that came running along the street, before plunging down the narrow alleys, where it shook the branches that reached out over the low roofs. Thanks to the wind, the night grew brighter. The great cloud was moving off, and here and there you could see patches of clear sky. It's not raining now, said the woman to her child, who was sleeping and, of the four, was the only one not to know the good news.

They came to a square in which a few trees were exchanging brief whispers. The man stopped the cart and said to the woman, Wait here, and walked under the trees toward a brightly lit doorway. It was a bar, a taberna, and inside three men were sitting on a bench while another was standing at the bar, drinking, holding his glass between thumb and forefinger as if posing for a photograph. And behind the bar, a thin, shriveled old man turned his eyes to the door, through which the man with the cart entered, saying, Good evening, gentlemen, the greeting of a new arrival wishing to gain the friendship of everyone in the room, either out of fraternal feeling or for more selfish commercial reasons, I've come to live here in São Cristóvão, my name's Domingos Mau-Tempo* and I'm a shoemaker. One of the men sitting on the bench joked, Well, you certainly brought the bad weather with you, and the man who was drinking and had just emptied his glass smacked his lips and added, Let's hope his soles are better than the weather he brings, and the others, of course, laughed. These were not intended as rude or unwelcoming words, but it's nighttime in São Cristóvão, all the doors are shut, and if a stranger arrives bearing a name like Mau-Tempo, only a fool could resist making a joke of it, especially after that heavy downpour. Domingos Mau-Tempo responded with a reluctant smile, but that's to be expected. Then the old man opened a drawer and produced a large key, Here's the key, I was beginning to think you weren't coming, and everyone stares at Domingos Mau-Tempo, taking the measure of this new neighbor, every village needs a shoemaker and São Cristóvão is no exception. Domingos Mau-Tempo offered an explanation, It's a long way from Monte Lavre, and it rained while we were on the road,

---

* Mau-Tempo means bad weather.

not that there's any need for him to account for himself, but he wants to be friendly, and then he says, Let me buy you all a drink, which is an excellent way of touching the pockets of men's hearts. The men who were seated stand up and watch the ceremony of their glasses being refilled, and then, unhurriedly, each man again picks up his glass with a slow, careful gesture, this is wine, after all, not cheap brandy to be drunk down in one gulp. Won't you have a drink yourself, sir, says Domingos Mau-Tempo, and the old man, who knows the ways of the big city, answers, Here's wishing good health to my new tenant. And while the men are engaged in these niceties, the woman comes to the door, although she doesn't actually come in, the taberna is reserved for men only, and she says quietly, as is her wont, Domingos, the child is restless, and what with the furniture and everything being so wet, we need to get unloaded.

She is quite right, but Domingos Mau-Tempo disliked being summoned by his wife like that, what will the other men think, and as they cross the square, he scolds her, If you do that again, I'll be very angry. The woman did not respond, too busy trying to quiet the baby. The cart went slowly on, jolting over the bumps. The donkey had stiffened up with the cold. They went down a side street where the houses alternated with vegetable gardens, and they stopped outside a low hovel. Is this it, asked the woman, and her husband replied, Yes.

Domingos Mau-Tempo opened the door with the large key. In order to enter, he had to lower his head, for this is no palace with high doors. There were no windows. To the left was the fireplace, with the hearth at floor level. Domingos Mau-Tempo made a small, flickering torch from a sheaf of straw and held it up so that his wife could see their new home. There was a bundle of firewood by the chimney breast. Enough for their immediate needs. In a matter of minutes, the woman had laid the child down in one corner to sleep, gathered together some logs and some kindling, and the fire had sprung into life, like a flower on the whitewashed wall. The house was once again inhabited.

Domingos Mau-Tempo led the donkey and the cart in through the gate to the yard, and started unloading the furniture and carrying it into the house, where he set it down willy-nilly, until his wife could come and help him. The mattress was wet on one side. The water had got into the clothes chest, and one leg of the kitchen table was broken. But on the fire was a saucepan of cabbage leaves and rice, and the baby had suckled again and fallen asleep on the dry side of the mattress. Domingos Mau-Tempo went out into the yard to do his business. And standing in the middle of the room, Sara da Conceição, Domingos's wife and João's mother, stood quite still, staring into the flames like someone waiting for a garbled message to be repeated. She felt a slight movement in her belly. And another. But when her husband came back in, she said nothing. They had other things to think about.

DOMINGOS MAU-TEMPO will not make old bones. One day, when he has given his wife five children, although not for that most mundane of reasons, he will put a rope around the branch of a tree, in a desolate place almost within sight of Monte Lavre, and hang himself. Before he does this, however, he will carry his house on his back to other places, run away from his family three times, but fail to make his peace with them on that third occasion because his hour will have come. His father-in-law Laureano Carranca had predicted just such an unfortunate end when he was forced to give in to Sara's stubbornness, for, so besotted was she with Domingos Mau-Tempo that she swore that if she could not marry him, she would marry no one. Laureano Carranca would roar furiously, He's a ne'er-do-well and a drunkard and will come to no good. And so the family war raged on until Sara da Conceição fell pregnant, a conclusive and usually highly effective argument when persuasion and pleading have failed. One morning, Sara da Conceição left the house, in May it was, and walked across the fields to the place where she had arranged to meet Domingos Mau-Tempo. They were there for half an hour at most, lying amid the tall wheat, and when Domingos returned to his lasts and Sara to her parents' house, he went off whistling with satisfaction, while she was left shivering despite the hot sun beating down on her. And when she crossed the stream by the ford, she had to crouch down beneath some willows and wash away the blood flowing from between her legs.

João was made, or to use a more biblical term, conceived, on that same day, which, it would seem, is most unusual, because, in the haste and confusion of the moment, semen does not necessarily do its job the first time, only later. And it's true that there was considerable consternation, not to say suspicion, regarding João's blue eyes, for no one else in the family had such eyes nor, as far as they could recall, had any relative, close or distant, we, however, know that such thoughts were grossly unfair to a woman who, after much soul-searching, had deviated from the straight virginal path and lain down in a wheatfield with that one man alone and, by her own choice, opened her legs to him. It had not been the choice, almost five hundred years before, of another young woman, who, standing alone at the fountain filling her jug with water, was approached by one of the foreigners who had arrived with Lamberto Horques Alemão, the governor of Monte Lavre appointed by Dom João the First, by a man whose speech she couldn't understand, and who, ignoring the poor girl's cries and pleas, carried her off into the bracken where, purely for his own enjoyment, he raped her. He was a handsome fellow with pale skin and blue eyes, whose only fault was the fire in his blood, but she, naturally enough, could not bring herself to love him, and when her time came, she gave birth alone. Thus, for four centuries those blue German eyes appeared and disappeared, like the comets that vanish and return when we least expect them or simply because no one has bothered to record their appearances and thus discover a pattern.

This is the family's first move. They came from Monte Lavre to São Cristóvão on a strangely rainy summer's day. They traversed the whole district from north to south, what on earth can have made Domingos Mau-Tempo decide to move so far away, well, he's a bungler and a good-for-nothing, and things were getting difficult for him in Monte Lavre because of drink and certain shady deals, and so he said to his father-in-law, Lend me your cart and your donkey, will you, I'm going to live in São Cristóvão, By all means go, and let's hope you acquire a little common sense, for your own good and for the sake of your wife and son, but be sure to bring that donkey and cart back promptly, because I need them. They took the shortest route, following cart tracks, or highways when they could, but mostly heading across country, skirting the hills. They lunched in the shade of a tree, and Domingos Mau-Tempo gulped down a whole bottle of wine that he soon sweated out again in the heat of the day. They saw Montemor in the distance, to the left, and continued south. It rained on them when they were just one hour from São Cristóvão, a deluge that presaged no good at all, but today it is sunny, and Sara da Conceição, sitting in the garden, is sewing a skirt, while her son, still rather unsteady on his legs, is feeling his way along the wall of the house. Domingos Mau-Tempo has gone to Monte Lavre to return the donkey and cart to his father-in-law and tell him that they're living in an excellent house, that customers are already beating a path to his door and that he won't lack for work. He will return on foot the following day, as long as he doesn't get drunk, because apart from his drinking, he isn't a bad man, and God willing he'll sort himself out, after all, there have been worse men than him and they've turned out all right in the end, and if there's any justice in the world, what with one small child and another on the way, he'll shape up to be a respectable father too, and as for me, well, I'll do what I can to give us all a good life.

João has reached the end of the wall, where the picket fence begins. He grips it hard, his arms being stronger than his legs, and peers out. His horizon is quite limited, a strip of muddy road with puddles that reflect the sky, and a ginger cat sprawled on the doorstep opposite, sunning its belly. Somewhere a cock crows. A woman can be heard shouting out, Maria, and another, almost childish voice answers, Yes, Senhora. And then the silence of the great heat settles again, the mud will soon harden and return to the dust it was. João lets go of the fence, that's quite enough looking at the landscape for the moment, executes a difficult half-turn and commences the long journey back to his mother. Sara da Conceição sees him, puts her sewing down on her lap and holds out her arms to her son, Come here, little one, come here. Her arms are like two protective hedges. Between them and João lies a confusing, uncertain world with no beginning and no end. The sun sketches a hesitant shadow on the ground, a tremulously advancing hour. Like the hand of a clock on the great expanse of the latifundio.

When Lamberto Horques Alemão stepped out onto the terrace of his castle, his gaze could not encompass all that lay before him. He was the lord of the village and its lands, ten leagues long and three leagues wide, and he had the right to exact a tribute, and although he had been charged to go forth and multiply, he had not ordered the rape of the girl at the fountain, it happened and that was that. He himself, with his virtuous wife and his children, will scatter his seed where he pleases, depending on how the mood takes him, This land cannot remain as uninhabited as it is now, for you can count on the fingers of one hand the number of settlements in the whole estate, while the uncultivated areas are as many as the hairs on your head, Yes, sir, but these women are the swarthy cursed remnants of the Moors, and these silent men can be vengeful, besides, our king did not call on you to go forth and multiply like a Solomon, but to cultivate the land and rule over it so that people will come here and stay, That is what I am doing and will do, and whatever else I deem appropriate, for this land is mine and everything on it, although there are sure to be people who will try to hamper my efforts and cause trouble, there always will be, You are quite right, sir, you obviously gleaned such knowledge from the cold lands of your birth, where people know far more than we natives of these remote western lands, Since we are in agreement, let us discuss what tributes should be imposed on these lands I am to govern. Thus, a minor episode in the history of the latifundio.

T HIS SO-CALLED SHOEMAKER is really nothing but a cobbler. He soles and heels and dawdles over his work when he
isn't in the mood, often abandoning last, awl and knife to go to the
taberna, he argues with impatient customers and, for all these reasons, beats his wife. Not just because he is obliged to sole and heel,
but also because he can find no peace in himself, he's a restless man
who has no sooner sat down than he wants to get up again, who
as soon as he has arrived in one place is already thinking about
another. He's a child of the wind, a wanderer, this bad-weather
Domingos, who returns from the taberna and enters the house,
bumping into the walls, glancing sourly at his son, and for no reason at all lashes out at his wife, wretched woman, let that be a lesson to you. And then he leaves again, goes back to the wine and
his carousing mates, put this one on the slate, will you, landlord,
of course, sir, but there's quite a lot on the slate already, so what, I
always pay my debts, don't I, I've never owed anyone a penny. And
more than once, Sara da Conceição, having left her child with the
neighbor, went out into the night to search for her husband, using the shawl and the darkness to conceal her tears, going from
taberna to taberna, of which there weren't many in São Cristóvão,

but enough, peering in from outside, and if her husband was there, she would stand waiting in the shadows, like another shadow. And sometimes she would find him lost on the road, abandoned by his friends, with no idea where his house was, and then the world would suddenly brighten, because Domingos Mau-Tempo, grateful to have been found in that frightening desert, among hordes of ghosts, would put an arm about his wife's shoulders and allow himself to be led like the child he doubtless still was.

And one day, because he had more work than he could cope with, Domingos Mau-Tempo took on an assistant, thus giving himself more time with his fellow drinkers, but then, on another ill-fated day, he got it into his head that his wife, poor, innocent Sara da Conceição, was deceiving him in his absence, and that was the end of São Cristóvão, which the guiltless assistant had to flee at knifepoint, and Sara, pregnant, quite legitimately, for a second time, underwent her own painful via dolorosa, and the cart was loaded up again, another trek to Monte Lavre, more toing and froing, We're fine, and your daughter and grandson are happy, with another on the way, but I've found a better job in Torre da Gadanha, my father lives there and will be able to help us out. And once more they set off north, except that this time the landlord was waiting for them on the way out of São Cristóvão, Just a moment, Mau-Tempo, you owe me for the rent and the wine that you drank, and if you don't pay up, me and my two sons here will make you, so pay me what you owe or die.

It was a short journey, which was just as well, because almost as soon as Sara da Conceição set foot in the house, she gave birth to her second son, who, for some forgotten reason, was named Anselmo. He was fortunate from the cradle on because his paternal grandfather was a carpenter by trade and very pleased to have his grandson born so close to home, almost next door. His grandfather worked as a carpenter and had no boss and no apprentice, no

wife either, and he lived among lengths of timber and planks, per-
manently perfumed by sawdust, and used a vocabulary particular
to laths, planes, battens, mallets and adzes. He was a serious man
of few words and not given to drinking, which is why he disap-
proved of his son, who was hardly a credit to his name. Given Domingos Mau-Tempo's restless nature, however, his father had little
time in which to enjoy being a grandfather, just long enough to
teach his oldest grandson that this is a claw hammer, this is a plane
and this a chisel. But Domingos Mau-Tempo could bear neither
what his father said nor what he didn't say, and like a bird hurling itself against the bars of its cage, what prison is this in my soul,
damn it, off he went again, this time to Landeira, in the extreme
west of the district. Preferring this time not to approach his father-
in-law, who would find such wanderings and uncertainties odd, he
had, at some expense, hired a cart and a mule, intending to keep
quiet about his plans and tell his father-in-law later. We never
seem to settle anywhere, we go from one place to another like the
wandering Jew, and it's not easy with two small children, Be quiet,
woman, I know what I'm doing, there are good people in Landeira
and plenty of work, besides, I'm a craftsman, not like your father
and brothers tied to their hoes, I learned a trade and have a skill,
That's not what I'm saying, you were a shoemaker when I married you and that's fine, but I just want some peace and to stop
all this moving around. Sara da Conceição said nothing about the
beatings, nor would it have been appropriate, because Domingos
Mau-Tempo was traveling toward Landeira as if to the promised
land and carrying on his shoulders his eldest son, holding on to his
tender little ankles, which were a bit grubby, of course, but what
does that matter. He barely felt the weight, because years of sewing
leather had given him muscles and tendons of iron. With the mule
trotting along behind, with a sun as warm as a cozy blanket, Sara
da Conceição was even allowed to ride in the cart. But when they

reached the new house, they found that their furniture was once again badly damaged, At this rate, Domingos, we'll end up with no furniture at all.

It was in Landeira that João, who already had his real godparents in Monte Lavre, found a new and more illustrious godfather. He was Father Agamedes, who, because he lived with a woman he called his niece, provided João with a borrowed godmother too. The child did not lack for blessings, being as protected in heaven as he had been on earth up until then. Especially when Domingos Mau-Tempo, encouraged by Father Agamedes, took on the duties of sacristan, helping at mass and at funerals, because thanks to this, the priest befriended him and adopted João. Domingos Mau-Tempo's sole aim in being received into the bosom of the church was to find a respectable reason for avoiding work and a respite from his persistent vagabond restlessness. But God rewarded him as soon as he saw him at his altar, clumsily performing the ritualistic gestures he was taught, for Father Agamedes also liked his drink, and thus celebrant and acolyte came together over that other sacrifice. Father Agamedes owned a grocery store, not far from the church, where he worked whenever his priestly duties allowed, and when they didn't, his niece would come down to the square and, from behind the counter, rule over the family's earthly business. Domingos Mau-Tempo would drop in and drink a glass of wine, then another and another, alone, unless the priest was there, and then they drank together. God, meanwhile, was up above with the angels.

But all heavens have their Lucifers and all paradises their temptations. Domingos Mau-Tempo began to look on his neighbor's companion with covetous eyes, and she, as niece, took offense and mentioned it to her uncle, and that was enough to create bad feeling between those two servants of the holy mother church, one permanent and the other temporary. Father Agamedes could not speak frankly for fear of giving credence to the evil thoughts of those parishioners who had their doubts about that niece-uncle relationship, and so, to drive away the threat to his own honor, he focused on the married status of the offending party. Deprived of his easy access to wine and weary of plying his trade here, there and everywhere, Domingos Mau-Tempo declared his intention at home of avenging himself on the priest. He did not say exactly what he was avenging himself for, and Sara da Conceição did not ask. She continued to suffer in silence.

The church had few parishioners and not all of them regular. It provided no remedy for their ills, nor was it obliged to, since, as far as one could see, it didn't increase them either. That was not the problem. The lack of apostolic action was not conducive to increased devotion, not so much because Father Agamedes lived with his so-called niece and ran a grocery store, because only those who are not of the people are ignorant of such basic needs, but because he mangled the words of the prayer book, and dispatched newborns, newlyweds and the dead with the same cold-blooded indifference with which he slaughtered and ate his pig and with equally scant attention to the letter or spirit of the holy writ. Ordinary people can be strangely sensitive. Domingos Mau-Tempo knew how to ensure that the church would be full. He let it be known that the next mass would be something special, that Father Agamedes had told him that in future he was going to take particular pains over the holy precepts, and would make use of sublime pauses and even vibrato, you'd be a fool to miss it, so don't come complaining to me afterward if you do. Father Agamedes was amazed when he saw the church packed with people. It wasn't the church's name day and the drought had not been so bad as to require celestial intervention, but he said nothing. If the flock came to the pen of its own free will, so much the better for the shepherd when it came to rendering accounts to his master. In short, so as not to appear ungrateful, he outdid himself and, all unknowing, confirmed Domingos Mau-Tempo's prediction. However, the shoemaker raised up to the position of sacristan, and already planning another escape, had his revenge prepared. When it came to the point in the mass where he had to ring the sanctus bell, he calmly raised the bell and shook it. It was as if he had waved a chicken feather in the air. At first, the faithful thought that they must all have gone deaf, others, out of habit, bowed their heads, while others watched distrustfully as Domingos Mau-Tempo, in dramatic silence, his face a mask of innocence, continued to shake the bell. The priest looked puzzled, the faithful muttered to each other, the younger members laughed. It was shameful, what with all the saints, not to mention all-seeing God, looking down on them. Father Agamedes could contain himself no longer, and he stopped the communion service there and then, grabbed the bell and felt inside it. There was no clapper. And yet no thunderbolt fell to punish such impiety. Terrible in his holy fury, Father Agamedes slapped Domingos Mau-Tempo hard about the face, right there in that sacred place, it scarcely seemed possible. But Domingos Mau-Tempo responded in kind, as though this were all part of the mass. And it was not long before the priest's vestments and the sacristan's surplice were caught up in a furious maelstrom, one on top, the other underneath, rolling sacrilegiously about, bruising their ribs on the altar steps, beneath the round-eyed gaze of the monstrance. The congregation rushed to separate the two warring powers, and some took advantage of that tangle of arms and legs to slake an ancient thirst for revenge on either one side or the other. The old ladies had gathered in one corner, praying to all the hosts of heaven, and, finally summoning up physical force and spiritual courage, advanced on the altar in order to save their priest, however unworthy. It was, in short, a triumph of faith.

The next day, Domingos Mau-Tempo left the village, followed by a noisy cortege of boys, who accompanied him and his family as far as the barren outskirts. Sara da Conceição bowed her head in shame. João looked about him with his stern blue eyes. The other boy was sleeping.

THEN THE REPUBLIC arrived. The men earned twelve or thirteen vinténs, and the women, as usual, less than half. Both ate the same black bread, the same cabbage leaves, the same stalks. The republic rushed in from Lisbon, traveled from village to village by telegraph, if there was one, advertised itself in the press for those who knew how to read, or passed from mouth to mouth, which was always by far the easiest way. The king had been toppled, and according to the church, that particular kingdom was no longer of its world, the latifundio got the message and did nothing, and the price of a liter of olive oil rose to more than two thousand réis, ten times a man's daily wage.

Long live the republic. So how much is the new daily rate, boss, Let's see, I pay whatever the others pay, talk to the overseer, So, overseer, how much is the daily rate, You'll earn an extra vintém, That's not enough to live on, Well, if you don't want the job, there are plenty more who do, Dear God, a man could die of hunger along with his children, what can I give my children to eat, Put them to work, And if there is no work, Then don't have so many children, Wife, send the boys off to collect firewood and the girls for straw, and come to bed, Do with me as you wish, I am my master's slave, and there, it's done, I'm pregnant, with child, in the family way, I'm going to have a baby, you're going to be a father, I've missed a period, That's all right, eight can starve as easily as seven.

And because far from there being any visible differences, only similarities, between the latifundio under the monarchy and the latifundio under the republic, and because the wages they earned could buy so little that they only served to increase their hunger, some innocent workers got together and went to the district administrator to demand better living conditions. The person with the best handwriting wrote out their request, remarking on the new joy felt among the Portuguese people and the new hopes that had sprung up with the coming of the republic, we wish you good health and send fraternal greetings, sir, and await your reply. Once the suppliants had been dismissed, Lamberto Horques sat down in his Hanseatic chair, meditated deeply on what would be best for the farms, himself and the people he governed, and having perused the maps on which the various parcels of land were marked, he placed his finger on the one most densely populated and summoned the captain of the guard. The captain had formerly belonged to the civil police force and now cut a martial figure in his new uniform, but he had a short memory and had, therefore, forgotten the days when he had worn the blue-and-white ribbon on his left sleeve.* Thanks to the captain's zeal and vigilance, Lamberto learned that the workers were agitating for change and protesting about the forced loans and other such impositions, they were complaining, too, about the poor-quality food, which, after paying the various taxes and tributes, was all they could afford, these complaints were all there in the letter of petition, albeit expressed in measured tones, but perhaps those tones only disguised other, worse intentions. An ill wind of insurrection was blowing

---

* Blue and white were the colors of the old monarchical flag.

through the latifundio, the snarling of a cornered, starving wolf that could cause great damage if it should turn into an army of teeth. It was necessary, therefore, to set an example, to teach them a lesson. Once the interview was over and he had received his orders, Lieutenant Contente clicked his heels and ordered the bugle to be sounded on the parade ground. There the republican national guard lined up, sabers at their side and reins tight, harnesses, mustaches and manes gleaming, and when Lamberto appeared at the window of his room, the guards saluted him as if they were waving goodbye, thus uniting in one gesture both affection and discipline. Then he withdrew to his chamber and summoned his wife, with whom he took his pleasure.

See how the guards go flying through the countryside. They trot, they gallop, the sun beats down on their armor, the saddle cloths swirl about the horses' legs, O cavalry, O Roland, Oliveros and Fierabras,* happy the country that gave birth to such sons. The chosen village is within sight, and Lieutenant Contente orders the squadron to prepare to charge, and when the bugle sounds, the troops advance in lyrical, warlike fashion, sabers unsheathed, the whole nation comes to the balcony to observe the spectacle, and when the peasants emerge from their houses, from barns and cattle sheds, they are mown down by the charging horses and struck from behind by the blades of the soldiers' swords, until Fierabras, frisky as an ox stung by a gadfly, grips his saber in his hand and cuts, scythes, slices, pierces, blind with rage, although quite why he doesn't know. The peasants lay moaning on the ground, and when finally carried back into their huts, they did not rest but tended their wounds as best they could, with lavish use of water, salt and

---

* In French and Italian chivalric literature, Fierabras was a Saracen giant who sacked Rome and stole two containers of the fluid in which Christ was said to have been embalmed. This fluid was reputed to be able to heal any wound. Fierabras was, in turn, defeated by Oliveros, who gave the containers to Charlemagne so that he could return them to Rome. Roland became, in legend, Charlemagne's chief paladin.

cobwebs. We'd be better off dead, said one. Our time has not yet come, said another.

The national guard, belovèd child of the republic, is leaving, the horses are still trembling, and flecks of foam still fill the air, and now they move on to the second phase of the battle plan, which is to ride into the hills and gullies and hunt down the workers who are inciting the others to rebellion and strikes, leaving the work in the fields undone and the animals untended, and thus thirty-three of them were taken captive, along with the main instigators, who ended up in military prisons. The guards led them off like a train of mules, their backs clothed in lashes, blows and mocking remarks, you bastards, mind you don't trip over your cuckold's horns, long live the republican guard, long live the republic. The farm workers were all individually bound and then tied as well to a single rope, like galley slaves, can you believe it, as if these were tales from barbarous times, from the days of Lamberto Horques Alemão, from the fifteenth century, at most.

And who is going to take the leaders of the mutiny to Lisbon? Eighteen soldiers from the seventeenth infantry, led by their lieutenant, also called Contente, set off secretly on the night train, thirty-eight eyes keeping watch over five farm laborers accused of sedition and incitement to strike. They will be handed over to the government, our solicitous correspondent informs us, this government is a regular almshouse, always eager to receive such deliveries. And it's May again, gentlemen, the month of Mary. There goes the train, there it goes, whistling away, there go the five farm laborers, to rot in Limoeiro prison. In these barbarous times the trains travel slowly, they stop for no apparent reason in the middle of nowhere, perhaps at some halt perfect for an ambush and sudden death, and the locked carriage in which the malefactors are traveling has its curtains closed, if there are curtains in the days of Lamberto Horques, if such extravagances are commonplace in third-class carriages, and the seventeenth infantry have their rifles cocked, perhaps even their bayonets fixed, who goes there, getting off the train ten at a time whenever it stops, to prevent any attacks or attempts to free the prisoners. The poor soldiers are under orders not to sleep, and they stare nervously at the hard, grimy faces of those five criminals, so like you. And when I get out of the army, my friend, who knows, perhaps another soldier will arrest me and carry me off to Lisbon on the night train, in the dark, We know our place now, but tomorrow, who can say, They lend you a rifle, but they never say anything about turning it on the estate workers, All that training, all that take aim and fire, is actually turned against yourself, the barrel of your weapon is staring at your own deceived heart, you have no idea what you're doing, and one day they'll give the order to fire, and you'll shoot yourself, Shut your mouth, you seditious bastards, you'll learn your lesson, who knows how many years you'll spend inside, Yes, Lisbon is a big city, the biggest in the world they say, as well as home to the republic, which should, by rights, set us free, We're perfectly within the law.

There are now two groups of workers face to face, a mere ten paces apart. Those from the north are saying, We're perfectly within the law, we were hired and we want to work. Those from the south say, You've agreed to work for less money, you come here to do us harm, go back where you came from, you rats,* you black-legs. Those from the north say, Where we come from there is no work, it's all stones and scrub, we're from the Beira, so don't insult us by calling us rats. Those from the south say, But you are rats, you come here to gnaw at our bread. Those from the north say, We're hungry. Those from the south say, So are we, but we refuse to accept this poverty, if you agree to work for such a low wage, we'll be left with nothing. Those from the north say, That's your fault, you shouldn't be so proud, accept what the boss offers you,

---

* *Ratinhos* in Portuguese; these were temporary workers from northern and central Portugal who went to seek work in the Alentejo.

better something than nothing, and then there'll be work for everyone, because there aren't many of you and we've come to help. Those from the south say, That's just a trick, they want to trick us all, we don't have to accept that wage, why not join forces with us and then the boss will have to pay everyone a better wage. Those from the north say, Each man knows his own heart and God knows them all, we don't want to make alliances, we've traveled a long way, we can't stay here and make war on the boss, we want to work. Those from the south say, Well, you're not going to work here. Those from the north say, Yes, we are. Those from the south say, This land is ours. Those from the north say, But you don't want to work it. Those from the south say, Not for this wage, no. Those from the north say, The wage is fine with us. The overseer says, All right, you've had your chat, now stand aside and let these men get to work. Those from the south say, Don't do it. The overseer says, Get working, if you don't do as I say, I'll call the guards. Those from the south say, There'll be blood spilled before the guards arrive. The overseer says, If the guards do come, still more blood will be spilled, so don't say I didn't warn you. Those from the south say, Brothers, listen to what we're saying, for pity's sake, join us. Those from the north say, Like we said, we want to work.

Then the first man from the north walked over to the wheat with his sickle, and the first man from the south grabbed his arm, and they grappled clumsily, awkwardly, roughly, brutishly, hunger against hunger, poverty against poverty, how dearly we buy our daily bread. The guards arrived and broke up the fight, attacking one side only, driving back with their sabers those from the south and corralling them as if they were animals. The sergeant says, Shall I arrest the lot of them. The overseer says, It's not worth it, leave the bastards there for a while to cool off. The sergeant says, But one of the other men has a wound to the head, he was attacked, and the law is the law. The overseer says, It's not worth it, Sergeant, why worry over spilling a mere animal's blood, it doesn't matter whether they're from the north or the south, they're worth about as much as the boss's piss. The sergeant says, Speaking of the boss, I need some firewood. The overseer says, We'll send you a cartload. The sergeant says, And a few roof tiles too. The overseer says, Well, we can't have you without a roof over your head. The sergeant says, Life is very expensive. The overseer says, I'll send you some sausages.

The men from the north are in the field now. The blond ears of wheat fall onto the dark earth, how lovely, it smells like a long-unwashed body, then, in the distance, a passing tilbury stops. The overseer says, It's the boss. The sergeant says, Give him my thanks, and let me know if you need any more help. The overseer says, Keep an eye on those rascals. The sergeant says, Don't worry, I know how to handle them. Some of the men from the south say, Let's set fire to the wheatfield. Others say, That would be a terrible shame. They all say, That lot don't know what shame is.

THEY HAD BEEN to Landeira, and to Santana do Mato, in and out of the parish, to Tarrafeiro and Afeiteira, and in the midst of all this traveling their third child was born, a daughter this time, Maria da Conceição, and a fourth, a boy named Domingos, like his father. May God give him better fortune, because there was nothing good to be said about his progenitor, who, caught between the wine and the cheap brandy, the mallet and the shoe stud, was going from bad to worse. And as for the furniture, the least said the better, for it continued to be bumped over hills and ditches as it was transported from house to cart and from cart to house and from village to village. A new shoemaker's arrived, his name's Mau-Tempo, let's go and see what this master craftsman is like, mind you, he drinks wine all year round the way you drink water in August, he's certainly a master at that. While living in Canha with her husband and children, Sara da Conceição suffered from tertian fever for two years, which, for those unfamiliar with the disease, is the sort of fever that comes and goes every four days. That is why, when his mother was ill in bed, João Mau-Tempo, he of the blue eyes, which were not repeated in his siblings, used to go to the well, and once, as he plunged the jug in, he lost his footing, proof that no one watches over the innocent, and fell into the water, which was very deep for a little seven-year-old. He was carried home by the woman who saved him, and his father beat him while his mother lay in bed trembling with fever, shaking so hard that even the brass balls on the bed shook, Don't hit the boy, Domingos, but she might as well have been talking to a brick wall.

Then came the day when Sara da Conceição called her husband and he did not answer. That was the first time Domingos Mau-Tempo spurned his family and went wandering off. Then, Sara da Conceição, who had kept silent for so long about her life, asked a literate neighbor to write a letter for her, and it was as if she were pouring her whole soul into it, because such behavior certainly wasn't what had made her fall in love with her husband. Dearest Father, for the love of God, please come and fetch me with your donkeys and your cart and take me back home with you where I belong and I beg you please to forgive me all the trouble and grief I've caused you as well as all you've had to put up with and believe me when I say how I regret not following the advice you gave me over and over not to make this unfortunate marriage to a man who has brought me only sorrow because I've suffered so much poverty disappointments beatings I was well advised but ill fated, this final phrase was drawn from her neighbor's literary treasure trove, marrying the classical and the modern with admirable boldness.

What would any father worthy of the name do, regardless of previous scandals? What did Laureano Carranca do? He sent his gloomy, ill-tempered son, Joaquim, to Canha to fetch his sister and however many grandchildren there might be. Not because he loved them dearly, they were, after all, the children of that drunkard cobbler, no, he didn't love those chips off the old block, and besides, he had other grandchildren he preferred. And so, that poor woman and her children, abandoned by husband and father, arrived in Monte Lavre with the ruins of their furniture piled high on the cart, and some were given house-room by parents or grandparents, out of a somewhat tetchy sense of pity, while others were deposited in a hayloft until a home could be found for them. And when they had to find shelter, mats on the floor served them as beds, and for food the older children went begging, as Our Lord once did, for it is a sin to steal. Sara da Conceição worked hard, of course, because she wasn't just there to bring children into the world, and her parents helped her out a little, her mother rather more generously, as is only natural, well, she was her mother. And thus they scraped along. A few weeks later, though, Domingos Mau-Tempo reappeared, prowling around Monte Lavre, trailing after his wife and children and finally ambushing them, contrite and repentant, to use his words, doubtless learned while he was sacristan. Laureano Carranca flew into a great rage, saying that he never wanted to see his daughter again if, heaven forbid, she went back to that useless, drunken scoundrel of a son-in-law. A much-chastened Domingos Mau-Tempo went to talk to him and assured him that he had changed his ways, and that this absence had shown him, blind as he was, how much he loved his wife and his dear children, I swear this to you, sir, on bended knee if necessary. Having somewhat assuaged their anger with all his tears, he and his family set off for a nearby hamlet, Cortiçadas de Monte Lavre, almost within sight of the paternal home. Having lost all the equipment that had allowed him, as he preferred, to work for himself, Domingos Mau-Tempo was forced to take employment with Master Gramicho, while Sara da Conceição labored away stitching uppers to soles, to help out her husband and keep her children fed and clothed. And the fates? Domingos Mau-Tempo once again began to slide into sadness, like a monster in exile, for that is the worst of all sadnesses, as you can see from the tale of Beauty and the Beast, and it wasn't long before he said to his wife, It's time to move on, I don't feel comfortable here, wait for a few days with the children while I go and look for work elsewhere. Sara da Conceição, not believing that her husband would come back, waited for two months, what else could she do, and was once more the abandoned widow, then up he popped again, happy as a lark, full of sweet words, Sara, I've found work and a really nice house in Ciborro. And so they left for Ciborro, and things went quite well for them, because the people there were pleasant and paid their bills promptly. There was no shortage of work, and the shoemaker seemed to have lost his taste for the taberna, not entirely, that would be asking too much, but enough to make him seem a respectable man. And this happened at an opportune moment because, meanwhile, a primary school had been set up there, and João Mau-Tempo, who was the right age, went there to learn to read and write and count.

And the fates? For some reason werewolves are drawn to cross-roads, the poor wretches, not that I claim to understand such mysteries, dear reader, it's as if they were under an evil spell, but on a particular day of the week, they leave their houses and at the first crossroads they come to, they take off their clothes, throw themselves on the ground, roll around in the dust, and are transformed into whatever animal has left its trail there, You mean any trail, or only the trail left by a mammal, Any trail, sir, once, a man was transformed into a cartwheel, and he went spinning and spinning along, it was terrible, but it's more common for them to be changed into animals, as was the case with a man, whose name I can't now recall, who lived with his wife in Monte do Curral da Légua, near Pedra Grande, and his fate was to go out every Tuesday night, but he knew what would happen, and so he warned his wife never to open the door when he was outside, no matter what noises she heard, because he uttered cries and howls that would freeze the blood of any Christian, no one could sleep a wink, but one night, his wife screwed up her courage, because women are very curious and always want to know everything, and resolved to open the door. And what did she see, oh dear God, she saw before her a huge pig, like a rampant boar, with a head this size, this big, and it hurled itself at her like a lion ready to devour her, but luckily she managed to slam the door shut, although not before the pig had bitten off a piece of her skirt, and imagine her horror when her husband returned home at dawn with that same piece of cloth still in his mouth, but at least it gave him an opportunity to explain that whenever he went out on Tuesday nights, he was changed into an animal, and that night he had been a pig, and he could have done her real harm, so next time she must on no account open the door, because he couldn't answer for his actions, How dreadful, Anyway, his wife went to speak to her in-laws, who were most upset to learn that their son had become a werewolf, because there weren't any others in the family, and so they went to a holy woman who recited the prayers of exorcism appropriate to such cases, and she told them that the next time he was changed into a werewolf, they must burn his hat, and then it would never happen again, and this proved to be a sovereign remedy, because they burned his hat and he was cured, Do you think burning his hat cured him because the sickness was in his head, I have no idea, the woman never said, but let me tell you of another, similar case, a man and his wife lived on a farm near Ciborro, why these things only happen between couples, I don't know, where they raised chickens and other livestock, and every night, because it happened every night, her husband would get out of bed, go into the garden and start clucking, can you imagine, and when his wife peered around the door, she saw that he had been turned into a huge chicken, What, the same size as that pig, You may laugh, but just hear me out, this couple had a daughter, and when their daughter was about to get married, they killed a lot of chickens for the wedding feast, because that was what they had most of, but that night, the wife didn't hear her husband get out of bed or hear him clucking, and you'll never guess what happened, the man went to the place where the chickens had been killed, picked up a knife, knelt down by a bowl, and stuck the knife in his own throat, and there he stayed until his wife woke to find the bed empty, went in search of her husband and found him dead in a great pool of blood, you see, like I said, it's the fates.

Domingos Mau-Tempo went back to his old ways, wine, idleness, beatings, fights and insults. Mama, is Papa cursed, Don't say such things about your father. These are words often spoken in such circumstances, and neither those intended as an accusation nor those intended to absolve should be taken seriously. Poverty was casting a dark shadow over the faces of these people, and the children who were old enough to do so went begging. However, there are still some kind, conscientious people, such as the owners of the house in which the Mau-Tempo family lived, who often gave them food, but children can be cruel, and although when bread was being baked in the owners' house they always reserved a bread roll for João Mau-Tempo, the boys of the family, who went to the same school and were all friends, used to play a practical joke on João Mau-Tempo, tethering him with a rope to the trough with the bread roll before him and refusing to let him go until he had eaten it. And people say there's a God.

Then, what had to happen, happened. Domingos Mau-Tempo reached the last of his misfortunes. One afternoon, he was sitting on his bench polishing the heel of a shoe when he suddenly put everything down, untied his apron, went into the house, made up a bundle of clothes, took some bread out of the bread bin, put everything in a knapsack and left. His wife was working, along with her two youngest children, João was at school, and the other one was idling about somewhere. This was the last time Domingos Mau-Tempo left home. He will still appear to say a few words and to hear others, but his story is over. He will spend the next two years as a wanderer.

NATURE DISPLAYS REMARKABLE callousness when creating her various creatures. Apart from those who die or are born crippled, some do manage to escape and thus guarantee the results of nature's engeneration, to coin an ambivalent and therefore equivocal noun that combines generation and engendering, with just the right cozy margin of imprecision that surrounds the many mutations of what one says, does and is. Nature does not itself parcel out the land, but uses the system to its advantage. And if after harvest time the granaries of the thousand anthills of the fields are not all equally full, the profits and losses feed into the great accounting department of the planet and no ant is left without its statistical quota of food. In the settling of accounts it matters little that millions of ants have died from being flooded out, dug up or urinated on: those who lived ate, and those who died left the others behind. Nature doesn't count its dead, it counts the living, and when there are too many of those, it organizes a new slaughter. It's all very easy, very clear and very fair, and as far as the memory of ants and elephants can recall, no one in the animal kingdom has as yet complained.

Fortunately, man is the king of the beasts. He can therefore do his accounts with pen and paper or by other, subtler means, murmured comments, hints, glances and nods. Such mimicry and onomatopoeia come together, in cruder form, in the songs and dances of struggle, seduction and enticement that certain animals use to obtain their goals. This may help in understanding Laureano Carranca, that rigid man of principle, think only of his inflexibility, his chill disapproval of his daughter's marriage, and the game of emotional weights and measures that he practiced daily, now that he has his grandson João at home with him, an act of reluctant charity, and another, much more favored grandson called José Nabiça. Let us explain why, although it won't really contribute much to our understanding of the story, only enough for us to know each other better, as the gospels urge us to do. José Nabiça was the child born to one of Sara da Conceição's sisters and a man whose anonymity consisted in everyone pretending not to know who he was, when in fact his identity was public knowledge. In such cases, there is often a general complicity, based on everyone knowing the truth but feeling curious as to how the protagonists will behave, and what's wrong with that, given how few distractions life provides. Such love children are often abandoned, sometimes by both mother and father, and consigned to the foundling hospital or left out on the road to be devoured either by the wolves or the Brothers of Mercy. Fortunately for José Nabiça, however, despite the taint of his birth, he was blessed with a father who had a little money and with grandparents who had an eye on a future inheritance, a remote possibility but of some substance nevertheless, enough to be a promise of wealth for the Carranca family. They treated João Mau-Tempo as if he wasn't of the same blood at all, and so he, as the son of a cobbler-turned-vagrant, would inherit neither money nor land. The other grandson, though he was the son of a sin unpurged by marriage, was treated like a prince by his grandfather, who remained deaf to what people said and blind to the evidence of his daughter's besmirched honor, and all because he had hopes of a legacy that never materialized. Proof perhaps that divine justice does exist.

João Mau-Tempo had more than a year of schooling, and that was the end of his education. His grandfather eyed that skinny little body, pondered for the nth time those blue eyes that were immediately lowered in fright, and decreed, You're to help your uncle in the fields, so behave yourself, because if you don't, you'll feel the weight of my hand. By work in the fields he meant clearing land and digging, a kind of brute labor quite unsuitable for a child, but it was as well for him to find out now what his place in the world would be when he grew up. Joaquim Carranca was himself a brute, and would leave João out all night in the fields, on guard in the cabin or on the threshing floor, when such duties were completely beyond the strength of a child. Worse still, during the night, out of pure malice, he would go and see if the boy was sleeping and then throw a sack of wheat on top of him and make the boy cry, and as if that were not enough, or, indeed, too much, he would prod him with a metal-tipped stick, and the more his nephew screamed and wept, the more the heartless wretch would laugh. These things really happened, which is why they're hard to believe when set down as fiction. In the meantime, Sara da Conceição gave birth to another daughter, who died eight days later.

There were rumors in Monte Lavre that a war was being waged in Europe, a place that few people in the village knew much about. They had their own wars to wage, and not small ones either, working all day, when there was work, and feeling sick with hunger all day, whether there was work or not. Not quite so many people died though, and generally speaking, any corpses entered the grave in one piece. However, as previously announced, the time had come for one of them to die.

When Sara da Conceição heard that her husband had been seen in Cortiçadas, she gathered together the children who lived with her and, putting little trust in her father's ability to protect

João, she picked him up en route and sought shelter in the house of some relatives, the Picanços, who were millers in a place called Ponte Cava, about half a league away, the place taking its name from the bridge that crossed the river there. The bridge in question, however, was now nothing but a crumbling arch and some large boulders on the riverbed, but João Mau-Tempo and the other children would bathe naked there, and when João lay on his back staring up at the sky, all he could see was sky and water. It was there in Ponte Cava that the family chose to hide, fearful of the threats emanating from Cortiçadas via the mouths of well-known tattletales. Domingos Mau-Tempo might never have come to Monte Lavre if the messenger, on his return journey, had not told him that his family had fled in terror. One day, he slung a saddlebag over his shoulder and, blinded by fate, set off along cart tracks and across plains, and when he reached the mill, he stood outside, demanding satisfaction and the return of his family. José Picanço came out to speak to him while, in the depths of the house, his wife kept guard over the refugees. Domingos Mau-Tempo says, Good morning, Picanço, And José Picanço says, Good morning, Mau-Tempo, what do you want. And Domingos Mau-Tempo says, I've come for my family, who, it seems, have run away from me, and someone told me that they're living in your house. And José Picanço says, Whoever told you that was quite right, they are living in my house. And Domingos Mau-Tempo says, Then send them out to me, because my wandering days are done. And José Picanço says, Who are you trying to fool, Mau-Tempo, you certainly can't fool me, I know you too well. And Domingos Mau-Tempo says, They're my family, not yours. And José Picanço says, Well, they're certainly in far better hands here, anyway, no one is coming out, because no one wants to go with you. And Domingos Mau-Tempo says, I'm the father and the husband. And José Picanço says, Get out of here, I saw how you treated your honest, hard-working wife when we were neighbors, and your poor children, and the misery you put them through, in fact, if it hadn't been for me and a few others, they would have died of hunger, and there would be no need for you to be here now, because they would all be dead. And Domingos Mau-Tempo says, Yes, but I'm still the father and the husband. And José Picanço says, Like I said before, get out of here and go where no one can hear or see or speak to you, because you're a hopeless case, a lost cause.

It's a beautiful day. A sunny morning after rain, because we're in autumn now, you see. Domingos Mau-Tempo draws a line on the ground with his stick, an apparent challenge, a sign that he is ready to fight, at least that is how Picanço interprets it, and so he, too, picks up a stick. These are not his problems, but often a man cannot choose, he simply happens to find himself in the right place at the right time. At his back, behind the door, are four frightened children and a woman who, if she could, would defend them with her own body, but the forces are so unequal, which is why Picanço draws his own line on the ground. He needn't have bothered. Domingos Mau-Tempo says nothing, makes no other gesture, he is still absorbing what has been said to him, but if he is truly to absorb it, he cannot stay there. He turns and goes back the way he came, taking the path that follows the river past Monte Lavre. Someone sees him and stops, but he doesn't respond. He might perhaps murmur, Wretched bloody place, but he says it with great sadness, with the grief of having been born, because he has no particular reason to hate this place, or perhaps all places are wretched and all are cursed, condemned and condemning. He goes down a grassy slope, crosses a fast-flowing stream via three steppingstones and climbs up the bank. There is a hill opposite Monte Lavre, each man has his mount of olives and his reason for going there. Domingos Mau-Tempo lies down in the sparse shade and looks up at the sky without knowing that he's looking at it. His eyes are dark, as deep as mines. He isn't thinking, unless thought is this slow parade of images, back and forth, and the occasional indecipherable word dropping like a stone that suddenly rolls for no reason down a hillside. He sits up and leans on his elbows, Monte Lavre is there before him like a nativity scene, at its highest point, above the tower, a very tall man is hammering at the sole of a shoe, raising his hammer and bringing it crashing down. Fancy seeing such things, and he's not even drunk. He is merely sleeping and dreaming. Now it's a cart passing by, piled with furniture and with Sara da Conceição perched precariously on top, and he is the one who's going to have to be the mule, fancy hauling all that weight, Father Agamedes, and around his neck is a bell without a clapper, he shakes it hard to make it ring, it must ring, but it's made of cork, oh, to hell with mass. And coming toward him is cousin Picanço, who removes the bell and replaces it with a millstone, you're a hopeless case, a lost cause.

He felt as if he had spent the whole afternoon daydreaming like this and yet it took only a few minutes. The sun has barely moved, the shadows haven't changed. Monte Lavre has neither grown nor shrunk. Domingos Mau-Tempo got up, ran his right hand over his beard and, when he did so, a piece of straw got caught in his fingers. He rubbed it between his fingertips, broke it in two and threw it away. Then he put his hand into his bag, produced a length of rope and walked in among the olive trees, out of sight now of Monte Lavre. He walked, looking about him as he went, like a landowner sizing up the harvest, he calculated heights and resistance, and finally decided where he would die. He slung the rope over a branch, secured it well, then climbed onto the branch, put the noose about his neck and jumped. No hanged man ever died so quickly.

JOÃO MAU-TEMPO IS now the man of the house, the oldest son. The firstborn with no firstborn's legacy, the owner of nothing at all, he casts a very brief shadow. He clomps around in the clogs his mother bought for him, but they're so heavy that they fall off his feet, and so he invents some rough-and-ready suspenders, which he loops under the soles of the clogs and through the holes he has made in his trouser bottoms. He cuts a grotesque figure, with his mattock, much larger than him, over his shoulder, as he rises from his thin mattress at dawn, in the cold, oily light of the lamp, so confused, so heavy with sleep, so clumsy in his gestures, that he probably leaves his bed with the mattock already on his shoulder and his clogs on his feet, a small, primitive machine capable of only one movement, raising the mattock and letting it fall, heaven knows where he gets the strength. Sara da Conceição said, Son, they've given me work for you so that you can earn a little money, because life is hard and we have no one to help us. And João Mau-Tempo, who already knows about life, asked, Shall I go and dig, Mama. If she could, Sara da Conceição would have said, No, my son, you're only ten years old, digging is no work for a child, but what is she to do when there are so few ways of

44

earning a living on the latifundio and when his dead father's trade proved so ill fated. It is still pitch-black when João Mau-Tempo gets up, but luckily for him, his path to the farm of Pedra Grande passes through Ponte Cava, a fortunate place for him despite all, the place where they, poor things, were saved from the wrath of Domingos Mau-Tempo, indeed, a doubly fortunate place because, even though his father killed himself in that cruel fashion, and despite his many sins, if that shoemaker is not at God's right hand, then there is no such thing as mercy. Domingos Mau-Tempo was a sad, unfortunate wretch, so let not good souls condemn him. His son, then, is setting off in the dim light of a still distant sun when Picanço's wife comes out to meet him and says, So, João, where are you off to. The blue-eyed lad answers, I'm off to Pedra Grande to clear the fields. And Picanço's wife says, You're far too small to use a mattock and the weeds are far too tall. One can see at once that this is a conversation between poor people, between a grown woman and a man still growing, and they speak of these lowly and insubstantial matters because, as you have seen, they are rough-and-ready types, with no education to enlighten them, or if they have, any light once shed is rapidly burning out. João Mau-Tempo knows what answer he will give, no one taught it to him, but any other reply would be out of time and place, That may be so, but I have to help my poor mother, well, you know what our life is like, and my brother Anselmo is going out begging for alms so that he can bring me something to eat in the fields, because my mother hasn't even enough money to buy food. Picanço's wife says, You mean you're going off to work without anything for your lunch, you poor lad. The poor lad answers, Yes, Senhora, I am.

This would be an appropriate moment for a Greek chorus to declare its horror and to create a suitably dramatic atmosphere for large, generous gestures. The best charity is that which one poor person gives to another, for, that way, at least it's between equals. Picanço was working in the mill and his wife called to him, Come here, husband. He came, and she said, Just look at João here. They had the same conversation over again, and it was decided there and then that on the days when he worked at Pedra Grande, he should stay in their house, and Picanço's wife, like the good woman she was, filled his lunch basket with food. She, too, is seated at God's right hand, doubtless in earnest conversation with Domingos Mau-Tempo, as they try together to understand why misfortune so outweighs reward.

João Mau-Tempo earned two tostões, which would have been the wage of a grown man four years earlier, but which was now a pittance, given how expensive life had become. He benefited from the good graces of the foreman, a distant relative, who pretended not to notice the boy battling with the roots of the weeds, far too tough for a small child. He spent the whole day, hours on end, half hidden in the undergrowth, slicing away with the mattock at those recalcitrant roots, why, Lord, do you make even children suffer so. Foreman, what's that boy doing here, you're not going to get much work out of him, commented Lamberto one day as he was passing. And the foreman answered, We took him on out of kindness, sir, his father was that wretch Domingos Mau-Tempo. I see, said Lamberto, and went into the stables to visit his horses, of which he was very fond. It was warm in there and smelled of straw, This one is called Sultão, this one Delicado, this one Tributo and this one Camarinha, and this as yet unnamed colt will be called Bom-Tempo, Fair-Weather.

When the land had been cleared, João returned to his mother's house. But he was in luck, because just two weeks later, he had found work again, on an estate belonging to another man, Norberto by name, and under the orders of a foreman called Gregório Lameirão. This Lameirão fellow was an utter brute. For him, the temporary workers were a mutinous rabble who would only respond to the stick and the whip. Norberto saw none of this, and yet he was said to be an excellent person getting on in years, a white-haired gentleman with a distinguished bearing and a large family, who were refined folk, albeit of the country kind, and who went sea bathing in Figueira in the summer. They owned property in Lisbon, and the younger members of the family were gradually moving away from Monte Lavre. The world lay before them like a vast landscape, although they knew this only by hearsay, of course, and the time was approaching when they would take their feet out of the mud and go in search of the paved streets of civilization. Norberto did not oppose them, and this new trend in his descendants and their collaterals even gave him a certain modest contentment. Thanks to cork trees and wheat, acorns and grubbing pigs, the latifundio rewarded the family with large surpluses, which were quickly converted into money, as long, of course, as the day laborers played their part, they and all the others. That is what the foremen were for, like rustic copies of Lieutenant Contente, with no right to a horse or a saber but invested with just as much authority. With a slender cane under his arm, which he used as a horsewhip, Gregório Lameirão would walk along the line of workers, keeping an eagle eye out for the slightest sign of slacking or sheer exhaustion. Fortunately he was a man who stuck to the rules and used his own sons as examples. They all suffered there, the younger ones, that is, because hardly a day passed without one of them getting a sound beating, or two or three if their father was in his angry vein. When Gregório Lameirão set out from his house or barracks, he left his heart hanging behind the door and thus walked with a lighter step, his only desire being to deserve the boss's confidence in him and to earn the larger wage and better food that were his due as foreman and scourge of his troops. He was also an arrant coward. Once, the father of one of his unfortunate victims met him on the road and made it quite clear that if he unjustly punished his boy one more time, he would see, if he could still see, his own brains spattering the door of his house. The threat worked in that case, but this only meant that he increased the number of punishments he meted out to the others.

In Norberto's household, the ladies had all the refinements of the female sex, they drank tea, knitted, and were godmothers to the daughters of the maids closest to them. Fashion magazines lay on the sofas in the living room, ah, Paris, a city the family was determined to visit once there was an end to this stupid war, which, quite apart from other inconveniences of a greater and lesser degree, was delaying their plans. It is not in our power, of course, to do anything about such problems. And when old Norberto listened to his foreman giving his mumbled report on how the work on the land was going, a report whose sole object was to make himself look good, Norberto would grow as impatient as if he were listening to communiqués from the front. His imperial tendencies, and perhaps some trace memory of the birthplace of Lamberto Horques, who might well have been his ancestor, meant that he was a natural Germanophile. And one day, in a playful spirit, he said as much to Gregório Lameirão, who simply stared at him, eyes wide, not understanding what he had heard, because he was stupid and illiterate. Just in case, he humbled himself still more and was even more rigorous with his workers. His oldest sons now refused to work for him and went in search of employment on other estates, which offered more humane foremen and more security, although more security meant only that they would not die quite so soon.

These were good times for discipline. Sara da Conceição, who, understandably enough, could not forget the bad example set by her husband nor the worm of guilt that gnawed away inside her for the unfortunate manner of his death, was always saying, João, if you don't toe the line, I'll give you a sound beating, we've got a living to make. That is what his mother told him, a sentiment reinforced by Lameirão, who used to say, According to your mother, all she wants from you are your bones to make a chair with and your skin to make a drum. When two such authorities were so clearly of one mind, what could João do but believe them. But one day, worn down by beatings and overwork, he braved the threat of being flayed and boned, and spoke frankly to his astonished mother. Poor Sara da Conceição, who knew so little of the world. Amid screams and sighs, she said, That wretched man, I never said any such thing, a mother doesn't give birth to a child in order to be the death of him, oh, how the rich despise the poor, that monster doesn't even love his own children. But we ourselves have said as much before.

João Mau-Tempo is not the stuff of heroes. He's a skinny little ten-year-old runt, a scrap of a boy who still regards trees as shelters for birds' nests rather than as producers of cork, acorns or olives. It's unfair to make him get up when it's still dark and have him walk, half asleep and on an empty stomach, the short or long distance to wherever his place of work happens to be, and then slave away all day until sunset, only to return home, again in the dark, mortally tired, if something so like death can be called tiredness. But this child, a word we use only for convenience's sake, because this is not how the latifundio categorizes its population, people are either alive or dead, and all one can do with the dead is bury them, you certainly can't make them work, anyway, this child is just one among thousands, all the same, all suffering, all ignorant of what evil they committed to deserve such a punishment. On his father's side, he comes from tradesmen's stock, his father a shoemaker, his grandfather a carpenter, but see how destinies are forged, there is no bradawl here, no plane, nothing but dry earth, killing heat, deathly cold, the great droughts of summer, the bone-deep chill of winter, the hard morning frost, lace, Dona Clemência calls it, cracked, bloody, purple chilblains, and if that swollen hand rubs against a tree trunk or a stone, the soft skin opens, and who can say what misery and pain lies beneath. Is there no other life than this drudgery, an animal living on the earth alongside other animals, the domestic and the wild, the useful and the harmful, and he himself, along with his human brothers, is treated as either harmful or useful, depending on the needs of the latifundio, now I want you, now I don't.

And sometimes there is no work, first the youngest are dismissed, then the women, and finally the men. Caravans of people set off along the roads in search of a miserable wage somewhere else. At such times, there's not a foreman or an overseer to be found, far less a landowner, they're all shut up in their houses, or far away in the capital or some other hiding place. The earth is either a dry crust or pure mud, it doesn't matter. The poorest boil up some weeds and live on those, their eyes burn, their stomachs bloat, and this is followed by long, painful bouts of diarrhea, the sense that the body is letting go, detaching itself, becoming fetid, an unbearable weight. You feel like dying, and some do die.

As we said before, there is war in Europe. And war in Africa too. But these things are like shouts from a hilltop, you know you shouted, and sometimes it might be the last thing you do, but down below, that shout grows fainter and fainter until it vanishes into nothing. Monte Lavre hears about these wars from the newspapers, but they are only for those who can read. When those who can't read see prices going up or basic foodstuffs running short, they ask why, It's the war, say those in the know. War ate a great deal and war grew fat and rich. War is a monster who empties men's pockets, coin by coin, before devouring the men themselves, so that nothing is lost and all is changed, which is the primary law of nature, as one learns later on. And when war has eaten its fill, when it is sated to the point of vomiting, it continues its skillful pickpocketing, always taking from the same people, the same pockets. It's a habit acquired in peacetime.

In some places, people put on mourning clothes because a relative had died in the war. The government sent condolences, deepest sympathies, and spoke about the nation. The usual mentions were made of Afonso Anriques and Nuno Álvares Pereira,* about how we Portuguese were the ones who discovered the sea route to India, and how Frenchwomen have a weakness for our soldiers, but nothing was said about African women apart from what we know already, the czar was deposed, the neighboring powers are concerned about the situation in Russia, there's a big offensive on the western front, aviation is the weapon of the future, but the infantry still reigns supreme in battle, you can't do anything without the artillery, dominion of the seas is indispensable, revolution in Russia, Bolshevism. Adalberto read his newspaper, looked anxiously out at the foggy weather, shared the indignation expressed in the newspaper and said out loud, It will pass.

It isn't all roses for one side or the other, although, as we have explained before, the distribution of thorns is made according to the old familiar rules of disproportion and gives the lie to the dictum, which may be true in the world of navigation, The larger the ship, the bigger the storm. On land, it's different. The Mau-Tempo family have only a tiny, flat-bottomed boat, and it's only by chance and because of the demands of the story that they haven't all drowned. However, their small craft was giving every sign of breaking up on the next reef or the next time the store cupboard was empty, when, unexpectedly, Sara's brother, Joaquim Carranca, lost his wife. He wasn't of a mind to remarry, nor did he have a list of potential brides, plus he had three children to bring up and a very bad temper, but hunger joined forces with a desire to eat, and this prompted brother and sister to unite lives and children. It balanced out nicely, the brother provided a new father, the sister a new mother, but it was all kept in the family, so let's see how things turned out. It wasn't any worse than what could have happened,

---

* Afonso Anriques, or Henriques, was the first king of Portugal, nicknamed "the Conqueror." Nuno Álvares Pereira (1360–1431) was a Portuguese military leader who played a crucial role in assuring Portugal's independence from Castile.

and possibly better. The Mau-Tempo children stopped begging from door to door, and Joaquim Carranca had someone to wash his clothes, which is something every man needs, and, in addition, someone to look after his children. And since it is not the custom for brothers to beat their sisters, or at least not as often as it is for husbands to beat their wives, this was the beginning of better days for Sara da Conceição. Some may consider this to be very little. They, we would say, clearly don't know much about life.

E VERY DAY HAS ITS story, a single minute would take years
to describe, as would the smallest gesture, the careful peel-
ing away of each word, each syllable, each sound, not to mention
thoughts, which are things of great substance, thinking about what
you think or thought or are thinking, and about what kind of
thought it is exactly that thinks about another thought, it's never-
ending. It would be best to say that for João Mau-Tempo, these
years will provide his professional education, in the traditional
country sense that a workingman has to know how to do everything, from scything to harvesting cork, from clearing ditches to
sowing seeds, and he needs a good strong back for carrying loads
and for digging. This knowledge is transmitted across the generations with no examinations and no discussions, and it has always
been the same, this is a hoe, this is a scythe, and this is a drop of
sweat. It is also the thick white saliva you get in your mouth on
furnace-hot days, it's the sun beating down on your head, and your
knees going weak with hunger. Between the ages of ten and twenty
you have to learn all this very fast, or no one will employ you.

Joaquim Carranca remarked one day to his sister how good
it would be to find a boss who would take them all on, and she

agreed, a habit born of years as a submissive married woman, but in this case what flickered before her was the hope of spending a whole year safe from unemployment, that would be her one modest but sure ambition, for they could hardly aspire to anything more. At this time, three brothers inherited Monte de Berra Portas following the death of the old owner, their father, who had sowed his seed in the womb of a very canny mistress, who, while appearing to submit to the patriarch's terrible whims and to his thunderous rants and rages, had gradually tamed him, like a lamb, so much so that he agreed, at the last, to disinherit his closest relatives in favor of his three natural sons. Pedro, Paulo and Saul took turns presiding over the estate, each taking a different season, and when Pedro was giving the orders, the other two obeyed, a system that could have worked well if each brother hadn't chosen to spy on his other siblings, with Saul declaring that when he wasn't in charge, the household went to rack and ruin, with Paulo stating that he was the only really capable administrator, and with all three becoming embroiled in domestic alliances and plots, as often happens in families. The story of this triumvirate would, alone, be enough to make an opera. And then there was the mother, who screamed that she had been plundered by her own sons, or to speak more plainly, robbed, after all she had done for them, putting up with being the servant of that old pig and now finding herself the slave of her own children, who kept her short of money and a virtual prisoner in the house. At night, when the countryside drew the silence up about it like a blanket, the better to hide itself away in the great secrets of the dark, you would hear what sounded like a sow having its throat slit and the loud stamping of feet, it was the war between mother and sons.

Joaquim Carranca found employment with these bosses, and João Mau-Tempo worked as a day laborer. All in all, they earned a pittance, enough, just about, for them not to be constantly hungry, but there was at least the advantage that they could all be together and have access to a vegetable patch where they could break their backs toiling away on high days and holidays. Joaquim Carranca's wage at this time consisted of lodging, firewood, sixty kilos of maize flour, three liters of olive oil, five liters of cowpeas, one hundred escudos and, at the end of the year, a modest handout. As for the younger members of the family, they earned forty kilos of maize flour, a liter and a half of olive oil, three liters of cowpeas and fifty escudos. And so it went on, month after month. They would take their sacks and bags to the granary, their jug to the cellar, where the foreman would measure out their rations of food and oil, and the administrator would pay their wages, and that was all they had to keep body and soul together and to recoup the energy expended every day. Of course, not all of them did recover, and they accepted this, time would inevitably take its toll, the skull beneath the skin becoming ever more evident, but then we are all born in order to die. Joaquim Carranca died, without having had a single day's illness, after coming back from working in his vegetable patch on one of those Sundays when it's easy to believe in the existence of God, even without the aid of Father Agamedes, it was just a shame that the mattock was so heavy that he had to sit down on a log at the front door, feeling unusually tired, and when Sara da Conceição came out to tell her brother that supper was ready, he had lost all appetite. There he was, eyes wide, his hands open on his lap, more peaceful than he could ever have dreamed of being when alive, and he wasn't a bad man really, despite his sudden rages, despite his cruelty to his oldest nephew, what's done is done. Death is like a great strickle that passes over the measuring jug of life, discarding any excess, although it is often hard to make out what exactly its criteria are, as in the case of Joaquim Carranca, who was still needed by his family.

Life, or whoever rules over life, with either a sure or an indifferent hand, expects us to acquire both our professional and our sentimental education at the same time. This conjunction is clearly a mistake, doubtless made necessary by the brevity of life, which is not long enough for things to be done in a more leisurely, timely manner, which means that one neither acquires enough nor feels enough. Since the world was not going to change its ways, João Mau-Tempo, as he acquired his working skills, also went courting in the local villages and dancing wherever the sound of an accordion was to be heard, and he was a good dancer too, and, who would have thought it, much sought after by the girls. As we know, he had inherited his blue eyes from that ancestor of four hundred years before, the same one who, not far from here, lying on the forebears of this same bracken, raped a young girl who had gone to the well for water, watched by birds whose plumage remains unchanged, and who gazed down on the pair struggling amid the greenery, a scene with which those creatures of the air had been familiar since the world began. And his blue eyes troubled the hearts of the young girls, which would melt when those eyes grew suddenly dark, though he himself was unaware of any ancient amorous rage rising up in him, such is the hidden force of past actions. Ah, youth. The fact is that João Mau-Tempo may have flirted a lot but he rarely went further than that. When he had had a few drinks, he might touch a girl rather more boldly or give her a clumsy kiss devoid of all the knowledge that the century was gradually accumulating for future general use.

In the eclogues of old, the shepherds played their lutes and the shepherdesses wove their garlands of flowers, but in this modern version, João Mau-Tempo, during a ten-week contract that took him off to Salvaterra to cut cork, ate a whole string of garlic in the hope of preserving himself from the mosquitoes, as a result, you could smell him ten paces away. He was learning the cork trade in the hope that he might one day earn the eighteen escudos paid to master cork cutters, and fortunately enough, he was far from his would-be girlfriends, who, while they might have been pretty tolerant of most smells, would perhaps have drawn the line at garlic. Happiness, as we know, depends on such small details.

And now João Mau-Tempo has received his call-up papers. He is full of daydreams, he imagines himself far from Monte Lavre, in Lisbon perhaps, having completed his military service, only a fool would miss the chance to find a job on the trams or on the police force or with the national guard, he has a smattering of education, he just has to push himself forward, he wouldn't be the first. Call-up day is a day of celebration, with fireworks and wine, the young lads who finally deserve to be called men are all there in their freshly washed clothes, and when they're lined up stark naked, they make macho jokes to disguise their embarrassment and stand at attention, red-faced, to answer the doctor's questions. Then the draft board meets and makes its selections. A few men were chosen, and of the four who weren't, only one went away downhearted. That was João Mau-Tempo, who watched his dream of wearing a uniform vanish into the realm of the impossible, his dream of standing on the platform of a tram, ringing the bell, or becoming a policeman and policing the streets of the capital, or, as a guard, guarding, ah, but on whose behalf, the very fields in which he labored now, and he found this possibility so troubling that it helped him get over his disappointment. One cannot think of everything all at the same time.

So what is João Mau-Tempo to do? He has just turned twenty, he has been let off military service, he hasn't filled out much since the days when he, tiny as a dwarf, battled with the weeds in Pedra Grande and ate the maize porridge that Picanço's wife used to make for him out of familial charity. In Salvaterra, he buys his first cape and struts about in it like a tomcat with its tail in the air. It's very full and reaches down to his heels, but the village doesn't expect people to be dressed in the height of fashion, he has reached heights enough simply by owning a new item of clothing, regardless of what it's like. When João Mau-Tempo plunges his mattock into the earth, he thinks about that cape, about the dances he goes to, about the girlfriends in his life, some more serious than others, and he forgets the pain of living here, bound to this place, so far from Lisbon, if he ever really had aspired to living there, if that wasn't all just a youthful dream, for what else is youth for but to dream.

A time of great storms is approaching, some will arrive with their natural boom and bluster, others more quietly, without a shot being fired, coming from far-off Braga, but we will hear more of these later on, when there is nothing to be done about them. However, although one should deal with each event in its proper order, and although, as we feel we should point out so as not to keep offending against the rules of storytelling, we have, in fact, already anticipated the death of Joaquim Carranca, which actually happened a few years later, let us nonetheless talk about the storm that remained fixed in people's memories for reasons of grief and loss. It was summer, ladies and gentlemen, when one doesn't really expect such things, though occasional solemn rolls of thunder boomed across the stubble, catapum, one moment distant and almost sleepy, the next flickering right above our heads and pounding the earth, whatever would we do without Saint Barbara's help. Now, the Mau-Tempo family may seem to have been singled out for grim happenings, but only someone of little understanding could possibly believe that. After all, so far only one member of the family has died, and if we're talking hunger and poverty, then any other family could serve as an example, for hunger and poverty are hardly in short supply. Besides, the uncle in question was not even a blood relative. Augusto Pintéu was married to one of Sara da Conceição's sisters, and although he was a farm laborer, he chose, in his spare time, to work as a carter. He, naturally, had his appointment with death, but how oddly things turn out, for this simple, mild-mannered, soft-spoken man met a very dramatic end, with much celestial and terrestrial brouhaha, like a character in a tragedy. This serene man did not leave life as serenely as Joaquim Carranca. And such contradictions provide much food for thought.

As we said, Augusto Pintéu also worked as a carter, traveling between Vendas Novas and Monte Lavre to be exact. The former had a train station, to which, with his pair of mules and his cart, he would take cork, coal and wood and bring back groceries, seeds and whatever else was needed, not many men enjoyed such a good life. On that day, which, being a summer's day, should have been long and bright, the sky suddenly filled with black clouds and there was an almighty thunderclap. The heavens opened and unleashed all God's store of water. Augusto Pintéu wasn't particularly worried, because these summer storms come and go, and so he continued his work of loading and unloading, fearing nothing worse than arriving home soaked to the skin. When he left Vendas Novas, night had already closed in, lit by lightning so bright that there seemed to be some celebration going on up above, some holy procession. The mules knew the route blindfold and could find and recognize it even when it was flooded, as the lower parts already were. With two thick sacks on his head to protect him, Augusto Pintéu consoled himself with the thought that, in such weather, there was, at least, little danger of being ambushed by thieves, as had happened in the past. In a storm like this, highwaymen would all be safe in their lairs, roasting their stolen slices of pork and drinking coarse wine, because they rarely stole anything else. It's three leagues from Vendas Novas to Monte Lavre, but Augusto Pintéu would not travel the last league, nor would his mules. By the time they reached the stream, the darkness had grown as black as pitch, and the waters roared and thundered loudly enough to frighten anyone. This was usually the place where, in good weather, you could ford the stream, with the water up to your knees, but for those on foot there was a broad wooden plank that went from shore to shore, past a giant ash tree that had been born there and grown up in the days before the course of the river had changed. In the midst of the water, the ash tree rustled furiously, defending with its thick roots its vital patch of earth, threatened now by the speed and force of the current. Augusto Pintéu had crossed there with his cart and his mules many times. He would not cross it again. Right at the beginning of the ford, the bed of the stream dropped away to form a deep, deep chasm, which was called, because everything has to have a name, Pego da Carriça, Wren's Pool. Augusto Pintéu put his trust in the Holy Virgin and in his mules and thus managed to reach the middle, where the water lapped against the bottom of his cart. At that point, fearing the current seething about them and fearing that he would be swept away with no hope of salvation, he tried to drive the mules upstream. They resisted as best they could, but being subject to the whip and the bit, they finally submitted. At one point, the right-hand mule lost its footing, one wheel slipped off the edge and into the chasm, and amid screams and rumbles of thunder, Augusto Pintéu and his mules, along with the cart, the groceries and the other merchandise, were all drowned, plunged forever into the thick blackness of the waters, into mortal silence. They touched bottom and there they remained, with Augusto Pintéu still held fast to the reins, and the mules to the cart, because down below the waters were absolutely calm, as if they had been like that since the world began. The following day, accompanied by the widow's screams and the orphaned children's tears, they were pulled out, thanks to some lengths of rope and the efforts of some very brave men, while a crowd, come from far and wide, gathered on the banks of the river. It had stopped raining by then. That was a summer of great afflictions. So great were the storms that men working in the cork forests fell from the trees and, as they fell, cut themselves on their axes. This is a life more filled with tribulations than one can say.

At the time, the Mau-Tempo family lived in Monte de Berra

Portas with their uncle and brother, Joaquim Carranca. The next year, when Portugal had been following the Braga road* for some six months, João Mau-Tempo, along with his siblings Anselmo and Maria da Conceição, went to work in the winter pastures for a different boss, in a place called, for some reason, Pendão das Mulheres, Ladies' Pennant. It was four long leagues away, on foot and on bad roads, from Monte de Berra Portas that is, whereas from Monte Lavre it was only a league and a half. There were quite a few girls in the party, which explained why the boys were so pleased, up there all week with those young women and only going home every other Saturday. The workers were mostly youngsters. The place was a hotbed of flirtations and dalliances, and quite a few got burned. At the time, João Mau-Tempo had a girlfriend elsewhere, but he didn't care, and pretended that he was a free agent, and his skill as a dancer made him a most attractive prospect.

What with work and romance, the weeks flew past, and then a girl from Monte Lavre joined them, a girl he knew well from having danced and sung with her countless times. But they had never been in love. Half serious, half joking, they addressed each other as Friend João and Friend Faustina, for that was her name. There would seem to be nothing more to say about them. However, this turned out not to be the case. Whether it was because of the freedom they enjoyed or because the time had come to tie that particular knot, João fell in love with Faustina, and Faustina with João. In matters of love, it can as easily bloom in diamond rings in shop windows as grow wild among the castor-oil plants, only the language differs. This love began to put down roots, and João Mau-Tempo forgot all about his other girlfriend, but since this new love was serious, they agreed to say nothing for the moment to Faustina's family, because although João Mau-Tempo himself had done

---

* On May 28, 1926, General Gomes da Costa led an uprising in Braga, which was the prelude to the so-called National Dictatorship, which, in turn, paved the way for Salazar's dictatorship.

nothing to be ashamed of, he had inherited his father's bad name, and these things stick, for as the saying goes, He who is born of a cat will run after mice. The secret nonetheless reached the ears of Faustina's family, and they made her life a misery. He can't be any good, he looks shifty with those strange blue eyes, and then there was that father of his, a loose-living, drunken fellow who only ever did one good thing, which was to hang himself. That is how some village evenings are spent, beneath the starry sky, while the male genet pursues the female genet and copulates with her amid the bracken. The lives of human beings are far more complicated, for we are, after all, human.

It was January and very cold, the sky was one solid sheet of cloud, the laborers were walking along the road toward Monte Lavre for their fortnightly rest, and as befitted a courting couple, João was talking to Faustina, and she, fearing the domestic storm awaiting her, was telling him her problems. Then suddenly they were assailed by the angry shouts and violent gestures of one of Faustina's sisters, who, given their mother's advanced age, had taken over as family spokesperson, and it was her treacherous ambush that so startled the couple. Natividade, for that was her name, said, Have you no shame, Faustina, you stubborn creature, it seems that no amount of good advice and beatings has any effect, Lord knows what will become of you. She said other things too, but Faustina did not leave João's side. Natividade stood in front of them, intending to block their path and their destiny, if it is in a sister's power to do such a thing, and it was then, so to speak, that João Mau-Tempo took hold of the world and felt its weight, because from then on, it would be a matter of world and man, house, children, the shared life. He placed one hand on Faustina's shoulder, for she would be his world, and said, trembling at his own daring, We can't go on like this, we either finish right here and now so that you don't suffer anymore, or you come and live with me in my mother's house, until I can get us a house of our own, and from now on I will do all I can to protect you. As we said earlier, the sky was one solid sheet of cloud, and it stayed like that, thus providing natural proof that the heavens care nothing about us, if they did, the clouds would have opened in glory. Because Faustina, a brave, trusting lass, the color of whose eyes and the expression of whose face we haven't described yet, said in a firm, loud voice, João, where you go, I go, if you will promise to love me and care for me always. And Natividade said, You ungrateful wretch, and with that, she turned abruptly and shot off home like an arrow to announce this latest catastrophe. The two lovers were left alone, evening was coming on, and João Mau-Tempo took her hands in his and said, I will care for you for as long as we live, in sickness and in health, but now let us go our separate ways, and when we reach the village, we'll set a time for our escape.

João Mau-Tempo's brother Anselmo and his sister Maria da Conceição were with him and had witnessed some of what had happened. He went over to them and said in a firm voice, Go to the village and tell our mother that I'm bringing my girl home with me, that I count on having her permission to do so, and that I'll explain everything later. Anselmo said, Think carefully before you act, don't get into something you can't get out of. And Maria da Conceição said, I hate to think what our mother and our uncle will say. And João Mau-Tempo said, I'm a grown man now, I've been turned down for the army, and if my future is to take a new direction, then why wait, better sooner than later. And Anselmo said, One day, Uncle Joaquim Carranca could get an idea in his head and simply go off, you know what he's like, and you're needed at home. And Maria da Conceição said, You might be doing the wrong thing. But João Mau-Tempo said, Be patient, these things happen. When they left him, Maria da Conceição had a tear in her eye.

During this time of weekly comings and goings between Pendão das Mulheres and Monte de Berra Portas, the Mau-Tempo children had lodgings in the house of Aunt Cipriana, who was the woman we saw weeping by the river after the waters of Pego da Carriça had swept her husband away. She is dressed in mourning and will remain so until she dies, many years later, lost from our sight. Her nephew's bold move, however, gave her a taste for acting as go-between, an honest one, of course, not a procuress, and as a protector of star-crossed lovers, and she never regretted this or suffered public censure for her actions. But that is another story. When João Mau-Tempo arrived, he said to his aunt, Aunt, will you please let Faustina come and meet me here until we can leave for my mother's house in Monte de Berra Portas. And Cipriana answered, Think about what you're doing, João, I don't want any problems, and I don't want to besmirch your late uncle's memory either. And João replied, Don't worry, we'll only be here until it gets dark.

This was what João agreed with Faustina afterward, when he went to meet her, and she had deliberately dawdled, well, that's only normal when you're in love, but he can't dissuade her from seeing her mother before they run away together, even if she doesn't tell her where she's going. João Mau-Tempo, not wanting to start his new life with a fortnight's growth of beard, decided to visit the barber's, where he got himself done up like a bridegroom, that is, with a clean-shaven face. Whenever such usually thickly bearded faces are shaven, they look somehow innocent, defenseless, their very fragility touches the heart. When he returned to Aunt Cipriana's house, Faustina was there waiting for him, still tearful from her sister's angry words, her father's terrible rage and her mother's grief. She had crept away unnoticed, but since her family would doubtless be scouring Monte Lavre to find out where the couple had gone, João and Faustina decided they had better make their escape as soon as possible. Cipriana said, It's going to be a very tiring journey, and we're in for a wet, dark night, take this umbrella and some bread and sausage to eat on the way, now that you've played this very unfunny joke on everyone, be sure to behave yourselves in future, that was what Cipriana said, but in her heart she was blessing them, vicariously enjoying this youthful transgression, ah, to be young again.

It was two and a half leagues from there to Monte de Berra Portas, the night had closed in completely, and rain was threatening. Walking two and a half leagues along paths that are all shadows and alarming shapes and noises, your thoughts inevitably turn to stories about werewolves, what's more, because there is no other way, they have to cross the plank bridge at Pego da Carriça. Let's say a prayer for my uncle, he was a good man and did not deserve such a sad death. The ash tree rustled gently, the water flowed like dark, whispering silk, and to think that in this very place, who would believe it. João Mau-Tempo was holding Faustina's hand, his calloused fingers trembled, he guided her beneath the trees and through the dense undergrowth and the wet grass, and suddenly, quite how they didn't know, perhaps it was due to exhaustion after so many weeks of work, perhaps to an unbearable shaking, they found themselves lying down. Faustina soon lost her maidenhood, and when they had finished, João remembered the bread and sausage, and it was as man and wife that they shared the food.

As we have seen, Lamberto, regardless of whether he's German or Portuguese, is not a man to work his vast estate with his own hands. When he inherited it or bought it from the friars or, since justice is blind, stole it, he found, clinging to the estate like a tree trunk to its roots, a few creatures with arms and legs who were created for precisely such a fate, by producing children and bringing them up to be useful. Even so, whether out of pragmatism, custom, etiquette or pure self-interested prudence, Adalberto has no direct contact with those who will work his land. And that is a good thing. Just as the king in his day, or the president of the republic in his, did not and does not go about bandying words and gestures with the common people in an overly familiar manner, it would seem quite wrong on a large estate, where the owner has more power than either president or king, were Floriberto to be too forward. However, this intentional reserve did allow for certain deliberate exceptions, intended as a more refined way of bending wills and attracting perfect vassals, namely, the subservient creatures who, receiving as they do both caresses and beatings, enjoy the former and respect the latter. This matter of relations between employer and employee is a very subtle thing which cannot be determined or explained in a few words, you have to be there and eavesdrop like a fly on the wall. Add to this, brute force, ignorance, presumption and hypocrisy, a taste for suffering, a large dollop of envy, guile and a taste for intrigue, and you have a perfect training in diplomacy, for anyone who cares to learn. However, a few empirical rules, tried and tested over the centuries, will help us understand such cases better.

As well as land, the first thing Lamberto needs is a foreman, the foreman being the whip that keeps order in the pack of dogs. He is a dog chosen from among the others to bite his fellow dogs. He needs to be a dog because he knows all a dog's wiles and defenses. You wouldn't go looking for a foreman among the children of Norberto, Alberto or Humberto. A foreman is, first and foremost, a servant, who receives privileges and payments in proportion to the amount of work he can get out of the pack. He is, nonetheless, a servant. He is placed among the first and the last, a kind of human mule, an aberration, a Judas, who betrays his fellows in exchange for more power and a slightly larger chunk of bread.

The biggest and most decisive weapon is ignorance. At his birthday supper, Sigisberto said, It's just as well that they know nothing, that they can't read or write or count or think, that they assume and accept that, as Father Agamedes will explain, the world cannot be changed, that this is the only possible world, exactly as it is, that they will find paradise only after death, and that work alone brings dignity and money, but they mustn't go thinking that I earn more than they do, the land, after all, is mine and when the time comes to pay taxes and contributions, I don't go to them asking for a loan, it's always been like that and always will be, if I didn't give them work, who would, it's them and me, I'm the land and they are the work, what's good for me is good for them, that is how God wanted it, as Father Agamedes will explain in simple terms, we don't want to make them even more confused than they are already, and if Father Agamedes doesn't do the trick, then we'll ask the guards to ride around the villages on their horses, just as a reminder that they exist, a message they're sure to understand. But tell me, Mama, do the guards beat the estate owners as well, You're clearly not quite right in the head, my boy, the national guard was created and is maintained in order to beat the people, But how is that possible, Mama, do you mean that the guard was made simply in order to beat the people, but what do the people do, They don't have anyone who can, in turn, beat the estate owner when he sends out the guards to beat them, Well, I think the people should ask the guards to beat the estate owner, If you want my advice, Maria, the child is slightly mad, don't let him go around saying such things, we have our work cut out as it is, keeping the guards in check.

The people were made to be hungry and dirty. People who wash regularly are people who don't work, well, maybe it's different in the cities, I don't deny that, but here on the estate they're hired to work away from home for three or four weeks, sometimes months, if that's what Alberto wants, and during that time it's a point of honor and of manhood with them to wash neither face nor hands and to remain unshaven. If they did wash and shave, if such a hypothesis were not so laughably improbable, they would be the butt of jokes from bosses and fellow workers alike. That's the great thing about this day and age, the sufferers glory in their suffering, the slaves in their servitude. This beast of the earth must remain a beast who never rubs the sleep from his eyes from morning to night, indeed the dirt on his hands, face, armpits, groin, feet, arsehole must be for him the glorious aura surrounding work on the latifundio, man must be lower than the beasts of the field, for they, at least, lick themselves clean, man, however, must degrade himself so that he respects neither himself nor his fellows.

More than that. The workers boast of the beatings they get when working the land. Each beating is a medal to be bragged about at the inn, between drinks, I got beaten *x* number of times when I was working for Berto and Humberto. That's a good worker for you, one who, when he gets whipped, will show off his raw welts, and if they're bleeding, all the better, these are the same sort of boasts that the urban rabble make, taking as proof of their virility the number of cankers and sores acquired from their labors in a hired bed. Ah, you people preserved in the grease or honey of ignorance, you have never lacked for exploiters. So, work, work yourself to death, yes, die if necessary, that way you'll be remembered by the foreman and the boss, but woe betide you if you get a reputation for being an idler, no one will ever love you then. You can go and stand at the doors of inns with your companions in misfortune, and they, too, will despise you, and the foreman, or the boss, if he deigns to notice, will eye you with disgust and you'll be given no work, just to teach you a lesson. The others have already learned their lesson, they go off every day to slave away on the latifundio, and when you get home, if the hovel you live in can be called a home, how are you going to explain that you have no work, that the other men have but you haven't. Mend your ways while there's still time, and swear that you've taken twenty beatings, crucify yourself, hold out your arm to be bled, open your veins and say, This is my blood, drink it, this is my body, eat it, this is my life, take it, along with the church's blessing, the salute to the flag, the march past, the handing over of credentials, the awarding of a university diploma, thy will be done on earth as it is in heaven.

Ah, but life is a game too, a playful exercise, playing is a very serious, grave, even philosophical act, for children it's part of growing up, for adults it's a link with their childhood, advantageous for some. Whole libraries of books have been written on the subject, all of them solid, weighty tomes, only a fool could fail to be convinced. The mistake lies in thinking that such profundity can be found only in books, when in fact a quick glance, a moment's attention, is all it takes to see how the cat plays with the mouse, and how the latter is eaten by the former. The question, the only one that matters, is knowing who exploits the initial innocence of the game, this game that was never innocent, for example, when the foreman says to the workers, Let's run, and see who gets there last, And the innocents, blind to the obvious deceit, run, trot, gallop, stagger from Monte Lavre to Vale de Cães, merely for the glory of arriving first or for the smug satisfaction of not being last. Because the last man, well, someone always has to be last, will have to put up with the jeers and mockery of the winners, who are already panting and breathless, they haven't even started work yet but the poor fools waste their breath on this explosion of scorn. Poor João Mau-Tempo won the booby prize, not that anyone knows what that is, a prize that marks you out as idle or not being fast enough on your feet, that says you're not a man but a mere nothing. Portugal is a country of men, there's certainly no lack of them, only the one who comes last in the race is not a man, get away, you lazy brute, you don't even deserve the bread you eat.

But the games have not ended. The last to arrive, if he has any self-respect, will offer to carry the first load, well, it's some compensation. The pile of wood that will eventually become charcoal is being prepared, and having placed a sack on your back to dull the pain to come, you say, Give me that big trunk, I'll carry that. The foreman is watching, you have to prove to your colleagues that you're as good a man as they, and besides, you can't afford to be without work next week, you have children to think of, and then, groaning with effort, two men lift the trunk, they're not your children but it's as if they were, and they place the trunk on your shoulders, you kneel down like a camel, if you've ever seen one, and when you feel the weight, your knees sag, but you grit your teeth, brace your back and gradually draw yourself up, it's a huge trunk, like the leg of a giant, it feels like a hundred-year-old cork oak on your shoulders, you take the first step, and how far away that pile of wood is, your colleagues are watching, and the foreman says, Let's see if you can do it, if you can you're a brave man. That's what it's about, being brave, bearing the weight of that trunk and the pain in your creaking spine and in your heart, just so as to look good in the foreman's eyes, who will say to Adalberto, He's a brave fellow that Mau-Tempo, although it could be any other name, you should have seen the piece of wood they gave him to carry, sir, it really was a sight to see, oh yes, he's a real man all right. Possibly, but so far you've taken only three steps. What you really want to do now is put the load down on the ground, at least that's what your tormented body is asking. Your soul, your spirit, if you have the right to one, tells you that you can't, that you would rather die than be humiliated in your own village and dubbed a weakling, anything but that. People have been going on for two thousand years or more about how Christ carried the cross to Golgotha with help from the Cyrenian, but no one has a word to say about this crucified man who dined last night on very little and has had almost nothing to eat today, and he's still only halfway there, his vision grows blurred, it's a real torment, ladies and gentlemen, with everyone watching and shouting, He can't do it, he can't do it, and although you have ceased to be yourself, at least you haven't yet been reduced to being an animal, a great advantage, because an animal would have fallen to its knees, crushed by the load, but you haven't, you're a man, the dupe at the universal gaming table, why not place a bet, your wage may not pay you enough to feed you, but life is this merry game, He's nearly there, you hear someone say, and you feel as if you were not of this world, carrying a load like that, have pity on me, help me, comrades, if we all carried it together it would be so much easier, but that's not possible, it's a matter of honor, you would never again speak to the man who helped you, that is how deceived you are. You deposit the trunk in precisely the right place, a huge achievement, and your comrades all cheer, you're no longer the last in the race, and the foreman says gravely, Well done, man. Your legs are shaking, you're as exhausted as an overladen mule, you have difficulty breathing, you have a stitch, dear God, it's not a stitch, you fool, what you have is a strain, a pulled muscle, you don't even know the words, you poor creature.

Work and more work. Now they travel far from Monte Lavre, some take their families with them, to work as charcoal burners in the area around Infantado, those men without wives bed down in this big hut, and those who brought their wives set up house in another, using mats or cotton curtains or improvised panels to separate the couples, with the children, if they have them, sleeping with their parents. The midges bite furiously, but it's worse during the day, when the mosquitoes come in clouds, so many you can barely see, and they fall upon us, whining, like a rain of ground glass, our grandmothers, who knew so much about life, were quite right when they said, I'll never see my grandchildren again, they'll die far from home. They know, these are not things one forgets, that the children's little bodies will become a running sore, a torment to them, little lepers who will lie down among rags at night, their stomachs crying out for food, it's never enough, they're growing up without any consolation from their parents, who very slowly touch each other, move and sigh, as if this were something they had to do in order to keep their senses more or less placated, while beside them another couple echoes that touching, moving and sighing, either because they want to or by suggestion, and all the children in the great hut lie listening, eyes open, experiencing their own gestures and disappointments.

From the tops of these hills, on a clear day, you can see Lisbon, who would have thought it was so close, we imagined that we lived at the end of the world, the mistaken ideas of those who know nothing and have had no one to teach them. The serpent of temptation slithered up the branch from which João Mau-Tempo can see Lisbon and promised him all the marvels and riches of the capital in exchange for the very modest price of a ferry ticket, well, not that modest for someone with nothing, but, in for a penny, in for a pound, he'd be a fool to refuse. We will disembark in Cais do Sodré and declare, wide-eyed, So this is Lisbon, the big city, and the sea, look at the sea, all that water, and then we walk through an archway into Rua Augusta, so many people, so much traffic, and we're not used to walking on pavements, we keep slipping and sliding in our hobnail boots, and we cling to each other in our fear of the trams, and you two fall over, which makes the Lisbonites laugh, What bumpkins, they cry, And look, there's Avenida da Liberdade, and what's that thing sticking up in the middle, that's Restauradores, oh, really, and I think to myself, Well, frankly, I'm none the wiser, but ignorance is always the hardest and most embarrassing thing to own up to, anyway, let's walk up Avenida da Liberdade and find our sister, who's working as a maid, this is the street, she's at number ninety-six, isn't that what you said, after all, you're the one who can read, No, there must be some mistake, it goes from ninety-five to ninety-seven, there is no ninety-six, but he who seeks always finds, here it is, they laughed at us because we didn't know that ninety-six was on the other side, the people in Lisbon laugh a lot. Here's the building where our sister works, it's really tall, the owner and resident of the first-floor apartment is Senhor Alberto, our sometime boss, everything belongs to the same family, Well, look who's here, Maria da Conceição will say, what a surprise, and how plump she's got, there's nothing like being a maid. We'll all go out together afterward, because the lady of the house is very generous and gives her time off, although it will be discounted from her next bit of leave, because normally she gets an afternoon off once a fortnight, between lunch and supper. We'll visit some cousins who live in the area, in streets and back streets, and there'll be the same joyful greeting, Well, look who's here, and we'll arrange to go to the show tonight, but first, you mustn't miss the zoo, the monkeys are so funny, and that's a lion over there, and look at the elephant, if you came across a monster like that in the countryside, you'd die of fright, and the show is called *The Clam*, starring Beatriz Costa and Vasco Santana, the man almost had me crying with laughter. We'll sleep here in the kitchen and in the corridor, don't worry, we're used to all sorts, the nights are different in Lisbon, it's the silence, the silence isn't the same, So, did you sleep well, and no one dares to say No, we spent all night tossing and turning, but now let's have a cup of coffee and then go for a stroll around the city, but this isn't a city, it's the size of a county, and in Alcântara we'll meet a group of men working on the railway line, and they say, Morning, bumpkins, and that's it, our brother-in-law takes umbrage and goes over to them, What did you say, a few blows are exchanged, then we flee in shame, and the men shout, Look at the one in the jacket, Look at that bumpkin run, but we're not bumpkins, and even if we were, that would still be no reason to scorn us. We will cross the river again, Look at the sea, and a gentleman traveling with us in the boat says very politely, Actually, this is the river, the sea starts over there, and he points, and then we realize that you can't see land in that direction, how is that possible. When we disembark in Montijo, we'll still have a few kilometers to walk, eight to be precise, until we reach our work camp, we spent an awful lot of money but it was worth it, and when we get back to Monte Lavre, we'll have a lot to tell, because life has its good points too.

Sometimes when people get married, there's already a baby on the way. The priest blesses the couple and the blessing falls on three, not two, as you can see by the sometimes quite prominent bump beneath the woman's skirt. But even when that isn't the case, whether the bride is a virgin or not, it would be very unusual for a year to pass without a child being born. And if God so wills it, it'll be one child out, another one in, for as soon as the woman gives birth, she falls pregnant again. They're real brutes these people, ignorant, worse than animals, because animals aren't in heat all the time, they follow the laws of nature. But these men arrive home from work or from the inn, get into bed, their blood inflamed by the smell of their wife or by the wine they've drunk or by the sexual appetite that comes with tiredness, and they get on top of her, they don't know any other way, they huff and puff, they're not exactly subtle, and leave their sap to soak in the mucous membrane inside the woman's incomprehensibly intricate innards. This is a good thing, better than going with other women, but the family is growing, more and more children are born, because they don't take precautions, Mama, I'm hungry, the proof that God does not exist lies in the fact that he did not make men sheep so that they could eat the grass in the fields, or pigs so that they could eat acorns. But even if they did eat acorns and grass, they couldn't do so in peace, because there's always a warden or the guards around, with eye and rifle cocked, and if the warden, in the name of Norberto's lands, doesn't shoot you in the leg or kill you right off, the guards, who will do the same if they're ordered to, or even if they're not, can choose the more benign options of prison, a fine and a beating. But this, ladies and gentlemen, is a bowl of cherries, you pull out one and three or four come out together, there are even estates that have their own private prison and their own penal code. Justice is done every day on the latifundio, what would become of us if the authorities weren't here.

The family grows, though many children die of diarrhea, dissolving in their own shit, poor little angels, snuffed out like candles, with arms and legs more like twigs than anything else, their bellies distended, until the moment comes and they open their eyes for the last time to see the light of day, unless they die in the dark, in the silence of the hovel, and when the mother wakes and finds her child dead, she starts to scream, always the same scream, these women whose children have died aren't capable of inventing anything, they're speechless. As for the fathers, they say nothing and, the following night, go to the taberna looking as if they're ready to kill someone or something. They come back drunk, having killed nothing and no one.

The men go far away to work, wherever they can earn some

money. At bottom they're all itinerants, they go here and there, and come home weeks or months later to make another child. Meanwhile, as they labor on the cork plantations, watched by the overseers, each drop of sweat is a drop of spilled blood, and the wretches suffer all day and sometimes all night as well, counting the number of hours worked on the fingers of three hands, except when they have to resort to a fourth hand, like the four-legged beasts they are, to count the rest, their clothes don't dry on their backs for a whole two weeks. To rest, if such a word can be used in the circumstances, they lie down on beds of heather with some straw on top of them, and, dirty and bruised, they moan all night, it's quite wrong, how can they believe in Father Agamedes when they see him coming back from his Sunday lunch at Floriberto's house. Judging from the loud belch that echoes around the estate, it was a very good lunch indeed.

This is the power of the heavens. It is, besides, an oft-repeated story. The men are in the hut, exhausted, still clothed, some are sleeping, others can't sleep at all, and through the gaps in the cane walls there enters a never-before-seen light, the morning is still far off, so it's not the morning light, one of the men goes outside and stands frozen with fear, because the whole sky is a shower of stars, falling like lanterns, and the earth is lit more brightly than by any moonlight. Everyone comes out to look, some are really terrified, and the stars fall silently, the world is going to end, or perhaps begin at last. One man, with a reputation as a sage, says, When the stars are restless, so is the earth. They are standing close together, looking up, their heads right back, and they receive on their grubby faces the luminous dust from the falling stars, an incomparable rain that leaves the earth with a different and much greater thirst. And a rather dim laborer who passed through there the following day swore on his mother's life that those celestial signs were announcing that in a ruined shepherd's hut, three leagues from there, a child had been born of another mother, probably not a virgin, a child who couldn't be said to be Jesus Christ only because he had been baptized with another name. No one believed him, and that general skepticism aided Father Agamedes, who, on the following Sunday in a church unusually full and abuzz with excitement, mocked the fools who believe that Jesus will return to the earth just like that, I, your priest, am here to tell you what he would say, I have my holy orders and instructions and am mandated by the Holy Roman Catholic Apostolic Church, do you hear, because if you can't, I'll open another ear on the top of your head.

He was quite right, that wise man who predicted that if the stars are restless, then the earth will be too, the Abyssinians were the first to confirm this, immediately followed by the Spaniards, and later by half the world. Here, the earth is moving according to the old customs. Saturday comes and brings with it the market, but so poorly stocked that it's hard to know how one will fill next week's lunch sacks, it makes you shudder to think of it. A woman went to the grocer and said, Can I owe you for this week's groceries, we've had a terrible week because of the bad weather. Or she would say the same thing in different words, but starting in the same way, Can I owe you for this week's groceries, there was no work this week and my husband hasn't earned a thing. Or perhaps, staring shamefaced at the counter, like someone with not a penny more to her name, Sir, my husband will earn more come the summer, then he'll sort things out with you and pay what he owes. And the grocer, thumping his account book with his fist, would reply, Don't come to me with that old story, I've heard it before, the summer comes and goes and the dog will still be barking, because debts are like dogs, a funny idea, I wonder who first thought of it, this is a people who come up with these sharp, urgent images, they imagine the account book of the grocer or the baker, the large numbers written in pencil, this much and this much, yes, it's like a small, soft puppy that can grow into a beast with wolf's teeth, last year's still unpaid debt, Pay up or I'll cancel your credit, But my children are hungry, and some are ill, my husband has no work, where can we find money, Too bad, you get nothing without paying for it. Everywhere the dogs are barking, we can hear them at the doors, they pursue those who can't pay, bite their shins, bite their souls, and the grocer comes out into the street and says loudly enough for everyone to hear, Tell your husband, and we know the rest. Some people peer out of their doors to see who is being shamed, a poor person's malice, today it's me, tomorrow it could be you, you can't really blame them.

When a man complains, it's because something must be hurting him. We are complaining about this nameless cruelty, and it's a pity it has no name, What will become of us today, this is all the money we have, and we're weeks behind in paying, the grocer won't give us any more credit, and every time I go there, he threatens to cut it off completely, not a penny more, Go and try again, the husband says, but that's just for the sake of saying something, he doesn't really have a stone for a heart, No, not on my own, I can't face going through that door again, only if you come with me, Then we'll both go, but men are not much good at these things, their job is to earn the money and the wife's to make it stretch, besides, women are used to it, they protest, swear, bargain, cry, are capable even of falling to the floor, give the poor woman a drink of water, she's fainted, but a man goes in there and he's shaking, because he should be earning and he isn't, because he should be keeping his family in food and he isn't, How can I do what I said I'd do when I married, Father Agamedes, tell me that. We reach the shop, and other customers are there, some are leaving, some are going in, not all are there simply to buy, and we keep getting pushed to the back of the queue, standing here in this corner next to a sack of beans, let's hope he doesn't think we're going to steal it. Finally, the other customers have all gone, and we make our move, I, the man, step forward, my hands shaking, Senhor José, you were kind enough to give me some credit, but I can't pay it all back today,

I've had a dreadful week, but believe me, as soon as my earnings increase I'll pay it back, then I won't owe you a penny. Needless to say, these are not new words, they were spoken on the previous page, spoken on every page of the book that is the latifundio, how could one expect the answer to be any different, No, I won't give you any more credit, but before the grocer said these words, his hand greedily snatched up the money I had put on the counter to placate him. And I said, with all the calm I could muster, and God knows that wasn't much, Senhor José, don't do this to me, how am I going to feed my children, have pity on me. And he said, I don't want to know, I won't give you any more credit, you already owe me a lot. And I said, Senhor José, please, at least give me something for the money you've taken from me, just so that I can give my children something to eat, until I can sort something out. And he said, I can't give you any more, this money won't pay even a quarter of what you owe me. He thumps the counter, defying me, and I make as if to hit him, perhaps with the strickle, or else to stick a knife in him, this penknife, or yes, this curved blade, this Moorish dagger, What are you doing, man, think of our children, take no notice of him, Senhor José, don't take it the wrong way, such is the despair of the poor. I'm bundled toward the door, Let me go, woman, I'll kill the bastard, but my thoughts are thinking, I won't kill him, I don't know how to kill, and from inside the shop he says, If I give credit to everyone and none of them ever pays me back, how will I live. We are all in the right, who, then, is my enemy.

It's because of these and other, similar deficiencies that we invent stories about hidden treasure, or search out ones that have been invented already, proof of a very ancient need, it's nothing new. There are always warnings that must be attended to, one false move and the gold turns into a fish and the silver into smoke, or a man goes blind, it's happened before. Some say that one cannot trust dreams, but if, on three consecutive nights, I dream of a treasure and tell no one about it nor about the place I saw in my dream, it's certain that I'll find it. But if I speak about it, I won't, because treasures have their fate too, they can't just be distributed as man wishes. There's that old story about a girl who dreamed three times that on the branch of a particular tree she would find fourteen coins and beneath the tree's roots a clay pot full of gold pieces. One should always believe these things even when they're invented. The girl told her dream to her grandparents with whom she lived, and they went together to the tree. There on the branch were the fourteen coins, so half the dream had come true, but they didn't want to dig down into the roots because it was a lovely tree, and with its roots exposed it would die, well, the heart has its reasons. Anyway, the news spread, no one knows how, and when she and her grandparents went back, having thought better of their scruples, they found the tree had been dug up and in the hole was a clay pot split in two, and nothing else. Either the gold had disappeared by magic or someone, less scrupulous or with a harder heart, had taken the treasure and made off with it. Anything is possible.

A still clearer case is that of the two stone chests buried by the Moors, one containing gold and the other containing the plague. It is said that, fearful of opening the wrong chest, no one had had the courage to look for them. But if that's true, how is it that the plague has spread throughout the world.

J OÃO MAU-TEMPO AND FAUSTINA are married, a peaceful
conclusion to the romantic episode which, on a rainy, overcast
night in January, with no moon and no nightingales, in a tangle
of half-unfastened clothes, satisfied the desires of both parties.
They have three children. The oldest is a boy called António, who
is the very image of his father, although he is of a stronger build
and lacks his father's blue eyes, which have not as yet reappeared,
where can they have gone to. The other two are girls, as gentle and
discreet as their mother was and continues to be. António Mau-
Tempo is already working, he helps out keeping pigs, for he isn't
old enough nor his arms strong enough to do any heavier work.
The foreman doesn't treat him well, but that's the custom in this
place and this time, so don't let's get steamed up over nothing. As
is also traditional, António Mau-Tempo's lunch sack is light as
a feather, a banquet consisting of half a mackerel and a hunk of
maize bread. As soon as he leaves the house, the mackerel vanishes, because some hungers simply cannot wait, and his is a very
old hunger. The bread is all he has left for the rest of the day, just
a mouthful now and then, as he nibbles away at the crust, taking scrupulous care not to let a single crumb fall into the grass,

where the ants, their noses in the air like dogs, are desperate to fill their stores with any leavings and leftovers. The foreman, in his role as foreman, would stand on a patch of bare ground and shout, Run over there, boy, and see to those animals on the other side, and António Mau-Tempo, like a small broom, would run around the herd of pigs as if he were a sheepdog. The foreman, now that someone else was doing all the work, passed the time picking ripe pine cones, which he would first roast and peel and then extract the kernels, which he would carefully toast and put away in his haversack, all the while enjoying the rustic peace of the lovely trees. The fire would glow red, the resin-scented pine cones would open in the heat of the fire, and if António Mau-Tempo, mouth watering, found a pine cone that had by chance fallen within sight of his yearning eyes, he quickly hid it, so that it didn't immediately go to increase the other man's wealth, as happened on a few dramatic occasions. Childhood has its just revenge. One day, near some wheatfields, when the foreman was engaged in roasting pine cones, he said to António Mau-Tempo, as he often did, Keep an eye on those pigs over there and make sure they don't get into the wheat. A really cutting wind was blowing that day, and, dressed as he always was in the skimpiest of clothes, António Mau-Tempo decided to give the pigs a holiday, while he took shelter behind a machuco, What's a machuco, A machuco is a young chaparro, everyone knows that, And what's a chaparro, A chaparro is a young cork oak, of course, So a machuco is a cork oak, Isn't that obvious, Ah, As I was saying, António Mau-Tempo sat down behind a machuco, wrapped in the sack that served as his coat in all weathers, come rain or ice, a guano sack was all he had, may God suit the cold to the covering, anyway, there was, for once, general contentment, the pigs in the wheatfield, the foreman roasting pine cones and António Mau-Tempo in his shelter, gnawing away at his crust of bread. And to think that some people still have nothing but bad things to say about the latifundio. Now the trouble was that the foreman had a dog, a clever creature who, suspicious of what An-tónio Mau-Tempo was up to behind the tree, started barking furi-ously, It's true what they say, that a dog is man's best friend, It was no friend of António Mau-Tempo's, however. The foreman leapt up in alarm and when he found the boy, he cried, So you're asleep, are you, and threw a stick at him, which, had it hit its mark, would have been the end of António Mau-Tempo. No boy worth his salt would have given him a second chance, so António Mau-Tempo grabbed hold of the stick himself and hurled it into the middle of the wheatfield, there, go and find it if you can, and then he legged it. The pigs' fun did not last very long either. Isn't it always the way.

Such episodes are all part and parcel of the pastoral life and of a happy childhood. You just have to see for yourself how easy it is to live happily on the latifundio. The pure air, for example, I'll give a prize to anyone who can find better. And the birds, sing-ing away above our heads when we stop to pick a little flower and study the behavior of the ants or this slow, black stag beetle afraid of nothing, impassively crossing the path on his long legs, but who dies beneath our boot, if we so choose, it depends on our mood, at other times, we might be more disposed to consider all life sacred and then even the centipedes escape with their lives. When the foreman comes to complain, António Mau-Tempo's father is there to defend him, Don't hit the boy, I know exactly what goes on, you sit there toasting pine kernels, talking to whoever happens by, and he has to play sheepdog, running from one side to the other, the boy isn't a beetle for you to crush. The foreman went off and found another assistant, and António Mau-Tempo went to keep pigs for a new boss, until he grew stronger.

Man has many jobs to do. We've mentioned some already, and now we add others for the purpose of general enlightenment, be-cause townspeople think, in their ignorance, that it's all a matter of sowing and harvesting, well, they're much mistaken unless they learn all the other verbs involved and realize just what they mean, harvesting, carrying sheaves, scything, threshing either by machine or by hand, flailing the barley, covering the hayrick, baling up straw or hay, shucking the maize, spreading manure, sowing seeds, digging, clearing land, cutting up the maize stalks and digging them in, shoeing, pruning, ringing, leveling, digging ditches and trenches, hoeing, making terraces, grafting vines, taping up the graft, spraying with copper sulfate, carrying the grapes, working in the cellars, laboring in the vegetable plots, preparing the ground, beating the olive trees, working the oil presses, cutting cork, shearing sheep, cleaning wells, hacking undergrowth, chopping firewood, staking, covering with straw, earthing up, plugging, bagging and whatever else needs doing, all those lovely terms enriching our lexicon, blessed be the workers, and if we were to start explaining how each task is performed and in which season, and the tools and the implements needed, and whether it was men's work or women's and why, we would never end.

Anyway, a man is hard at work, in this case he happens to be a man, or rather, he is at home after work, when a hunting hound comes in through the door, his name isn't Ranter or Ringwood, he has two legs and a man's name, but he's a vicious beast all the same, and he says, I've got a piece of paper here for you to sign, you're to go to Évora on Sunday to a rally in support of the Spanish nationalists, it's an anticommunist rally, transport's free, you'll be taken there in a truck, all expenses paid by the bosses or the government, it comes to the same thing. The man feels like saying no, but can't find the will to say it, he sits there chewing, pretending he hasn't heard, but there's no point, the other man repeats what he's said, but in a different, somewhat threatening tone, and João Mau-Tempo looks at his wife, who is there as well, and Faustina looks at her husband, who wishes he weren't there, and at the hound grasping the piece of paper, waiting for a reply, what shall I say to him, what do I care about such things, I don't know anything about communism, well, that's not quite true, last week I found some papers wedged under a stone, with one corner sticking out, as if they were trying to attract my attention, and I dropped behind and picked them up, no one saw me, but what's this hound doing here, baring his teeth, perhaps someone' told him, perhaps he came here to see if I would dare to say that I don't want to go to Évora, that I won't sign, the worst thing is that afterward, because everyone knows this dog, his name's Requinta, he'll go and tell on me, there's sure to be someone with a grudge against me, but if I come up with an excuse, tell him I've got a pain in the gut or that I have to mend the rabbit hutch, he won't believe me, and they might arrest me, All right, Requinta, I'll sign.

João Mau-Tempo signed where others had signed before him, or put their mark because they didn't know how to write, which was most of them. And when Requinta left to continue collecting signatures, his nose in the air, sniffing the wind, the impudent creature, João Mau-Tempo felt a great thirst and drank straight from the jug, drowning in water the sudden fire that was merely a wave of unexplained embarrassment, other men would have drunk wine. Faustina had heard something of the conversation and hadn't liked what she heard, but she preferred to console her husband, Well, at least it will mean a trip to Évora, it will be a distraction, and it's free too, with transport there and back, it's a shame you can't take António, he'd love it. This wasn't all that Faustina said, she continued to murmur something or other without really thinking what she was saying, and João Mau-Tempo knew that her words were like gestures that bring no hope of salvation, but which the patient receives gratefully like a soft hand on his brow, or rather a rough hand, given that we're in the country, but all the same. All the same, they shouldn't force a man to go, because that's what they're doing, I'd rather pretend to be ill. Faustina said, It's not so dreadful, treat it like an outing, I'm sure the government knows what it's doing. João Mau-Tempo said, Yes, you're right. Anyone overhearing this conversation might declare that these people are a lost cause, but he or she has no idea what it's like here, the people live miles from anywhere, they either get no news at all or don't understand it when they do, and only they know what a struggle it is simply to survive.

The day came, and at the appointed time, the men gathered in the street, and while they waited, some went into the taberna and drank as much wine as their pockets could afford, each drinker sticking out his lips to catch the surface bubbles bursting under his nose, ah, wine, blessed be the man who invented you. The more refined and better-informed among them were expecting great things of Évora and kept their appetites for later, but they soon learned their lesson, because they were dropped at the door of the bullring and picked up from there at the end of the rally. Forewarned is forearmed, a bird in the hand is worth two in the bush, that's what people say, some live their whole lives according to such wisdom, and it does them no harm. This time the drinkers were right and were pleasantly merry by the time the trucks arrived, with their bellies singing hosannas and uttering the holy belch of wine, and enjoying the aftertaste that lingers in the mouth, the taste of paradise.

It's quite a journey. On the bends, even when not taken at speed, the truck leans to one side and the men have to cling to each other so as not to be thrown out, they totter about, the wind catches their hats and they have to hang on to them so they don't fly away, Go more slowly, driver, we don't want a man overboard. One of the wittier men said this, well, that's what gives a little spice to life, if not, life would be very dull indeed. They stopped in Foros to take on more people, and then it was plain sailing, they glimpsed Montemor, but there was no time to visit, and Santa Sofia and São Matias, I've never actually been there myself but I have family there, a cousin of my sister-in-law, he's a barber and has done really well for himself, it would be a different story, of course, if men's beards stopped growing, it would be the same for prostitutes if men's cocks stopped growing too. The man who says this knows what he's talking about, well, once in a while never hurts, I haven't been to a whorehouse since I did my national service, this time, though, I'm going to fill my boots. Men's talk. Humanity has done its best to improve communications, even the estate has trucks at its disposal, Évora lies before them, and the hound Requinta, because he came too, barks, When we get out, follow me, and those fateful words cast a pall over the various appetites for wine and women, for that imagined long, restless night in bed with some woman, but dreams are never to be trusted.

The bullring is packed. Hordes of farm laborers have been herded in there, sometimes by a landowner, smiling and chatty, and there's always some lackey toadying up to him, shaming those who came for the sensible reason that they feared being left jobless. On the whole, though, they do their best to appear happy. That's the kindness of the crowd, not wishing to disappoint the person who expects us to be contented, and although it's true that this doesn't look much like a party, it's no one's funeral either, so tell me what face to wear, should I cheer or boo, cry or laugh, tell me. They're sitting on the benches in the stands, others fill the arena, it would be better if there were some bulls there, and they still have no idea what's going to happen or what exactly a rally is. Where has Requinta got to, Requinta, when does the party begin. Friends and acquaintances wave to each other, the more timid among them change places in search of some braver souls, Come over here, and then Requinta says, Keep together and pay attention, this is serious business, we came here to find out who is on the side of good and who on the side of evil, that would be useful, wouldn't it, to have Requinta lead us by the hand toward a knowledge of good and evil, who would have thought it could be so easy, Father Agamedes, all you have to do is stop thinking and plunk your bum down on a bench, Where do we go to take a piss, Requinta, such talk is the first sign of a lack of respect, and Requinta frowns and pretends not to hear, but now the rally is about to start, Ladies and gentlemen, that's funny, so in the bullring in Évora I'm a gentleman, am I, I don't remember being a gentleman anywhere else, not even by my own choice, what's he saying, Viva Portugal, I can't hear him, We are gathered here today, united by the same patriotic ideal, in order to say to our government that we are pledged to continue the great Lusitanian adventure and that we promise to follow in the footsteps of those ancestors who gave the world whole new worlds and spread both faith and empire, and when the trumpet sounds, we will come together, as one man, around Salazar, the genius who has dedicated his life, here there are shouts of salazar salazar salazar, the genius who has dedicated his life to the service of the country, against the barbarous threat from Moscow, against those wretched communists who threaten our families and who would kill your parents, rape your wives and daughters, who would send your sons to labor camps in Siberia and destroy the holy mother church, for they are atheists, godless men with no morals and no shame, down with communism, death to all traitors, the bullring bawls out the slogan, some still have no idea what they're doing here, others have begun to understand and are saddened, some are convinced, or deceived, a worker makes a speech, then another speaker, he's from the Portuguese legion, he stretches out one arm and bawls, Who gives the orders, who gives us life, well, that's a good question, the boss gives the orders, and as for life, what's that. But the obedient bullring gives the expected response, and no sooner has the legionnaire stopped speaking than another man is there, mouth open, they certainly talk a lot, these people, something about Spain, about how the nationalists are fighting the reds, and how the lands of Castile and Andalusia are defending the sacred, eternal values of western civilization, that it's every man's duty to help our fellow believers, and that the remedy for communism is to be found in a return to the Christian morality whose living symbol is Salazar, goodness me, we have a living symbol, we must not be soft on our enemies, words words words, and then he goes on to talk about the good people of the region, expressing their gratitude to that immortal statesman and great Portuguese citizen who has devoted his whole life to serving his country, may God preserve him, and I will tell the president what I saw today in this historic city of Évora, and promise him that each of the thousands of hearts was beating in unison with that of the fatherland, that each heart is the fatherland, that deathless, sublime and most beautiful of all fatherlands, because we are blessed with a government that places the interests of the nation above the interests of any one social class, because men pass and the nation remains, death to communism, or is it down with communism, who cares, among so many people who's going to notice, we must remember that life in the Alentejo, contrary to what many may think, is not propitious to the development of subversive ideas, because the workers are the true partners of the landowners, sharing the profits and losses, ha ha, ha, Where do I go to take a piss, Requinta, that's just a joke, no one here would dare say such a thing at a moment of such gravity, when the nation, which never has to take a piss, is being evoked by that well-dressed gentleman on the platform, who is opening wide his arms as if he wanted to embrace us all, and since he can't do that, the men on the platform embrace each other, the commander of the legion, the major from Setúbal, the members of parliament, the man from their national union, the captain of cavalry regiment five, a man from the en-i-double-u-double-u, if you don't know what that means, just ask, the national institute of work and welfare, and all the others who have traveled from Lisbon, they look like rooks perched on top of a holm oak, but that's where you're wrong, we are all rooks, lined up on the benches, flapping our wings, cawing away, and now it's time for the music, it's the national anthem, everyone stands up, some because they know it's the thing to do, others out of pure imitation, Requinta reviews his men, Come on, sing, I wish I could, who knows the national anthem, if it was some popular song we all knew, that would be another matter, oh, are we leaving, no, it's not time to leave yet, if only we could fly, spread our wings and fly far from here, over the fields, watching from on high the trucks driving back, how sad, it was all so sad, and we shouted as if we had been paid to do it, I don't know what's worse, it's not right, it was like a carnival farce. So you didn't enjoy yourself, João, Not a bit, Faustina, we went like sheep and we came back like sheep. By the time they're in the truck again, evening is falling, an aid to melancholy, someone tries singing and two men join in, but when sadness weighs heavy, even that sad voice falls silent, and then they hear only the sound of the engine, and they sit in silence, being thrown about, a badly tied load, a loose load, this was no work for men, João Mau-Tempo. The truck drops the men off outside Monte Lavre, like a flock of dark birds who scatter, not knowing quite where to go, some go to the taberna to slake their thirst and their bitterness, others mumble to themselves, the saddest go back to their houses, We're just like dolls to be traipsed back and forth, who's going to pay us for today, I had work to do in the vegetable garden, it's that wretch Requinta's fault, I'll find some way to get my own back, words and promises born only of the pain underneath, but they can give full expression to little of that pain, it's too vague, it may not hurt but it cripples. That's why Faustina asks, Are you ill. João Mau-Tempo says no, he isn't, and if he says nothing more, it's because he doesn't know how to explain how he feels. Lying in bed, they talk a little more, So you didn't enjoy yourself, Not a bit, and by way of pouring out his heart and confessing his feelings, João Mau-Tempo rests his head on Faustina's shoulder and falls asleep.

The gentlemen of the estate go up the hill so that the sun will warm them alone, at least they do in João Mau-Tempo's rough-and-ready dream, because the gentlemen have no faces and the hill has no name, but that's how it is when João Mau-Tempo wakes up, and when he falls asleep again, a procession of gentlefolk are walking along and he goes ahead of them, digging up weeds with his mattock, clearing the way for that gay company of men, he pulls up the gorse with his bare hands, his hands are bleeding, and the gentlemen of the estate are laughing and talking, they are generous and patient when he falls behind in his weeding, they wait, they don't mistreat him or summon the guards, they simply wait, and while they wait, they picnic, and João Mau-Tempo dredges up the strength from somewhere and lays in with his mattock, breaking the earth and slicing through the roots, he's a man now, and above him, on the side of the hill, he sees trucks passing, bearing a sign that says Surplus Goods from Portugal, they're heading for Spain, don't give the reds an inch, as for those others, the saints, the pure ones, those who save me, João Mau-Tempo by name, from falling into hell, down with them, death to them, and now a man on horseback is coming after me, and the horse is the only thing in the dream to have a name, it's called Bom-Tempo, well, horses have a long life, Wake up, João, it's time to go to work, says his wife, and yet it's still pitch-black outside.

Others, though, had already got up, not in the sense of someone who, sighing, drags himself from the dubious comfort of a mattress, if he has one, but in that other, peculiar sense of waking in the middle of the day to discover that, only a minute before, it was still black night, for man's true time and the changes to which he is subject are not ruled by the rising of the sun or the setting of the moon, objects that are merely part of the celestial and terrestrial landscape. It is true that there is a time for everything, and this particular event was fated to happen during harvest time. Sometimes, a physical impatience, not to say exasperation, is required for souls finally to move, and when we say soul, we mean that thing with no real name, which is perhaps merely the body, the whole body. One day, if we don't give up, we will all know what these things are and how far they are from the words that attempt to explain them, and how far those words are from the things themselves. But this looks far more complicated when you try to write it down.

This machine looks complicated too, and yet it is so simple. It's a thresher, never better named because that is precisely what it does, it removes the grain from the ear of wheat, separating stalks and husks from grain. From the outside, it looks like a large wooden box on metal wheels, connected by a chain to an engine that trembles, roars, rumbles and, if you'll forgive the word, pongs. It was originally painted egg yolk yellow, but the color has faded beneath the dust and the harsh sun, and now it looks more like another feature of the landscape, alongside others, like the piles of straw, in this sun it's even hard to tell them apart, nothing is still or quiet, the engine is throbbing, the thresher is vomiting out straw and grain, the slack chain is vibrating, and the air shimmers as if it were the reflection of the sun in a mirror held in the sky by the small, unsteady hands of angels with nothing better to do. A few shapes can be seen in the midst of this mist. They have been working all day, and yesterday and the day before, and before that, ever since the threshing began, there are five of them, one older man and four younger men, whose seventeen or eighteen years are not enough to cope with such strenuous work. They sleep on the threshing floor, in between the bales, but it's already dark by the time the engine falls silent, and the sun is still far off when this beast fed on cans of sticky, black liquid first groans into life and then proceeds to batter their ears with noise all the blessed day. It's the machine that sets the pace of work, the thresher cannot chew on nothing, as becomes immediately obvious when the foreman emerges from his hiding place and bawls at them to keep it fed. The inside of the machine's mouth is a volcano, a giant gullet, and the older of the five men tends to be in charge of feeding the monster. The others are responsible for helping the piles of straw to grow higher and higher, they spin like mad things in that fog of chopped-up straw, they haul the rough, dry wheat, the stiff stalks, the bearded ears, the dust, where is the tender springtime green of the fields when the earth really does seem like paradise. The heat is unbearable. The older man steps down and one of the younger men takes his place, and the machine is like a bottomless pit. All it needs is for a man to fall in. The bread would then take on the correct blood-red color, rather than its usual innocent white or neutral brown.

The foreman comes over and says, Go and work down at the chaff end. The chaff is that weightless monster, that straw-cum-dust that blocks your nostrils, that creeps in through every gap in your clothing and sticks to your skin like a layer of mud, it itches like crazy and gives you the very devil of a thirst. The water they drink from the clay jug soon grows lukewarm and slimy, as if you were drinking directly from a swamp full of worms and bloodsuckers, which is what we call leeches around here. The lad goes down to the chaff end and receives it full in his face like a punch, and his body begins slowly to protest, it doesn't have the strength to do more than that, but then, and only those who have experienced this themselves will know what I mean, the despair feeds on the body's exhaustion, grows steadily stronger, and that strength feeds back into the body, and finally, with that redoubled energy, the lad, whose name is Manuel Espada, and who will reappear later in this story, steps away from the chaff, calls to his colleagues and says, I'm off, this isn't work, it's slow death. The older man is once more standing on the thresher, What about the straw bales, but he's left with his words hanging in the air and his arms by his sides, because the four lads leave together, brushing off their clothes, they're like clay figures ready for the kiln, grayish brown, their faces striped with sweat, they look just like clowns, except that they're not funny at all. The older man jumps down from the thresher and turns off the engine. The silence is like a blow to the ears. The foreman comes running over, panting, What's going on, and Manuel Espada says, I'm leaving, and the others say, We're leaving too, the threshing floor is stunned, So you don't want to work. Anyone looking around can see the air trembling, it's only heat haze but it feels as if the whole estate were trembling, and yet it's just these four young men, who are free to leave, having no wife and no children to feed, for as João Mau-Tempo says to Faustina, That's the reason why I agreed to go to Évora. His wife answers, Don't think about that now, get up, it's time.

Manuel Espada and his friends go to the overseer, squint-eyed Anacleto, to ask for the money they're owed for the days they've worked, and to tell him that they're leaving because they can't take any more. Anacleto fixes his wandering eye on the four young rascals, ah, if only he could give them a good whipping, You're not getting any money, and be warned, I'm going to put you down as strikers. The insurrectionists are too young and innocent and ignorant to know what this word means. They walk back to Monte Lavre, which is a long way, taking the most direct route they can along old paths, feeling neither happy nor regretful, that's how it is, a man cannot spend his whole life obeying orders, and these four men, if we can call them that, stroll along talking and saying the kind of things lads of their age always say, one of them even throws a stone at a hoopoe that fluffs up its wings as it crosses their path, the only thing they regret is leaving behind those women from the north who worked alongside them on the threshing floor, there being a great shortage of labor that season.

Anyone traveling by foot has all the time in the world, but when speed is of the essence, and especially when one is athirst for justice, when evil deeds and evildoers threaten to put the latifundio at risk, it's understandable that Anacleto should go by cart to Montemor, he is furious and trembling, his face tinged with the holy blush that marks the faces of all those who struggle passionately for the preservation of the world, yes, it's understandable that he should rush to Montemor where these matters can be dealt with properly and that he should inform the guards that four men from Monte Lavre have declared themselves to be on strike, What will become of me, what shall I tell the boss when he wants to know how the threshing is going, now that I've lost these men. Lieutenant Contente said, Don't worry, we'll take care of it, and Anacleto returned to the threshing floor with his mind at rest, and as he was driving back, in less of a hurry now, enjoying the warm glow of one who has performed a pleasant duty, a car laden with men passed him, and someone inside waved, it was the district administrator, and with him, shouting, Goodbye, Anacleto, were the lieutenant and a whole patrol, bearing down on the enemy in a panzer sherman tank bristling with weapons of all calibers, from the standard-issue pistol to the recoilless rifle, and off they go, with the nation watching them, they offer their breasts to bullets, sound their horn, and it's like a bugle giving the order to charge, while somewhere on the estate, walking, as we have said, along old paths, those four hardened criminals have stopped for a moment to see who can pee highest and farthest.

At the entrance to Monte Lavre, the dogs bark at the would-be tank, it would seem unreal without that detail, and since it's a steep road, the patrol gets out and advances in formation, with the administrator at the front this time and his back protected. Their first call, carried out with the efficiency of someone on maneuvers, in the knowledge that they are only firing blanks, leads them to the local parish councilor, who is, so to speak, dumbstruck when he sees the lieutenant and the administrator coming into his shop, while outside, the patrol scans the surrounding area with suspicious eyes. On the other side of the street, some boys have gathered, and in places invisible or unidentifiable, mothers call for their children, as they did at the time of the massacre of the innocents. Let them call, much good may it do them, and let's go to the shop, where the parish councilor has recovered his voice and is now all politeness and flourishes, unctuously addressing both the administrator and the lieutenant as sir, he stops short of calling the soldiers sir, because that would sound odd, and the administrator takes from his pocket Anacleto's statement, on which he had noted the names of the criminals, Can you tell me where Manuel Espada, Augusto Patracão, Felisberto Lampas and José Palminha

live, and not contented with his role as informer, the parish councilor summons his wife to keep watch over the counter and the
cash drawer, and then the company, enlarged by one, sets off into
the labyrinths of Monte Lavre, with one eye peeled for ambushes,
just like the Spanish civil guard, may God preserve them. Monte
Lavre is a desert under the blazing heat of the sun, even the boys
have lost interest, it's like an oven, all doors are shut, but some are
open just a crack, cracks being the resort of those who do not wish
to show themselves, and when the guards march past, they are followed by the eyes of women and by those of the occasional inquisitive old man with nothing else to do. Imagine if now we were to
launch into a detailed explanation of the expression in those eyes,
we'd never get to the end of the story, and yet all those things, the
seemingly unimportant and the seemingly important, form part of
the same narrative, and might be as good a way as any to explain
the latifundio.

Some things are innately funny, for example, the armed forces
and the civil authority coming to arrest four dangerous agita-
tors and finding none of them. The strikers are still a long way
off. You wouldn't be able to see them from the highest point in
Monte Lavre, even from the tower, if it is the tower, which it is,
from which Lamberto Horques witnessed the charge of his cavalry in that fifteenth century we mentioned earlier. In the midst of
that tangled landscape, not even the sun would help them spot the
four tiny ruffians, who are probably lying down in the shade, perhaps dozing, waiting for the relative cool of evening. Not everyone
finds their exploits so amusing, their mothers, for example, who
have been informed by the lieutenant and the administrator that
their sons are to present themselves in Montemor the next morning, if not, the guards will come to Monte Lavre and drag them to
Montemor kicking and screaming, as they rather extravagantly put
it. The tank sets off down the road, throwing up dust all around,
but before it does, the administrator goes to present his respects to

the largest landowner resident there, whether Lamberto or Dago-berto it doesn't matter, who receives them all, apart from the sol-diers, who are dispatched to the cellar, but Lieutenant Contente and that bestower of respects, the administrator, are ushered into a cool reception room on the first floor, how delightful it is here in the dark, your wife and daughters are well, I hope, and your-self, have another glass of liqueur, and on the way out, the lieuten-ant stands at attention and gives the most perfect salute, the ad-ministrator is trying to speak man to man, but the latifundio is so very large, and Alberto holds out one strong hand and says, Don't let them get away with it, and the administrator, who bears the singular name of Goncelho, says, I can't understand them, when there's no work, they complain there's no work, and when there is, they're not up to it. He's not exactly eloquent, but that's how it came out, among neighbors one can speak freely on the latifundio, and Norberto smiles sympathetically, The poor devils don't know what they want, Ungrateful wretches, says the administrator, and the lieutenant salutes again, he doesn't know what else to do, well, his knowledge lies elsewhere, especially in military matters, but he lacks opportunities to apply it.

The condemned men arrived at sunset. No sooner had they ar-rived than their mothers cried, What have you done, and they re-plied, We haven't done anything, we left because we couldn't face working with that machine anymore. There seems nothing wrong with that, but if you did do wrong, then what's done is done, to-morrow you must go to Montemor, don't worry, they won't arrest you, said their parents. And so the night passed in stifling heat, the lads would have been sleeping on the threshing floor now, and per-haps some woman from the north would have come out for a pee and lingered there, breathing in the night air and perhaps hoping that the world might take a turn for the better, Shall I go or will you, until one of the lads decides to chance it, his heart beating fast and his groin tense, well, he is only seventeen, what do you expect, and the woman doesn't move away, she stands there, perhaps the world really is going to take a turn for the better, and this space between the bales seems tailor-made for the purpose, big enough for two bodies lying one on top of the other, it's not the first time, the boy doesn't know who the woman is, and the woman doesn't know who the boy is, it's better like that, come morning, there'll be no need for embarrassment if there was none at night, it's a game played fairly, with each player giving his or her all, and the slight giddiness they feel when they slip in between the bales, the sweet smell, and then the flailing limbs, the trembling body, but that way we'll get no sleep, and tomorrow I have to go to Montemor.

The four travel in a small cart pulled by José Palminha's parents' most precious possession, a rather rickety-looking mule, who nevertheless trots tirelessly on, they are silent, their hearts filled with dread, they cross the bridge and go up the hill beyond, and now they're in Foros, with one house here, another one there, that's what these far-flung hamlets are like, and then on the left-hand side is Pedra Grande, and shortly afterward, rising above the horizon, in the already hot morning air, stands the castle of Montemor, what remains of the city walls, it makes you sad. A man of seventeen starts speculating about the future, what will become of me, denounced as a striker by Anacleto, and the only thing my three friends are guilty of is keeping me company, our only other unforgivable fault being that we lacked the strength to keep up with the killing pace set by a thresher that was threshing me as it threshed the wheat, in I go through the machine's mouth and out it spits my bare bones, turning me into straw, dust, chaff, I'm being forced to buy the wheat at a price not of my choosing. Augusto Patracão, who is a great whistler, does so to calm his nerves, but his stomach hurts, he's no hero and doesn't even know what a hero is, and José Palminha keeps his mind occupied driving the mule, a task he performs to perfection, as if the mule were a high-stepping steed. Felisberto Lampas may be called Felisberto, but that's just a coincidence, and he sits sulkily, legs dangling, his back turned on his destiny, as he will do for the rest of his life. Then suddenly Montemor is upon them.

They leave the cart under a plane tree, and the mule with its nosebag on, what more can life have to offer a mule, and the four of them go up to the barracks, where a corporal tells them brusquely that they're to be at the town hall at one o'clock. The four lads kick their heels in Montemor for the rest of the morning without even the possibility, given their youth, of waiting inside the local taberna, it's impossible to describe the hours that precede any interrogation, so much happens in them, all the fear and dread inside each person's head, ill-disguised anxiety etched on every face, and the knot in the throat that neither wine nor water can dissolve. Manuel Espada says, It's all my fault you're here, but the others shrug, what difference does it make, and Felisberto Lampas answers, We just have to put on a brave front and show no weakness.

For these callow youths, things turned out well. At one o'clock, they were waiting in the corridor of the town hall listening to administrator Goncelho's voice booming around the building, Are the men from Monte Lavre here. Manuel Espada answered as he should, after all, he was the leader of the rebellion, Yes, sir, we're here, and they stood in a line, waiting to see what would happen next. The administrator played his part as the representative of the authorities, and Lieutenant Contente stood by him, You young rascals, do you have no shame, you're going to be sent across the sea to Africa, that will teach you to respect authority, Manuel Espada, come here, and the interrogation began, Who taught you to be strikers, who taught you, because you've obviously had good teachers, and Manuel Espada answered, with all the force of his innocence, No one taught us, we don't know anyone, we know nothing about strikes either, it was the machine, it kept eating and eating and the piles of straw were getting higher and higher. And the administrator said, I know your sort, that's what they taught you to say, and who is going to speak on your behalf, the administrator was preparing the ground because, when it was known in Montemor that some lads from Monte Lavre had been accused of being strikers, a few people of good sense had already spoken to him and to Lieutenant Contente, There's no point taking these things too seriously, they didn't mean any harm, what do they know about strikes. Nevertheless, all four were questioned, and once this was over, the administrator made a speech, in which, of course, he stated the obvious, Be more sensible in the future, learn to respect the people who give you work, we'll let it go this time, but don't let me see you here again or you'll end up in prison, so be careful, and if anyone comes along wanting to give you things to read or to engage in subversive conversations, tell the guard and they'll deal with it, and be grateful to the people who spoke up for you and don't let them down, you can go now, say goodbye to Lieutenant Contente here, he is your friend, as am I, for I only want what's best for you, don't forget that.

That's what this part of the country is like. The king said to Lamberto Horques, Cultivate and populate it, watch over my interests without forgetting your own, I give you this counsel because it suits me too, and if we follow this advice to the letter, we will all live in peace. And to his pastured sheep, Father Agamedes said, Your kingdom is not of this world, I suffered so that you might enter heaven, the more tears you shed in this vale of tears, the closer to the Lord you will be when you cast off the world, which is nothing but perdition, the devil and the flesh, and you can be sure that I'll be keeping my eye on you, for you are greatly deceived if you think that the Lord Our God has left you free to do both good and evil, everything will be placed in the balance come the day of judgment, better to pay in this world than be in debt in the next. These are excellent doctrines and are probably the reason why the four from Monte Lavre had to accept that the wages they had earned but not been paid, nine escudos a day, for three and a quarter days during the week in which they committed their crime, would go to the old folks' home, although Felisberto Lampas did mutter on the journey home, They'll probably spend our money on beer. We must forgive the young, who so often think ill of their elders. Far from being spent on beer, those one hundred and seventeen escudos given into the hand of the administrator meant that the old people enjoyed better food, a positive orgy, you can't imagine, all these years later they still talk of that feast, and one very ancient resident was heard to say, Now I can die.

They're strange creatures, men, and boys are perhaps stranger, for they are quite a different species. We have said enough about Felisberto Lampas, who is in a bad mood, and for whom the matter of the stolen wages is just a pretext. However, they all returned to Monte Lavre feeling sad, as if something more valuable had been stolen from them, perhaps their sense of pride, which they hadn't lost, of course, but there had been something offensive about the whole situation, they had been treated with scorn, stood in line to hear the administrator's sermon, while the lieutenant watched from the sidelines, memorizing their faces and features. They were even angry at the people who had interceded on their behalf, and whose pleas probably wouldn't have helped at all if the incident hadn't taken place two days before a bomb attempt on Salazar's life, from which he escaped unharmed.

That Sunday, the four went to the square, but could find no one to take them on. The same thing happened on the following Sunday and the Sunday after that. The estate has a long memory and good communications, it misses nothing and passes on the word, it will forgive only when it chooses to, but it will never forget. When they finally did find work, they each went their separate ways. Manuel Espada had to go and tend pigs, and during his time as a pigherd, he met António Mau-Tempo, who, later on, when the time comes, will become his brother-in-law.

S ARA DA CONCEIÇÃO IS not well. She has taken to dreaming about her husband, barely a night passes when she doesn't see him lying on the ground in the olive grove with the purple mark of the rope on his neck, she can't let his body go to the grave like that, and then she starts washing his neck with wine, because if she can make the mark disappear, she will have her husband back again, alive, which is the last thing she would want when awake, but that, inexplicably, is how it is in the dream. This woman, who traveled around so much when young, lives a very quiet, stable life now, but then she always did really, she helps out in the house of her son João Mau-Tempo and her daughter-in-law Faustina, she takes care of her granddaughters, Gracinda and Amélia, tends to the chickens, darns and redarns the clothes, patches up trouser seats, a skill learned during her short time as a stitcher of uppers to soles, and she has a strange habit that no one can understand, which is to go out walking at night when all her family is sleeping. True, she doesn't go very far, fear won't let her, the end of the street is quite far enough. The neighbors say she's slightly mad, perhaps she is, because if all the old mothers came out into the street at night so that their sons and daughters-in-law or their daughters and sons-in-law could take their pleasures in peace, it would be worthy of being recorded in the very brief history of small human gestures, imagine seeing lots of old ladies wandering about in the shadows or in the moonlight or sitting on the ground next to the low walls or on the steps outside the church, waiting silently, what would they talk about, remembering their own past pleasures, what it had been like or what it had not been like, how long those pleasures had lasted, until one of them says, We can go back now, and they all get up, See you tomorrow, and return to their houses, quietly lifting the latch, and the young couple are perhaps sleeping, quite innocent of any conjugal activities, which can't happen every night. But Sara da Conceição prefers to err on the side of caution, finding it difficult only when the weather is bad, and then she stands under a porch in the garden, but thanks to Faustina, who understood her, that's women for you, they would call her in, a sign that the night would be as pure as the cold stars, unless it was on one of those starry nights when João Mau-Tempo sought his legitimate wife beneath the sheets.

Perhaps Sara da Conceição, with all that coming and going, is merely fleeing the dreams that await her, but one thing is sure, at dawn, she will once more find herself in the olive grove, the day after the death, which was when they found the body, as she knows in her dream, and with a bottle of wine and a rag she rubs and rubs, and the head sways from side to side, and when it turns in her direction, her husband fixes her with his cold eyes, and when it turns away, the corpse has no face, which is even worse. Sara da Conceição wakes up in a cold sweat, hears her son snoring, her grandson tossing and turning, but not her granddaughters or her daughter-in-law, they're women after all, and therefore silent, and she moves closer to the two girls, with whom she sleeps, who can say what fate awaits them, let's hope a better fate than that of the woman who dreams such dreams.

One night, Sara da Conceição went out and did not come back. They found her in the morning, outside the village, quite lost and talking about her husband as if he were still alive. So sad. Her daughter, Maria da Conceição, who was working as a maid in Lisbon, asked her employers to help, and they did, and yet still people speak ill of the rich. Sara da Conceição traveled from Monte Lavre and, for the first time, took a taxi from the boat in Terreiro do Paço, south and southeast, to the insane asylum in Rilhafoles, where she lived until she died like a wick burning out for lack of oil. Sometimes, but not often, well, we all have our own lives to lead, Maria da Conceição went to visit her mother, and they would sit looking at each other, what else could they do. When, some years later, João Mau-Tempo was brought to Lisbon for reasons we will learn in due course, Sara da Conceição had died, surrounded by the laughter of the nurses, because the poor fool kept humbly asking for a bottle of wine, imagine that, for some task she had to finish before it was too late. Isn't that sad, ladies and gentlemen.

IN THE INVENTORY OF WARS, the latifundio plays its part, although not a large one. Those Europes, where another war has just begun, play a far greater part, and from what one can ascertain, which is not very much in a land of such ignorance, so removed from the rest of the world, Spain is in such a state of ruin it would break your heart. But any war is a war too many, that would surely be the view of those who died in a war they never wanted.

When Lamberto Horques took charge of the lands in Monte Lavre and environs, the soil was still fresh with the blood of Castilians, although as to freshness, that is merely a rather bloodthirsty image when set beside the far more ancient blood spilled by Lusitanians and Romans, or by the confusing tumult of Alanis, Vandals and Swabians, if they got this far, as the Visigoths certainly did, followed later by the infernal, swarthy caravan of Moors, and then the Burgundians arrived to spill their blood and that of others, and a few crusaders, not all of them heroes like Osberno,* and then more Arabs, how much death these lands have seen, and the

---

* Osberno was a crusader who took part in the siege of Lisbon in 1147, when the city was taken from the Moors by King Afonso I, and who received decisive help from crusaders from northern Europe. Osberno left a written record of the siege.

only reason we haven't mentioned Portuguese blood is because all the blood spilled was Portuguese, or came to be, once enough time had passed for it to be naturalized, which is why we haven't mentioned the French or the English, for they truly are foreigners.

Things did not change after Lamberto Horques took over. The frontier is an open door, you can almost step across the Caia river, and the plain seems to have been deliberately and lovingly made smooth by warrior angels so that combatants can face each other with no obstacles to get in the way of arrows or, later on, all the many different kinds of bullets. The vocabulary of the armory is very beautiful, from the helmet to the cuirass, from the halberd to the harquebus, from the bombard to the ballista, and if the knowledge that such an arsenal walked, trod and fought in these lands sends a tremor of fear through you, you would tremble again if you saw the efficacy of such inventions. Anyway, blood was made to flow, whether from this wound in the throat or from that belly slit open, and would make an excellent ink in which to write such secret enigmas as whether those people were resigned to their deaths and aware of why they were dying. The bodies are carried away or buried where they fell, the latifundio is swept clean, and the land is left ready for the next battle. That is why the relevant trades have to be learned thoroughly and practiced assiduously, without a thought for expense, as when the Conde de Vimioso wrote this detailed letter to his majesty, Sir, the men of the cavalry should be armed with a carbine and two pistols per soldier, the carbines will take musket bullets or smaller and the barrel will be no more than three spans in length, which will be quite sufficient, because if they had to be reinforced, as such bullets require, thus making the barrel longer, the carbines would no longer be manageable, they will also need a metal charger for their powder flask, the pistols, too, will be of good quality, with a two-span barrel, and come with saddle holsters and two chains to hang them from, it would be useful if I could have some spare pistols and carbines so that we can make more of them, and a good quantity of iron should be sent to Vila Viçosa to be distributed to the riflemen, some of the iron can stay in Montemor and in Évora, those are my requirements for the cavalry, however, I leave it up to your majesty to decide what is most convenient.

His majesty, because of financial difficulties, did not always prove to be a prompt and generous paymaster, In Montemor we have been working on the fortifications with the two thousand cruzados that your majesty was kind enough to send and with the further two thousand donated by the people, and since the agreement was that your majesty would give six and the people another six, the town council has written to say that your majesty needs to give a further two thousand which they will then match, I told them that they should try to come up with that amount, and I, meanwhile, would ask your majesty to send your two thousand so that the people can then make their contribution. These are bureaucratic negotiations with distrust on both sides and a lot of buck-passing, but there is no haggling over blood, no one says, Why doesn't your majesty give a liter of your own blood, red or blue, it doesn't matter, because within half an hour of being spilled on the ground, it will be the same color as the earth. People don't dare go that far, because even if the blood of the whole royal household, including that of all the heirs to the throne and any bastard children the king or queen may have had, were poured into the same vat, it would still not be enough for the necessities of war. Let the people give their blood and their money, and his majesty will give the same amount of money that the people paid him earlier in taxes and tributes.

There are, of course, always calamities. All this talk of cavalry, crusades and fortifications, as well as the blood that binds them all together, belongs to the seventeenth century, a long, long time ago, but things have never improved, that's how, during the war of the oranges, we lost Olivença and never got it back, and thus, embarrassingly, without a shot being fired, Manuel Godoy, meeting with no resistance, marched in, and to our shame and his gallantry, he sent a fruit-laden branch from an orange tree to his lover, Queen María Luisa,* all that was lacking was for us to lie back and serve as their bed and mattress. Infinite misfortune, inconsolable grief, both of which lasted from the nineteenth century to the day before yesterday, there's something about oranges, they have a bad effect on both personal and collective destinies, if not, why would Alberto order any windfall oranges to be buried and say to the overseer, Bury the oranges, and if anyone picks them up and eats them, they'll be dismissed as of Saturday, and some men were dismissed because, in secret, they did eat the oranges, that forbidden fruit, while they were still good, rather than leaving them to rot beneath the earth, buried alive, poor things, what did we or the oranges do wrong. But there is a reason for everything, let us take a closer look at the situation, because, toward the end of the war that has just begun in Europe, a certain Hitler, Germany's very own Horques Alemão, will send children of twelve or thirteen to form the last battalions of the defeat, wearing uniforms so big they fall from their shoulders and hang about their ankles, carrying recoil rifles that their shoulders are too frail to withstand, and that's precisely what the owners of the large estates complain about, that there are no longer any children of six or seven who can tend the pigs or the turkeys, what will happen if they can't earn their daily bread, they say to the brutalized parents who have already given their blood and their money and still haven't caught on, or are just

---

* In 1800, Bonaparte and his ally, the Spanish prime minister Manuel de Godoy, issued an ultimatum to Portugal demanding that it enter into an alliance with France in the war against Britain and cede to France most of its national territory. Portugal refused, and in April 1801, French troops arrived in Portugal. On May 20, they were joined by Spanish troops under the command of Godoy. In a disastrous battle for Portugal, Godoy took the Portuguese town of Olivença and, following his victory, picked some oranges and sent them to his mistress, the queen of Spain. The conflict thus became known as the War of the Oranges.

beginning to feel the stirrings of mistrust, as, in another century, they distrusted the king's scornful rebuffs.

Wars are the least of it. A man can get used to anything, and between one war and another, he has time to make a few children and hand them over to the latifundio, without a spear thrust or a rifle shot cutting short the dream that the boy might be lucky enough to be made a foreman or an overseer or a trusted servant, or might choose to go and live in the city, which provides at least for a cleaner death. The worst of all things are the plagues and the famines that occur most years, and which are the ruin of the people, leaving the fields empty, whole villages closed down, you can travel for leagues without seeing a soul, although now and again you might spot ragged, wretched bands walking paths that the devil would walk only if carried on the shoulders of men. Some fall by the wayside, it's an itinerary of corpses, and when the plague relents and the famine eases and the living are counted, you don't have to count very high, because there are so few left.

These are all evils, and great evils at that. One might say, to use the language of Father Agamedes, that they are the three horsemen of the apocalypse, of whom there were once four, and if you start to count, on your fingers if you know no better system, the first is war, the second is plague and the third is famine, and there's always the fourth, the wild beasts of the earth. The last is the most commonly seen and has three faces, the face of the latifundio, the face of the guards who defend property in general and the latifundio in particular, and then there's the third face. He's a serpent with three heads and but one desire. He who gives orders is not necessarily the best fitted to do so, and the best fitted to give orders does not necessarily look the part. But we should perhaps speak more clearly. This horse can be seen in all the cities, towns, villages and hamlets, and he trots along with his leaden eyes and his legs that resemble human hands and feet, but are not human. What human being would say to Manuel Espada, years later, when on military service in the Azores, and forgive us if we jump forward a little in the story, When I get out of here, I'm going to join the police for the vigilance and defense of the state,* and Manuel Espada asked, What's that, and the other man answered, It's the political police, and it's just great, say there's someone you don't like, you simply arrest him, haul him off to the civil authorities and, if you like, shoot him in the head before you get there and say he tried to resist. This horse kicks down doors, eats at the same table on the latifundio as Father Agamedes and plays cards with the guards, while the colt called Bom-Tempo kicks in the prisoner's head. You can find these horses in cities, towns, villages, everywhere, they neigh, rub noses, exchange secrets and allegations, invent persuasive tortures and tortuous persuasions, which is what first made us realize that they did not belong to the equine race, Father Agamedes is a fool to believe that the horses he read about in the bible were real horses, a fundamental error revealed to Manuel Espada in the Azores by his promising fellow recruit. The roots of the tree of knowledge are not fussy about where they grow and are not put off by distance.

Father Agamedes bawls from the pulpit, There are certain men sneaking around who are intent on undermining your common sense, and yet in Spain, by the grace of God and the Virgin Mary, they were crushed, vade retro Satanas et abrenuncio, you must flee from them as if from plague, famine and war, for they are the worst misfortune that could befall our holy land, like the plague of locusts in Egypt, and that is why I will never tire of saying to you that you must heed and obey those who know more about life and the world, look upon the guards as your guardian angels, don't resent them, because sometimes even a father is obliged to beat the child he so loves and cares for, and we all know that sooner

* The PVDE was created in 1933 by Salazar himself in order to prevent, repress and punish crimes of a social or political nature. In 1945, this body was dissolved and replaced by the PIDE (Polícia Internacional e de Defesa do Estado), whose task was to investigate, detain and arrest anyone suspected of plotting against the State.

or later the child will say, It was for my own good, the only blows that were wasted were those that struck the ground, that, my children, is how it is with the guards, not to mention the other authorities, both civil and military, the mayor, the administrator, the regimental commander, the civil governor, the commander of the legion and all those other gentlemen in positions of power, beginning with those who give you work, yes, what would become of you if there were no one to give you work, how would you feed your families, tell me that, answer me, all right, I know that the congregation does not normally speak during mass, but it is your own conscience you must answer to, and for all these reasons, I urge, demand and order you to pay no heed to those red devils who want only your unhappiness, because that was not why God created the earth, he created it that it might be rocked in the loving arms of the Virgin Mary, and if you believe that someone is trying to lead you astray with seductive words, then go straight to the guards' barracks, for then you will be carrying out God's work, but if you lack the courage, if you are afraid of reprisals, I will hear you in the confessional and do with your confession what my soul and my conscience deem to be the right thing, and now let us say a pater noster for the salvation of our country, a pater noster for the conversion of Russia and a pater noster for those who govern our nation, who have so sacrificed themselves and who so love us, our father, who art in heaven, blessed be thy name.

Father Agamedes is quite right. There are men roaming the latifundio, they can be found hiding away in groups of three or four, in solitary places or abandoned houses, where they keep watch, or in the shelter of a valley, some from here, some from elsewhere, and they hold long conversations. They take turns to speak, and the others listen, anyone seeing them from a distance would say, They're itinerant workers, gypsies, apostles, and when they have finished talking, they scatter, taking out-of-the-way paths and carrying with them papers and decisions. This is what is called organization, and Father Agamedes is purple with rage, with righteous anger, May they be damned, may their souls fall into the very depths of hell, they are a harmful infection that seeks to destroy you, only yesterday I was talking to the president of the council, and he said to me, That fatal disease is already afflicting our village, Father Agamedes, we must do something to counteract the pernicious doctrines being spread among our families by these enemies of faith and civilization, O ingrates, do you not realize that the peace and order we enjoy in our country is the envy of other nations, and you come to me saying that you are willing to lose all that, you're just spoiled, that's your problem.

João Mau-Tempo has never been a man for going to mass, but now that he lives in Monte Lavre, he goes to church now and then both to please his wife and out of necessity. He hears Father Agamedes's fiery sermons and compares them in his head with what he has picked up from the papers handed to him in secret, he makes his own judgment as a simple man, and while he believes some of the things written on those papers, he doesn't believe a word the priest says. It seems that Father Agamedes himself finds it hard to believe, with all that ranting and raving and foaming at the mouth, which does not look good on one of God's ministers. When mass is over, João Mau-Tempo goes out into the square along with the rest of the congregation, and there he finds Faustina, who had been sitting with the other women, and he walks part of the way home with her before going to join some friends to have a drink, just one, though the others laugh at him, You drink like a little boy, Mau-Tempo, but he merely smiles, a smile that says everything, so much so that the others say nothing more, it's as if the body of a hanged man had suddenly dropped down from one of the beams in the inn. Then one of his friends says, Did Father Agamedes give a good sermon today, a question that has no answer, because he is one of the few men in Monte Lavre who never goes to mass, he only asks in order to provoke, João Mau-Tempo smiles again and says, Oh, it was the usual thing, then says nothing more, be-cause he's nearly forty now and never drinks so much that he loses control of his tongue. It was that same friend who gave him the papers, and they look at each other, and Sigismundo, for that is his friend's name, winks and raises his glass of wine to him, Good health.

I T WAS WHILE ANTÓNIO Mau-Tempo was employed tend-
ing pigs that he met Manuel Espada, who had been forced to
take such unskilled work because he could find nothing else once
he and his companions had become dubbed locally, and for two
leagues around, as strikers. Like everyone else in Monte Lavre, António Mau-Tempo knew what had happened, and in his still childish imaginings, he found some similarities with his own rebellion
against the pine-nut-roasting, stick-wielding foreman, although
he never confessed as much, especially given that Manuel Espada
was six years older than him, long enough to separate a mere child
from a lad and a mere lad from a man. The foreman of these pigs
didn't work any harder than the other one, but he, at least, had age
as an excuse, and the lads he employed didn't mind taking orders
from him, after all, someone has to be in charge, him in charge
of us and us in charge of the pigs. The working day of the swineherd is very long, even in winter, the hours pass so slowly they positively dawdle, like a shadow moving from here to there, and pigs
are creatures of little imagination, their snouts always pressed to
the ground, and if they do wander off, they mean no mischief, and
a well-aimed stone or a sharp thump on the back with a stick will

bring them, ears twitching, back to the rest of the herd. The pig soon forgets such incidents, having a poor memory and being little prone to bearing grudges.

There was, then, more than enough time to talk, while the foreman dozed under the holm oak or tended the animals farther off. Manuel Espada spoke of his adventures as a striker, although he never exaggerated, that wasn't in his character, and he shed a little light on the kind of thing that can happen on the threshing floor at night with the female workers, especially the ones from the north who have no men with them. The two became friends, and António Mau-Tempo greatly admired the older lad's serenity, a quality he lacked, for, as we will see later on, he was always itching to be up and off. He had inherited the vagabond tendencies of his grandfather Domingos Mau-Tempo, with the great and praiseworthy difference that he had a naturally sunny temperament, which didn't mean, however, that he was always laughing and joking. Nevertheless, he had the same tastes and anxieties of any lad his age, and took on the ancient and never resolved question of what separates boys from sparrows, he always spoke his mind and was, on occasions, impetuous, and those qualities will make him a touch impatient and something of a wanderer. He'll enjoy dances, as his father did in his youth, but will care little for large gatherings. He will be a great teller of tales about things he has either seen or invented, experienced or imagined, and he will possess the supreme art of being able to blur the frontiers between the two. But he will always work hard at acquiring all the rural skills. We're not reading this future in the palm of his hand, these are simply the elementary facts of a life that contained many other things, including some that appeared not to be promised to his generation.

António Mau-Tempo did not spend long with the pigs. He left Manuel Espada there and went off to learn skills that the latter, being older, already knew, and at thirteen, he was working with grown men, burning undergrowth, digging ditches, building dams, tasks requiring good strong arms. By the time he was fifteen, he had learned to cut cork, a precious skill at which he became a master, as, to be frank, he did with everything he turned his hand to. When he was still very young, he left his mother and father and traveled to places where his grandfather had left his mark and a few bad memories. But he was so very different from his grandfather that it never occurred to anyone that they could possibly belong to the same family, despite having the same surname. He was very drawn to the sea, he discovered the banks of the river Sado, and walked its whole length, which is no small journey, just to earn a bit more money than the pittance being offered in Monte Lavre. And one day, much later, as we will describe in due course, he will go to France to exchange a few years of life for a little hard currency.

The latifundio has its pauses, the days are indifferent or so it seems, what day is it today, for example. It's true that people die and are born just as they did in more remarkable times, hunger still doesn't always take account of the needs of the stomach, and the heavy workload hasn't grown much lighter. The biggest changes happen outside, there are more roads and more cars on them, more radios and more time to listen to them, understanding them is another skill entirely, more beers and more fizzy drinks, but when a man lies down at night, in his own bed or on the straw in a field, the pain in his body is just the same, and yet he should consider himself lucky to be employed. There's nothing much to say about the women, their fate as beasts of burden and bearers of children remains the same.

However, when one looks at this apparently lifeless swamp, only someone born blind or choosing not to see could fail to notice the watery tremor rising suddenly from the depths to the surface, the result of accumulated tensions in the mud, caught up in a chemical process of making, unmaking and remaking, until the liberated gas explodes. But to notice this, you have to look hard and not say as you pass by, There's no point hanging around here, let's go. If we were to go away for a while, distracted by different landscapes and picturesque events, we would notice, on our return, how, contrary to appearances, everything is finally changing. That is what will happen when we leave António Mau-Tempo to his life and return to the thread of the story we began, though all this is merely hearsay, including the story about José Gato and the misfortune that befell him and his companions, as António Mau-Tempo can witness and testify.

This isn't one of those tedious tales about the Brazilian bandit Lampião, nor of others nearer to home, such as João Brandão or José do Telhado, who were bad people or, who knows, just wrongheaded. I don't mean by this that there had never been any shady characters on the latifundio, no bandits who would leave a traveler dead and stripped of everything he had, regardless of how little that was, but the only one I knew of was José Gato, he and his companions, or should I say gang, whose names, if I remember rightly, were Parrilhas, Venta Rachada, Ludgero, Castelo and others whose names I've forgotten, well, one can't remember everything. I'm not even sure they were bandits. Itinerant workers, yes, that's what they were. If they wanted to work, they would work as hard as anyone else, they weren't criminals, but one day, it was as if they suddenly got the wind up their tails or something, and they put down their hoes or their axes, went to the overseer or foreman to receive what was owed to them, because no one ever dared to withhold their pay, and then they vanished. At first, they went their separate ways, each silent, solitary man for himself, and only later did they get together and form a gang. When I met them, José Gato was already the head of the gang, and I don't think anyone would have tried to take his place. They stole mainly pigs, of which, it must be said, there was no shortage. They stole in order to eat and also to sell, of course, because a man cannot live only by what he eats. At the time, they had a boat anchored in the Sado

river, and that was their slaughterhouse. They slaughtered the animals and placed the meat in the salting trough for times of need.
And speaking of the salting trough, they once ran out of salt and
were discussing what to do and what not to do, and José Gato,
who was a man of very few words indeed, told Parrilhas to go to
the saltworks. Normally, José Gato only had to say, Do this, and
like the word of God, it was done, but for some reason Parrilhas
refused to go, a decision he lived to regret. José Gato snatched off
Parrilhas's hat, threw it in the air, picked up his rifle and blasted
the hat to pieces with two shots, then he said to Parrilhas in the
quietest of voices, Go and get the salt, and Parrilhas saddled up
the donkey and went to get the salt. That was the kind of man José
Gato was.

For anyone living in one of the work camps nearby and who was
brave enough, José Gato was the main supplier of pork meat. One
day, Venta Rachada turned up, in secret, of course, at the place
where I was working, to ask if anyone wanted to buy some meat. I
did, as did two of my companions, and we arranged to meet Venta
Rachada in a place called Silha dos Pinheiros. We went there, each
carrying our coarse linen bag and a little money, and, just in case,
those of us who had some money put by left it back at the camp,
we didn't want to go looking for wool and come back shorn. I
had fifty mil réis on me, and the others had more or less the same
amount. It was pitch-black outside, and the place where we were to
meet Venta Rachada was enough to give anyone the creeps, in fact,
he was hiding there, waiting, and he played a trick on us by leaping
out, pointing his rifle at us and saying, I could rob you of all you
have, we all laughed, of course, and I, my heart thumping, managed to say, It would hardly be worth the bother, and then it was
Venta Rachada's turn to laugh and say, Don't worry, I won't hurt
you, follow me.

At the time, José Gato was based in the Loureiro hills, near
Palma, you probably know the place. It was full of cane apple trees

as big as a house and no one ever went there. An abandoned farm laborers' hut served as their slaughterhouse. They all lived there and moved on only when they noticed any suspicious activity, strangers prowling around, or heard rumors that the guards were closing in. We walked and walked and when we got within sight of the hut, we saw two men on guard, rifles at the ready. Parrilhas gave his name, we went in and found José Gato and the other men playing the mouth organ and dancing the fandango, now I don't know much about such things, but I thought they danced pretty well, and besides, everyone has a right to enjoy themselves now and then. Looped over one of the beams above the fire were some wires from which hung a large stewpot containing pigs' innards. José Gato said, So these are our buyers, are they. Venta Rachada said, They are, and the only ones, too. José Gato said, Don't worry, boys, before we do business, join us for a bite to eat, these were welcome words indeed, because the smell was already beginning to make my mouth water. They had wine, they had everything. To sharpen our appetite, we had some slices of ham and a few glasses of wine, José Gato played the mouth organ and kept an eye on the pot, he was wearing chaps made of donkey skin, with big buttons on them, as was the fashion, the rascal looked just like any other farmer. In one corner of the hut there were various rifles, the gang's arsenal, one was a five-shot rifle and belonged to Marcelino, but more of that later. We were happily engaged in eating and drinking when suddenly we heard a bell ringing, *ting-a-ling*, and I must confess that I shuddered, this could all end very badly indeed. José Gato noticed my unease and said, Don't worry, they're friends, they've come to buy meat. It was Manuel da Revolta, so called because he owned a shop in Monte da Revolta, and I could tell you a few stories about him too, but another time. Anyway, Manuel da Revolta arrived, loaded six pigs onto his cart and carried them off, the next day, of course, he would be doing the rounds of the work camps, selling them, pretending he had slaughtered them himself, even the guards would buy meat from him, and I still don't know to this day whether the guards were suspicious or whether it simply suited their purposes to say nothing. Then a fishmonger we all knew arrived, he kept us all supplied with fish and tobacco and a few other things that José Gato needed. He loaded one pig onto his bicycle, but left the head behind. Then someone else arrived, without a bell this time, he simply whistled and those on guard responded, that was the arrangement, just in case. He took away two pigs, one slung on either side of his mule, again with no head, the pigs that is, because obviously the mule needed his head to see where he was putting his feet. In the end, there were only two pigs left, lying on a couple of old sacks. A few rashers of bacon were fried and added to the stew, along with the seasonings, onions and so on, and then down it went into our stomachs, and boy, was it good that stew, washed down with a fair bit of wine. Then José Gato said, addressing me, António Mau-Tempo, Right, to business, how much money did you bring with you, and I said, I've brought fifty escudos, that's all I've got. Said José Gato, It's not a lot, but you won't leave empty-handed, and he sliced a pig in two, a piece weighing four and a half or five arrobas, Open your bag, but first he made sure to take the money and slip it into his pocket. It was the same with the others, to all of whom he said, Not a word to anyone, if you tell a soul, you'll live to regret it, and so we left, laden down with meat, and his warnings and threats stood us in good stead, because it turned out later that the pigs had been stolen from the very estate we were working on. The overseer bombarded us with questions, but all three of us kept our word. I dug a hole in the ground, lined it with cork, put in the meat and covered it with a cloth, having first sliced it up and salted it. It kept really well, too, and we had meat for a good long time.

That's just one story. Had it been João Brandão, I'm not sure how it would have turned out, but the man I dealt with was José Gato, with someone else it might have been different. Later, the gang moved to Vale de Reis, you city folk just can't imagine how wild it is around there, grottoes and caves and evil-looking swamps, no one else would go anywhere near, not even the guards, they didn't dare. The gang set up camp there, and they had a warning system in Monte da Revolta, whenever the guards appeared, Manuel da Revolta's mother would stick a pole up the chimney with a rag tied on top, and that was the sign. One of the gang always kept an eye on that chimney, and as soon as he saw that old rag, he would warn the others and they would all vanish, disappear without trace. The guards never caught any of them. Those of us who knew the signal, when we were out in the fields working, we'd say, Something's up.

Let me tell you now about Marcelino. He was the overseer in Vale de Reis and owned a famous rifle that the boss had bought him so that he could shoot any member of José Gato's gang he caught stealing. But before I tell you about that, I want to tell you another story about a rifle. Once, when Marcelino was out riding, José Gato ambushed him and, with his gun pointing straight at him, said mockingly, which was very much his style, Just open your arms nice and wide and I'll take the rifle, and Marcelino had no alternative but to do as asked, however much it galled him. José Gato was a small man, but he had a very big heart. Then it was the turn of the five-shot rifle, you know how it is, you start telling one story and other stories get in the way. Marcelino was riding along a path, no one bothered to clear the paths then, they were too busy cutting cork and slicing it up into small pieces, so the undergrowth was really thick. Marcelino was riding proudly along with his five-shot rifle loaded with five cartridges, thinking, If anyone tries to attack me now, that'll be their goose well and truly cooked, but José Gato was hiding behind a slender holm oak, aiming straight at him, Give me that rifle, I need it, and off he went. Later, the boss said to Marcelino, I'll buy you a carbine, I don't want you being made to look a fool, and Marcelino replied tartly, I don't want a carbine, from now on, it'll be just me and my stick, that's the best way to keep watch.

Marcelino had no luck at all with rifles. He even lost the one he owned himself and kept at home. The swineherd's dogs started barking, they could smell that something was up, and the swineherd went to Marcelino and said, The dogs are barking, there's someone trying to steal the pigs. Marcelino immediately picked up his rifle and his cartridge box and stood there guarding the pigs. Now and then he fired a shot, and José Gato's men, hiding in the bushes, knew that these shots were intended for them and responded, although without wasting much ammunition. And where was José Gato all this time, why, up on the roof, onto which he had climbed unnoticed and where he remained all night, crouched like a lizard so that no one would spot him, he was nothing if not bold. Come the morning, at daybreak or shortly afterward, just as it was beginning to grow light, and when any shots from the other side had long since ceased, Marcelino said, They must have run away, I'll just go home and have my breakfast, I'll be back in a jiffy. And the swineherd, whose own appetite was stirred by those words, thought, Yes, I'll go and have a bite to eat as well, why not. With his enemies gone, José Gato jumped down from the roof, ah, I forgot to mention that Marcelino had left his rifle inside the swineherd's hut, anyway, José Gato jumped down from the roof, took the rifle and the swineherd's new boots and a blanket, perhaps they were short of those as well, and meanwhile, his companions, there were five of them at the time, grabbed a pig each and carried them off into the undergrowth. Sows are like us, they have a joint just here, and if you cut it, they can't move, and that's what happened with these, only about a hundred and fifty yards from the pen, if that. And with someone keeping watch all the time. The boars noticed the sows were missing, but went looking for them far away, down the road, and none of them thought of looking closer to home. That night, José Gato went to fetch the sows, and so Marcelino's third rifle was lost.

There's another, more important story. Marcelino was standing guard, without his rifle this time, for they had all been stolen, and José Gato decided to set about stealing the broad beans, which had all been harvested and were lying on the threshing floor. It was close to the gang's current hideout which we found out was there only when we were felling trees in the area, by which time they had moved on. They had dug a deep ditch and carved out caves along the walls. There were some high hills all overgrown with willows, and they had cut a path through them, rather the way mongoose do, and created alcoves furnished with comfortable beds made out of reeds and twigs. Anyway, José Gato went out nightly to steal some of the beans, and Marcelino realized that someone had been taking them because some had been crushed underfoot and you could see the empty shells underneath. Marcelino said to himself, The bastards, they're after my beans, and so what did he decide to do, I'm going to confront them, he said, and so he tethered his horse out of sight, took a large sack with him, because in summer you don't need a blanket, and a big stick. Shortly afterward, he heard rustling, it was José Gato tossing three or four bundles of beans in a cloth to shell them, but everything was so dry that the beans crunched underfoot, and then, at the agreed hour, a member of the gang came to help him carry away the beans, about a hundred liters of them. They were probably going to sell them to Manuel da Revolta in exchange for bread and other essentials, I'm not sure. José Gato was completely absorbed in his work, and Marcelino, barefoot, was drawing closer and closer, his own description of it was very funny, I was barefoot, you see, gradually edging nearer, and I got within about six or seven meters of the guy, another three or four meters and I could have hit him with my stick, but he was too sharp and he heard me, and just when I thought I'd deal him a blow with my stick, in two hops he was gone, now you see him, now you don't, and I was pretty quick off the mark myself, but there he was pointing his rifle at me. José Gato said, or so Marcelino said, You're lucky, you were kind to a friend of mine once, that was at a time when the guards were doing their worst and Marcelino had given shelter and food to one of the gang, You're lucky, otherwise, I would have shot you dead. But Marcelino was a brave man too in his own way, Hang on, this calls for a smoke, and he pulled out his tobacco pouch, rolled himself a cigarette, stuck it in his mouth, lit it, then said, Right, I'm off now.

Later, the gang were all arrested. It started in Piçarras, in an out-of-the-way place between Munhola and Landeira. There was a showdown with the guards, shots were fired, it was like a war. The guards caught them, but every one of them was given a job by local farmers, Venta Rachada became a watchman on a vineyard in Zambujal, and others the same. I would love to have heard one of those conversations between guards and farmers, We've arrested a man, Oh good, I'll have him, I don't know who was the more brazen of the two. José Gato was only arrested some time later, in Vendas Novas. He was living with a woman who sold vegetables there and he always went about in disguise, which is why the guards never caught him. Some say she gave him away, but I don't know. He was taken prisoner at his lover's house, in the cellar, when he was sleeping, in fact, he had said once, If they don't catch me while I'm sleeping, they won't catch me at all. Rumor had it that he was taken to Lisbon, and just as the others were given jobs by farmers, it was said that he had been sent to the colonies as a member of the PVDE. I don't know if he would ever have agreed to that, I find it hard to believe, or perhaps they killed him and that was the story they made up, it wouldn't be the first time.

José Gato had many good qualities. He never stole from the poor, his intention being to steal only from the rich, as people say José do Telhado used to. Once, Parrilhas came across a woman who had gone shopping for her family, and he robbed her, the wicked devil. Unfortunately for him, José Gato found the poor woman sobbing. He asked what was wrong and realized from what she said that Parrilhas had been her attacker. He gave the woman enough money for three loads of shopping and Parrilhas got the worst beating of his life. Quite right, too.

José Gato was a man with no illusions, small in stature but brave, as you'll see from something that happened in Monte da Revolta. At the time, it was a very international place, you got people there from all over, suffice it to say that a man from the Algarve who was working on clearing the land managed to build a little cabin for himself, and there were others like him, with no house and no home, or if they had one, they kept quiet about it. A man there tried to provoke an argument between Manuel da Revolta and José Gato, telling Manuel da Revolta that José Gato had boasted about how he was going to sleep with Manuel's wife. But Manuel da Revolta, who trusted José Gato, said to him straight out, So-and-so told me this. José Gato said, The bastard, let's go and see him, and so they did, and when they got there, he said, This is what you told Manuel, and I'd like to hear you say the same to my face. The other man answered, Look, I was a bit drunk at the time, but you never said anything of the kind, and that's the honest truth. José Gato said very calmly, Walk a hundred paces ahead of me, that way he knew he had no chance of killing the man, then he fired two or three shots at his back, so that a couple of pellets just stuck in his flesh while the others ricocheted off, then he gave him a couple of lashes with a whip as he lay on the ground, Behave like a man from now on, and don't go playing any more childish pranks on people. It always seemed to me that José Gato got involved in a life of crime only because he couldn't earn enough to eat.

He was in this area when I was a little boy. He was the foreman in charge of clearing the area between Monte Lavre and Coruche. The road was built entirely by itinerant laborers, lots of people worked like that, putting in three or four weeks until they had earned enough cash and then others came to take their place. José Gato arrived and clearly knew what he was doing, so he was made foreman, although he kept away from the low-lying valleys. I was herding pigs at the time, before I got to know Manuel Espada, so I saw it all. It came to be known that he'd had a few run-ins with the guards, and then the guards learned, or someone told them, that he was in the area, and they hunted him down and caught him. They didn't quite have the measure of him though. He was at the head of the patrol, looking all meek and mild, and the guards were following behind him, looking smug, then suddenly he bent down, grabbed a handful of earth and threw it in the eyes of one of the guards, and was gone. Until his final arrest, they never saw him again. José Gato was a true wanderer. And I reckon he was always a very solitary man.

THE WORLD WITH ALL its weight, this globe with no beginning and no end, made up of seas and lands, crisscrossed by rivers, streams and brooks carrying the clear water that comes and goes and is always the same, whether suspended in the clouds or hidden in the springs beneath the great subterranean plates, this world that looks like a great lump of rock rolling around the heavens or, as it will appear to astronauts one day and as we can already imagine, like a spinning top, this world, seen from Monte Lavre, is a very delicate thing, a small watch that can take only so much winding and not a turn more, that starts to tremble and twitch if a large finger approaches the balance wheel and seems about to touch, however lightly, the hairspring, as nervous as a heart. A watch is solid and rustproof inside its polished case, shockproof up to a point, even waterproof for those who have the exquisite taste to go swimming with it, it is guaranteed for a certain number of years, possibly many years if fashion does not laugh at what we bought only yesterday, for that is how the factory maintains its outflow of watches and its inflow of dividends. But if you remove its shell, if the wind, sun and rain begin to spin and beat inside it, among the jewels and the gears, you can safely bet that the happy days are over. Seen from Monte Lavre, the world is an open clock, with its innards exposed to the sun, waiting for its hour to come.

Having been sown at the right time, the wheat sprouted, grew and is now ripe. We pluck an ear from the edge of the field and rub it between the palms of our hands, an ancient gesture. The warm, dry husk crumbles and we hold cupped in our hand the eighteen or twenty grains from that ear and we say, It's time to harvest. These are the magic words that will set in motion both machines and men, this is the moment when, to abandon the image of the watch, the snake of the earth sheds its skin and is left defenseless. If we want things to change, we must grab the snake before it disappears. From high up in Monte Lavre, the owners of the latifundio gaze out at the great yellow waves whispering beneath the gentle breeze, and say to their overseers, It's time to harvest, or, if informed of this in their Lisbon homes, indolently say the same thing, or, more succinctly, So be it, but having said these words, they are trusting that the world will give another turn, that the latifundio will respect the regularity of its customs and its seasons, and they are relying, in a way, on the urgency with which the earth accomplishes these tasks. The war has just ended, a time of universal fraternal love is about to begin. They say that soon the ration books will be unnecessary, those little bits of colored paper that give you the right to eat, if, of course, you have the money to pay with and always assuming there is something for that money to buy. These people aren't much bothered really. They have eaten little and badly all their lives, they have known only scarcity, and the hunger marches practiced here are as old as tales of the evil eye. However, everything has its moment. As anyone can see, this wheat is ripe and so are the men.

There are two slogans, not to accept the daily rate of twenty-five escudos and not to work for less than thirty-three escudos a day, from morning to night, because that's how it must be, fruits do not all ripen at the same time. If the wheatfields could speak, they would say in astonishment, What's going on, aren't they going to harvest us, someone isn't doing his job. Pure imagination. The wheatfields are ripe and waiting, it's getting late. Either the men come now or, when the season is over, the stems will break, the ears crumble, and all the grain will fall to the ground to feed the birds and a few insects, until, so that not everything is lost, they let the livestock into the fields, where they will live as if in the land of Cockaigne. That is pure imagination too. One side will have to give in, there is no record of the wheat ever being left to fall to the ground like that, or if it did, it was the exception that proved the rule. The latifundio orders foremen and overseers to stand firm, the language is warlike, No going back, the imperial guard will die rather than surrender, oh, if only they would die, but there are faint echoes here of bugle calls, or are they merely a nostalgia for battles lost. The guards are beginning to emerge from their cocoons, the corporals and sergeants appear at the windows of their barracks to sniff the air, some are oiling their rifles and giving their horses double rations from the emergency reserves. In the towns, men stand shoulder to shoulder, muttering. The overseers come to talk to them again, So, have you reached a decision, and they reply, We have, and we won't work for less. In the distance, on this hot evening, a warm wind blows as if it came from the earth itself, and the hills continue to hold tight to the roots of those dry stalks. Hidden in the forest of the wheatfield, the partridges are listening hard. No sound of men passing, no roaring engine, no tremulous shaking of the ears of wheat as the sickle or the whirlwind of the harvester approach. What a strange world this is.

Saturday comes. The overseers have been to speak to the owners, They're very determined, they said, and the owners of the latifundio, Norberto, Alberto, Dagoberto, replied in unison, each from his particular place in the landscape, Let them learn their lesson. In their houses, the men have just had supper, the little or nothing they dine on every day, the women are looking at them in

silence, and some ask, What now, while some men shrug glumly
and others say, They're sure to come to their senses tomorrow, and
there are those who have decided to accept what they are being offered, the same pay as last year. It's true that from all sides comes
news that many men are refusing to work for such a pittance, but
what is a man to do if he has a wife and children, the little urchins
who are all eyes and who stand, chin resting on the edge of the table, using one saliva-moistened fingertip to hunt breadcrumbs as
if they were ants. Some of the luckier men, although they might
not seem so to those who know little of such things, have found
employment with a smallholder, a man who cannot risk losing his
harvest and who has already agreed to pay them thirty-three escudos. The night will be a long one, as if it were winter already.
Above the rooftops is the usual wasteful sprawl of stars, if only
we could eat them, but they're too far away, the ostentatious serenity of a heaven to which Father Agamedes keeps returning, he
has no other topic, stating that, up above, all our hardships in this
vale of tears will end and we will all stand equal before the Lord.
Empty stomachs protest, grumbling away at nothing, proof of that
inequality. Your wife beside you isn't asleep, but you don't feel like
rolling over on top of her. Perhaps tomorrow the bosses will come
to an agreement, perhaps we'll find a pot full of gold coins buried
at the back of the fireplace, perhaps the chicken will start laying
golden eggs, or even silver would do, perhaps the poor will wake
up rich and the rich poor. But we do not find such delights even in
dreams.

Dearly beloved children, says Father Agamedes at mass, because it's Sunday already, Dearly beloved children, and he pretends
not to notice how sparse the congregation is and how ancient most
of its members are, nothing but old ladies and altar boys, Dearly
beloved children, and it's only natural that the old ladies should be
thinking vaguely that they long ago ceased to be children, but what
can one do, the world belongs to men, Dearly beloved children, be

very careful, the winds of revolution are blowing across our happy lands, and once more I say to you, pay them no heed, but why bother writing down the rest, we know Father Agamedes's sermon by heart. The mass ends, the priest disrobes, it's Sunday, that holiest of days, and lunch, blessings be upon it, will be served in the cool of Clariberto's dining room, although Clariberto goes to mass only when he really wants to, which is rare, and the ladies are equally lazy, but Father Agamedes doesn't take it to heart, if they should be overcome by devotion or overwhelmed by fears of the beyond, they have a chapel in the garden, with newly varnished saints, including a Saint Sebastian generously sprinkled with arrows, may God forgive me, but the saint does seem to be enjoying it rather more than virtue should allow, and Father Agamedes enters through the same door that the overseer Pompeu has just left, carrying in his ear the consoling message, Not a penny more, there's nothing quite like a man with authority, be it on earth or in heaven.

A few men are hanging around outside, and although the labor market normally starts later on, some of them go to the overseer and ask, So what has the boss decided, and he replies, Not a penny more, well, why waste a nice turn of phrase or spoil it with redundant variations, and the men say, But some farmers are already paying thirty-three escudos, and Pompeu says, That's their business, if they want to bankrupt themselves, good luck to them. This is when João Mau-Tempo opens his mouth, and the words come out as naturally as water flowing from a good spring, The wheat won't get harvested then, because we're not working for less. The overseer did not reply, because his lunch was waiting for him and he wasn't in the mood for such unsettling conversations. And the sun beat down hard, glinting like a guard's saber.

Those who could eat ate, and those who couldn't starved. The labor market has begun now, all the rural workers from Monte Lavre are there, even those who have already been hired, but only the ones who are being paid thirty-three escudos, anyone who accepted the old rate is sitting at home, chewing on his own shame, getting annoyed with his children who can't keep still and giving them a clip on the ear for no reason, and the wife, who is always the voice of justice in any punishment, protests, We're the ones who bore them, besides, you shouldn't hit an innocent child, but the men in the square are innocent too, they're not asking for the moon, just thirty-three escudos for a day's work, it's hardly an outrageous amount, by which they mean that the boss isn't going to lose out. This isn't what Pompeu and the other overseers say, but perhaps he speaks more brusquely because of his Roman name, What you're asking for is outrageous, you'll be the ruin of agriculture. Various voices cry, Some farmers are already paying that, and the chorus of overseers replies, That's their choice, but we're not paying it. And so the haggling continues, retort and counter-retort, who will tire of it first, it's hardly a dialogue worthy of setting down, but there is nothing else.

The sea beats on the shore, well, that's one way of describing it, but not everyone would know what we meant, because there are many around here who have never been to the sea, the sea beats on the shore and if it meets a sandcastle in its path or a rickety fence, it will flatten both, if not at the first attempt, then at the second, and the sandcastle will have been razed to the ground and the fence reduced to a few planks being washed back and forth by the waves. It would be simpler to say that many men accepted the twenty-five escudos, and only a few dug in their heels and refused. And now that they are alone in the square, asking each other if it was worth it, and Sigismundo Canastro, who is one of those men, says, We mustn't get discouraged, this isn't happening only in Monte Lavre, if we win, then everyone will benefit. What makes him think this, when there are just twenty men unemployed. If only there were more of us, says João Mau-Tempo gloomily. And these twenty men seem about to go their separate ways, with nowhere to head but home, which is not a good place to be today. Sigismundo Canastro tells them his idea, Tomorrow, let's go together to the fields and ask our comrades not to work, tell them that everywhere people are fighting for their thirty-three escudos, we in Monte Lavre can't be seen to weaken, we're as brave as they are, and if the whole district refused to work, the bosses would have to give in. Someone in the group asks, What's happening in those other places then, and someone answers, either Sigismundo Canastro or Manuel Espada or someone else, it doesn't matter, It's the same in Beja, in Santarém, in Portalegre, in Setúbal, this isn't just one man's idea, either we all work together or we're lost. João Mau-Tempo, who is one of the older men present and therefore has a greater responsibility, stares into the distance as if he were gazing inside himself, judging his own strength, and then he says, We should do as Sigismundo says. From where they are standing, they can see the guards' barracks. Corporal Tacabo appeared at the door to enjoy the cool of the evening, and it was doubtless purely by chance that the first bat also appeared at the same moment, cutting smoothly through the air. It's a strange animal, almost blind, like a rat with wings, and it flies as fast as lightning and never bumps into anything or anyone.

A scorching June morning. Twenty-two men left Monte Lavre, separately, so as not to attract the guards' attention, and met up on the riverbank, just beyond Ponte Cava, among the reeds. They discussed whether they should set off together and decided that, since there were so few of them, it would be best not to break up the group. They would have to walk farther and more quickly, but if things went well, they would soon find others to join them. They drew up an itinerary, first Pedra Grande, then Pendão das Mulheres, followed by Casalinho, Carriça, Monte da Fogueira and Cabeço do Desgarro. They would see how they felt after that, assuming there was sufficient time and enough people to send to other places. They crossed at the ford, where the water formed a sort of natural harbor, and they were like a band of boys, wearing very serious smiles, or playful recruits with few weapons, taking off their shoes and putting them on again, with someone saying, as a joke of course, that he'd rather spend the day swimming. It's three kilometers to Pedra Grande, along a bad road, then another four to Pendão das Mulheres, three to Casalinho, and beyond that, it's best not to count, otherwise people might give up before they take the first step. Off they go then, the apostles, they could certainly do with a miracle of the fishes, preferably grilled over hot coals, with a drizzle of olive oil and a pinch of salt, right here underneath this holm oak, if duty were not calling to us so softly that it's hard to know whether it's coming from inside us or from outside, if it's pushing us from behind or is there up ahead, opening its arms to us like Christ, how amazing, it's the first comrade to leave the fields of his own free will, without waiting for someone to give him a reason, and now they are twenty-three, a veritable multitude. Pedra Grande comes into sight, and the fields lie before us, they've nearly cleared them already, as if they were working out their rage, who is this talking to them, it's Sigismundo Canastro, who knows more than the others, Comrades, don't be deceived, we workers must remain united, we don't want to be exploited, what we are asking for wouldn't even pay for a filling in one of the boss's teeth. Manuel Espada steps forward, We cannot be shown to be weaker than our comrades in other towns, who are also demanding a fairer wage. Then a Carlos, a Manuel, an Afonso, a Damião, a Custódio, a Diogo and a Filipe speak, all saying the same thing, repeating the words they have just heard, repeating them because they have not yet had time to invent their own, and now it's João Mau-Tempo's turn, My only regret is that my son António isn't here, but I hope that wherever he is, he will be saying the same things his father is saying, let us join together to demand a decent wage, because it's high time we spoke out about the value of the work we do, it can't always be the bosses who decide what they should pay us. Appetite comes with eating, and the ability to talk comes with talking.

The foremen arrive, gesticulating, they look like scarecrows frightening off sparrows, Get out of here, if these people want to work, let them, you're nothing but troublemakers, you lot, you deserve a good thrashing. But the workers have stopped, they have set down the sheaves, men and women are coming toward them, dark with dust, too baked dry with heat even to sweat. Work has stopped, the two groups join together, Tell the boss that if he wants us here tomorrow, all he has to do is pay us thirty-three escudos a day. Christ's age when he died, says one joker who knows about religious matters. There may have been no multiplying of the fishes, but there was a multiplying of men. They split into two groups and divided up the itinerary, with some going to Pendão das Mulheres and others to Casalinho, and they will meet back here on this hill to divide up again.

In heaven, the angels are leaning on the windowsills or over that long balcony with the silver balustrade that runs right around the horizon, you can see it perfectly on a clear day, and they are pointing and calling mischievously to each other, well, it's their age, and one angel higher up the scale runs off to summon a few saints formerly linked with agriculture and livestock, so that they can see what's going on in the latifundio, such upheavals, dark knots of people walking along the roads, where there are roads, or along the almost invisible tracks across the fields, taking shortcuts, in single file, around the edges of the wheatfields, like a string of black ants. The angels haven't enjoyed themselves so much in ages, the saints are giving gentle lectures about plants and animals, although their memory isn't what it used to be, but still they expound on how to grow wheat and bake bread, and how you can eat every bit of a pig, and how if you want to know about your own body, just cut open a pig, because they're just the same as us. This statement is both daring and heretical, it brings into question the whole of the Creator's thinking, had he run out of ideas when it came to creating man and so simply copied the pig, well, if enough people say so, it must be true.

The saints live so high up and so far away, and have so completely forgotten the world in which they lived, that they can find no explanation for the trail of humans walking from Casalinho to Carriça, from Monte da Fogueira to Cabeço do Desgarro, and now, while some head off in that direction, others are going farther afield, to Herdade das Mantas, to Monte da Areia, all of which are places where the Lord never trod, and even if he had, what would he or we have gained. They're heretics, Father Agamedes will bawl each day, and he's bawling these words out now from the window of his house, because the pilgrims are beginning to arrive in Monte Lavre, can this be the new Jerusalem, it's like the morning procession on Ascension Day, and the corporal has just run across the road, heading who knows where, someone must have summoned him, The boss wants to speak to you, and he pulls on his beret and tightens his belt, that's military discipline for you, because the guards fall just short of being an army, and it is precisely that shortfall that makes them feel hard done by, he enters the perfumed cool of the cellar where Humberto is waiting, Right, you know what's been happening, and Corporal Tacabo does know, it's his duty to know, that's what he's paid for, Yes, sir, the strikers have been visiting the workers on the estates and now they're back, So what are we going to do, I've asked for orders from Montemor, we're going to find out who's behind the mutiny, Don't worry, I have a list of names here, twenty-two of them, they were seen at Ponte Cava before they set off, and while he's saying this, Corporal Tacabo has poured himself a drink, Norberto paced back and forth, bringing his heels down hard on the flagstones, They're troublemakers, idlers, that's what they are, they don't want to work, if the right side had won the war, they wouldn't dare to so much as wag a finger, they'd be quiet as mice, happy to be working for whatever we were prepared to pay them, this is what Alberto says, and the confused corporal doesn't know what to say, he doesn't like the Germans and wants nothing to do with the Russians but he has a soft spot for the English, and when he thinks about it, he's not quite sure who it was who won the war, but he takes the list of names, it will look good on his service record, twenty-two proven strikers is no small thing, even though the angels find it all terribly amusing, they're young, you can't really blame them, one day they will learn the harsh realities of life, if they start having children, always supposing there are girl angels, as is only right and proper, and then they'll have to feed them, and if heaven becomes a latifundio, then they'll see.

But the ants won. In the fading evening light, the men gathered in the square and the overseers came, grim-faced and silent, but defeated, Tomorrow you can work for thirty-three escudos, that was all they said and then they withdrew, humiliated, thinking vengeful thoughts. That night, joy was unconfined in the tabernas, João Mau-Tempo, most unusually, dared to drink a second glass of wine, the shopkeepers are hoping to get some of their debts repaid and are considering raising their prices, at the mention of money the children cannot even think of what they would want to buy, and since the body is sensitive to the contentments of the soul, the men moved closer to the women, and the women closer to the men, and they were all so happy that if heaven understood anything about human lives, you would have heard hosannas and the clamor of trumpets, and the moon was its usual bright, lovely June self.

And now it's morning again. Each day's work is worth an extra eight escudos, which is less than a ten-tostão increase per hour or almost nothing per minute, so little that there isn't a coin small enough to represent it, and each time the sickle cuts into the wheat, each time a left hand grasps the stems and a right hand deals a final, decisive blow with the blade at ground level, only someone versed in higher mathematics could say how much that gesture is worth, how many zeros you would have to add to the right of the decimal point, in what thousandths we could measure out the sweat, the tendon in the wrist, the muscle in the arm, the strained back, the eyes fogged with fatigue, the broiling noonday heat. So much suffering for so little reward. And yet there are still some who sing, although not for long, because they soon hear the news that yesterday, in Montemor, the guards rounded up agricultural workers in the area and put them in a bullring, penned in like cattle. Those with long memories remembered what had happened in Badajoz,* the carnage that took place there, again in the bullring, it doesn't seem possible, they machine-gunned the whole lot of them, but it won't be like that here, we're not that cruel. Dark presentiments fill the countryside, the line of reapers advances hesitantly, unrhythmically, and the furious foremen take out their anger on the workers, anyone would think it was their money, Now that you're earning more, I've suddenly got a fieldful of malingerers. The line grows livelier, they don't want to seem to be in the boss's debt, they move more quickly, but then their imaginations turn back to the bullring in Montemor full of our people, from all over the latifundio, and fear so dries the mouth that some call to the water carrier to let them drink, Who knows what will happen to us. The guards know, as they walk over the clods of earth, a few at each end of the line, rifles at the ready and fingers on the trigger, If anyone makes a run for it, shoot in the air first, then aim at their legs, and if you have to fire a third time, make sure you don't have to shoot again. The reapers straighten up when they hear the names, Custódio Calção, Sigismundo Canastro, Manuel Espada, Damião Canelas, João Mau-Tempo. These are the local mutineers, the others are being rounded up right now, or they already have

---

* In August 1936, during the Spanish Civil War, between 1,300 and 4,000 Republicans — civilian and military — were rounded up and killed by Nationalist troops.

been or soon will be, if they thought they wouldn't have to pay the price for their insubordination, they were roundly deceived, they clearly didn't know the latifundio. Those left behind lower head and arms, bow their whole trunk with heart and lungs, their back struggling to keep them upright, and the sickle again slices through the wheat, cutting what, why, the dry stalks of course, what else. And beside the workers, the foreman growled like a wolf, You're lucky you weren't all taken away, that's what you deserve, if it was up to me, I'd teach you a lesson you wouldn't forget.

The five conspirators are flanked by the guards, who taunt them, So you thought you could lead a strike and get off scot-free, did you, well you've got another think coming. None of the five men replies, they hold their heads high, but have pangs in their stomachs that are not hunger pangs, and they're strangely unsteady on their feet, that's what fear does, it takes you over and it makes no difference if you speak or keep silent, but it will pass, a man is a man, whereas, even today, we can't be quite sure whether a cat is an animal or a human. João Mau-Tempo makes as if to say something to Sigismundo Canastro, but we never find out what it is because, as one man, one commander, with one will, the guards say, If you open your gob, we'll hit you so hard you'll leave teeth marks in the road, and so no one else dares say a word, and they arrive in Monte Lavre in silence, go up the ramp to the guards' post, because they had been arrested by then, all twenty-two of them, so someone had obviously betrayed us. They put them in an enclosure in the yard at the back, piled them in with nowhere to sit but the ground, although what does that matter, they're used to it, weeds can survive the hardest of frosts, they have skin as thick as donkey hide, which is just as well, because that way they get fewer infections, if it were us, frail city dwellers, we wouldn't stand a chance. The door is open, but in front of it, under a porch, stand three guards, rifles at the ready, one of them doesn't seem too happy in his sentry box, he averts his gaze, the barrel of his rifle pointing at the ground, and he doesn't have his finger on the trigger, He looks quite sad, who would have thought it. The prisoners only think this, they don't speak, they're under strict orders, but Sigismundo Canastro does manage to murmur, Courage, comrades, and Manuel Espada says, If we're questioned, the answer is always the same, we simply want to earn a just wage, and João Mau-Tempo says, Don't worry, they're not going to execute us or send us to Africa.

From the street comes a sound like that of waves breaking on a deserted beach. It's their relatives and neighbors come to ask for news, to plead for the men's impossible release, and then the voice of Corporal Tacabo is heard, a roar, Get back all of you or I'll order my men to charge, but this is purely a tactical threat, how are they going to charge if they have no horses, and one can hardly imagine the guards advancing with fixed bayonets to pierce the bellies of children or women, some of whom aren't bad-looking as it happens, and old ladies who can barely stand and who are about ready for the grave anyway. But the crowd draws back and waits, and all you can hear is the soft weeping of the women, who don't want to cause a scandal for fear that it might redound on their husbands, sons, brothers, fathers, but they are suffering too, what will become of us if he goes to prison.

Then, as evening comes on, a truck arrives from Montemor with a large company of guards, they're strangers here, we're used to the local ones, but so what, it's not as if we're going to forgive them, how can they have sprung from the same suffering womb only to turn on ordinary people who have never done them any harm. The truck reaches the fork in the road, and one branch leads off to Montinho, where João Mau-Tempo once lived, as did his late mother Sara da Conceição and his brothers and sisters, some of whom live here and others over there, but none in Monte Lavre, but this is the story of those who stayed, not those who left, and before we forget, the other road is the one the owners of the latifundio usually drive along in their cars, now the truck turns and comes bumping down toward them, belching out smoke and kicking up dust from the parched road, and the women and children, the older people too, find themselves pushed out of the way by the truck's swaying carcass, but when it stops, right by the wall that surrounds the guards' barracks, they cling to the sides in desperation, a foolish move, because the guards inside use the butts of their rifles to strike the people's dark, dirty fingers, they don't wash, Father Agamedes, it's true Dona Clemência, they're impossible, worse than animals, and Sergeant Armamento from Montemor shouts, If anyone comes too near, we'll shoot, so we can see at once who is in charge. The rabble falls silent, retreats to the middle of the road, between the barracks and the school, O schools, sow your seeds,* and it is then that the prisoners are called out, with the patrol forming up in two lines from the door of the barracks to the truck and inside it, too, like a hedge, or like a net into which the fish, or men, were drawn, for when men or fish are caught, there are few differences between them. All twenty-two came out, and each time one appeared on the threshold, there came from the crowd an irrepressible shout or cry, or, rather, shouts, because by the time the second or third man had appeared, there was an incessant clamor, Oh, my dear husband, Oh, my dear father, and the rifles were trained on the malefactors, while the local garrison kept their eyes fixed on the crowd, in case there should be a rebellion. It's true that there are hundreds of people there and that they are desperate, but there are the barrels of the rifles saying, Come any closer and you'll see what happens. The prisoners emerge from the barracks, look frantically around them, but there's no time, they are forced onward and when they reach the edge of the wall, they have to jump into the truck, it seems like a spectacle put on to terrify the people, and meanwhile the light is fading, and in the gloom they can't make out individual faces, barely has the first man

* The opening lines of the Republican hymn to public education.

emerged than they are all in the truck and the truck is setting off, it swerves wildly as if to scythe through the crowd, someone falls, but fortunately suffers only a few scratches, downhill it's easy, the men sitting in the back of the truck are thrown around like sacks, and the guards hang on to the sides, forgetting all about keeping their rifles trained on the crowd, and only Sergeant Armamento, with his back to the cab, legs straddled, faces the crowd running after the truck, the poor things are getting left behind, they gain on it slightly at the bottom, when the truck has to slow down to turn left, but then they can do nothing more, for the truck accelerates in the direction of Montemor, and the poor, panting people wave and shout, but both cries and gestures are lost as the vehicle moves away, they can't hear us now, the faster runners among them try to keep up, but what's the point, the truck disappears around the first bend, we'll see it later on going over the bridge, there it is, there it is, what kind of justice is this and what kind of country, why is our portion of suffering so much greater, they might as well kill the whole lot of us, thus sealing our fate once and for all.

Each man is immersed in his own thoughts. From what they heard while they were waiting to leave the barracks, Sigismundo Canastro, João Mau-Tempo and Manuel Espada know that they have been named as the main leaders of the strike. Of the three, Sigismundo Canastro is the calmest. Sitting on the floor along with all the other men, he began by resting his head on his folded arms, which were, in turn, resting on his knees, you get the picture. He wants to be able to think more clearly, but suddenly it occurred to him that his companions might think, from his posture, that he was discouraged, and he didn't want that, so he unfolded his arms and sat up straight, as if to say, here I am. Manuel Espada is remembering and comparing. He recalls how, eight years ago, he made the same journey in a smaller truck with his youthful companions, only Augusto Patracão is with him this time, Palminha had come to his senses and made other plans, and Felisberto Lampas became an itinerant worker and hasn't been seen since. Manuel Espada says to himself that there's really no comparison, this time things are serious, then they were just a bunch of boys, this time they're grown men, the level of responsibility, as no one would deny, is quite different. These three, for we cannot speak for every man there, are caught up in a never-ending stream of thoughts, a mixture of determination, fear and bravery, a trembling in hands and legs, no one's immune from that, João Mau-Tempo is lost in a kind of dream, it's almost dark now, and if his eyes fill with tears, so be it, no man is made of stone, his comrades mustn't see this though, he doesn't want them to lose courage too. Once past Foros, there is only open countryside, soon the moon will rise, well, it's June and the moon rises early, and ahead lie some large rocks, what giants could have rolled them there, a good place for an ambush, imagine if José Gato was there along with his fellow gang members, Venta Rachada, Parrilhas, Ludgero and Castelo, suddenly leaping out from behind the log they've rolled across the road, after all, they've had plenty of practice, and shouting, Stop, and the truck braking sharply and skidding on the tarmac, bloody hell, I hope the tires don't burst, and then, One move and you're dead, each bandit with his rifle at the ready, and they're not joking either, you can tell from their faces, there's the five-shot rifle that José Gato stole from Marcelino, Sergeant Armamento does make a move, well, it's what his superiors would expect of him, but he falls from on high with a hole right through his heart, and José Gato puts a second cartridge in the chamber and says, The prisoners can get out, meanwhile, the guards are standing with their hands in the air like in a Wild West film, and Venta Rachada and Castelo start collecting the rifles and the cartridge belts, behind the rocks they've tethered two of the mules they use to carry sides of pork, a little more dead weight won't bother them. João Mau-Tempo ponders whether to go straight back to Monte Lavre or to stay there in hiding until things quiet down a little, but he would have to send a message to his family to reassure them that everything has turned out for the best.

Everyone jumps out, Quick, quick, says a resuscitated Sergeant Armamento, with no hole through his heart. They're at the gate of the barracks in Montemor, and there's no sign of José Gato. The guards line up, they're not so tense now they're back on home ground, and there's no danger of riots or armed attacks, and as you'll have guessed, well, it wasn't that hard, José Gato's bold intervention was all in João Mau-Tempo's imagination. The rocks are still there at the side of the road, where they've been for centuries and centuries, but no one leapt out from behind them, the truck passed by with its usual mechanical calm, dropped the men off at the barracks and left, having done its duty. The twenty-two men are bundled down a corridor and across a courtyard, where two guards are standing by a door, one of them opens the door to reveal a room packed with people, some standing, some sitting on the floor, on the straw from two bales that have been pulled apart and strewn about to serve as bedding. The floor is made of concrete, and the room is strangely cold, considering how many people are crammed inside and that this is the hottest time of the year, perhaps it's because the back wall is built onto the side of the castle. Including those who were there already, there are nearly sixty men, who would make a good gang of workers. The door clangs shut, deliberately loud, and the sound of the key turning in the lock grates on the nerves like one of those bits of broken glass that the latifundio places on top of the walls surrounding its gardens, when the sun catches them, they look quite pretty, glinting away, and beyond lie trees heavy with oranges, and not just oranges, but pears, another fine fruit, and roses twine about the arches that line the orchard paths, any worker passing through would smell the perfume, but frankly, Father Agamedes, I doubt they have soul enough to appreciate such beauty. The ceiling is very low and is lit by one lightbulb, twenty-five watts at most, we haven't yet lost our frugal habits, and in the end, there's no denying it, the heat becomes unbearable. The men recognize each other or introduce themselves, there are people from Escoural and Torre da Gadanha, they say that the men from Cabrela were taken to Vendas Novas, but that's not certain, and so what are they going to do with us now. Whatever it is, says one of the men from Escoural, they can't take those thirty-three escudos away from us, now we just have to wait.

They wait. The hours pass. Now and then the door opens, more men are bundled in, the dungeon is beginning to be too small for so many people. Most have had nothing to eat since morning, and there's no sign that the guards have any intention of feeding their prisoners. Some lie down on the straw, the more trusting or those with the strongest nerves fall asleep. They hear the town hall clock strike midnight, nothing more will happen today, it's too late, they'd better get some sleep, their empty stomachs are protesting but not too much, and as the men are about to abandon themselves to slumber, made drowsy by the smell and the heat from all those bodies, the door is flung open and Corporal Tacabo and six guards appear, the corporal is clutching a piece of paper and the guards their rifles as if they had emerged fully armed from their mothers' wombs, and the corporal bawls, João Mau-Tempo from Monte Lavre, Agostinho Direito from Safira, Carolino Dias from Torre da Gadanha, João Catarino from Santiago do Escoural. The four men, four shadows, stand up and go out through the door. Their companions feel as if their hearts were in their mouths, what will happen to the poor things. Then comes the voice of a man who can no longer keep the secret, Apparently they killed a man here yesterday.

This time, they do not cross the courtyard. They continue along by the wall, between the guards, before being pushed toward a door. The light from the lamp there is much brighter, the prisoners screw up their eyes against the aggressive brightness, the first aggression of the night. The guards left, leaving only the corporal, who went over and put the piece of paper down on a desk behind which were seated two men, one in uniform, Lieutenant Contente, and the other in plain clothes. João Mau-Tempo, Agostinho Direito, Carolino Dias and João Catarino were ordered to stand next to each other in a line. Lift your snouts up high so we can see if you resemble your whores of mothers, said the man wearing civilian clothes. João Mau-Tempo couldn't resist retorting, My mother is dead, to which the man responded, Do you want your face smashed in, you may speak only when I tell you to, it won't be long before you lose your taste for talking, but that's precisely when you'll have to talk. Then Lieutenant Contente began to give orders, Stand up straight, you're not at home in your nice soft bed now, the usual military talk, and pay attention to the policeman here. The other man stood up, reviewed the ragged troop, staring at them hard, damn the man, it's as if he were trying to look right inside me, fixing me with a lingering, intimidating look, What's your name, and the man questioned answered, João Catarino, and you, Carolino Dias, and you, Agostinho Direito, and you, the one with the dead mother, what's your name, João Mau-Tempo. The PIDE agent smiled broadly, That's a fine name and very appropriate for the situation. Then he strode over to the desk, took his pistol out of its holster, slammed it down and turned angrily on the poor men, I want you to know that you won't get out of here alive unless you vomit up everything you know about this strike, about the organization, the people who gave you orders, the propaganda they've fed you, everything, I want it all out in the open, and woe betide you if you don't talk. Lieutenant Contente picked up four school exercise books that were in a pile at one end of the desk, You are each going to be locked in a room with one of these exercise books and a pencil, and you're to write down everything you know, names, dates, meeting places and houses, how and when any leaflets and so on were delivered, do you understand, and you won't be let out until it's all there in black and white. The PIDE agent returned to the desk, put his pistol back in the holster, having completed his show of force, and said, It's enough to drive a man crazy, you see before you an exhausted man, unable to sleep because of this wretched strike, so be sensible and write down everything you know and hide nothing, because if I find out later that you have left anything out, all the worse for you. João Catarino says, I can barely write, Agostinho Direito says, I can only write my name, João Mau-Tempo says, I can hardly write at all, Carolino Dias says, Nor can I. You know enough for our purposes, says the agent, we chose you because you know how to read and write, if you don't like it, tough, you shouldn't have learned, now you're going to regret not having stayed as stupid as you were born. The agent laughed at his own joke, the corporal laughed as did the private, and Lieutenant Contente, of course, laughed contentedly. The lieutenant gives an order to the corporal, the corporal tells the private, the private opens the door, and the four rascals leave, outside are the other troops, it's a public event, and like someone putting pigs in a pigsty, they march the four men down the corridor, opening doors and shoving them in, each with his own exercise book, Dias, Direito, Catarino and Mau-Tempo, they're just scum, Father Agamedes, if you'll forgive the expression.

In the barracks a great silence falls, full of noises as silences always are. The men locked up in the dungeon moan and sigh, unable to sleep, as is usual with weary bodies, and even when they do sleep, there's that ache from the day when they were working at the charcoal pit and tried to carry a great heavy log, if it was now, they'd tell them to piss off, I wonder what's happening to our comrades, I can't hear anything, only the footsteps of the sentries outside, and the clock chiming, I wish that bloody owl would shut up, it gives you gloomy thoughts. Locked in their rooms, the four make the same gestures, they look around them, there's the table and the pencil, it felt like a game, like being back at school and having to do a dictation, except that there was no teacher to read and mark the lesson, their conscience would have to be their teacher, deciding what they would write in their slow, crooked hand, and each of them, at some point, wrote his name on the first line of the first page, right in the margin, as if they wanted to make sure they had enough paper to write down all they were going to write, my name is Agostinho Direito, my name is João Mau-Tempo, my name is João Catarino, my name is Carolino Dias, and then they sat staring at the page, all those lines to fill, and then on and on until the final page, it was like a wheatfield, but for some reason this pencil-cum-sickle won't cut, won't move forward, it gets stuck on this root, this stone, what on earth am I supposed to write, they're waiting for me to tell them all I know, here on these crooked lines, or do they only look crooked because I'm so tired, João Catarino is the first to push the exercise book to one side, he wrote his name, he will write nothing more, his name will stay there so that people will know that the owner of that name wrote nothing more than his name, not a word more, and then, at different times, each of the other men pushed the exercise book to one side with a large, dark hand, some closed the book, others left it open so that the name was the first thing that would be seen when they came for them, and nothing more.

At the first crack, which is a very picturesque and rural way of speaking that came into being perhaps along with the unboarded roof, especially the thatched variety, in which cracks and holes appear with wear and tear and no thanks to the skills of the thatcher, and it is through those cracks and holes that the dawn light enters, although the light could have entered earlier from a star which, on its journey, was caught there by the eyes of some sleepless person. The idea of the exercise books was probably a ruse on the part of the PIDE agent and the lieutenant to be able to get a decent night's sleep while the criminals made their confessions, or a subtle way of dispensing with a scribe and getting the work done for free. We'll never know the truth until it is confirmed, or not, in this account of prison and interrogation. At the first crack, we have to go back to that phrase because the sentence was left unfinished and the meaning lost, when the doors opened and the dapper PIDE agent, as dapper and fresh as if he really had slept at home and in a good bed, went from room to room, his anger growing, because each exercise book told him only what he knew already, that this villain is called João Catarino, that this turd is called Agostinho Direito, that this piece of shit is called Carolino Dias, and that this son-of-a-bitch, yes, son-of-a-bitch, is called João Mau-Tempo. They must have planned it together, the bastards, Come here, there's to be no more joking now, I want to know who organized the strike, who your contacts are, or the same thing will happen to you as happened to that other man. They don't know who that other man is, they don't know anything, they shake their heads, determined, weary, brave, hungry heads, oh dear, my eyes are filling with tears. And Lieutenant Contente, who was also there, says, You'll end up being sent to Lisbon, you'd be better off confessing here on your home territory, among people who know you. But for some reason the agent softened, Send them back inside, we'll decide what to do with them later. The four were almost dragged down the corridor into the courtyard, look up there, my friend, at the sky, it's bright even though the sun's not out, and then were plunged, stumbling over the bodies on the floor, into the darkness of the dungeon where their comrades were still being kept. Those who were asleep had to wake up, or else, grumbling, turn over, but all finally settled down again, because the four men, before they, too, lay down and slept, as was their perfect right, all said, hand on heart, that they had told them nothing, not a single word. That sleep did not last long, for these are people accustomed to sleeping little and rolling up their blanket when the sun is still hidden among the mountains in Spain, and besides, there is the nagging, cruel anxiety that slips in between the folds of the unconscious mind, shakes and distends them, breaking the chrysalis, and on top of that is the hollow ache in the stomach, which has not been fed for who knows how many hours, you wouldn't even treat an animal like this.

It's midmorning when the door opens again, and Corporal Tacabo says, João Mau-Tempo, you have a visitor, and João Mau-Tempo, who was talking to Manuel Espada and Sigismundo Canastro about what fate might await them, jumps to his feet in surprise and sees the astonishment on his companions' faces too, it's only natural, everyone knows that in situations like this there are no visitors, such kindness is unheard of, and there are even those who wonder if their comrade really did say nothing, which is why João Mau-Tempo leaves, flanked by two silent, serious groups of men, and why he drags his feet as if he were carrying the guilt of the world on his shoulders. He is like a spinning wheel, going round and round, with the sky above full of sunlight, who can possibly have come to visit me, it must be Faustina and the kids, no, it can't be, the lieutenant wouldn't give permission, and there's no way that the PIDE agent, that foul-mouthed dog, would allow it.

The corridor seems far shorter, it was behind that door that he spent the night gazing at a school exercise book, a particularly hard lesson, my name is João Mau-Tempo, and now, while the guard is knocking at the next door and waiting for the order to enter, it must be Faustina, or else they're just saying that to get my hopes up, when in fact they're going to question me again, perhaps beat me, what did that policeman mean when he said that if we didn't talk, the same thing would happen to us as happened to the other man, what other man. Thoughts move quickly, which is why João Mau-Tempo had time to think all this while he was waiting, but when the door opened, his brain emptied of ideas, as if his head were filled with the blackness of night, and then he felt a great sense of relief, because standing between the agent and the lieutenant was Father Agamedes, they wouldn't beat me up in front of a priest, but what's he doing here.

This is how it will be in heaven, with me in the middle as befits the spiritual obligation that has been mine ever since I have known myself and you have known me, with you, Lieutenant, at my right hand as protector of the law and those who make the law, and you, Senhor Agent, on my left hand as the man who does the dirty work, about which I would really rather not know. The door to this house of discipline opens, and what do I see, O my poor eyes, better to have been born blind than to see this, tell me you're deceiving me, can this be João Mau-Tempo from Monte Lavre, the home of my somewhat troublesome flock, you must be mad, according to the lieutenant and the policeman, or the policeman and the lieutenant, you have refused to tell them all that you know, well, it would be best if you did, for your own sake and that of your family, they are not to blame for the mistakes and follies of their father, you should be ashamed of yourself, João Mau-Tempo, a grown man, a respectable man caught up in such foolishness, this so-called insurrection, how often have I told you and the other men at the church, Beloved brethren, the road you are taking will lead you only to perdition and to hell, where there shall be wailing and gnashing of teeth, I have told you that so often, I've grown weary of repeating it, but what good did it do, João Mau-Tempo, it's not that I don't care about the others, I don't know them, but the policeman and the lieutenant told me that of the men from Monte Lavre, you were the one they asked to write in that exercise book, but you wrote nothing, you refused to help, as if you were mocking them, mocking these poor, patient gentlemen, who spent a sleepless night, because they have families too, you know, sitting at home waiting for them, and because of you, they had to say to them, I won't be home until late or I have to work tonight, don't wait up for me, have your supper and go to bed, I won't be home until morning, or not even then, because it's almost lunchtime now, and the lieutenant and the policeman are both still here, I just can't believe it, João Mau-Tempo, you clearly have no consideration for the authorities at all, if you did, you wouldn't behave like this, what would it cost you to tell them who organized the strike and who distributed the leaflets, where they come from and how many there are, what would it cost you, you wretched man, what could be simpler than to give them the names, the policeman here and the lieutenant would do the rest, you could then go home to your family, what could be nicer, a man in the bosom of his family, tell me, although, obviously, as a priest, I can't reveal the secrets of the confessional, but was it So-and-so and Whatsisname, was it, tell me, a nod will do if you prefer not to speak, only we four will ever know, was it them or wasn't it, that's what I've heard, but I can't be sure and I'm not saying it was them, I'm simply asking, really, João Mau-Tempo, I find your attitude most disappointing, aren't you ashamed to make your family suffer like this, speak, man.

Speak, man, there's no one else here, just me, Father Agamedes, the lieutenant, the policeman and you, there are no other witnesses, why can't you tell us what you know, which probably isn't much, but each man does what he can, you can't do more than that, Look, Father Agamedes, I don't know anything, I can't repent of something I didn't do, I would give anything to be back with my wife and my daughters, but I can't give you what you're asking me, I can't say anything because I don't know anything, and even if I did, I'm not sure I would tell you, Now you've shown your true colors, you bastard, shouts the policeman, Stop, says Father Agamedes, as I never tire of saying, they're nothing but poor brutes, I said as much the other day when I was at Dona Clemência's house, he probably really doesn't know anything and was just led astray by the others, He's down as one of the strike leaders, says Lieutenant Contente, Right, says the policeman, send him back inside.

João Mau-Tempo leaves, and as he walks down the corridor for what seems like the nth time, he sees, coming out of another door, flanked by a large escort of guards, So-and-so and Whats-isname, their eyes meet in recognition, they've been badly beaten, poor things, and João Mau-Tempo, as he walks across the court-yard, feels his eyes fill with tears, not because he's dazzled by the sun, he's used to that now, but out of an absurd feeling of content-ment and relief to know that the two men have already been ar-rested, and that he wasn't the one who betrayed them, no, it wasn't me, what a relief that they've been arrested, but what am I saying, and he weeps twice over, once out of contentment and once out of sorrow, and both times he weeps to have seen them here, they've obviously been beating them up, as sure as my name is João Mau-Tempo, that policeman was spot-on when he said I have the right name for the times we're living through.

He went back into the dungeon and told the others what had happened. They saw that he had tears in his eyes and asked if he had been beaten. He said no, he hadn't, but continued to weep, his heart filled with sorrow, any contentment he had felt quite gone, re-placed by a feeling of mortal sadness. The men from Monte Lavre gathered around him, those of the same age, that is, because the younger ones moved away, embarrassed to be near a man whose hair was already white but who was crying like a child, is that what awaits us as well, they thought. These are scruples it would be best to accept without further analysis or discussion.

It was after midday when the situation took a turn for the bet-ter. They were led out into the courtyard, where they were re-united with their families, who had come from far and wide, those who could, and who were only now allowed into that anteroom of authority, having been kept waiting outside the barracks, penned in by the guards, where they redoubled their sighing and sobbing, but when Corporal Tacabo turned up to give the order to let them in, they were filled with hope, and there were Faustina and her two daughters, Gracinda and Amélia, who had walked the four leagues from Monte Lavre, what a wearisome life they lead, along with

others, mostly women, There they are, and the guards finally relaxed their security measures, ah, what hungry kisses might then
have been heard throughout the glade,* what do you mean glade,
the poor creatures embraced and wept, it was like the resurrection
of the dead, and as to kisses, that is not something in which they
have much practice, but Manuel Espada, who had no family there,
stood looking at Gracinda, who had her arms about her father, but
she was already taller than him and so could look at Manuel over
her father's shoulder, of course, they had met before, and this was
hardly love at first sight, but afterward she said, Hello, Manuel,
and he replied, Hello, Gracinda, and that was that, and anyone
who thinks more is required is quite wrong.

The families were still engaged in this festival of embraces when
Lieutenant Contente and the PIDE agent came out into the courtyard, and the speech they gave emerged from their two mouths
simultaneously, it was impossible to know which of them was im-
itating the other, or if there was some mechanism at work, connected to Lisbon perhaps by electric cables, that made them speak
like that, like two phonographs, Lads, be careful from now on, this
time we're letting you walk free, but be warned, if you get involved
in any such terrorist activities again, you will pay twice over, so
don't be so foolish as to be taken in by false doctrines, doctrines
spread by the enemies of our nation, if you come across pamphlets
on the roads or in the streets of a village, don't read them, or if you
do read them, burn them immediately afterward, don't give them
to anyone else or repeat what you read, because that is a crime, and
then both you and your innocent families will suffer, if you have a
problem to resolve, don't go on strike, go to the authorities, who
are there to inform and help, that way you will be given whatever
is fair and lawful, with no need for fuss or upsets, that's why we're
here, and now go and work in peace, and may God go with you,

---

* A reference to canto IX, verse 83, of *The Lusiads* by Luís Vaz de Camões.

but before you leave, you have to pay the cost of gas for the truck that brought you from Monte Lavre to Montemor, you're the ones who did wrong and you're the ones who have to pay, the State can't be expected to do that.

They scraped together the necessary money, having rummaged around in bags and pockets and handkerchiefs, there's the money, Lieutenant Contente, at least we won't be in debt to the State, because we know how hard up it is, it's just a shame the trip wasn't longer, because we already know the Monte Lavre road. These words were not, in fact, spoken, the narrator took the liberty of adding them, but the following words were spoken, by the PIDE agent, alone this time, Now that you've settled your bill, go back to your homes and may God go with you, and be sure to thank the priest here, who has shown what a friend he is to you all. At these words, Father Agamedes raises his arms, as if he were standing before the altar, and people don't know quite what to do, some go over and thank him, others pretend to have neither heard nor seen him and gaze off into space or talk to their wives and families, and Manuel Espada, who, by some strange coincidence, is standing right next to Gracinda Mau-Tempo, mutters, as if the words were biting into his heart, I feel quite ashamed, and just when he thought things could get no worse, Father Agamedes, smiling broadly, says, And now for some good news, there is transport for everyone outside in the street, provided by your employers, with no charge either, you're to be driven home in your employers' cars and carts, and to think that some people still speak ill of them. And off Father Agamedes goes, his black, wax-spattered cassock fluttering in the breeze, carrying along in his blessed wake his wretched flock frantically chewing on the tiny quantity of food brought from home, and Manuel Espada, who, by some strange coincidence, is still standing right next to Gracinda Mau-Tempo, said, And they expect us to be grateful to them, it's just despicable. Gracinda Mau-Tempo did not reply, and Manuel Espada returned to his theme, Well, they're not taking me, I'm walking. Then the anxious girl did move and said, part shyly, part boldly, It's an awfully long way, but immediately corrected herself, unsure who to praise and who to censure, whether those who accepted the offer of a lift or this rebel, It's up to you, of course, Manuel Espada replied that he knew it was a long way, took three steps, then turned back, Would you be my girl, and she responded with a look, which was all that was needed, and when Manuel Espada had already turned the first corner, that was when Gracinda Mau-Tempo said Yes in her heart.

During the days that followed, Father Agamedes stocked up his already well-stocked larder with the gratitude of his parishioners, It's not very much, I'm afraid, but it comes from the heart, this is for all you did for us, a pint of beans, a little bag of maize, a laying hen, a bottle of olive oil, three drops of blood.

O LÉ. ON THE ORDERS of the president of the bullring, the constable enters the arena, inspects the locks on the corrals, counts the number of halters, decides that there are enough, takes a turn about the arena to get a good view of the whole thing, the tiered benches, the boxes, the bandstand, the seats in the shade and in the sun, sniffs the odor of fresh dung on the air and says, They can come in now. The doors are opened and the bulls enter, these are the bulls that will be fought today according to the rules and precepts of the art, taunted with a cape, stuck with darts, beaten with sticks and finally crowned with the hilt of the sword, whose point and blade pierce my heart, olé. They are brought in by the guards, they come from near and far, from places we have already mentioned, but not, as chance would have it, from Monte Lavre, and gradually the ring fills up, not the benches, the very idea, no, the audience is composed entirely of guards, who stand around, in the shade where possible, their rifles at the ready, well, they don't feel like men without them. The ring starts filling up with dark cattle, captured from leagues around in heroic combat, with the guards on the attack, at the charge, there they are bearing down on those beastly strikers, those lions of the sickle, those

158

men of sorrows, These are the captives from the battle, and at your feet, lord, we lay the flags and cannon seized from the enemy, see how red they are, but not as red as they were at the beginning of the war because, meanwhile, we have heaped dust and spit upon them, you can hang them in the museum or in the regimental chapel where the recruits kneel, waiting to have revealed to them the mystical fate of being a guard, but perhaps it would be preferable, lord, to burn them, because the sight of them offends the feelings you taught us to have, and we want no other feelings. The constable, with the benign authorization of the president of the bullring, had ordered the arena to be scattered with straw, so that the men, because they are men not lions and have neglected to bring their sickles with them, can sit or lie down, grouped more or less according to their village of origin, such gregarious instincts are hard to give up, but there are a few others, too, who go from group to group, offering a word here, a hand on the shoulder there, a glance or a discreet gesture, so that everything, as far as possible, is safe and clear, and now it's just a matter of waiting.

The guards are keeping watch from their viewing platform, and one of them says to the other, with a hearty, military laugh, It's like the monkey house at the zoo, all we need are some nuts to throw to them, that would be funny, watching the monkeys scrabbling for food. This implies that some of the guards have traveled, that they have visited a zoo, practiced the rules of summary observation and of expeditious classification, and if they say that the men of sorrow herded into the bullring in Montemor are monkeys, who are we to contradict them, especially when they are pointing their riffles in our direction, we say riffle to provide a sort of half rhyme with pistol, although piffle would be funnier, and there's plenty of that about. The men talk to pass the time or to prevent it from passing, it's a way of putting your hand on your heart and saying, Don't go forward, don't move, if you take another step, you'll crush me, what did I ever do to you. It's also like bending down, placing one hand on the earth and saying, Stop turning, I want to see the sun for a while longer. While all this is going on, this heaping of words one upon another, just to see if they come out differently, no one has noticed that the constable has entered the ring in search of a man, just one, who is not even a lion with a sickle and who has not even come very far, and that man, if he were given an exercise book in which to write down all he knows, as the four from Monte Lavre, Escoural, Safira and Torre da Gadanha will do the following day, that man would write on the first line or on every line, so that there could be no doubt and so that there could be no change of heart from one page to the next, as I say, if he were to write his name, he would write Germano Santos Vidigal.

They have found him. Two guards lead him away, and whichever way we turn, that is all we see, they lead him out of the ring, to the exit door from sector six, where two more guards join them, and now it seems deliberate, it's uphill all the way, as if we were watching a film about the life of Christ, up there is Calvary, and these are the centurions in their stiff boots and warriorlike sweat, their spears cocked, it's suffocatingly hot. Halt. A few men are coming down the road, and Corporal Tacabo, fearing that they might be José Gato and his gang, says, Keep walking, this man is under arrest. The passersby stay as far away as they can, pressed against the wall, they're in no danger, it's almost as if they were grateful for that order and for the information, and the cortege has only a hundred meters or so to go now. Up above, we can see her over the wall, a woman is hanging a sheet out on the line, it would be funny if that woman was called Verónica, but she isn't, her name is Cesaltina and she's not much of a one for churches. She sees the man pass by under guard, follows him with her eyes, she doesn't recognize him, but she has a presentiment and presses her face to the damp sheet as if it were a shroud, and says to her son, who insists on playing outside in the sun, Let's go indoors.

The guards cross the road that leads up to the castle, where it widens out to form a square, only a few more steps to go and so little profit in them, but if you think that is what the prisoner is thinking, you're quite wrong, we can't know what his thoughts are or will be, but now it's up to us to start thinking. If we were to stay outside, if we followed that woman, Cesaltina, and sat down, for example, to play with her son, well, who doesn't like children, but then we wouldn't find out what is about to happen, and we can't have that. Two sentries are at the door, the guards are on a war footing, raise up once again the grandeur of Portugal,* you get a good view of the countryside from here, the chapel of Our Lady of the Visitation, who is as miraculous as they come, but we don't want any pilgrimages here, and a few gardens, but in this cramped space there's no room to see more. Let's go indoors, says Cesaltina to her son, Let us go indoors too, through here, past the sentries, they can't see us, that's our privilege, let's cross the courtyard, no, don't go in there, that's a kind of dungeon, a kind of wholesale warehouse for criminals, tomorrow the men from Monte Lavre and elsewhere will come here, minor cases, this is the way, but don't take that corridor, it's around this corner, another ten paces or so, mind you don't trip over that bench, here it is, we need go no further, we've arrived, it's just a matter of opening the door.

We have missed the preliminaries. We lingered to look at the landscape, to play with the little boy who so loves to play in the sun, however often his parents call him indoors, and to ask questions of Cesaltina, whose husband is not involved in these troubles, he works for the council and is called Ourique, but all these things were merely excuses, delaying tactics, ways of averting our eyes, but now, in between these four whitewashed walls, on this tiled floor, notice the broken corners, how some tiles have been worn smooth, how many feet have passed this way, and look how interesting this trail of ants is, traveling along the grooves between tiles

---

* A line from the Portuguese national anthem.

as if they were valleys, while up above, projected against the white sky of the ceiling and the sun of the lamp, tall towers are moving, they are men, as the ants well know, having, for generations, experienced the weight of their feet and the long, hot spout of water that falls from a kind of pendulous external intestine, ants all over the world have been drowned or crushed by these, but it seems they will escape this fate now, for the men are occupied with other things. The hearing apparatus and musical education of ants do not allow them to understand what men say or sing, so they cannot catch every detail of the interrogation. But that doesn't matter, in the morning, in this same barracks, albeit in a less secret place, the men from Monte Lavre, Torre da Gadanha, Safira and Escoural will be questioned too, and then we'll hear everything, along with the insults, son-of-a-bitch, bastard, son-of-a-bitch, piece of shit, son-of-a-bitch, faggot, all of which is very trivial, and we won't be offended by such trifles, it's like a scurrilous form of the tittle-tattle exchanged by gossips, she said this, then she said, who cares, in a couple of days they'll have made up, but not in this case.

Let's take this ant, or, rather, let's not, because that would involve picking it up, let us merely consider it, because it is one of the larger ones and because it raises its head like a dog, it's walking along very close to the wall, together with its fellow ants, it will have time to complete its long journey ten times over between the ants' nest and whatever it is that it finds so interesting, curious or perhaps merely nourishing in this secret room, before this episode doomed to end in death is over. One of the men has fallen to the ground, he's on the same level as the ants now, we don't know if he can see them, but they see him, and he will fall so often that, in the end, they will know by heart his face, the color of his hair and eyes, the shape of his ear, the dark arc of his eyebrow, the faint shadow at the corner of his mouth, and later, back in the ants' nest, they will weave long stories for the enlightenment of future generations, because it is useful for the young to know what happens out there in the world. The man fell and the others dragged him to his feet again, shouting at him, asking two different questions at the same time, how could he possibly answer them even if he wanted to, which is not the case, because the man who fell and was dragged to his feet will die without saying a word. Only moans will issue from his mouth, and in the silence of his soul only deep sighs, and even when his teeth are broken and he has to spit them out, which will prompt the other two men to hit him again for soiling State property, even then the sound will be of spitting and nothing more, that unconscious reflex of the lips, and then the dribble of saliva thickened with blood that falls to the floor, thus stimulating the taste buds of the ants, who telegraph from one to the other news of this singularly red manna fallen from such a white heaven.

The man fell again. It's the same one, said the ants, the same ear shape, the same arc of eyebrow, the same shadow at the corner of the mouth, there's no mistaking him, why is it that it is always the same man who falls, why doesn't he defend himself, fight back. This is the reasoning of the ant and of ant civilization, they do not know that Germano Santos Vidigal is not fighting with those two thugs Escarro and Escarrilho,* but with his own body, with the searing pain between his legs, or his testicles, to use the language of a physiology manual, or his bollocks, to use the more easily acquired and cruder language of the street, fragile balls, balloons full of some imponderable ether which raise us men up to ecstasy, that carry us between heaven and earth, but not these pathetic objects anxiously protected by hands that suddenly release them when the heel of a boot thuds brutally into the small of the back. The ants are surprised, but only fleetingly. After all, they have their own duties, their own timetables to keep, it is quite enough that they raise their heads like dogs and fix their feeble vision on the fallen man to check that he is the same one and not some new variant in the

---

* Literally, Big Spit and Little Spit.

story. The larger ant walked along the remaining stretch of wall, slipped under the door, and some time will pass before it reappears to find everything changed, well, that's just a manner of speaking, there are still three men there, but the two who do not fall never stop moving, it must be some kind of game, there's no other explanation, let's hope Cesaltina's son never plays this game, they are engaged in hurling the other man against the wall, they grab him by the shoulders and propel him willy-nilly in the direction of the wall, so that sometimes he hits his back, sometimes his head, or else his poor bruised face smashes into the whitewash and leaves on it a trace of blood, not a lot, just whatever spurts forth from his mouth and right eyebrow. And if they leave him there, he, not his blood, slides down the wall and he ends up kneeling on the ground beside the little trail of ants, who are startled by the sudden fall from on high of that great mass, which doesn't, in the end, even graze them. And when he stays there for some time, one ant attaches itself to his clothing, wanting to take a closer look, the fool, it will be the first ant to die, because the next blow falls on precisely that spot, the ant doesn't feel the second blow, but the man does, and his stomach, not he, gives a lurch, and again he collapses, retching, from that violent kick to the stomach, followed by another to his private parts, which is an expression too widespread to cause offense.

One of the men leaves the room to rest from his exertions. His name is Escarrilho, he has a mother and father and is married with children, which isn't saying much, because the one who stayed behind to guard the prisoner, Escarro, also has a mother and father, and is married with children, the men are distinguishable only by their features, although only just, and by their names, one is Escarro and the other Escarrilho, they are not related and yet they belong to the same family. He walks down the corridor and, in his weariness, stumbles over the bench, These guys who won't talk will be the death of me, but screw the bugger, I'll get something out of him or my name's not Escarrilho. He takes a long, long drink of water, he's burning up with fever, then a kind of nervous fit comes upon him, and, energies replenished, he irrupts into the room again like a typhoon, and launches himself at Germano Santos Vidigal like a dog, he is a dog called Escarrilho, and it's as if Escarro were urging him on, Go on, bite him, and perhaps he really does bite him, later on they'll find teeth marks here and there, but whether they're from a man or a dog is hard to tell, for sometimes, as everyone knows, men are born with dogs' teeth. Poor dogs, trained to bite those they should respect and to bite parts of the body they should never bite, here, for example, the place that marks me out as a man, no more than they should bite a man's arm or jaw, or this other place, the heart, our inner eye, or the head, where our real eyes are. But I was told as a child that this restless piece of machinery is what makes me a man, and although I didn't really believe them, I'm fond of it, and it isn't something that a dog should bite.

The large ant is on its fifth journey, and still the game continues. This time it was Escarro's turn to go out for a rest, he went into the courtyard to smoke a restoring cigarette, then visited Lieutenant Contente in his office to ask about the progress of the field operations, the great maneuvers, and the lieutenant told him they were making a general sweep of strikers in the area, deploying all their manpower, it was good that they finally sent us reinforcements, he said, enough to arrest as many men again as we've got penned up in the bullring. And has that guy Germano Vidigal talked yet, asks Lieutenant Contente discreetly, because it really has nothing to do with him and Escarro is under no obligation to answer, but he does, Not yet, he's a tough nut to crack, and the lieutenant, solicitously, helpfully, adds, You'll have to tighten the screws still more. This mini-Torquemada of Montemor makes a good adjutant, offering them a roof over their heads and protection, and also throwing in a little free advice, but as he lights a cigarette, he hears Escarro's ill-tempered response, We know what we're doing, he snarls, then leaves, slamming the door and muttering, Imbecile, and, feeling perhaps put out by this exchange, he went into the room where the ants were and removed from the drawer a deadly weapon, a steel-tipped cat-o'-nine-tails, he looped the handle about his wrist to get a better grip, and as Germano, that foolish man of sorrows, tried to crawl away from his attacker, Escarro unleashed the whistling whip upon his shoulders, moving slowly down his back, centimeter by centimeter, as if he were threshing green rye, as far as the kidneys, where he lingered, blind even though his eyes were open, for there is no more dangerous form of blindness, rhythmically thrashing the man now lying on the floor, beating him methodically so as not to tire himself too much, because tiredness is the real killer, but gradually he began to lose all self-control and became a kind of manic whipping machine, a drunken automaton, until Escarrilho placed one hand on his arm, Don't get carried away, man, you'll kill the guy. Ants know about death, because they're used to seeing their own dead and to making instant diagnoses, sometimes, on their travels, as they're dragging along a grain of wheat, they stumble upon some small, shriveled, almost indecipherable thing, but they don't hesitate, despite being encumbered by their load, they thoroughly investigate the object with their antennae, but their Morse code is quite explicit, This is a dead ant, and you only have to glance away for a moment, and when you look again, the corpse has gone, that's what ants are like, they don't leave behind those who fall in the line of duty, and for all these reasons, the large ant, which was on its seventh trip back and forth and happened to be passing, raises its head and studies the great cloud before its eyes, but then makes a special effort, adjusts its visual mechanism and thinks, How pale this man is, he doesn't look the same at all, his face is all swollen, his lips are cut, and his eyes, poor eyes, you can't see them for the bruises, he's so different from when he first arrived, but I know him by his smell, because smell is the keenest of the ants' senses. The ant is still thinking all this when the face is removed from view because the other two men turn the man over and lay him on his back, they throw water on his face, a whole jug of cool water, pumped up from the deep, dark well, little did that water suspect the fate awaiting it, coming as it did from the depths of the earth, after who knows how many years traveling underground, having known other places, the stony steps of a spring, the harsh brilliance of sand, the soft warmth of mud, the putrid stagnation of the swamp, and the fire of the sun that slowly erased it from the earth, vanished, gone, until it reappears in a passing cloud long, long afterward and suddenly falls to earth, falling helplessly from above, the earth seems beautiful to the water, and if the water could choose the places where it fell, if it could, there would be far less thirst or far less surfeit, yes, long, long afterward it fell to earth and went traveling, gradually evolving into pure, crystal-clear water, until it found a course to follow, a secret stream, this dark, echoing well, this surface perforated by a suction pump, and suddenly it's trapped inside a transparent trap, a jug, is its fate perhaps to slake someone's thirst, no, it's being poured from on high onto a face, an abrupt fall, abruptly broken as it runs slowly over lips, eyes, nose and chin, over gaunt cheeks, over a forehead drenched in sweat, another kind of water, and thus it comes to know this man's as yet still-living mask. But the water drips onto the floor, spattering everything around and the tiles turn red, not to mention the ants who were drowned, apart from this larger one tirelessly making its eighth journey.

Escarro and Escarrilho grab Germano Santos Vidigal under the arms, lift him bodily, he hates to be a bother, and sit him on a chair. Escarro is still holding the cat-o'-nine-tails, the handle is still looped over his wrist, the fury that had gripped him has passed, but he still yells, Bastard, and spits in the face of the man who sits slumped in the chair like an empty jacket. Germano Santos Vidigal opens his eyes, and, incredible though it may seem, what he sees is the trail of ants, perhaps because there are so many of them in the place where his gaze happens to fall, it's hardly surprising, human blood is a delicacy for ants, when you think about it, they live on nothing else, and three drops of blood have fallen there, Father Agamedes, and three drops of blood make a well, a lake, an ocean. He opened his eyes, if you can use the word open to describe the narrow slits through which light barely penetrates, and what light does enter is too much, piercing his pupils with pain, which he is aware of only because it is a new pain, a knife sticking into flesh already pierced by another one hundred revolving knives, and then with a moan he stammered out a few words that Escarro and Escarrilho both hastened to hear, regretting now having beaten him so badly that they may have rendered him incapable of speech, but what Germano Santos Vidigal wants, poor man, still subject to his bodily needs, is to relieve his bladder, which for some reason is suddenly sending out an urgent signal, and will, if not heeded, empty itself right here and now. Escarro and Escarrilho don't want to get the floor any dirtier than it already is, and they also cherish the hope that they have finally broken this stubborn man's resistance and that this request is the first sign, one of them goes to the door to check that no one is in the corridor, nods, then goes back inside, and together the two men help Germano Santos Vidigal to walk the five meters that separate them from the latrine, they lean him up against the urinal and leave the poor man to unbutton his fly with clumsy fingers, feeling for and extracting his tortured penis, his cock, not daring to touch his swollen testicles, his torn scrotum, and then he concentrates, calls on all his muscles to help him, asking them first to contract and then to relax so that the sphincters soften and relieve the terrible tension, he tries once, twice, three times, and out it spurts, blood, mingled perhaps with urine, although it's impossible to tell from that one red stream, as if every vein in his body had burst and found an outlet there. He tries to hold it back, but the stream continues to pour forth as strongly as ever. It's his life pouring out of him, and it's still dribbling out when he finally puts his cock away, lacking the strength now to rebutton his fly. Escarro and Escarrilho lead him, feet dragging, back to the room of the ants and sit him down again on the chair, and Escarrilho asks, in a voice full of hope, So now will you talk, he has the idea that having been allowed to go to the toilet, the prisoner has a duty to speak, after all, one good turn deserves another, but Germano Santos Vidigal's arms drop to his sides, his head slumps onto his chest, and the light goes out inside his brain. The larger of the ants disappears under the door, having completed its tenth journey.

When it returns from the ants' nest, it will find the room full of men. Escarro and Escarrilho are there, along with Lieutenant Contente, Sergeant Armamento, Corporal Tacabo, two nameless privates and three specially chosen prisoners who state that the policemen left the room for a minute, no more than that, to deal with some urgent matter, and when they returned, found the prisoner had hanged himself on a piece of wire, just as we see him now, with one end tied around that nail there, and the other wound twice around Germano Santos Vidigal's neck, yes, his name's Germano Santos Vidigal, it's important to know that for the death certificate, the official doctor must be called, yes, as you can see, he's kneeling, yes, kneeling, but there's nothing odd about that, if someone wants to hang himself, even if it's only from a bedstead, it's all a matter of will, does anyone have any questions, Not me, say the lieutenant, the sergeant and the corporal, and the two privates and the three prisoners, who thanks to this stroke of luck will probably be set free today. There is great indignation among the ants, who witnessed everything, at different times, but meanwhile they have joined forces and pieced together what they saw, they know the whole truth, even the larger of the ants, who was the last to see the man's face close up, like a vast landscape, and it's a well-known fact that landscapes die because they are killed, not because they commit suicide.

The body has been removed. Escarro and Escarrilho put away the tools of their trade, the stick, the cat-o'-nine-tails, they rub their knuckles, inspect the tips and heels of their shoes, in case some thread of clothing or some bloodstain should reveal to the sharp eyes of Sherlock Holmes the weakness of their alibi and the conflicting times, but there's no danger of that, Sherlock Holmes is dead and buried, as dead as Germano Santos Vidigal, buried as deep as Germano soon will be, and the years will pass and these cases will remain swathed in silence until the ants acquire the gift of speech and tell the truth, the whole truth and nothing but the truth. Meanwhile, if we hurry, we'll still be in time to catch up with Dr. Romano, he's over there, head bowed, small black bag over his left arm, which is why we can ask him to raise his right hand, Do you swear to tell the truth, the whole truth and nothing but the truth, that's how it is with doctors, they're used to such solemn acts, Speak up, Dr. Romano, doctor of medicine, you who have sworn the Hippocratic oath with its various modern revisions to form and sense, speak up, Dr. Romano, here beneath the bright sun, is it really true that this man hanged himself. The doctor raises his right hand, looks at us with candid, innocent eyes, he's a much-respected man in the town, a regular churchgoer and punctilious in carrying out his social duties, and having shown us what a pure soul he is, he says, If someone has a wire wound twice around his own neck, with the other end tied to a nail above his head, and if the wire is pulled taut enough, even by only the partial weight of the body, then there is no doubt that, technically speaking, the man has hanged himself, and having said this, he lowered his hand and went about his business, Not so fast, Dr. Romano, doctor of medicine, it's not time for supper yet, if you still have any appetite after what you've just seen, I envy you your strong stomach, tell me, didn't you see the man's body, didn't you see the welts, the bruises, the battered genitals, the blood, No, I didn't, they told me the prisoner had hanged himself and he had, there was nothing else to see, You're a liar, Dr. Romano, medical practitioner, how and why and when did you acquire the ugly habit of lying, No, I'm not a liar, it's just that I can't tell the truth, Why, Because I'm afraid, Go in peace, Dr. Pilate, sleep in peace with your conscience, and give her a good screwing, because she deserves both you and the screwing, Goodbye, Senhor Author, Goodbye, Senhor Doctor, but take my advice, keep well away from ants, especially those that raise their heads like dogs, they're very observant creatures, you can't imagine, you will be watched from now on by all ants, don't worry, they won't harm you, but you never know, one day your conscience might make a cuckold of you, and that would be your salvation.

The street we are on is Rua da Parreira, or the street of the vine trellis, presumably because in days gone by, it was shaded by a trellis of fine grapes, and since the council couldn't come up with the name of a saint or a politician or a benefactor or a martyr to bestow on the street, it will for the time being continue to be called Rua da Parreira. What shall we do now, given that the men from Monte Lavre, Escoural, Safira and Torre da Gadanha only arrive tomorrow, given that the bullring is closed and no one can get in, what shall we do, let's go to the cemetery, perhaps Germano Santos Vidigal has arrived there already, the dead, when they choose to, can move very fast, and it's not that far and it's cooler now, you go down this street, turn right, as if we were going to Évora, it's easy enough, then left, you can't go wrong, there are the white walls and the cypresses, the same as everywhere else. The mortuary is here, but it's locked, they lock everything and they've taken away the key, we can't go in, Good afternoon, Senhor Ourique, no rest for the wicked, eh, That's true, but what's a man to do, people may not die every day, but you still have to straighten their beds and

sweep the paths, Yes, I saw your wife Cesaltina and your son earlier on, he's a lovely child, That's true, True is a good word, Senhor
Ourique, That's true, Tell me, is it true that the body in the mortuary died of a beating or simply because its former owner decided
to hang himself, It's true that my son is a lovely boy, always wanting to be out playing in the sun, it's true that the body in there is
that of a hanged man, it's true that given the state he was in, he
wouldn't have had the strength to hang himself, it's true that his
private parts were battered and bruised, it's true that his body was
caked in blood, it's true that even after death the swellings didn't
go down, the size of partridge eggs, they were, and it's true that
I would have died of far less, and I'm used to death, Thank you,
Senhor Ourique, you're a gravedigger and a serious man, perhaps because you're so fond of your son, but tell me, whose skull
is that you're holding in your hand, does it belong to the king's son,
That I don't know, I wasn't working here then, Goodbye, Senhor
Ourique, it's time to close the gates, give my regards to Cesaltina
and my love to your boy who so likes to play in the sun.

    We have said our farewells, from down here you can see the cas-
tle, who could recount all its stories, those from the past and those
to come, it would be quite wrong to think that just because wars
are no longer fought outside castles, such military actions, however
petty, however inglorious, are a thing of the past, as the Marquis de
Marialva put it, Have you noticed, your majesty, how poorly Manuel Ruiz Adibe, governor of Montemor, runs the barracks there,
because quite apart from his general incompetence, if the workers give him enough money, he excuses them from having to help
build the fortifications, which is why so little work has been done,
as anyone can see, and so I am asking your majesty if I might suggest someone more suited to the post, notably the lieutenant general of artillery, Manuel da Rocha Pereira, who possesses all the
necessary qualities, efficiency, energy, zeal, as well as a desire to occupy said post, so if your majesty would be so kind as to write the

requisite letter of appointment, giving him the title of field marshal, then Manuel Ruiz Adibe can still enjoy his salary, as do the other cavalry captains whom your majesty has retired, he's not so needy nor does he have so many responsibilities that he need live uncomfortably, even if his salary isn't always paid promptly. Devil take Adibe, who took such poor care of your majesty's service and such good care of his own, the times have changed, now there are zealous functionaries willing to kill a man in the Montemor barracks, then go outside to smoke a cigarette, wave goodbye to the sentry courageously gazing out at the horizon to make sure no Spaniards are approaching, and set off down the road with a firm step, chatting serenely and totting up their day's work, so many punches, so many kicks, so many blows with a stick, and they feel proud of themselves, neither of them is called Adibe, their names are Escarro and Escarrilho, they're like twins, they pause outside the cinema, where the film being shown tomorrow, on Sunday, is advertised, the summer season is getting off to a good start with an interesting comedy called The Magnificent Dope. Bring your wives, they'll enjoy it, poor ladies, when things calm down a bit, it's sure to be worth seeing, but if you want a really good film, don't miss the Thursday showing, with Estrellita Castro, the goddess of song and dance, starring alongside Antonio Vico, Ricardo Merino and Rafaela Satorrés in that marvelous musical Mariquilla Terremoto, olé.

THESE MEN ESCAPED from among the dead and the wounded. We will not name them one by one, it's enough to know that some went to Lisbon to languish in prisons and dungeons, and others returned to the threshing machine, being paid the new wage for as long as the harvest lasted. Father Agamedes issues a paternal admonishment to these madmen, reminds them directly or indirectly how much they owe him and how they, therefore, have still more of an obligation to fulfill their Christian duties, for did not the Holy Mother clearly demonstrate her power and influence by touching the bolts on the prison doors and making them fall away and by prying open the bars on the windows, hallelujah. He makes these grand statements to a church almost empty apart from old ladies, because the other parishioners are still brooding over how much that gratitude has cost them and are not consoled. In Monte Lavre, they know little of the arrests, it's all very vague, however often Sigismundo Canastro tells them how many there were, and only tomorrow will it become known how many deaths there were, as worker talks to worker, but the weariness of the living seems to hang heavier than a death about which they can do nothing, My father is ill and I don't know what to do with him, these are private concerns particular to each household, not to mention that the harvest is coming to an end, and then what will happen. It will be no different from other years, but now Norberto, Alberto and Dagoberto are saying, through the mouths of the overseers, that this rabble will regret ever going on strike, and the extra money they earned will cost them dearly. Adalberto has already sent written instructions from Lisbon to the effect that, once the harvest and the threshing are over, he will keep on only the swineherds and shepherds and the watchman, because he doesn't want his land trampled by strikers and idlers, later we'll see, it depends on the olives, how are the olives doing, by the way. The overseer will reply, but this is the kind of correspondence no one bothers to keep, you receive the letter, do what it tells you to do or send an answer to the question asked, and then it's, Now where did I put that letter, it would be amusing to base a whole history on such letters, it would be another way of doing it, our problem is that we think only the big things are important, and so we talk about them, but then when we want to know how things really were, who was there and what they said, we're in trouble.

Her name is Gracinda Mau-Tempo and she is seventeen. She will marry Manuel Espada, but not just yet. She's young, she can't simply get married from one day to the next, with no trousseau, they will have to be patient. Quite apart from these obvious social obligations, they have nowhere to live, It would mean having to move somewhere else, You don't want to be like your brother, always having to live so far away, I know it's not the same thing, because you're a girl, but it's bad enough never seeing one child, ah me, that boy of mine. These are Faustina's words, and João Mau-Tempo nods, he always feels a pang in his heart whenever they talk about his son, the little devil, who was only eighteen when it became clear that he had inherited his late grandfather's wanderlust. Gracinda Mau-Tempo will tell Manuel Espada the substance of these conversations later, and he will say, I want to marry you

and I don't mind waiting, and he says this gravely, as is his custom on all occasions, a manner that makes him seem older than
his years, and there was already quite an age difference, as Faustina
had pointed out to Gracinda when Gracinda told her that Manuel
Espada had asked her to be his girl, But he's much older than you,
What's that got to do with it, Gracinda had replied, offended, and
quite right, too, because that wasn't what mattered, what mattered
was that she had liked Manuel Espada ever since that June day in
Montemor, what did age have to do with anything, although Manuel Espada, when he spoke to her, had also pointed this out, I'm
seven years older than you, and she, smiling, not sure quite what
she was saying, had replied, The husband should be older than the
wife, and then she had blushed because she realized that she had
said yes without actually saying yes, as Manuel Espada realized,
and he passed on to the next question, So that's a yes, is it, and
she said, Yes, and from then on they spent time with each other as
the rules of courtship demanded, at the front door of her house,
because it was too soon for him to be allowed into the house, but
where Manuel Espada did not follow the rules was in speaking
to her parents right away, rather than waiting until both he and
she were sure of their feelings and of their ill-kept secret. It was
then that João Mau-Tempo and Faustina explained, and this was
hardly news, that marriage was an economic impossibility just
then, and that they would have to wait, I'll wait as long as I have
to, said Manuel Espada, and then he left, determined to work and
save, although he also had to help his own parents, with whom he
still lived. These are the problems of ordinary life, which change
little or so little in two generations that one hardly notices, and
Gracinda Mau-Tempo knows that in future she will have to agree,
by negotiation with her mother, how much of her wage she can
put aside for her trousseau, as is her duty.

We have spoken a great deal about men and a little about
women, but only in passing, as fleeting shadows or occasionally es-

sential interlocutors, as a female chorus, albeit usually silent because weighed down either by some burden or by the weight in their bellies, or else, for various reasons, in the role of mater dolorosa, a dead son or a prodigal son, or a daughter dishonored, there's never any shortage of them. We will continue to talk about men, but also more and more about women, and not because of this particular courtship and future marriage, because we have already witnessed the respective courtships and marriages of Sara da Conceição and Faustina, Gracinda's grandmother now long gone and her mother happily still alive, and we said little about them, there are other reasons, as yet somewhat vague, and that's because the times are changing. Declaring their feelings at the door of a prison, or, rather, in a barracks and a place of death, which comes to the same thing, goes against all the traditions and conventions, and at a time of such suffering too, doubtless compensated by the joys of an as yet timorous freedom, fancy a young man saying to a young woman, Will you be my girl, ah, it's all very different from when I was their age.

Gracinda was born two years before her sister Amélia, who, because she had filled out early, looked, to the ill informed, about the same age. There was little physical resemblance, perhaps because the family blood was so mixed and so prone to produce singularities. We have only to think of that ancestor who came from the cold north and raped a girl at the fountain, a crime that went unpunished by his lord and master, Lamberto Horques, who was more concerned with origins of another kind and with horses. However, so as to confirm how small and modest a world this is, here we have Manuel Espada asking Gracinda Mau-Tempo to marry him next to that very same fountain, next to a field of bracken, which will not this time be trampled and broken until the body of the rape victim gives in, defeated. If only we could tie up all the loose ends, the world would be a stronger and better place. And if the fountain could speak, for example, which it would be perfectly justified in doing, given that it's been a constant source of pure, bubbling water for over five hundred years, or longer if it was a Moorish fountain, anyway, if it could speak, we think it would say, This girl has been here before, an understandable mistake, over time even fountains get confused, not to mention the vast difference in how Manuel Espada behaves toward Gracinda, merely taking her hand and saying, So that's a yes, is it, and then the two of them walking back, leaving the bracken for another occasion.

These three children know a lot about many different things. There are only four years between António Mau-Tempo, the oldest, and Amélia Mau-Tempo, the youngest. Once, they were just three bundles of ill-nourished, ill-dressed flesh and bone, as they continue to be today as adolescents, if that word isn't too refined for these lands and these latifundios. They were carried on the backs of father and mother or in baskets on their parents' heads, when they could still not walk or their little legs got tired quickly, or on their father's shoulders or in their mother's arms, or on their own two feet, they traveled more, given their age, than the wandering Jew. They battled with mosquitoes in the ricefields, poor, defenseless innocents who didn't even know to brush from their faces the squadrons of flying lancers that whined with pure, intense pleasure. However, since mosquitoes have very short lives and since none of the children died, it is of them that we speak, not of some others who died of malaria, so if there were any winners in the war, they were those who practiced passive resistance. It doesn't often happen, but in this case it did.

Look at these children, it doesn't matter which one, the oldest boy, or the middle child, or the youngest, lying in a box in the shade of the holm oak while her mother, let's say the child is a girl, works nearby, not so near that she can see her, and like all children, especially when they can't yet talk, she gets a pain in her belly, or not even that, just the usual outpouring of poo, at least she hasn't got dysentery this time, and by the time Faustina comes back, it's lunchtime, and Gracinda is covered in excrement and flies like the dung heap she has, alas, become. By the time her mother has washed, and washed not just Gracinda's little body, which is smeared all over, but also the rags covering her and which she hopes will dry draped over this pile of firewood, lunchtime has passed and so has her appetite. At this point, we don't know who to take care of first, Gracinda, who, though clean and fresh, is all alone, or Faustina, who returns to work, gnawing on a bit of dry bread. Let's stay here, beneath this holm oak, fanning the child's face with this branch as she tries to sleep, because the flies are back again, but also to save the parents any grief, because you never know, a cortege of kings and knights might pass by, and the barren queen's nursemaid might spot this little angel and carry her off to the palace, and how awful it would be if, later, she didn't recognize her real parents, because in the palace she wears only velvets and brocades and plays the lute in her room in a tower, with its view of the latifundio. Later on, Sara da Conceição used to tell such stories to her grandchildren, and Gracinda wouldn't believe us if we told her what danger she would have been in if we weren't here, sitting on this stone, fanning her with this branch.

But children, if they get the chance, grow up. Until they are of an age to work, they are left in the care of their grandmother or their mother, if there's no work for the mother, or with their mother and father, if there's no work for the father either, and if, when they're older, there are no children and all are workers, if there's no work for fathers, mothers, children or grandmothers, there you have it, ladies and gentlemen, the ideal Portuguese family gathered around the same hunger, depending on the season. If it's acorn time, then the father goes to gather them, as long as Norberto, Adalberto or Sigisberto doesn't send the guards to patrol at night, which is why, as soon as it came into being, the dear republic set up the national republican guard. That's all a very long story. But nature is prodigal, a generous teat that spills forth its milk in every ditch. Let's go gathering thistles, dockweed, watercress, what better diet could there be. Dockweed is just the same as spinach, it looks the same, although it tastes quite different, but once cooked, fried with a little of the onions we have left, it's enough to make your mouth water. And as for thistles. Strip those thistles, add a few grains of rice, and you have a banquet, please, Father Agamedes, help yourself, he who ate the meat can gnaw the bones. Every Christian, and even a non-Christian, needs his three meals a day, breakfast, lunch and supper, or whatever you choose to call them, what matters is having a full plate or bowl, or, if it's only bread and scrape, then it should be rather more than just a nice smell. It's a rule as golden as any other noble rule, a human right for both parents and children, which means that I don't have to eat only once in order for them to eat three times, although those three meals serve more to keep hunger at bay than to fill the stomach. People talk and talk, but they don't know what real need is, it means going to the bread bin knowing that the last crust of bread was eaten yesterday, and yet still opening the lid, just in case there's been another miracle of the roses,* which would, in any case, be quite impossible, because neither you nor I can remember putting roses in the bread bin, to do that we would have had to pick them, and have you ever seen roses growing on a cork oak, if only they did, hunger, as you see, can bring on delirium. Today is Wednesday, Gracinda, take your sister Amélia and go up to the big house, hold her hand, Gracinda, António won't go this time. Encouraging children to beg, that's the kind of education the parents give their children, I don't know why my tongue doesn't form a knot in my mouth or fall to the floor and leap about like a lizard's tail, that would teach me to be more care-

---

* Queen Isabel of Aragon, the wife of the Portuguese king Dom Dinis, was devoted to helping the poor. When her husband upbraided her for giving money to beggars, the queen drew back her cloak to reveal not money but a magnificent bunch of roses. The king, seeing this miracle, allowed her to continue her good works.

ful what I say and not speak about hunger on a full stomach, because it's not polite.

Wednesday and Saturday are the days when Our Lord God comes down to earth consubstantiated into bacon and beans. If Father Agamedes were here, he would cry heresy, call for the holy inquisition, and all because we said that the Lord was a bean and a slice of bacon, but the trouble with Father Agamedes is that he has little imagination, he has grown used to seeing God in a wafer and was never able to think of him in any other way, except, of course, as the Father with the full beard and dark eyes and the Son with the short beard and pale eyes, was there perhaps some incident involving a fountain and bracken at some point in the sacred story, do you think. Dona Clemência knows more about such transfigurations, having been the wife and fount of virtue from Lamberto down to the last Berto, because on Wednesdays and Saturdays she presides over how much food should be given to whom, advising on and checking the thickness of the slice of bacon, the piece with the least meat, of course, because if it's pure fat, all the better, so much more nourishing, she also levels off the measure of beans with the strickle, purely in the interests of fairness and charity, you understand, we don't want the children to quarrel, You've got more than me, I've got less than you. It's a lovely ceremony, it quite makes one's heart melt with saintly compassion, not a dry eye in the house, or a dry nose, well, it's winter now, especially outside, where the children of Monte Lavre are leaning against the wall, waiting to receive alms, how they suffer, barefoot, in pain, see how the girls lift first one foot and then the other to escape the icy ground, they would lift both at once if they ever grew the wings it's said they will have once they're dead, if they have the sense to die early, and see how they keep tugging at their dresses, not out of injured modesty, because the boys are too young to notice such things, but because they're terribly cold. They form a queue, each holding a small tin, all of them snotty and snuffling, waiting for the

window above finally to open and for the basket to descend on a
rope from the skies, very slowly, magnanimity is never in a hurry,
oh no, haste is plebeian and greedy, just don't eat the beans as they
are, because they're raw. The first child in the queue places his tin
in the basket, and then the basket ascends, off you go and don't be
long, the wind cuts along the wall like a barbed razor, who can possibly bear it, well, they all do in the name of what is to come, and
then the maid sticks her head out of the window, and down comes
the basket with the can full or half full, just to show any smarty-
pants or novices that the size of the tin has no influence over the
donor of this cathedral of beneficence. Anyone seeing this would
think he had seen just about everything. But that's not true. No
one leaves until the last one has received his ration and the basket
has been taken in until Saturday. They have to wait until Dona
Clemência comes to the window, warmly wrapped up, to make
her gesture of farewell and blessing, while the dear little children
chorus their thanks in various ways, apart from those who merely
move their lips, Oh, Father Agamedes, it does my soul so much
good, and if someone were to assert that Dona Clemência was
nothing but a hypocrite, they would be much mistaken, because
only she can know how different her soul feels on Wednesdays and
Saturdays, in comparison with other days. And now let us recognize and praise Dona Clemência's Christian act of mortification,
for although she has both the time and the money to hand out
bacon and beans every day of the week, as well as the permanent,
assured comfort of her immortal soul, she doesn't do it, and that,
dear readers, is her personal penance. Besides, Dona Clemência,
these children mustn't be allowed to acquire bad habits, imagine
what demanding creatures they would grow into.

When Gracinda Mau-Tempo grew up, she did not go to school.
Nor did Amélia. Nor had António. A long time before, when
their father was a child, the propagandists for the republic urged
the people, Send your children to school, they were like apostles

sporting goatees, mustaches and trilby hats and proclaiming the good news, the light of education, a crusade they called it, with the signal difference that it wasn't a matter of driving the Turk out of Jerusalem and from the tomb of our Lord, it wasn't a question of absent bones, but of present lives, the children who would later set off with their bag of books slung over one shoulder with a piece of twine, and inside it, the primer issued to them by the same republic that ordered the national guard to charge if these same children's progenitors demanded higher wages. That is how João Mau-Tempo learned to read and write, enough to have misspelled his name in that exercise book in Montemor as João Mau-Tenpo, although, unsure which was the correct version, he sometimes wrote João Mautempo, which is better but still not quite right, Mau-Tempo, of course, being clear evidence of grammatical presumption. The world progresses, but within certain limits. In Monte Lavre it didn't advance enough for him to be able to send his own three children to school, and now how will Gracinda Mau-Tempo write to her fiancé when he's far away, a good question, and how will António Mau-Tempo send news if the poor thing never learned how to write and has apparently joined forces with a gang of ne'er-do-wells, I just hope he's leading a respectable life, says Faustina to her husband, You always set such a good example.

João Mau-Tempo nods, but in his heart of hearts he's not sure. It wounds him not to have his son by his side, and to see only women around him. Faustina is so different from what she was as a young woman, and she was never pretty, and his daughters, whose freshness and youth still survive despite a life of hard labor in the fields, it's just a shame that Amélia has such dreadful teeth. But João Mau-Tempo isn't so sure about having set a good example. He has spent his whole life simply earning his daily bread, and some days he doesn't even manage that, and this thought immediately forms a kind of knot inside his head, that a man should come into a world he never asked to be born into, only to experience a greater than normal degree of cold and hunger as a child, if there is such a thing as normal, and grow up to find that same hunger redoubled as a punishment for having a body capable of withstanding such hardship, to be mistreated by bosses and overseers, by guards both local and national, to reach the age of forty and finally speak your mind, only to be herded like cattle to the market or the slaughterhouse, to be further humiliated in prison, and to find that even freedom is a slap in the face, a crust of bread flung to the ground to see if you'll pick it up. That's what we do when a piece of bread falls to the ground, we pick it up, blow on it as if to restore its spirit, then kiss it, but we won't eat it there and then, no, I'll divide it into four, two large pieces and two small, here you are Amélia, here you are Gracinda, this is for you and this is for me, and if anyone asks who the two larger pieces are for, he is lower than the animals, because I'm sure even an animal would know.

The parents cannot do everything. They bring their children into the world, do for them the little they know how to do and hope for the best, believing that if they're very careful, or even when they're not, for fathers often deceive themselves and think they have been attentive when they haven't, no son of theirs will become a vagabond, no daughter of theirs will be dishonored, no drop of their blood poisoned. When António Mau-Tempo spends time in Monte Lavre, João Mau-Tempo forgets that he is his father and older than him and starts dogging his footsteps, as if he wanted to find out the truth behind those absences, as far away as Coruche, Sado, Samora Correia, Infantado and even the far side of the Tejo river, and the true stories he hears from his son's mouth both confirm and confuse the legend of José Gato, well, legend is perhaps an exaggeration, because José Gato is nothing but an inglorious braggart, he allowed us to be driven from Monte Lavre to prison, the stories are important more because they involve António Mau-Tempo, who either was there himself or heard about it

later, than because they are picturesque facts that contribute to the
history of minor rural crimes. And João Mau-Tempo sometimes
has a thought that he cannot really put into words, but which,
from the glimpse we've had of it, seems to say that if we're talking
about good examples, perhaps that of José Gato is not so very bad,
even if he is a thief and doesn't turn up when he's needed. One day,
António Mau-Tempo will say, In my life I've had a teacher and an
explainer, but now I've gone back to the beginning to learn everything over again. If you need an explanation, let's say that his father
was the teacher, José Gato the explainer and that what António
Mau-Tempo is learning now he will not be learning alone.

   This Mau-Tempo family learn their lessons well. By the time
Gracinda Mau-Tempo marries, she will know how to read. This
formed part of her engagement, a reading primer by João de
Deus,* with the words in black and gray so that you could distinguish the syllables, but it's not natural that such refinements
should take root in memories born to remember other things, she
just has to continue hesitantly reading and pausing between the
words, waiting for her brain to light up her understanding, It's not
acega, Gracinda, it's *acelga*.† Manuel Espada is now allowed into
the house, if it wasn't for the primer he would still be lingering on
the threshold, but it seemed wrong that they should sit outside
learning to read where other people could see them, and besides,
their relationship is clearly a serious one, Manuel Espada's a good
lad, Faustina would say, and João Mau-Tempo watched his future
son-in-law and saw him walking from Montemor to Monte Lavre,
scorning cars and carts so as to stay true to his beliefs and not be in
debt to the very people who had refused him his daily bread. That,
too, was a lesson, and João Mau-Tempo took it as such, although

---

* João de Deus (1830–1896) was the greatest poet of his generation, but he turned his attention to education. His *Cartilha maternal*, a reading primer published in 1876, was used
in schools for more than fifty years.
† Chard.

Sigismundo Canastro had said, What Manuel Espada did was good, but that doesn't mean we acted wrongly either, he gained nothing by walking, and we lost nothing by traveling back in the cart, one has to act according to one's conscience. And Sigismundo Canastro, who had a mischievous, albeit rather toothless smile, added, And of course he's still a young man, whereas our legs are getting old and heavy. That may well be, but even if there were thirty-three other reasons why Gracinda's parents should welcome Manuel Espada's courtship of their daughter, the very first, if João Mau-Tempo were ever to confess as much to himself, would be those twenty kilometers, Manuel Espada's out-and-out rejection of help, his affirmation of himself as a man during the almost four hours it took him to walk, with the sun beating down and his boots pounding the tarmacadam road, it was as if he were carrying a large flag that would not submit to being carried in the cars and carts owned by the latifundio. In this way, and as has always happened since the world began, the old learn from the young.

MAY IS THE MONTH of flowers. Let the poet go on his way in search of the daisies he has heard of, and if he doesn't come up with an ode or a sonnet, he'll produce a quatrain, which is much more to the common taste. The sun hasn't reached the crazy temperatures it does in July and August, there is even a cool breeze, and wherever you look, from this high vantage point, which would once have served as a lookout post, everything is green fields, no spectacle can more easily soften souls, only someone very hard of heart would not feel a tremor of joy. Over there, the thick growth of bushes resembles a garden lacking both irrigation and a gardener, these are plants that have had to learn by themselves how best to adapt to nature, to the brute stone that resists their roots, and perhaps for that very reason, because of the stubborn energy expended in these places that men avoid, here where the struggle is between vegetable and mineral, the scents are so penetrating, and when the sun blazes down upon the hillside, all the perfumes open and might lull us to sleep forever, we might perhaps die with our face to the earth, while the ants, raising their heads like dogs, advance, protected by gas masks, for this is their home as well.

These are easy poems to write. The odd thing is that there are no men to be seen. The fields grow green and lush, the undergrowth is steeped in peace and perfume, but a second look tells us that the wheat has lost its first tender freshness, there are tiny dabs of yellow in that vast space, barely noticeable, and the men, where are the men in this happy landscape, perhaps they are not, in fact, the serfs of this glebe, tethered to a stake like goats so that they can eat only what is within reach. There are long periods of idleness while the wheat grows, man has sown the seed in the earth, and if the year is favorable, then lie down and sleep, and call me when it's harvest time. It's hard to understand that this May of flowers is actually a sullen month, we don't mean the weather, which is lovely and seems set fair, but these faces and eyes, this mouth, this frown, There's no work, they say, and if nature sings, good luck to her, we're not in the mood for singing.

Let's go for a walk in the country, up into the hills, on the way the sun glints on this one stone, and we, who are suckers for happiness, say, It's gold, as if all that glittered were gold. We see no men working and immediately declare, What an easy life, the wheat is growing and the workers are resting. However, the truth is rather different. The winter passes, as we have described, in grand banquets and feasts of thistles, dockweed and watercress, with a little fried onion, a few grains of rice and a crust of bread, taking the food from our own mouths so that our children don't go hungry, we shouldn't really need to repeat this, you'll think we're boasting about the sacrifices we make, the very idea, it was the same for our parents and for their parents, and for the parents of those parents, in the days of Senhor Lamberto and before, as far back as anyone can remember, the winter passed, and while some died of starvation, there are plenty of other ways of describing the cause of death, names that are far less offensive to modesty and decency. It's mid-January, men are needed to prune the trees, whether for Dagoberto or Norberto, it doesn't matter, we start to earn a little money, but there's not enough work for everyone, Make a choice, don't get into arguments, and then, once the trees have been pruned, there's the wood on the ground, and the charcoal burners arrive to buy from here and there, and then it's time for them to perform their fiery art, and while we savor the vocabulary of charcoal-burning, staking, earthing up, plugging and firing, the words are doing what they say, it's nothing to do with us, we just know the words, but we didn't know them before, we had to learn them fast, out of necessity, and if everything's ready, let's bag the charcoal up and carry it away, and that's that until next year, my name's Peres, I own twenty-five charcoal kilns in the Lisbon area, as well as several others in the environs, and you can tell your mistress that my charcoal is good stuff, oak, so it burns nice and slow, which is why, of course, it's more expensive. We're burning up in this dryness, this dust, this smoke, there's water to drink over there, I put the jug to my lips, lean back my head, the water gurgles down, a shame it's not cooler, it dribbles from the corners of my mouth and traces rivers of pale skin among the banks of coal dust. We must all have experienced such things and others, because life, despite being short, has room for these and many more, but there are some who lived but briefly, and their whole lives were consumed in this one task.

The charcoal burners and sellers have gone, and now it's May, the month of flowers, may those who write verses try eating them. There are sheep to be sheared, who knows how to do that, I do, I do, cry a few, and the others return to the good life, so called, to weeks of the bad life, going in and out of their houses, until the wheatfields are ready to be harvested, earlier here, later there, yes, we need you now or we might need you later, the goat is tethered to the stake and has no more to eat. It hasn't for some time. So what's the daily rate, ask the workers in the labor market, and the overseers stroll along the unarmed battalions, the sickle has been left at home and we don't use hammers in our trade, and as they stroll along or pause, drumming with their fingers on their waistcoat pockets, they say, We pay whatever the others pay. This is a very old conversation, that's what they said in the days of the monarchy, and the republic changed nothing, these are not things that can be changed by replacing a king with a president, the trouble lies elsewhere, in other monarchies, Lamberto gave birth to Dagoberto, Dagoberto gave birth to Alberto, Alberto gave birth to Floriberto, and then came Norberto, Berto, and Sigisberto, and Adalberto and Angilberto, Gilberto, Ansberto, Contraberto, it's no surprise that they all have such similar names, they simply mean the latifundio and its owners, names don't count for much, which is why the overseer mentions no names but simply says "the others," and no one will ask who those others are, only city folk would make that mistake.

And so when someone asks, How much are we going to be paid, the overseer will say only Whatever the others pay, thus closing the circular conversation of I asked and you didn't answer with a nonresponse, You'll find out when you go to work. The man says more or less the same thing to his wife, I'll go to work and see what happens, and she thinks, or says out loud, and perhaps she shouldn't say anything, because such things hurt, Well, at least you've got work, and on Monday, the workers are out in the fields doing their duty, and they say to each other, How much do you reckon it will be, and they don't know, What about them over there, I've asked, but they don't know either, and so we arrive at Saturday, and the foreman comes and says, The wages are this much, and they have worked the whole week not knowing how much their work was worth, and at night their wives will ask, Do you know yet, and the husbands will reply irritably, impatiently, No, I don't, stop asking me, and she will say, I'm not asking for myself, the baker wanted to know when we could pay off our debt, such wretched conversations, which continue, That's not much, Well, when the others pay more, so will I. Pure lies, we all know that, but they are lies agreed upon between Ansberto and Angilberto, between Floriberto and Norberto, between Berto and Latifundio, which is another way of saying everything and everybody.

EVERY YEAR, ON CERTAIN dates, the nation summons its sons. That's a somewhat exaggerated way of putting it, a skillful imitation of some of the proclamations used in time of national need, or by the person speaking, when necessary, on the nation's behalf, for overt and covert reasons, to show that we are all one big happy family of brothers, with no distinction made between Abel and Cain. The nation summons its sons, can you hear the voice of the nation calling, calling, and you, who up until now were worth nothing, not even the bread you need to satisfy your hunger, nor the medicine for any illness you might have, nor the knowledge to end your ignorance, you, the son of this great mother who has been waiting for you ever since you were born, you see your name on a piece of paper at the door of the town hall, not that you can read it, but someone who can indicates the line where a black worm coils and uncoils, that's you, you discover that the worm is you and your name, written by the clerk at the local recruitment office, and an officer who doesn't know you and is interested in you for only this one purpose writes his name under yours, an even more tangled and confusing worm, you can't make out what the officer's name is, and from now on, there's no running away, the nation is staring at you hard, hypnotizing you, to flee would be to offend against the memory of our grandfathers and the Discoveries. Your name is António Mau-Tempo, and since you came into this world, I have been waiting for you, my son, for I am, you see, a devoted mother, and you must forgive me if, during all these years, I haven't paid you much attention, but there are so many of you, and I can't possibly keep my eye on everyone, I've been preparing my officers who will be in charge of you, one can't live without officers, how else would you learn to march, one two left right, right turn, halt, or to use a gun, careful when you load the breech, country boy, make sure you don't get your finger caught, and yet they tell me you can't read, I'm astonished, didn't I set up primary schools in all the strategic places, not secondary schools, of course, because you wouldn't need them for the kind of life you lead, and yet you come and tell me that you can't read or write or do arithmetic, well, you're putting me to a lot of trouble, António Mau-Tempo, you're going to have to learn while you're in the army, I don't want illiterate sons bearing my standard, and if, later on, you forget what I'm ordering you to learn, never mind, that won't be my fault, you're the one who's stupid, a bumpkin and a yokel, truth be told, my army is full of bumpkins, but it's not for long, and once your military service is over, you can go back to your usual job, although if you want another, equally difficult job, that can be arranged too.

If the nations were telling the truth, this is the speech we would hear, give or take a comma or two, but then we would have to suffer the disappointment of ceasing to believe in the sweet fairy tales of yesterday and today, which are sometimes clothed in armor and gauntlets, sometimes in epaulettes and jambeaux, for example, the story about the little soldier in the trenches who missed his real mother, the heavenly one having already died, and who would gaze for hours at the portrait of she who brought him into the world, until a stray bullet, or an extremely well-aimed one from a skilled marksman on the other side, shattered the portrait, and the young soldier, mad with grief, clambered over the parapet and ran toward the enemy trenches, brandishing his rifle, he didn't get very far, though, he was mown down in a hail of bullets, that's what they say in war stories, said hail of bullets coming from a German soldier, who also had a portrait of his dear old mother in his pocket, we add this information so as to round out these stories about mothers and nations and about who dies or kills for such stories.

António Mau-Tempo left his work unfinished and headed for Monte Lavre, getting off the train in Vendas Novas, where he viewed from outside the barracks he would have to enter in three days' time, before setting off to walk the three leagues home, and since it was fine weather, he walked at a steady but relaxed pace, leaving behind him on his left the firing range, an ill-fated place, and, like certain men, punished with sterile upheavals, he finally loses sight of it, or, to be more exact, when he can no longer see it, he puts it out of his mind, and feels upset just to think that he is about to lose his freedom for a year and a half. He thinks of José Gato, and wonders if he ever did his military service, and feels a great weight lifting off his heart, as if destiny were opening a door to the empty road before him and saying, Leave it all behind, why be stuck in a barracks, trapped between four walls, only to go back afterward to cutting cork, digging, scything, don't be a fool, look at José Gato, now that's what I call living, no one dares lay a finger on him, and besides, he has his gang, he's the boss, what he says goes, and though you're not the boss now, you could learn, you're young, it wouldn't be a bad beginning. Temptations, we all have the temptations available to us according to our class and background, as well as those we have learned. His plan may seem rash in a lad who comes from an honest family, apart from the stain left by the life and death of his grandfather Domingos Mau-Tempo, but you can't spend your whole existence thinking about that, let he who has never dreamed of these and worse things throw the first stone, especially since, at this point, António Mau-Tempo doesn't yet know the whole of José Gato's story, which is still to come, and all he can think of is the delicious smell of pork bought clandestinely with his honestly earned money.

With fifteen kilometers to walk, a man has plenty of time to think, to weigh up his life, yesterday he was just a kid and soon he'll be a recruit, but the young man walking determinedly along the road is the best cutter of cork of his nine fellow trainees, perhaps he'll meet one of them in the army. The weather has warmed up, his bag doesn't weigh that much, but it jogs against him and keeps sliding from his shoulder, I'll stop here for a rest, a few meters off the road, not too far, but out of sight, on the grass because the earth is damp, I'll lay my head on my bag and sleep, I've plenty of time to get to Monte Lavre. An old lady sits down next to me, bad luck for me and good luck for her, I don't know what she wants from me, what power she has, perhaps she's a witch, she takes my hand, opens my closed fingers, and says, According to your hand, António Mau-Tempo, you will never marry or have children, you will make five long journeys to distant countries and will ruin your health, you will never own any land of your own apart from the plot that will be your grave, you're no different from other men, and that plot will be yours only until you're nothing but dust and a few bones the same as everyone else's, which will end up somewhere or other, my predictions don't go that far, but as long as you're alive, you will do no wrong, even if others tell you otherwise, but you must get up now, it's time. But António Mau-Tempo, who knew he was dreaming, pretended he hadn't heard this order and continued sleeping, a bad move because he never knew that a weeping princess had been sitting beside him, and that she had held his hand, so hard and calloused though he was still young, so young, and then, having waited a long time, the princess left, trailing the satin of her gown over the gorse and the rockroses, which is why, when António Mau-Tempo finally woke up, the shrubs and bushes were covered in white flowers such as he had never seen before.

These apparently impossible but entirely true incidents often occur on the latifundio. However, the reason António Mau-Tempo was deep in thought from there to Monte Lavre was that he had found two drops of water in the palm of his hand and couldn't work out where they had come from, especially since they refused to mingle into one, but rolled around like pearls, such prodigies are also common in the latifundio, and only the presumptuous would doubt them. António Mau-Tempo would, we believe, still have those drops of water if, when he arrived home and embraced his mother, they had not slipped from his hand and flown out of the door, fluttering white wings, What birds were those, António, I don't know, Ma.

SOME PEOPLE SLEEP very heavily, some lightly, some, when they fall asleep, detach themselves from the world, some have to sleep in a particular position in order to dream. We would say that Joana Canastra belongs to the latter category. If she's left to sleep peacefully, which is the case when she's ill, and if she's not in too much pain, she lies there just as she did in the cradle, or so someone who knew her then would say, resting her dark, weary cheek on her open palm and immersed in a long, deep sleep. But if she has things to do, things that have to be done at a particular time, then fifteen minutes before the designated hour, she abruptly opens her eyes, as if in obedience to an internal clock, and says, Get up, Sigismundo. Now, if this story were being told by the person who lived it, you would see that already dastardly changes have been made, some involuntary, some premeditated and in accordance with certain rules, because what Joana Canastra really said was, Get up, Sismundo, and one can see how little such minor errors matter when both parties know what they're talking about, the proof being that Sigismundo Canastro, who has his own doubts about how his name should be spoken or spelled, throws off the blanket, jumps out of bed in his long johns, walks over to open the shutters and peers out. It's still black night, and only a very sharp eye, which Sigismundo no longer has, or millennia of experience, which he has in abundance, could distinguish the imponderable change taking place in the east, perhaps it is the fact, and who can comprehend such natural mysteries, that the stars are shining more brightly, when you would expect quite the opposite to be the case. It's a cold night, which is hardly surprising, November is a good month for cold, but the sky is clear and will remain so, for November is also a good month for clear skies. Joana Canastra gets up, lights the fire, puts the blackened coffeepot on to heat up the coffee, the name that continues to be given to this blend of barley and chicory or ground toasted lupine seeds, for even they are not always sure what they are drinking, then goes over to the bread bin to fetch half a loaf and three fried sardines, leaving little if anything behind, and places them on the table, saying, Coffee's ready, come and eat. These may seem trivial words, the poor talk of people with little imagination, who have never learned to enlarge life's small actions with superlatives, compare, for example, the words of farewell spoken by Romeo and Juliet on the balcony of the room in which she has just become a woman, and the words spoken by the blue-eyed German to the no less maidenly, albeit plebeian girl who became a woman against her will after being raped amid the bracken, and, of course, the words she said to him. If these dialogues were being held on the elevated level demanded by the circumstances, we would know that, although this is hardly the first time Sigismundo Canastro has left the house, there's more to this departure than meets the eye, which is why we're telling you about it. Sigismundo ate half a sardine and a crust of bread, with no plate and no fork, slicing into the sardine and cutting chunks off the loaf with the keen blade of his penknife, and once this pap was safely in his stomach, he topped it off with the comforting warmth of that ersatz coffee, there are those who swear blind that the existence and harmonious coexistence of cof-

fee and fried sardines is sufficient proof that God exists, but these
are theological matters that have nothing to do with early-morning
journeys. Sigismundo then put his hat on his head, laced up his
boots, pulled on a worn sheepskin coat and said, See you later, and
if anyone asks for me, you don't know where I've gone. There was
no need for him to give this advice, it's always the same, besides,
Joana Canastra would have little to say, because, although she
knows what her husband is going to do, and she wouldn't tell anyone that, even if they killed her, but since she doesn't know where
he's going, she couldn't tell them even if they did kill her. Sigismundo will be out all day and won't return until after dark, more
because of the path taken and the distance covered than because
of the actual time it takes, although one never knows. The woman
says, Goodbye, Sismundo, she insists on calling him this, and we
shouldn't laugh or even smile, after all, what's in a name, and once
he'd gone out through the gate, she went and sat down on a cork
stool by the fire and stayed there until the sun came up, her hands
clasped, but there's no evidence that she was praying.

Faustina Mau-Tempo, at the other end of Monte Lavre, is not
used to this, it's the first time, which is why, although she knew
her husband wouldn't have to leave the house until sunrise, she
couldn't sleep all night, alarmed that the usually restless João Mau-
Tempo should be sleeping so peacefully, like a man afraid of nothing, though he should be afraid. This is the body's way of soothing
the troubled soul. It's daybreak, not daylight, when João Mau-
Tempo wakes up, and the memory of what he is about to do suddenly enters his eyes, so much so that he immediately closes them
and feels a pang in his stomach, not of fear but of quiet respect,
the kind one feels in a church or a cemetery or when a child is
born. He's alone in the room, he can hear the sounds of the house
and those outside, the cold trilling of a lone bird, the voices of his
daughters and the crackle of burning wood. He gets up, he is, as
we have said before, a small, wiry man with ancient, luminous blue

eyes, and at forty-two his hair is thinning and what hair he has is turning white, but before standing up, he pauses to accommodate his body to the sharp pain in his side that always resuscitates after he's been lying down all night, when it should be quite the opposite if his body has rested properly. He dresses and goes over to the fire in the kitchen, as if still wanting to savor the warmth of bed, you would never think he was a man accustomed to bitter weather. He says, Good morning, and his daughters come and kiss his hand, it's good to see the family all together, all are currently unemployed, although they have plenty of things to do to fill the day, be it darning clothes or, in Gracinda's case, working on her trousseau as best she can, though the marriage won't be until next year, and that afternoon, she'll go with her sister to wash clothes in the stream, a whole load of laundry from the big house, well, twenty escudos is better than nothing. Faustina, who is going deaf, didn't hear her husband, but she felt him, perhaps the seismic tremor of the earth as he approached or the movement through the air that only his body makes, each body is different, but these two have been together for twenty years, probably only a blind man would make a mistake, and she has no problems with her eyesight, it's her hearing that's going, although it seems to her, and this is her usual excuse, that people nowadays gabble when they speak, as if they were doing so on purpose. This may sound like the sort of thing only the very old complain about, but these are simply people tired before their time. João Mau-Tempo is stoking up for the day, he drinks his coffee, which is as disgusting as Sigismundo Canastro's coffee, eats some bread made from various flours, just which part of the wheat do they use in the flour, he wonders, and devours a raw egg, making a hole in each end, one of life's great pleasures, when he can get it. The tightness in his stomach has gone, and now that the sun has risen, he's suddenly in a great hurry, See you later, he says, and if anyone asks for me, you don't know where I've gone, this is no pre-planned formula, they are merely the words that come naturally, and there's no need to search for other reasons. Neither Gracinda nor Amélia know where their father is going, they ask their mother when he's left, but she makes the most of her deafness and pretends not to hear. We shouldn't blame the girls, they're young and curious, certainly not irresponsible, an imputation that would doubtless offend Gracinda, who knows all about the exploits of Manuel Espada and his friends when they were only lads, and he was Monte Lavre's first known striker.

The meeting is in Terra Fria. Places are given names doubtless for some comprehensible reason, but to find out why this place was called Terra Fria, Cold Land, on a latifundio that is as hot in summer as it is cold in winter, you would have to go right back to the origins, and those, as lazy people say, are lost in the mists of time. Before they get to Terra Fria, Sigismundo Canastro and João Mau-Tempo will meet at Atalaia hill, not on the very top, of course, they wouldn't want to make themselves too visible, although in this particular area and on this occasion, the latifundio is not exactly as busy as the main square in Évora. They will meet in the dense woods at the foot of the hill. Sigismundo Canastro knows the place well, João Mau-Tempo less well, but all roads lead to Rome. And they will travel on to Terra Fria together, along paths that God never walked and along which the devil would walk only if forced to.

There is no one on the circular balcony of the sky, which is the angels' usual viewing platform above the horizon whenever there is any significant activity on the latifundio. This is the great and fatal mistake made by the heavenly hosts, they measure everything against the crusade. They ignore small patrols, bold sorties, like these tiny dots, the volunteers for this mission, two men here, another farther off, another up ahead and another as yet far away and lagging behind, but all converging, even when they seem not to be, on a place that has no name in heaven, but which down here on earth is called Terra Fria. Perhaps above, in the peaceful empyrean, they think these humans are merely going to work, though there's none to be had, as even heaven must know thanks to the occasional messages sent by Father Agamedes, and it's true that the meeting is work-related. This is a different kind of work, however, and such a great responsibility that João Mau-Tempo will ask Sigismundo Canastro when he meets him and they have taken their first few steps together, or when he has finally managed to overcome his shyness, Do you think they'll accept me, and Sigismundo Canastro will answer, with the confidence of someone older and more experienced, You've been accepted already, you wouldn't be coming with me today if there was any doubt.

One man has come on his bike. He will hide it in the bushes, in some easily identifiable place, just in case he gets disoriented afterward and can't find it. No need, of course, to worry about number plates, if he was in a car, the guards might stop him out of sheer pigheadedness or because they felt a sudden twinge of suspicion, Where are you going, where have you come from, show me your license, and that wouldn't be good, this man happens to be called Silva, but he's also Manuel Dias da Costa, Silva to those he's going to meet in Terra Fria, Manuel Dias da Costa to the guards, with a different name in the registry office and known by a different name again to Father Agamedes, who baptized him far from here. There are those who say that without a name we wouldn't know who we are, which seems a perceptive and philosophical view to take, but this man Silva or Manuel Dias da Costa pedaling along a muddy cart track, for he's now left the road where the guards occasionally appear or else don't appear for days on end, but you never know, your guess is as good as ours, this cyclist is utterly at peace with his soul, quite untouched by these subtle questions of identity. Although that's not quite true, he is actually far more certain of who he is than of the documents that name him. And since he is a thoughtful fellow, he thinks how odd it is that the guards put more faith in a piece of stamped paper, worn thin from being unfolded and refolded, than in what they can actually see, a man and his bicycle, All right, on your way, but as the man puts his foot on the pedal and presses down, he thinks that it would be best not to come this way again in the near future, this is his first time here, and he's been lucky, no one has ordered him to stop.

Some come by train, getting off at São Torcato, on the Setil line, or at Vendas Novas, or even Montemor, if the meeting is being held in Terra da Torre, and at the nearer stations if they're meeting in Terra Fria. It's just a hop and a jump for anyone coming from São Geraldo, but anyone leaving São Geraldo on similar business today will have gone farther afield, and this is not just chance, but doubtless in accordance with very sensible rules. It's midmorning now and there's no bicycle to be seen, the trains are far away somewhere, you can hear them whistling, and a red kite is hovering over Terra Fria, a lovely sight to see, but even lovelier is first seeing it and then hearing its cry, the thin, piping call that no one can quite put into words, but when we hear it, we immediately want to say what it sounded like and can't, there's no shortage of singing birds, but that cry of the red kite is different, so wild it almost sends a shiver down your spine, it wouldn't surprise me to learn that if you heard it often enough, you would sprout wings yourself, well, stranger things have happened. Hovering high up, the red kite drops its head a little, the smallest of movements, because it doesn't need to be that tiny bit closer to see, we're the ones troubled by myopia and astigmatism, a word that should be used with caution on the latifundio, in case the angels mistake it for stigmatism and rush to the balcony expecting to see Francis of Assisi and finding instead a red kite calling and five men approaching Terra Fria, some nearer, some farther off. Only the red kite sees them from on high, but it's never been a telltale.

The first to arrive were Sigismundo Canastro and João Mau-Tempo, who have made a special effort to be early because one of them is new. While they waited, sitting in the sun so as not to get too cold, Sigismundo Canastro said, If you take off your hat, always place it on the ground crown uppermost, Why, asked João Mau-Tempo, and Sigismundo Canastro replied, So as not to reveal your name, we shouldn't know each other's names, But I know yours, Yes, but don't say it, the other comrades will do the same, it's just in case anyone should be arrested, if we don't know each other's names, we're safe. They talked of other things too, just for talking's sake, but João Mau-Tempo was still thinking about how careful they had to be, and when the man with the bicycle arrived, he realized at once that here was someone whose real name he would never know, perhaps because of the great respect with which he was treated by Sigismundo Canastro, who nevertheless addressed him as *tu*, but then perhaps that was the most respectful thing he could do. This is our new comrade, said Sigismundo Canastro, and the man with the bicycle held out his hand, it wasn't the large, coarse hand of an agricultural worker, but strong and with a firm grip, Comrade, the word is not a new one, that's what one's work colleagues are, but it's like saying *tu*, it's the same and, at the same time, so utterly different that João Mau-Tempo's knees buckle and his throat tightens, which is odd in a man past forty who has seen a great deal of life. The three men chat together while they wait for the others to arrive, We'll wait half an hour, and if they don't come, we'll start anyway, and at some point João Mau-Tempo takes off his hat and, before putting it down on the ground, crown uppermost as Sigismundo Canastro had recommended, he quickly looked inside it and saw his name written on the band, in the hatter's fine lettering, as was the custom in the provinces at the time, whereas city folk were already favoring anonymity. The man with the bicycle, as we know him, although João Mau-Tempo assumes that he has come all the way on foot, the man with the bicycle is wearing a beret, which might or might not have his name in it, and if it did, what would it be, after all, you can buy berets at markets and from cheap tailors who don't take such pride in their craft and have no tools for doing poker work or gilding, and who don't care whether their client loses a beret or finds it.

The other two men arrived within a few minutes of each other. They had all met on other occasions, apart from João Mau-Tempo, who was there as the prime exhibit, if you like, and at whom the others stared long and hard in order to memorize his face, which was easy enough, you certainly wouldn't forget those blue eyes. The man with the bicycle asked gravely and simply for better punctuality in future, although he recognized that it was hard to calculate precisely how long it would take to cover such long distances. I myself arrived after these two comrades, and I should have been here first. Then money was handed over, only a few coins, and each man received small bundles of pamphlets, and if names had been permitted, or if the red kite had overheard and repeated them, or if the hats had sneaked a furtive look at the names on each other's respective hatbands, we would have heard, These are for you, Sigismundo Canastro, these are for you, Francisco Petinga, these are for you, João dos Santos, none for you this time, João Mau-Tempo, you just help Sigismundo Canastro, and now tell me what's been happening. The person he addressed was Francisco Petinga, who said, The bosses have found a new way of paying us less, when they have to take us on by order of the workers' association,* they dismiss us all on the Saturday, every single one of us, and say, On Monday, go to the workers' association and tell them I said I want the same workers back, that's the boss speaking, and the result is that we waste all of Monday going to the workers' association, and the boss only has to start paying us on Tuesday, what are we supposed to do about that. Then João dos Santos said, Where

---

* *Casa do povo* in Portuguese. The organization was set up in 1933 to protect the rights and welfare of agricultural workers.

I live, the workers' associations are in cahoots with the bosses, if they weren't, they wouldn't act the way they do, they send us off to work, we go where we're sent, but the bosses won't accept us, and so back we go to the workers' association, but they won't accept us either and tell us to leave, and that's the way things stand now, the bosses won't accept our labor, and the workers' association either has no power to force them to or is simply having fun at our expense, what are we supposed to do about that. Sigismundo Canastro said, The workers who do get jobs are earning sixteen escudos for working from dawn to dusk, while many can't get any work at all, but we're all of us starving, because sixteen escudos doesn't buy you anything, the bosses are just playing with us, they have work for us to do, but they're allowing the estates to go to rack and ruin and doing nothing about it, we should occupy the land, and if we die, we die, I know you say that would be suicide, but what's happening now is suicide too, I bet there's not a man here can boast of having eaten anything you might call supper, it's not just a matter of feeling downhearted, we must do something. The other men nodded their agreement, they could feel their stomachs gnawing, it was past midday, and it occurred to them that perhaps they could eat the bit of bread and scrape they had brought with them, but at the same time they felt ashamed to have so little, though they were all equally familiar with such dearth. The man with the bicycle is wearing clothes so threadbare that it's as plain as day he has no lunch concealed in his pockets, and what we know and the others don't is that the ants could walk up and down his bicycle all they liked, but they wouldn't find a single crumb, anyway, the man with the bicycle turned to João Mau-Tempo and asked, And what about you, do you have anything to add, this unexpected question startled the novice, I don't know, I have nothing to say, and he said no more, but the other men sat silently looking at him, and he couldn't let the situation continue like that, five grave-faced men sitting under an oak tree, and so, for lack of anything else to say, he added, When there is work, we wear ourselves out working day and night, and still we starve, I keep a few bits of land they give us to cultivate, and I work until late into the night, but now there's no paid work to be had, and what I want to know is why are things like this and will it be like this until we die, there can be no justice as long as some have everything and others nothing, and all I want to say really is that you can count on me, comrades, that's all.

Each man gave his arguments, they are sitting so still that from a distance they look like statues, and now they are waiting to hear what the man with the bicycle will say and what he's already saying. As before, he speaks first to the men as a group, then to Francisco Petinga, then to João dos Santos, more briefly to Sigismundo Canastro and then at length to João Mau-Tempo, as if he were putting together stones to make a pavement or a bridge, a bridge more like, because over it will pass years, footsteps, heavy loads, and below it lies an abyss. From here, it's like watching a dumb show, we see only gestures, and there are few enough of those, everything depends on the word and the stress laid upon it, and on the gaze too, but from here, we cannot even make out João Mau-Tempo's intensely blue eyes. We don't have the keen vision of the red kite, which is still circling around, hovering over the oak tree, sometimes dropping down whenever the air current slackens, and then with a slow, languid beat of its wings rising up again in order to take in the near and the far, this and that, the excesses of the latifundio and just the right measure of patience.

The meeting has ended. The first to leave is the man with the bicycle, and then, in a single expansive movement, like a sun exploding, the other men head off to their respective destinations, at first keeping within sight of each other, as they would know if they were to turn around and look, which they don't, that's another of the rules, and then they are hidden, they don't hide, but are hidden by a dip or vanish into the distance behind a hill, or simply into the distance and the intense cold, which they are aware of now, and which makes them screw up their eyes, you have to look where you're putting your feet too, you can't just amble along willy-nilly. The red kite utters a loud cry, which echoes throughout the celestial vault, then it moves northward, while the startled angels rush to the window, bumping into each other, only to find no one there.

MEN GROW, AND WOMEN grow, everything in them grows, both the body and the area occupied by their needs, the stomach grows commensurate to our hunger, the sex grows commensurate to our desire, and Gracinda Mau-Tempo's breasts are two billowing waves, but that's just the usual lyrical tosh, the stuff of love songs, because the strength of her arms and the strength of his arms, we are referring here, by the way, to Manuel Espada, for three years have passed and there has been no inconstancy of feelings, but, rather, great steadfastness, anyway, the strength of their arms, male and female, is, by turns, required and rejected by the latifundio, after all, there is not such a big difference between men and women, apart from the wages they are paid. Mother, I want to get married, said Gracinda Mau-Tempo, here's my trousseau, it's not much to look at, but it will have to do if Manuel Espada and I are ever to lie down together in a bed that is his and mine, and in which we can be husband and wife, and for him to enter me and for me to be in him, as if we had always been together, because I don't know much about what happened before I was born, but my blood remembers a girl who, at the fountain in Amieiro, was violated by a man who had blue eyes like our father, and I know, although quite how I don't know, that out of my womb will come a son or a daughter with the same eyes.

If Gracinda Mau-Tempo really had said these words, there would have been a revolution on the latifundio, but it is our duty to understand what her actual words meant, mean or will mean, because we know how hard it is to express the little we do say each day, sometimes because we don't know which word best fits which meaning, or which of the two words we know is the more exact, often because no word seems right, and then we hope that a gesture will explain, a glance confirm and a mere sound confess. Mother, said Gracinda Mau-Tempo, the little I have is enough for us to make a home, or perhaps she said, Mother, Manuel Espada says that it's time we married, or perhaps she said neither of those things, but gave the great cry of a solitary red kite, Mother, if I don't marry now, I'm going to lie down in the bracken by the fountain and wait for Manuel Espada to come and enter my body, and then I will lift up my dress and wash myself in the stream, and my blood will flow off to some unknown place, but at least I will know who I am. And perhaps it wasn't like that either, perhaps one night Faustina said to João Mau-Tempo, possibly interrupting his thoughts about leaving some pamphlets in the hollow of a particular tree, She should get married now, she has her little trousseau ready, and João Mau-Tempo would have replied, It'll have to be a modest affair, I'd like it to be a really special occasion, but that's not possible, and António won't be able to help now that he's doing his national service, tell Gracinda to sort out the paperwork and we'll do what we can. As ever, it's still the parents who have the last word.

They have a house, one that suits their pocket, and since their pocket is small, the house is small too, and rented of course, just in case you were thinking that Gracinda Mau-Tempo and Manuel Espada were about to announce proudly, This is our house, no, they would rather hide the fact and say, I live over there somewhere, as if they were playing hide-and-seek or hunt the thimble, except, of course, those are games played at school or in the city, simply so that no one will know exactly where they live, in this house which is just walls and a door, with one room up and one down, a rickety ladder that wobbles when you climb it and no fire in the grate when we're out. We're going to live on the side of this hill in Monte Lavre, in this little yard, there's not enough space to swing a hoe if we wanted to grow some cabbage, after all it does get the sun all day, although I don't know that it's worth the trouble, we're hardly going to get fat on cabbage. We'll sleep downstairs, in the kitchen, except it won't be a kitchen when we're sleeping in it, just as it won't be a bedroom when we're up and about, what should we call it then, a kitchen when we're cooking, a sewing room when Gracinda Mau-Tempo is doing the darning, and a waiting room when I'm sitting looking at the hills opposite, with my hands in my lap, this may seem as if they're just playing with words, but it's simply their mutual excitement, each tumbling over the other in their eagerness to speak.

If we start to get too far ahead of ourselves, we'll soon be talking about children and the problems they bring. Today is a holiday, Manuel Espada is going to marry Gracinda Mau-Tempo, there hasn't been a marriage like this in Monte Lavre for a long time, that is, with such an age difference between bride and groom, he's twenty-seven and she's twenty, but they make a handsome couple, he's the taller of the two, which is as it should be, although she's not short either, she doesn't take after her father in that respect. I can see them now, she's wearing a pink, calf-length dress with a high neck and long sleeves buttoned at the cuff, if it's hot, she's not aware of it, as far as she's concerned it might as well be winter, and he's wearing a dark jacket, more like a three-quarter-length coat than the jacket of a suit, a pair of rather tight trousers and shoes that no amount of polishing will bring a shine to, a white shirt and a tie bearing a pattern of branches as indecipherable as the tops of trees no one has bothered to prune, but let there be no misunderstanding, the trees are just a simile, nothing more, because the tie is new and will probably never be worn again, unless it's at another wedding, should we be invited. It's not a big wedding party, but there are plenty of friends and acquaintances, and children attracted by the prospect of sweets, and old ladies at the door talking about heaven knows what, one never knows what old ladies talk about, whether they are uttering blessings or reproaches, poor things, what is the point of their lives.

The ceremony takes place after the mass, as is the custom, and people look a bit cheerier than usual because, luckily, there's plenty of work around at the moment, plus it's a nice day. Doesn't the bride look lovely, the boys don't dare make many jokes about marriage, because, after all, Manuel Espada is older, nearly thirty, a different generation from us, that's a bit of an exaggeration, of course, since he's only twenty-seven, but it's an interesting situation, even the married men refrain from teasing him, the bridegroom is hardly a boy, and he always looks so serious, he was the same when he was a child, you can never tell what he might be thinking, just like his mother, who died last year. They're quite wrong, though, it's true that Manuel Espada has a grave face or countenance, as people used to say, but even if he wanted to, he wouldn't be able to explain quite what he is feeling, it's like water singing as it rushes over the rocks up there in Ponte Cava, which is a bleak place and a bit frightening at night, but then, come the dawn, you see there was no reason to be afraid, it was just the water singing among the rocks.

Great injustices are committed because of how people look, that was the case with Manuel Espada's mother, a woman who seemed to be made of granite, but who melted sweetly at night in bed, which is perhaps why Manuel Espada's father is slowly weeping, some say, It must be tears of joy, and only he knows that it isn't. Let's see, how many people are here, twenty, and each one of them would make a story, you can't imagine, years and years of living is a lot of time, and a lot of things can happen in that time, if we were all to write our life story, think how big that library would be, we would have to store the books on the moon, and when we wanted to find out who So-and-so is or was, we would travel through space to discover not the moon, but life. It makes us feel, at the very least, like turning back and recounting in detail the life and love of Tomás Espada and Flor Martinha, if we weren't driven on by events and by the new life and love of their son and Gracinda Mau-Tempo, who have now entered the church, surrounded by a throng of excited children, take no notice, boys will be boys, while the older people, who are familiar with rituals and sermons, enter, looking composed and slightly constrained, wearing old clothes from a time when they were slimmer. Just this coming into church and being here, these faces, feature by feature, each line and wrinkle, would merit chapters as vast as the latifundio that laps around Monte Lavre like a sea.

Father Agamedes is at the altar, and I don't know what exactly has got into him today, what fair wind greeted him when he got up, perhaps it was the Holy Spirit, not that Father Agamedes is one to boast of his closeness to the third person of the Holy Trinity, he himself doubts the simplicity of these theological formulae, but for whatever reason, this old devil of a priest is in a good mood, he's very composed, but his eyes are shining, and that can't be because he's looking forward to satisfying his greedy appetite, there will hardly be an abundance of food at the wedding feast. Perhaps it's simply the pleasure of blessing this marriage, Father Agamedes is a very human priest, as we have seen throughout this story, and even if, for the moment, he chooses not to think about the latifundio's variable need for workers, he must be pleased that this man should join flesh with this woman and make children who will then grow up and who are sure to bring some benefit to the church by being born, marrying and dying, as the other people here present have and will. This is a flock that brings him little wool, but it's better than nothing, out of these crumbs comes a sponge cake, Have another slice, Father, and drink this glass of port, and then another slice, I couldn't eat another thing, Senhora Dona Clemência, Go on, make a sacrifice, Father Agamedes, after all, that's what he does every day, the sacrifice of the holy mass, come closer now and I will make you man and wife.

There is some confusion among the witnesses, none of whom can remember which side they should be standing on, and Father Agamedes says the necessary words, folds and unfolds his stole, steals a suspicious glance at the sacristan, who arrives late, but what are you thinking, he's not Domingos Mau-Tempo, that was years ago, and this isn't the same priest, people don't live forever. Nothing happened, the light didn't change, the church didn't fill up with thrones and seraphim, and a turtledove cooing in the garden continues to coo, preoccupied perhaps with other weddings, and Gracinda Mau-Tempo can now look at Manuel Espada and say, This is my husband, and Manuel Espada can look at Gracinda Mau-Tempo and say, This is my wife, which, as it happens, will only be true from this moment on, because the bracken at the fountain has never received these two bodies, though that once seemed a distinct possibility.

The bride and bridegroom are just crossing the tiny nave when the door of the church opens and in comes António Mau-Tempo in his army uniform, he's late for his own sister's wedding, a matter of delayed trains, missed connections, which left him furiously counting the kilometers between him and home, but finally, after António Mau-Tempo had uttered oaths capable of melting the bronze bearings on a train and alternately run and strode along the verge of the road, the driver of a passing fish truck succumbed to the magic spell of his uniform and asked, Where are you going, To Monte Lavre for my sister's wedding, and dropped him off at the bottom of the hill, saying, Congratulate the happy couple for me, and António Mau-Tempo bounded up that hill like a mountain goat, walked straight past the big house and the guards' barracks without so much as a glance, bastards, and then it suddenly occurred to him that perhaps the wedding was over, but no, there are still people outside, only a few more meters, up the steps in two strides, and there's my sister and there's my brother-in-law, I'm glad you could make it, brother, Oh, I'd have made it if I had to set fire to the whole regiment. Out in the street now, the main topic of conversation isn't the wedding but António Mau-Tempo, who was given leave to come to his sister's wedding, and since he then has to embrace everyone, father and mother, relatives and friends, the wedding cortege is slightly disrupted, patience, not that Gracinda Mau-Tempo is jealous, she has her magnificent husband, Manuel Espada, by her side, she stands arm in arm with him the way couples at the very smartest weddings stand, and she's blushing furiously, Lord in heaven, why can you not see these things, these men and women who, having invented a god, forgot to give him eyes, or perhaps did so on purpose, because no god is worthy of his creator, and should not, therefore, see him.

The disruption was short-lived. Manuel Espada and Gracinda Mau-Tempo are once more the king and queen of the party, António Mau-Tempo having now joined his childhood friends, with whom he always needs to reinforce and refresh the bonds of friendship after his long absences in such places as Salvaterra, Sado and Lezírias, farther north toward Leiria, and now, during his national service. The wedding feast is being held in someone else's house, lent for the day. There is wine, lamb and bread stew, with more bread than lamb, bride cakes, two bottles of fortified wine and a few tasty pigs' ears, this is no banquet but the wedding of poor people, so poor that João Mau-Tempo would clutch his head if we were cruel enough to mention the expense and the quadrupled debt at the grocer's and the haberdasher's, the all too familiar dogs that will soon be snapping at the debtor's heels, but which for the time being remain treacherously silent, Is there anything else you need, after all, it's not every day your daughter gets married.

Until Father Agamedes joins them, no one can eat, wretched priest, he's obviously not as hungry as I am, the smell of that stew is making my stomach rumble, I don't know how I've lasted this long really, I deliberately didn't eat supper last night so that I'd have more appetite today. One doesn't own up to such feelings, of course, admitting that one didn't have supper so as to be able to eat more at other people's expense, but we're all familiar enough with such human frailties, and therefore with our own, to be able to forgive them in others. Especially now that Father Agamedes has finally arrived and goes over to say a few words to Tomás Espada and the Mau-Tempos, words that Faustina doesn't quite understand, although she nods vigorously and adopts an expression of filial unction, not that she's a hypocrite, poor woman, it's just that the timbre of Father Agamedes's voice makes her ears buzz, otherwise she would be able to understand him perfectly. Father Agamedes is very fatherly with the bride and groom, he gestures with his right hand, blessing people on either side, and they forget about their hunger for a moment, but now it comes roaring back, at last we're going to start. In came the platters and tureens, all borrowed, well, two of them weren't, and as for Gracinda Mau-Tempo's own meager collection of crockery, her mother was very firm, You're not taking that to the wedding, we'll sort something out, don't you worry, you can't start married life with a load of broken crockery, it might bring bad luck. Finally they ate, at first greedily, then more slowly, because everyone knew that there wouldn't be much more to eat, and common sense dictated, therefore, that they make the stew and the pigs' ears last, at least there was plenty of wine, which was something.

After a while, Father Agamedes got to his feet, made a gesture calling for silence, just a gesture, nothing more, he was a tall, extremely thin man, indeed it was a matter of great perplexity among his parishioners as to just where Father Agamedes put the considerable quantity of food that he ate, as was evident at the weddings and christenings he presided over, he got to his feet, looked at the people seated around him, wrinkled his sensitive nose at the sight of the dirty, disorderly table, oh, they're so ill bred, Senhora Dona Clemência, but then felt himself filled with charity, doubtless Christian charity, and said, My dear children, I address myself to you and especially to the newlyweds on this happy day on which I have had the great good fortune to unite in holy matrimony Gracinda Mau-Tempo and Manuel Espada, she, the daughter of João Mau-Tempo and Faustina Gonçalves and he, the son of Tomás Espada and the late Flor Martinha. You have made the vows of faithfulness and mutual support that the holy mother church requires of all those who come to her in order to sanctify the joining together of man and wife until death do them part. Father Agamedes was wrong to mention death at this point, because Tomás Espada closed his eyes to hold back his tears but failed, tears are like water oozing out from a painful crack in a wall, everyone, very wisely, pretended not to notice, and Father Agamedes proceeded regardless, This land of ours may be small, but fortunately we share a great friendship, there are no dissensions or disputes such as I have seen in other places, and although it's true that the people here are not great frequenters of our beloved mother church, who is always waiting patiently for her children to come to her, it is also true that almost no one omits to attend the sacraments, and those who don't attend are lost sheep whom I, alas, have long given up all hope of saving, may God forgive me, for a minister should never lose hope of leading his entire flock into the arms of God. One of those stray sheep was present, as was his wife, who compared very favorably with her husband in the stray-sheep stakes, namely Sigismundo Canastro and Joana Canastra, both of whom were beaming as if Father Agamedes's words were bouquets of roses, far be it from me to boast, but I have proven to be a constant and caring shepherd, for example, three years ago, at the time of the strike, as I hope you will all remember, some of you here today were among those I freed from prison, as you yourselves can attest, and were it not for Monte Lavre's good standing with the Lord, all twenty-two of you could have been taken to the bullring, as happened to other men in lands less blessed by Our Lord and the Virgin Mother, although I know, of course, that I, poor repentant sinner than I am, cannot take the credit for such things.

At this point, João Mau-Tempo turned red and, needing to look at someone, he looked at Sigismundo Canastro, whose grave and now unsmiling eyes were fixed on the priest, and then António Mau-Tempo spoke up, This is my sister's wedding, Father Agamedes, it's no time to speak of strikes or who should take credit for what, and his voice was so serene that he didn't seem the least angry, although he was, and everyone else kept silent, waiting to see what might happen next, but the priest merely proposed a toast to the health of the newlyweds and sat down. That was not a good idea, Father Agamedes, Norberto said afterward, what possessed you to say such things, it's like mentioning rope in the house of a hanged man, You're quite right, said Father Agamedes, I don't know what came over me, I just wanted to show them that if it weren't for us, the church and the latifundio, the two persons of the Holy Trinity, of which the third is the State, that purest of doves, if it were not for us, how would they keep body and soul together, and, come election time, who would they give their votes to, but I confess I was wrong, mea culpa, mea maxima culpa, that's why I didn't stay there much longer, I gave my pastoral duties as an excuse and left, I was, admittedly, slightly tipsy, though I didn't drink much of that rough fortified wine of theirs, far too acidic for my stomach, not like the excellent wine from your cellar, Senhor Lamberto.

Then António Mau-Tempo, as spokesman, said, Right, now that Father Agamedes has gone and we're among family, we can say what we like, according to our inclinations and our hearts' choosing, so Manuel Espada will talk to Gracinda, his wife and my sister, while my other sister, Amélia, doubtless has her eye on someone too, though she might not be free to speak to him, and if he's not here, then she can think about him, and we will all understand, because sometimes that's the most we can do, and my parents will think back over their lives and over ours and what they were like when they were young, and they will forgive us our mistakes, and the rest of you will think about yourselves and your nearest and dearest, some of whom are already dead, I know, but if you call them, they will come back, that's all the dead are waiting for, indeed, I can already feel the presence of Flor Martinha, someone must have summoned her here, but since I'm the one speaking, I will keep the floor, and don't be surprised at my fine way of speaking, you don't only learn about fighting in the army, if you really want to, you can learn how to read and write and do arithmetic, and that way you can begin to understand the world and a little about life, which isn't simply a matter of being born, working and dying, sometimes we have to rebel, and that's what I want to talk to you about.

Any conversations going on around him stopped, Gracinda Mau-Tempo and Manuel Espada ceased gazing at each other, although they continued to hold hands, Flor Martinha said her farewells, Goodbye, Tomás, the guests put their elbows on the table, they have no manners these people, and if someone sticks a finger in his mouth to extract from some cavity in his teeth a bit of gristle from the lamb, don't be angry, we live in a land where food cannot be wasted, and António Mau-Tempo, in his cotton uniform, is talking about just that, about food. It's true that there's a lot of hunger hereabouts, sometimes we're obliged to eat weeds, and our stomachs are as swollen and tight as drums, and perhaps that's why the commander of the regiment believes that if a donkey is hungry enough it will eat thistles, and since we are donkeys, because we hear nothing else on the parade ground, well, actually we hear far worse than that, we do eat thistles, but I can tell you that I would rather eat thistles than the food they serve at the barracks, which is fit only for pigs, although even they might turn up their snouts at it.

António Mau-Tempo paused, took a sip of wine to clear his throat, wiped his mouth with the back of his hand, after all, what more natural napkin is there, and resumed his speech, They believe that because we are starving at home, we should accept anything, but that's where they're wrong, because our hunger is a clean hunger, and the thistles we have to strip, we strip with our own hands, which even when they're dirty are still clean, no one has cleaner hands than us, that's the first thing we learn when we enter the barracks, it's not part of the weapons drill, but you sense it, and a man can choose between outright hunger and the shame of eating what they give us, they came to Monte Lavre to summon me to serve the nation, or so they said, but I don't know what that means, the nation is my mother and my father, they said, well, I, like everyone else, know my real mother and father, who took the food from their own mouths so that we could eat, in that case, the nation should also take the food from its own mouth so that I can eat, and if I have to eat thistles, then the nation should eat them too, if not, that means that some are the sons of the nation and others are the sons of whores.

Some of the women were shocked, some of the men frowned, but António Mau-Tempo, who has something of the vagabond about him despite his uniform, will be forgiven anything for having put Father Agamedes firmly in his place, and besides, he says these other words that taste to his listeners like the excellent wine from Senhor Lamberto's cellar, although that's purely a hypothesis, because our lips have never actually touched the stuff, Anyway, in the barracks we decided to hold a hunger strike, we wouldn't eat a single crumb of what they put before us, just like pigs who refuse to eat from the trough in which there's more rubbish in the swill than even a pig will eat, we don't mind eating two quarts of earth a year, the earth is as clean as us, but not that food, and I, António Mau-Tempo, speaking to you now, was the one who had the idea, and I'm proud of that, you don't know how different you feel until you've done these things, I talked to my comrades and they agreed that the situation could only be worse if they were actually spitting on us, and when the day came, the cookhouse bell rang and we went and sat down as if we were going to eat, but the food arrived and it stayed there on the plates uneaten, the sergeants bawled and yelled, but no one picked up his spoon, it was the revolution of the pigs, and then the officer on duty turned up, made a speech like the one Father Agamedes made, but we pretended we didn't understand a word of it, as if he were talking Latin, first he tried to win us over with sweet words, but then he lost his rag and started screaming at us, ordering us to form up on the parade ground, an order we did understand, because what we wanted more than anything was to get out of that cookhouse, so out we went, whispering words of encouragement to each other, Don't give up, courage, my friend, stick to your guns, we're all in this together, and there we stood for half an hour, and that, we assumed, was the punishment until we saw them setting up three machine guns trained on us, all in accordance with the regulations, with gunners and their assistants, and boxes of ammunition, and then the officer said that if we didn't go and eat, he would give the order to fire, that was the voice of the nation speaking, it was as if my mother had said to me, either eat your food or I'll slit your throat, none of us believed he would do it, but then they started loading the machine guns, and from that point on we had no idea what was going to happen, I can tell you I felt a shiver go down my spine, what if they really did shoot and there was a bloodbath over a bowl of soup, was it worth it, not that we were weakening, but in situations like that, you can't help such thoughts running through your mind, and then, from within the ranks, we never did find out who it was, even the comrades standing nearest never said, we heard a very calm voice say, as if it were someone politely inquiring after our health, Comrades, stand your ground, and then another voice at the other end of the line said, Go on, shoot us, and then, even now it brings a lump to my throat, every single soldier in the ranks repeated those defiant words, Go on, shoot us, I don't think they would have fired on us, but if they had, I know that we would all have stood our ground, and that was our real victory, rather than getting them to improve the food, it's odd how sometimes you start out fighting for one thing and end by winning something else, and that second thing was the best of the two. António Mau-Tempo paused again, and then, much wiser than his years, he added, But to win that second thing, you have to start fighting for the first.

The women are weeping and the men's eyes are filling with tears, this is the best wedding you could possibly imagine, Monte Lavre has never seen the like, and then Manuel Espada stood up and went to embrace António Mau-Tempo, thinking how different this army is from the one he served in, and he remembers his national service in the Azores and hearing his fellow soldier issuing that vague threat, When I get out of here, I'm going to join the police for the vigilance and defense of the state, it's great, say there's someone you don't like, well, you simply arrest him, haul him off to the civil authorities, and if you like, shoot him in the head before you get there and say he tried to resist.

Now Sigismundo Canastro, tall and thin, has got to his feet, he toasts the newlyweds, and when everyone has downed some of the fortified wine, he announces he's going to tell a story which, while not quite the same as António Mau-Tempo's, is nevertheless similar, because with stories and anecdotes you can always find some similarity, however unlikely, Many years ago, and at this point he pauses, just to make sure everyone is listening, and they are, their eyes fixed on him, some are rather sleepy, it's true, but can still manage to keep awake, and then he goes on, Many years ago, I was out hunting, oh, no, not another hunting story, all lies and exaggeration, but Sigismundo Canastro isn't joking and doesn't respond to this interruption, he merely looks around him as if pitying such a lack of seriousness, and whether it was that look or mere curiosity to find out how big a lie this will be, silence falls, and João Mau-Tempo, who knows Sigismundo Canastro very well, is sure there will be more to this story than meets the eye, the problem will be understanding it, At the time, I didn't have a rifle of my own, I used to borrow one from whoever I could, and I was a pretty good hunter too, just ask the people who knew me then, and I had a little dog I was training up, a real gem with a really keen nose, and one day I went out with some friends, there were quite a few of us, each of us with our dog, and we had already walked a long way and were somewhere over near Guarita do Godeal when a partridge suddenly flew up, as fast as you like, I put my rifle to my eye, and the bird fell just as I was about to pull the trigger, I certainly didn't hit it, fortunately, though, for my good name as a hunter, there was no one else around, but Constante, my dog, ran to where the partridge had fallen, thinking perhaps that the bird was wounded, lost amid the gorse, because the undergrowth was really thick, and there were some large rocks blocking your view, but anyway, the dog disappeared, and I called and called, Constante, Constante, and I whistled and whistled, but no response, it would be even more embarrassing having to return home without the dog, besides, I was really fond of him, he was one of those dogs who could almost speak. His audience was hanging on his every word now, listening and digesting, it doesn't take much to make a man happy and a woman content, and even if the story turned out to be pure hokum, it was a good story well told, as Sigismundo Canastro went on to show, Two years later, I happened to be in those parts again, and I came across a vast area of land which they had begun to clear but then, for some reason, abandoned, and I remembered what had happened with Constante, and I plunged in among the rocks and the undergrowth, it was the devil of a job, but something was leading me on, as if someone were saying, don't give up, Sigismundo Canastro, and suddenly what did I see but the skeleton of my dog standing there, guarding the skeleton of the partridge, and they had been like that for two years, both equally determined. I can see it now, my dog Constante, his nose pointing forward, his front leg poised and lifted, and no wind could knock him over and no rain dissolve his bones.

Sigismundo Canastro said no more and sat down. No one else spoke a word, no one laughed, not even the younger people, who belong to a less credulous generation, and then António Mau-Tempo said, They're still there, the dog and the partridge, I dreamt about them once, what more proof could you want, and having said that, everyone cried out together, They're still there, they're still there, and then they believed the story and burst out laughing. And after they had laughed, they carried on talking, and they talked all afternoon, about this and that, come on, have another drink, at this same hour, the parade ground at the barracks will be deserted, while the empty sockets of Constante the dog stare at the empty sockets of the partridge, both equally determined. When night fell, they said their goodbyes, some accompanied Gracinda Mau-Tempo and Manuel Espada to the door of their house, tomorrow there's work to be done, we're lucky to have it, Don't be long, Gracinda, Just coming, Manuel. In the next yard a dog barks, surprised to have new neighbors.

J OSÉ CALMEDO IS JUST one guard among many. You wouldn't notice him on parade, he's no more striking than any of his colleagues, and when he's not on parade, but on patrol or otherwise on duty, he's a quiet, easygoing fellow who always seems to have his mind on other things. One day, quite unexpectedly, perhaps even to himself, he will hand in his application for discharge to the commander of the Monte Lavre barracks, who will then begin the necessary procedures, and he will take his wife and two children far from there, learn to live the life of a civilian and spend his remaining years forgetting that he was once a guard. He is, however, a man with a history, which we do not, alas, have time to go into here, except to mention his family name, a story that is both brief and charming, and illustrative of the beauty of names and their unusual origins, for it is the fault of our feeble memory and our lack of curiosity that makes us ignore or forget, for example, that the name Sousa* means wild dove, isn't that lovely, and is not just the very ordinary name set down in the register of births, which

---

* Sousa was Saramago's father's name, Saramago being a family nickname, meaning wild radish, accidentally incorporated into Saramago's name when his birth was recorded in the register of births.

immediately clips its wings, that's the trouble with writing things down. But best of all are the names born out of the distortion of other names or of words that never had any intention of becoming names, for example, Pantaleão became Espanta Leões, pity the poor family who has to go through life with a duty to drive away lions in city and country. But we were talking about the guard José Calmedo and the brief and charming history of his name, born, or so the story goes, from the unintentional bravado of an ancestor of his, who, unaware of the very real danger he was in, was not as frightened as he ought to have been, and responded to the person asking about his lack of fear, *Qual medo*, what fear, and people were so amazed by the spontaneous effrontery of that question that this unintentional hero and his descendants, including this guard and his children, were known ever after as Calmedo, although later, another version was born, because Calmedo means very hot, windless weather, which is what it's like as he leaves the barracks now, carrying his secret orders.

It's three kilometers there and three kilometers back on foot, but that's what a guard's life is like, although not, of course, for the mounted guard, anyway, there's José Calmedo heading down the hill in Monte Lavre to the valley, he skirts around a village toward the west, then heads north along the road, with ricefields to his left, it's a beautiful July morning and hot, as we said before, but it will be even hotter later. There's a little stream down below, much thirst and little water, his boots strike the surface of the road, and he feels very much a man as he strides it out, while his head is full of stray clouds, words that once had meaning but have lost it, well, we were walking along the road, but now we've gone down the bank to the right, into the cool shade beneath the viaduct, and are now sitting beneath the whispering branches of the poplars, the place is deserted, who would have thought it, the empty pool, the ruined water wheel and, beyond it, the brick kiln with the broken roof, it seems that the latifundio corrodes everything that gets in its way. José Calmedo rests his rifle on his shoulder, takes off his cap and uses his handkerchief to wipe the sweat from his brow, where the dark and the light skin show the effect of the sun or the lack of it, it's almost as if the top part of his head belonged not to him but to his cap, although these, of course, are pure imaginings.

It's not much farther, he's going to Cabeço do Desgarro and should arrive there in time for lunch. He will return with João Mau-Tempo, on the pretext of some insignificant matter that has nothing whatever to do with João Mau-Tempo, it doesn't need to be a complicated story, the simpler the better, the more credible. He can see the hut among the trees and the men, who stand around the fire, removing the pot before it boils over or burns, it won't take long, he just has to go over to him and say, Come with me to the barracks, but José Calmedo doesn't take the few steps that would place him where he could be seen by everyone, should they look. He hides behind some high bushes and stays there, allowing time for João Mau-Tempo to finish his sparse lunch, while in the sky occasional clouds continue to pass, so few that they don't cast a shadow. José Calmedo is sitting on the ground smoking a cigarette, he has propped his rifle against the trunk of a tree. He has a good life, this guard, with few duties, simply watching the days pass by, only occasionally are there a few more serious cases, although there will be more, otherwise, the months come and go, the latifundio is calm and peaceful, the barracks and his beat are calm and peaceful, apart from report writing and patrols, court proceedings and the kind of complaints bickering neighbors always have. Life goes by, and before you know it you've reached retirement age. These are the thoughts of a peace-loving man, you would never think he had a rifle and a cartridge belt at his side and was wearing seven-league boots, above his head a bird is singing, its name doesn't matter, it hops from branch to branch, you can see its silhouette from here, just the fan of its tail and a wing. If we looked down at the ground, we would see the crawling fraternity of insects, the ant that raises its head like a dog, the other that always keeps it lowered, the tiny spider, wherever does it put its food, but we mustn't let ourselves be distracted, we have to go and arrest a man, we're simply letting him finish his lunch, well, just because we're guards doesn't mean we don't have a heart, you know.

There are no great feasts on the latifundio. José Calmedo peers between the bushes, everyone has finished eating. He gets up, sighing perhaps at the effort made or about to be made, puts his rifle over his shoulder with measured gestures, not because these gestures are important, but because they are crutches, things a man can hold on to in order not to get lost amid the meaninglessness of his actions, and then he heads off down the hill toward the men. They see him coming from a distance, their hearts perhaps beat a little faster, the laws of the latifundio are strict, whether they're to do with who owns the acorns or where you can collect firewood, or far worse misdemeanors. José Calmedo approaches, then stops and summons the foreman, he doesn't want everyone to hear, men may not be girls, but they have their modesty, Tell João Mau-Tempo I want to have a word with him.

João Mau-Tempo's heart beats as fast as that of a little bird. Not that he feels himself guilty of any heinous crime, of the kind that merits rather more than just a fine or a beating. He senses that he is the man the guard has come for, that from the moment the foreman says, João Mau-Tempo, go and talk to the guard, it will be like removing a layer of cork, you hear the creak and know that the efforts of both man and tree are working as one, all that's lacking is the man's grunt, Uh, and the scream of the bark as it comes away, craaack, So, Senhor José Calmedo, what can I do for you, asks João Mau-Tempo with the apparent calm of someone congratulating the guard on his appearance, fortunately our hearts are hidden, otherwise all men would be condemned sooner or later, either for their innocence or their crimes, because the heart is an impulsive, impatient thing, incapable of restraint. The person who made hearts clearly didn't know what he was doing, but fortunately one can learn to be sly, otherwise how could José Calmedo say, without anyone having told him to, Oh, it's nothing important, we just want to clear up a case involving two guys who stole a couple of sheaves of wheat, the owner swears it was them, but they say you're a witness to the fact that it wasn't, I don't really understand the situation myself, to be honest. It's always the same, however well intentioned, a man tends to get in a tangle when he shouldn't and whatever he says becomes like the devil's cape, which, being short, both covers and uncovers, but even when João Mau-Tempo, who is, in this case, completely innocent, even when he says, But what have I got to do with it, why should I get involved, the guard responds with the old argument, You have nothing to worry about, just come along with me, say your piece and leave.

So be it. João Mau-Tempo is about to go off and pick up his few tools and what's left of his lunch, but José Calmedo, still carried along on the wave of his invention, says, Don't bother doing that, you'll be back soon, it won't take long. And having fulfilled his quota of lies, he moves off, with an uneasy João Mau-Tempo following behind, clacking along in the clogs he wore when working. From there to Monte Lavre, José Calmedo's face is a picture of rage, as befits a guard who has made an arrest and is escorting his prisoner, but that wasn't the reason, rather, the sadness of having won such a pathetic victory, is this what two men were born for. And João Mau-Tempo, deep in his own thoughts and anxieties, was trying to convince himself that some sheaves of wheat really had been stolen and that his testimony really could save two innocent men.

João Mau-Tempo enters the same barracks where he had been held prisoner some four years before. Everything looks the same, as if time hadn't passed. José Calmedo goes to tell the corporal that the arrested man is here, that there have been no hitches, mission completed, but please, keep the medals for another occasion, just leave me alone to get on with my life and my cloud-thoughts, one day, I will present a sheet of paper bearing an official stamp and addressed to the Commander General of the National Republican Guard, Sir, meanwhile, Corporal Tacabo orders João Mau-Tempo to come in and says, Sit down, Senhor Mau-Tempo, such politeness is not so very odd, guards don't always behave like cruel executioners, Do you know why you've been summoned. João Mau-Tempo is about to say that if it's about some sheaves of wheat, he has nothing to tell, but he doesn't have time to open his mouth, and it's just as well, because if he had, José Calmedo would have been found to be a liar, fortunately, Corporal Tacabo went on, well, it's best to get this over with quickly, What were you doing in Vendas Novas, You must be mistaken, I wasn't doing anything, Well, I have an order from the Vendas Novas barracks to arrest you as a communist.

Here is an example of simple, straightforward dialogue, with no harmonies and no arpeggios, unaccompanied and unadorned by thoughts and subtleties, it's as if they weren't dealing with serious matters, but were saying, So, how have you been, Very well, thank you, and yourself, A friend of yours in Vendas Novas sends you his regards, Do give him mine when you next see him. A bell has just rung inside João Mau-Tempo's head, there is a great clanging sound like that of castle doors being slammed shut, no one enters here. But the owner of the castle is trembling, his hands and voice are trembling, Defend yourself, my soul, but this lasted only a second, time enough to feign horror, surprise, offended, outraged innocence, How can you say that, sir, I haven't been involved in anything like that for four years, not since I was arrested and taken to Montemor, there must be some mistake, and Corporal Tacabo says, Well, I certainly hope so, if you know nothing about it, the authorities will release you immediately. Perhaps it will be all right, perhaps it was a false alarm, perhaps no one is drowning, perhaps the fire will die down without him burning his hands, Could you send for my wife so that I can speak to her, Corporal. A perfectly natural request, but Monte Lavre, you see, is such an unimportant place, just a tiny village in the latifundio, that here the corporal is the commander, and he responds as firmly as the commander in Lisbon who gives him his orders, No, your wife can't speak to you, nor can anyone else, regardless of what you may say, you have been judged to be a dangerous element, a soldier will go and fetch anything you need from your house.

João Mau-Tempo, a dangerous element. He was taken to the room that served as a cell, again it was José Calmedo who took him, there didn't seem to be anyone else on duty, and João Mau-Tempo, before he was locked up, says, So you tricked me, and José Calmedo doesn't respond at first, he feels offended, he was only doing his job and this is his reward, but he can't remain silent as if he really had committed some crime, and so he replies, I didn't want to worry you, José Calmedo really shouldn't be wearing the uniform of the national guard, which is why he will take it off one day and go and live in a place where no one knows he was a guard, and that is all we will ever learn about his life.

Faustina Mau-Tempo and her two daughters come and go outside the barracks. They are in tears and anxious, they don't know what their husband and father stands accused of, only that he will be taken to Vendas Novas, and as ill luck would have it, as the saying goes, the three of them, for one reason or another, are absent when the jeep from Vendas Novas arrives, complete with a patrol armed with rifles and bayonets, to fetch the criminal. When mother and daughters return, they will learn that João Mau-Tempo is no longer there, and they are left standing out in the street, at the door of the barracks, to which entry is barred, He's not here now, that's all we know, go home and you'll be kept informed, they say these words to the poor women, but they are pure mockery, just as the guards who came from Vendas Novas to get João Mau-Tempo mocked him when they said, Hop in, we're off on a little trip. The guard would never normally invite him to go anywhere, with transport paid for by the nation, which pays for all these things and out of our pockets too, and João Mau-Tempo would love to travel, to leave the latifundio and see other lands, but now that he has been dubbed a dangerous element, no thought is given to the inconvenience caused to the guards, who enjoy their rest, nor to the price of gasoline, nor to the depreciation in the value of the vehicle, and they immediately provide a jeep and a patrol complete with rifles and bayonets to go to Monte Lavre to find the malefactor and bring him safely to Vendas Novas, Hop in, we're off on a little trip, if that isn't mockery, I don't know what is.

The journey is brief and silent, the guards' fount of jokes, always the same, soon runs dry, and João Mau-Tempo, after much thought, says to himself that he might as well be hanged for a sheep as for a lamb, and that no one will get any compromising information out of him, if I were to talk, it would be better if all the mirrors in the world were shattered and all the eyes of those who come to see me were closed, so that I would never have to see my own face again. This road has many memories, it was here that Augusto Pintéu died crossing the stream with his mule cart, and over there, behind that hill, was where I first lay with Faustina, it was winter and the grass was wet, I wouldn't do it now, but that's youth for you. And he can taste in his mouth the bread and chorizo they ate afterward, their first meal as man and wife according to the laws of nature. João Mau-Tempo puts his hand to his eyes as if they were burning, all right, they're tears, and a guard says, Don't cry, man, and another adds, His sort only cry when they're caught, but that isn't true, I'm not crying, retorts João Mau-Tempo, and he's right, even though his eyes are full of tears, it's not his fault that the guards lack any understanding of their fellow man.

João Mau-Tempo is in the barracks at Vendas Novas now, the journey was all a dream, and this PIDE agent, there's no mistaking him, once you've seen one, you've seen them all, and João Mau-

Tempo has more than enough experience of them, this agent says, while the barracks commander is picking at his teeth, Yep, this is the gentleman who'll be coming on a little trip to Lisbon with me, what is it with these people, they all talk about going on trips, let's go on a little trip, they say, and sometimes these are trips from which you don't return, that's what you hear anyway, but meanwhile, the agent turns to a guard and gives an order, the commander is here to obey, he's a stooge, a toady. Take this man to the recreation room so he can rest until tomorrow, and João Mau-Tempo feels someone grab his arm roughly and take him out the back, into a garden, the guards love gardens, perhaps their many sins will be forgiven them because of their love of flowers, which means that not everything is lost in their hardened souls, a moment of beauty and grace redeems the worst of crimes in the eyes of the supreme judge, like this crime of taking João Mau-Tempo from Monte Lavre and throwing him into a temporary dungeon and into other, more permanent ones, not to mention what will happen later. For now, it's a provincial cell, and over there is a truckle bed with a mat and a bundle of foul blankets, and here's a jug of water, he's so thirsty, he raises it to his lips and finds that the water is warm, but he drinks only after the guard has left, and now I can cry, don't laugh at me, I'm forty-four, but forty-four is nothing, you're still a lad, in the prime of life, don't say that on the latifundio and to my face, when I feel so tired and when there's this pain in my side that never leaves me and these lines and wrinkles that the mirror can still, for the time being, show me, if this is the prime of life, then allow me to weep.

We will pass over the night during which João Mau-Tempo did not sleep but merely paced up and down, not wanting to rest his body on the bed. Day dawns, he is weary and anxious, what will become of me, and when nine o'clock struck, the door opens and the guard says, Come out where I can see you, that's how he speaks, he hasn't been taught any other way, and the PIDE agent says, It's time to catch the train and set off on our little trip. And they leave, accompanied to the door by the commander of the barracks, who is very scrupulous and polite in such matters, See you, then, he says, and although João Mau-Tempo may be innocent, he is not so innocent as to think that this farewell is intended for him, but on the way to the station, he says, Sir, I swear I'm innocent. If the train wasn't about to leave, we could sit here and debate what it means to be innocent, and whether João Mau-Tempo truly believes in that oath and how he can believe in what appears to be a perjury, and we would discover, if we had time and intelligence enough, the difference between being innocently blameless and blamelessly innocent, although such subtleties are lost on João Mau-Tempo's companion, who responds angrily, Stop your bellyaching, they'll straighten you out in Lisbon.

Let us pass over the journey too, since it does not appear in the history of railways in Portugal. Such is the body's sovereign power over us that João Mau-Tempo even dozed a little, lulled to sleep by the swaying carriage and the clatter of the wheels over the rails, clackety-clack, but each time, he started awake, terrified to discover that he wasn't dreaming. Then there was the boat to Terreiro do Paço, what if I threw myself into the water, these are black thoughts, I want to die and not heroically either, what is unusual about João Mau-Tempo is that he has never seen a film and therefore doesn't know how easy and much applauded is that leap from the side of the boat, the impeccable dive and the swim American-style that carries the fugitive to the mysterious chartered yacht that waits at a distance, along with the veiled countess who, in order to be there, has broken the sacred bonds of family and the rules of her aristocratic heritage. But João Mau-Tempo will only learn later that he is the son of the king and sole heir to the throne, three cheers for King João Mau-Tempo, king of Portugal, the boat moors at the pontoon, and the man who was asleep wakes up, and by the time he does so, there are two men standing over him, Is he the only one, they ask, and the man who came with João Mau-Tempo answers, Yes, he's the only one this time.

Let us also pass over without much comment the journey through the city, the trams, the many cars, the passersby, the statue of Dom José on his horse,* now which one is the horse's right leg, João Mau-Tempo recognizes the various places, how could one forget such a big square and the arches, bigger than those in Giraldo square in Évora, but then suddenly everything is new to him, these steep, narrow streets, and just when he is finding the journey long, it becomes all too short, this half-door opening obliquely, the fly has been caught in the spider's web, we need no better or more original image.

And now there are stairs to climb. João Mau-Tempo is still flanked by the two men, well, you can't be too careful, high security, he is, after all, a dangerous element. Above and below, it's like a termites' nest, a hive of buzzing drones and ringing telephones, but as they go up, first floor, second floor, across wide landings, the noise and bustle diminish, they meet fewer people, and on the third floor there is almost complete silence, only the muted sounds of car engines and the vague murmur of the city in the heat of the afternoon. These are the attic rooms and this corridor leads to a long, low chamber where the ceiling is almost at head height, and some other men are sitting on long benches, and I am going to sit down next to them, I, João Mau-Tempo, native and inhabitant of Monte Lavre, forty-four years old, the son of Domingos Mau-Tempo, shoemaker, and Sara da Conceição, madwoman, and I have been dubbed a dangerous element, as Corporal Tacabo at the local barracks was kind enough to inform me. The other men sitting there look at João Mau-Tempo, but no one says a word. This is the house of patience, and here we await our immediate destiny. The roof is

---

* In Portuguese, this is an untranslatable joke: "Qual é a pata direita do cavalo de Dom José?," "Which is the right leg of Dom José's horse?," because the horse's left leg is straight (*direita*) and the right leg (*direita* also means right) is bent.

right above our heads, it creaks in the heat, if you poured water on it, it would boil, and João Mau-Tempo hasn't eaten for more than twenty-four hours, and for him there is no heat, it's a winter's day, he shivers as if he were exposed to the December wind blowing across the latifundio, with no more protection than his own bare skin. That is exactly what it is like, for this is the bench of the naked, every man for himself, they will not help each other, you must clothe yourself in strength and determination, in the loneliness of the moors, in the high soaring flight of the red kite who finally descends to ground level to count his own and test their courage.

However, the victims must be fed, we don't want to lose them sooner than would be convenient. Half an hour passed, and another, and finally in came some kitchen servant or other, bringing each prisoner a bowl of prison soup and two deciliters of wine, a kind thought from the nation to these her stepchildren, I hope they're grateful. And as João Mau-Tempo was scraping the bowl with his spoon, he heard one policeman say to the other, they were standing by the door keeping watch over the flock and shuffling papers, That guy's being handed over to Inspector Paveia, and the other replied, Rather him than me, and João Mau-Tempo said to himself, That's me they're talking about, and, as he found out later, it would have been far better not to have known. The plates and glasses were taken away, and the waiting continued, what will become of us, it was nearly night when they got their marching orders, some were being sent here and some there, Caxias or Aljube, provisional billets, there would be further moves, all of them to worse places, as the name became a face, so the face became a target. And the voice of Dona Patrocínio, a functionary in this socially useful service, was definitely the voice of the nation, So-and-so is to go there, So-and-so somewhere else, she could not have a better name as patron of displacements, it's the same with Dona Clemência, who is now doubtless chatting with Father Agamedes, I hear that João Mau-Tempo has been arrested, Yes, Senhora, he's paid for all his sins at once, and to think I went out of my way to help him and others, He seemed such a decent fellow, They're always the worst, Senhora Dona Clemência, they're always the worst, He wasn't even a drinking man, If only he had been, then he wouldn't have been tempted into such evil actions, What evil actions, Ah, that I don't know, but if he was innocent, they wouldn't have arrested him, Perhaps we should give his wife some help, You're a saint, Senhora Dona Clemência, if it wasn't for your kind patronage, I don't know what would become of these wretches, but leave it for a while, and see if they learn to be less proud, because that's their worst defect, pride, You're quite right, Father Agamedes, and pride is a mortal sin, The worst of all sins, Senhora Dona Clemência, because it is pride that causes a man to rise up against his employer and his god.

On the way back, the truck passed through Boa-Hora to pick up some prisoners who were being tried there. All of this is carefully measured and calculated, according to the order of service, the police van must be used to capacity, it's like saying, you have to take the rough with the smooth, and given how poor the nation is, the prisoners would be the first to agree, indeed, they might even suggest it, Let's pass through Boa-Hora, and some will think, Hmm, Boa-Hora, Good-Hour, what an inappropriate name, and pick up those who are being judged by the worthy judges, and then we can all go together, it'll make for better company, it's just a shame we don't have a guitar with which to accompany our sorrows. João Mau-Tempo has never traveled so much in his life. Or, rather, as much as any other man in the latifundio, but not as much as his son António, now a soldier, but who traveled a lot in the past, driven by life's obligations and the needs of his stomach, with his knapsack on his back, with hoe and scythe, ax and adze, but the latifundio is the same everywhere, some parts have more cork oaks or holm oaks, some have more wheat or rice, some have guards or overseers or managers or foremen, it makes no difference, this, however, is quite different, a good tarmacked road, and if it were daytime, you'd be able to see more clearly. The nation really looks after its disobedient sons, as one can tell from these high, secure walls and the care the guards take over their work, they're a real plague, they're everywhere, or were they cursed at birth and this is their fate, to be wherever the suffering are, although not to minister to their misfortunes, that is why they have neither eyes nor hands, but say, Hop into the jeep, we're off on a little trip, or Move along, or Go on, we're off to the barracks, or You stole some acorns, so pay the fine and take a beating, they must have studied, otherwise they wouldn't be guards, because no one was born a guard.

Which, do you think, are the narrator's thoughts, and which are João Mau-Tempo's, both are right, and if there are any mistakes, they are shared mistakes. This bureaucracy of registers, index cards and papers is there from the day we're born, we take no notice of it, unless one day we're allowed to come here and find out in detail what actually went on, from the dotted line on which his name is written, João Mau-Tempo, forty-four years old, married, native and inhabitant of Monte Lavre, where's that, in the district of Montemor-o-Novo, well, you must be a good sort. They take João Mau-Tempo into a room along with other prisoners, sleep if you can, and if you're hungry, tough, because suppertime is long gone. The door closes, the world vanishes. Monte Lavre is a dream, and Faustina is deaf, poor thing, however, let us not say, out of some foolish superstition, that this is the hour of bats and owls, poor creatures, it's not their fault they're ugly, you perhaps are convinced that you're handsome, now who's a fool.

João Mau-Tempo will be here for twenty-four hours. He won't have much opportunity to talk, although the following day, a prisoner will come up to him and say, Listen, friend, we don't know why you're here, but for your own sake, take my advice.

THIRTY DAYS IN SOLITARY confinement is a month that doesn't fit in any normal calendar. However carefully you make your calculations, there are always too many days, it's an arithmetic invented by mad people, you start counting, one, two, three, twenty-seven, ninety-four, then find you've made a mistake, only six days have passed. No one interrogates him, they brought him from Caxias, this time during the day, so he at least knew where he was, although trying to see the world through those cracks was like trying to see it through the eye of a needle, and then he was ordered to undress, the nation does things like that, it happened to me once before, the doctors did it when I was called up, to decide whether or not I was good enough, well, I'm obviously good enough for these people, they're not going to send me away, they empty my pockets, they rummage and search and ransack, they even remove the insoles in my shoes, these clever folk know where we stash our secrets, but they find nothing, of the two handkerchiefs I brought with me, they take one, of the two packs of cigarettes, they take one, farewell, knife, these police aren't always so thorough, only now do they take my knife off me, what if

I'd tried to kill myself. They read me the rubric, While in solitary confinement, you will not be allowed any visitors nor can you write to your family, and so on and so forth, otherwise, you will be punished. But one day, much later, he was given permission to write a letter, and back came some clean clothes, washed and ironed by Faustina herself and sprinkled with a few tears, for they're a sentimental people whose fountains of tears have not as yet dried up.

On the twenty-fifth day, at three o'clock in the morning, João Mau-Tempo was, as usual, sleeping badly, and so he woke at once when the cell door opened and the guard said, Get dressed, Mau-Tempo, you're leaving. What, you're going to let me go, the imaginations of the wretched know no bounds, they always think the best or the worst, depending on their mood, that's the attraction of extremes, let's hope he's not disappointed. He's taken down to the ground floor, where there are people waiting, plus a fierce-looking hound, Here's that good-for-nothing you're taking for a walk, jokes the guard, they're clearly obsessed with this idea of walks and trips and rides, we know exactly what they mean, they're not fooling anyone, but they keep saying it, with a few minor variations, as if they didn't know what else to say. The hound goes on ahead, To show you the way to brigade headquarters, that's what the dog barks at João Mau-Tempo, and the guard from Aljube prison is such a card, just fancy, at this time of the morning and in these painful circumstances he can still manage to say, Have a good journey. Words were not presented to mankind as a gift, far from it, each word was hard won and occasionally abused, and there are some words that should only be sold at a high price, bearing in mind who is saying them and to what end, as in this case, Have a good journey, he says, when he knows full well that the journey will be far from good, animals are kinder to each other, for at least they don't speak. But here is this hound leading me through the deserted streets, at least it's a lovely night, although all I can see of it is this corridor of sky between the buildings, and to the left the cathedral and to the right another, smaller church, Santo António, and farther on the Madalena, neither small nor large, it's a street of churches, I am under the protection of the heavenly host, and perhaps that's why the hound speaks rather gently, Don't tell anyone I told you, but things aren't looking good, apparently a comrade of yours gave them your name, you'd best tell them everything you know, that's the only way to get back to your family, you won't gain anything by being stubborn. This street is called São Nicolau and the one over there São Francisco, and if I left some saint or other behind me along the way, you can have him, Sorry, I don't know what you're talking about, officer, I haven't done anything wrong, I've been working ever since I was born, I don't know anything about these things, I was arrested once but that was years ago, and I've had nothing to do with politics since, these are João Mau-Tempo's words, some true, some false, and he won't say anything else, that's the good thing about words, they're like a river flowing over rocks, it always does so in the same way, be careful not to stumble, the water flows so quickly it can dazzle you, watch out. The hound barks, João Mau-Tempo recognizes the place, this slope with the tram lines shining, Ah, so that's it, well, just you wait, and the soft dawn is bruised by the bad words hurled at him, you this and you that, words barely known in the latifundio. And now João Mau-Tempo feels his strength leaving him, he's been stuck in a cell for twenty-five days, scarcely moving, or only from cell to latrine and from latrine to cell, with his poor mind working overtime, tying up loose ends that immediately come undone again with more anxious thinking, not to mention the sleepless nights, and now there's this walk, which seems so long and yet it's nothing compared to the distances his legs used to cover on the latifundio, and suddenly he's afraid he won't make it, afraid he'll tell all he knows as well as what he could never possibly know, but then he hears again the prisoner in Caxias, Listen, friend, we don't know why you're here, but for your own sake, take my advice, and he remembered this just in time, he covered the final meters as if in a dream, he's through the door, going up the steps, up to the first floor again, there's no one to be seen, a terrifying silence reigns, second floor, third floor, we're here, João Mau-Tempo's fate has been waiting for him, legs crossed, that's the trouble with fates, they do nothing but wait, and we are the ones who have to do everything, for example, learn when to speak and when to keep silent.

The hound shoved João Mau-Tempo into a room and remained on guard outside. After a few minutes, the door burst open and in came a very spruce-looking gentleman, freshly shaved and smelling of cologne and brilliantine, he gestured to the other man to leave and immediately started shouting, Because of this bastard, this bloody communist, I can't go to mass today, that really is what he said, although I doubt anyone will believe me, but it's true, probably the influence of the ecclesiastical neighbors mentioned earlier while we were walking over from the Aljube prison, not to mention the Church of the Martyrs and the Square of the Two Churches, the Church of the Incarnation and that other one, now what the devil is it called, Father Agamedes would love it here, he'd be able to hear the confession of this Inspector Paveia, who is so upset about having missed mass you would think he'd have his own chaplain really, and now, to complete this edifying picture, imagine if João Mau-Tempo were to say, Oh, sir, please don't miss mass on my account, if you like, I'll go with you. We can't believe our ears, and not even João Mau-Tempo knows why he said it, but we don't have time now to examine these bold or spontaneous words, because Inspector Paveia doesn't give us time to think, Bastard, faggot, swine, I'm sorry, Father Agamedes, but that's exactly what he said, it's not my fault, and, Shut up or it's the trapeze for you, what circus arts these are João Mau-Tempo has no idea, but he sees Inspector Paveia go over to a desk, he's rather ill named really, when you think that *paveia* means a sheaf of wheat of the kind I used to clutch to my chest, and he takes a pistol out of the drawer, along with a stick and a heavy ruler, He's going to kill me, thought João Mau-Tempo, and the inspector said, See this, it's for you if you don't tell me the whole story, and be warned, you won't leave here until you've told me everything you know, stay standing, don't move, not so much as a finger, if you move, you're in for it.

Every three hours, one man leaves and another enters. The victim doesn't change his story, So what were you up to in your village, Working to earn enough money to feed my family, the first question and the first answer, the question is as predictable as the answer is true, and this man should be allowed to go free because he has told the truth, Do you mean working or do you mean distributing communist newspapers, you can't fool us, you know, But I wasn't involved in that kind of thing, sir, All right, so you weren't distributing newspapers, you were taking it up the bum, you and your friends were taking it up the bum from the man in charge so that he would teach you the Moscow doctrine, isn't that right, look, if you want to go back to Monte Lavre and see your children again, tell us the full story, don't cover up for the buddies you held meetings with, think of your family, think of your own freedom. And João Mau-Tempo is thinking about his family and his freedom, but he remembers the story about the dog and the partridge told by Sigismundo Canastro, and says nothing, Go on, tell us the story, what is it you lot say, you bastards: Those thieves in government won't give us what we want, so we're going to get rid of them, we're going to rebel against them and against Salazar's laws, isn't that what you say to each other, isn't that what you intend doing, tell me the truth, commie, don't cover up, if you tell us the whole story, you can leave for Monte Lavre tomorrow and see your children again, and João Mau-Tempo, thinking of the skeleton of the dog face to face with the partridge, says again, Sir, I've told you my story, I was arrested in nineteen forty-five, but since then I've never been involved in anything political, and if someone has told you otherwise, he's lying. They hurled him against the wall, beat him, called him every name under the sun, and this they did over and over, without letup, but the victim still did not change his story.

João Mau-Tempo will stand there like a statue for seventy-two hours. His legs will swell up, he'll feel dizzy, and every time his legs give way, he'll be beaten with the ruler and the stick, not that hard, but enough to hurt. He didn't cry, but he had tears in his eyes, his eyes swam with tears, even a stone would have taken pity on him. After a few hours, the swelling went down, but beneath his skin, his veins became as thick as fingers. His heart shifts position, it's a thudding, deafening hammer echoing inside his head, and then finally his strength deserts him, he can no longer remain on his feet, his body droops without his realizing it, and he's crouching now, he's a poor farm laborer from the latifundio, squeezing out a final turd, the turd of cowardice, Get up, you swine, but João Mau-Tempo couldn't get up, he wasn't pretending, this was another of his truths. On the last night, he heard screams and moans coming from the room next door, then Inspector Paveia came in, accompanied by a large number of policemen, and when the screams started again, growing ever shriller, Paveia walked over to him with calculated slowness and said in a voice intended to terrify, So, Mau-Tempo, now that you've been to Monte Lavre and back, you can tell us your story. From the depths of his misery, his hunched body almost pressed against the floorboards, his eyes clouded, João Mau-Tempo answered, I have no story to tell, I've said all I have to say. It's a modest sentence, it's the skeleton of the dog after two years, a sentence barely worth recording compared to what others have said, From the top of those pyramids, forty centuries look down on you, I'd rather be queen for a day than duchess for a lifetime, Love one another, but Inspector Paveia's blood is boiling, And what about the twenty-five newspapers you distributed in your village, if you deny it, I'll kill you right now. And João Mau-Tempo thought, Life or death, and said nothing. Maybe Inspector Paveia was once again late for mass, or perhaps leaving his prisoner seventy-two hours on his feet was enough for the first round, but what he said was, Take the bastard back to Aljube and let him rest there, then bring him back here again to tell his story, otherwise he goes straight to the cemetery.

Two dragons approach, grab João Mau-Tempo by the arms and drag him down the stairs, from the third floor to the ground floor, and while they're hauling him along, they say, Tell him your story, Mau-Tempo, it will be better for you and for your family, besides, if you don't, the inspector will pack you off to Tarrafal,* he knows everything, a friend of yours from Vendas Novas told him, all you have to do is confirm what he said. And João Mau-Tempo, who can barely stand, who feels his feet flopping from step to step as if they belonged to someone else, answers, If they want to kill me, let them, but I have nothing to tell. They bundled him into the police van, it was a short journey, there had been no earthquake, all the churches were still triumphantly standing, and when they reached Aljube and opened the door, Out you jump, he missed the step and fell, and again was dragged inside, his legs were slightly steadier now, but not much, and then they shoved him into a cell, which, either by chance or on purpose, was the one he had been in before. Almost fainting, he collapsed face-forward onto the rolled mattress, but although he felt as if he were in a dream, he had just enough strength to unroll and fall on top of it, and there he lay for forty-eight hours, as if dead. He is clothed and shod, a broken statue held together only by his internal wiring, a puppet from the latifundio who peers over the top of the curtain and makes faces while he dreams, his beard continues to grow, and from one corner of his mouth a trickle of saliva forges a slow path through the stubble and the sweat. During those two days, the guard will look in now and then to see if the cell's occupant is alive or dead, the

---

* A prison camp in Cape Verde, known as the Camp of Slow Death, where Salazar sent opponents of his regime.

second time he looks in, he feels relieved, because the sleeper has, at least, changed position, but the guard knows the routine, whenever these men come back from playing statues, they always sleep like this, they don't even need to eat, but now the prisoner has slept enough, he's sleeping less profoundly, Wake up, your lunch is here on the shelf, and João Mau-Tempo sat up on the mattress, uncertain as to whether he had dreamed those words or not, because although no one else is in the cell, he can smell food, he feels a great and urgent hunger, but when he makes a first attempt to stand, his legs buckle and his eyes grow dim from the sheer effort, he tries again, it's only two steps from there to the shelf, the worst thing is that he won't be able to sit down to eat, because in prison you eat standing up so as to get the food down more quickly, and João Mau-Tempo, who had been small for his age as a child and never grew much taller, has to stand on tiptoe, a torment for someone in his weakened state, and if he drops any food on the floor, he knows he'll be punished, he who gives the food gives the orders.

Five days passed, which would have had as much to tell as any of the others, but that is the trouble with stories, sometimes they have to leapfrog over time, because suddenly the narrator is in a hurry, not to finish, not yet, but to reach an important episode, a change of plan, for example, the beat that João Mau-Tempo's heart skips simply because the guard comes into his cell and says, Mau-Tempo, get ready to leave, I want those blankets returned to the stores, along with the bowl and the spoon, have this place shipshape by the time I come back. The problem with these men from the latifundio, especially when they're innocent, is that they take everything so literally, call a spade a spade, which is why João Mau-Tempo is so happy, hoping for the best, Perhaps they're going to set me free, the man's a fool, as becomes immediately evident when the policeman returns to accompany him to the quartermaster's store, where he deposits blankets, spoon and bowl, and where he receives the few personal items that have been kept there, and now,

We're taking you to the mixed cell, you're not incommunicado anymore, which means you can write to your family and ask them to send anything you need, and then he opened the door and inside was a whole world of people, of all nationalities, well, that's just a manner of speaking, meaning that there were a lot of people, some of whom were foreigners, but João Mau-Tempo is too shy and too constrained by his strong Alentejo dialect ever to be on friendly terms with them, however, as soon as the door closed, all the other Portuguese men surrounded him, wanting to know why he was there and if he had any news from outside. João Mau-Tempo has nothing to hide, he tells them everything that has happened to him, and so steadfast is he in his declaration that he hasn't been involved in any political activities since nineteen forty-five that he repeats it there and then, though there's no need, because no one has asked him.

João Mau-Tempo proved very popular, and once, coming across a fellow prisoner smoking, he asked him for a cigarette, which was rather cheeky given that he didn't know him from Adam, but other prisoners immediately offered him tobacco too, and best of all was when another man, who had overheard their conversation, came bearing an ounce of superior tobacco, a pack of cigarette papers and a box of matches, Just say if you need anything, comrade, it's share and share alike here, you can imagine João Mau-Tempo's feelings, with the first puff he grew six inches, with the second he returned to his normal height, but greatly fortified, a diminutive figure among the other men, who smiled as they watched him smoking. And since even in the lives of prisoners there are happy events and coincidences, two days later, João Mau-Tempo was summoned to a room outside the mixed cell, where the guard, beaming as if he himself were the donor, for guards are contradictory creatures, said, Mau-Tempo, a gentleman from your village has brought you these clothes, four ounces of tobacco and twenty escudos. João Mau-Tempo was touched, more by the reference to

Monte Lavre than by the unexpected gift, and he asked, Who was the gentleman, and the guard answered, It doesn't matter, to us a donor is a donor, which was something João Mau-Tempo didn't know. He went back into the room clutching his treasure, and as soon as he did, he let out a shout that could have been heard all over the latifundio, Right, comrades, if anyone wants to smoke, here's tobacco for you, and another voice responded equally loudly, for these are things that need to be trumpeted abroad, That's how it is, comrades, share and share alike, we're all brothers here and we all have the same rights. Normally, one would choose quite different substances as proof of solidarity, but everyone takes what he needs or gives what he has, in this case cigarettes, little threads of tobacco rolled up inside the white cigarette paper, and now the tremulous tip of the tongue running along the edge and sealing it up, job done, humanity would be in a bad way indeed if it failed to understand such large gestures.

Some leave, others do not, new faces arrive, but they are rarely strangers, there is always someone who says, Well, fancy seeing you here, and after a few days, a policeman comes to the door of the room and says, Mau-Tempo, put your jacket on, we're going for a stroll, but you'll be right back, no need to take anything else. Perhaps he'll be back, perhaps he won't, but João Mau-Tempo is there to say that his heart dropped into his boots, and this is far truer than his statement that he hasn't been involved in political activities for four years. He repeats the journey with a hound at his side, this time a big, almost beardless lad who seems nervous, perhaps he's not yet used to this work, he keeps reaching around to feel his back pocket and doesn't utter a word, but at least João Mau-Tempo can look at the people passing by, they must know I'm a prisoner, he can see the trams, peer in at shop windows, this time it really is almost a stroll, so much so that he nearly forgets to feel afraid, then the fear comes flooding back, jumbling his thoughts, troubling his blood, and he misses the mixed cell, the shared ciga-

rettes and the conversations. He feels a sudden sympathy for statues, because for all we know the bronze and marble variety might
find it hard to stay standing, how is it that they don't get a cramp,
those men with their arms outstretched, those animals frozen in
the same posture, never giving in, never running away, though they
lack man's strength of will, despite which a man so often weak-
ens and crouches down, and no amount of kicking will make him
stand, he could die for all he cares, as long as his tongue doesn't
speak, except to repeat the same lie over and over. But the idea that
the torment is about to start again, that he is going to experience
the same pain or worse, this is what fills João Mau-Tempo's mind,
and suddenly a great darkness falls on the city, despite its being
broad daylight and hot, as it always is in August, but all the ungrateful creature can think is, what will become of me, what tor-
ture awaits me.

The door opened again, João Mau-Tempo went up the steps,
followed by the hound, and entered the room, and look who's here,
it's the man from Vendas Novas who traveled with João Mau-
Tempo as far as Terreiro do Paço, his name is Leandro Leandres,
and now he says in a scornful voice, Do you know why you've been
brought here, and João Mau-Tempo, always polite and respectful, says, No, sir, I don't, and Leandro Leandres says, You've come
to tell the rest of your story, but there's no point now describing
what happens next, it's the same old thing, the same conversation,
how many newspapers were distributed, and how local commit-
tees were formed and why did they stop meeting, and how many
members were there, and who, look, someone here gave us your
name, so it must be true, and if you don't confess, you won't get out
of here alive, it would be best for you if you talked, you know, but
João Mau-Tempo isn't at all sure about that, and even if he was, It's
been four years since I so much as touched any political papers,
and they were only ones I picked up in the streets or along the
way, apart from that I can't remember anyone actually giving them

to me, that was years ago, all I think about is my work, I swear. The conversation was always the same, the same questions and answers, the same grilling and the same lying, but this time there were no beatings and the statue that is João Mau-Tempo remained in his natural position, sitting on a chair, he looked as if he were posing for a portrait, except that his soul was jumping about inside his heart like a poor, frightened lunatic, and his pale but constant will kept saying, You mustn't talk, lie all you want but don't talk. There was another difference too, the fact that a hound of a lower category was typing out all the questions and answers, but after a few pages there was nothing more to write, because the conversation was like dredging up water with a wheel equipped with bottomless buckets, going round and round, the mule was treading in its own dung now and the sun sinking, and that was where the statements ended, and the man at the typewriter asked, Where's this guy's original statement, and Leandro Leandres, not realizing what he was saying, answered, It's over there, along with Albuquerque's statement, João Mau-Tempo had tormented himself over and over as to who had given them his name, and now he knew, it was Albuquerque, and knowing this was so painful and so sad, what must they have done to him to make him talk, or did he do so willingly, what could he have been thinking, well, it happens, and João Mau-Tempo cannot know that some years later, he will see Albuquerque, the squealer, in Monte Lavre, and remember that he was the one who once said, If they turn up here, I'll shoot them, I mean it, and yet in the end he had squealed on him, and when Albuquerque got out of prison, he became a Protestant priest, not that we have anything against religion, but why go around proclaiming the salvation of all men when he couldn't even save his few comrades, what will he have to say for himself at the hour of his death, but now all that João Mau-Tempo feels is a great sorrow and a great sense of relief that at least he has not talked, perhaps they won't beat me again or make me play the statue, I'm not sure I could take it.

João Mau-Tempo returned to Aljube, then, after a few days, he was taken from there to Caxias, and news of this finally reached Monte Lavre. Letters will come and go, everything has to be meticulously arranged between Faustina and João Mau-Tempo, because these things are no joke, everything has to be worked out to the last detail if a person is traveling a long way to be at a certain place at a certain time, even when the meeting is not a clandestine one, even when it's the police themselves who open the door and say, Come in. No, you have to take account of every eventuality, from Monte Lavre to Vendas Novas by cart, then from Vendas Novas to Barreiro by train, possibly in the same carriage that brought João Mau-Tempo and Leandro Leandres, and then by boat, it's only the second time Faustina Mau-Tempo has seen the sea, this vast estuary, and then again by train to Caxias, where the sea is suddenly much bigger, This is real sea, she says, and the woman who met her at Terreiro do Paço and who lives in the city smiles sympathetically and kindly at her friend's limited experience and says, Yes, that's the sea all right, but says nothing of her own ignorance about what the sea really is, not this modest opening of arms between two towers, but an infinite, liquid longing, a continuous sifting of glass and foam, a mineral hardness that softens and chills, the home of the great fish and of sad shipwrecks and of poems.

It is very true that while one may know some things, one cannot know everything, and Faustina Mau-Tempo's friend knows where to get off the train in Caxias but not where the prison is, however, she doesn't want to admit that she doesn't know and sets off in one direction, saying, It must be down here. It's August, and it's baking hot at this hour, which is fast approaching the hour so laboriously communicated and memorized, the hour of the visit, in the end, they had to ask a passerby, realized they had gone entirely the wrong way and turned back, already weary with all the toing and froing, and Faustina Mau-Tempo took off her tight shoes, to which her feet were unaccustomed, and was left in her stocking feet, this, however, was a big mistake, and only someone with no heart could laugh, this is the kind of humiliation that burns itself into the memory for the rest of one's life, the tarmac had half melted in the heat, and her stockings stuck fast as soon as she planted her feet on it, and the more she pulled, the more the stockings stretched, it was like a circus act, the funniest of the season, enough, enough, the clown's mother has just died, and everyone is crying, the clown isn't funny, he's frightened, and that is how we feel about Faustina Mau-Tempo, and we form a screen so that her friend can help her off with her stockings, modestly, for women who have only ever known one man are incurably shy, and now she's barefoot, and we can go home, and if any of us do smile, it's out of tenderness. But when Faustina Mau-Tempo arrives at the fort, her feet are in a terrible state, made worse by wearing shoes without stockings, they are black with tarmac and bleeding from where the skin has been rubbed raw, what a hard life the poor have.

The visitors have left, the hour has passed, and no one came to see João Mau-Tempo, his companions tease him in that stupid, joshing, manly way, She's forgotten all about you, You certainly weren't expecting to be stood up, while at the entrance, poor Faustina Mau-Tempo is demanding to be allowed in, Is this where my husband is, she asks, his name's João Mau-Tempo, and the man at the door responds jokingly, No, there's no one here by that name, and the other says mockingly, Do you mean your husband's in prison, this is their way of passing the time, for they lead very dull lives, they don't even get to beat up the prisoners, other men do that, but Faustina Mau-Tempo can't tell the difference, Yes, he is, and you're the ones who brought him, so he must be here, but her anger was like the fury of a sparrow, the rage of a chicken, the wrath of a lamb, finally, though, the man leafed through a book and said, Yes, you're right, he is here, in room six, but you can't visit him now, visiting time is over. Faustina Mau-Tempo is perfectly within her rights to burst into tears. She is a pillar crumbling, we can see the cracks appear and bits break off, and this pillar of the latifundio has painful feet too, she can cry about that now as well, and for everything else she has suffered and will suffer in her life, now is the moment to cry out your tears, pull out all the stops, Faustina Mau-Tempo, dissolve into tears, perhaps you'll manage to touch the hearts of these two iron dragons, or, if they have no heart, they might at least prefer not to be embarrassed, and since you're just a poor woman, they're not going to throw you out bodily, so weep, demand to see your husband, All right, all right, woman, I'll go and see if they'll let you in on a special dispensation, but this is an expression Faustina Mau-Tempo doesn't understand, what is a dispensation, let alone a special one, and how will they let her in on one, will it help her to see her husband. Those who travel by crooked paths also arrive, and though the visit will last no more than five minutes, that's long enough for two people who haven't seen each other for far too long, João Mau-Tempo is there, full of hope, his comrades tell him, It must be your wife, and it is, Faustina, João, and they embrace, and both shed copious tears, and he wants to know about the children and she wants to know how he is, and three minutes have gone, and are you well, and how have you been, have you had work, and Gracinda, and Amélia, and António, they're all fine, but you're a lot thinner, be sure not to get ill, five minutes, goodbye, goodbye, send them my love, ah, so much love, come back soon, I will, I know where it is now and I won't get lost, and I won't either, goodbye.

There will be other visits, different, less rushed, his daughters will come, his brother Anselmo will come, and António Mau-Tempo will come, only to leave feeling angry, no one made him angry, but that is how he feels when he leaves, he will stand some way off, a picture of rage, staring at the prison, he is not the António

Mau-Tempo we know, Manuel Espada will come, he will enter looking grave-faced and leave lit up by a serene light, and cousins and uncles will come too, some of whom live in Lisbon, but they will only be allowed in the corridors, peering in through a screen so fine that it's hard to see the people on the other side, and with a policeman patrolling up and down, listening for any complaints from the prisoners. And the months will pass, the long days and the even longer prison nights, the summer will end, the autumn will go and winter will arrive, João Mau-Tempo is still there, he is no longer summoned for interrogation, they have forgotten he exists, perhaps he'll stay there for good. Sigismundo Canastro had also been arrested, as João Mau-Tempo will find out later, when he is back in Monte Lavre and hears that Sigismundo has been freed, and then there he is, they embrace with free hearts, I didn't talk, Neither did I, It was Albuquerque. Sigismundo has had a much harder time, and yet he laughs, while João Mau-Tempo cannot help but feel a certain melancholy about the injustice done to them. There is much talk in room six, they discuss politics and other matters, some men study, others teach, there are lessons in reading, arithmetic, some do drawings, it's a people's university, about which we will say no more, because eternity would not be long enough.

Today he is to be freed. Six months have passed, it's January. Only last week, João Mau-Tempo was working on the access road along with other residents of room six, working in rain so cold it was like melted snow, and now he is sitting wondering what life holds in store for him, many men have been tried, but he has not, and some say this is a good sign, then the door opens and a guard says in his usual arrogant tone, João Mau-Tempo, and João Mau-Tempo stands at attention as the prison rules dictate, and the guard says, You're leaving prison, get your things ready and be quick about it. Those who are staying are so delighted, it's extraordinary, it's as if they themselves were being freed, and one says, The sooner they empty the prisons, the better, we're not achieving anything here, it's as logical as saying, The sooner they give me the tools, the sooner I can get down to work, and then everyone joins in, it's like a mother dressing her child, someone is putting on his shoes for him and another is pulling on his shirt or shaking out his jacket, anyone would think João Mau-Tempo was going to meet the Pope, it's amazing, they're like children, any moment now they'll all burst out crying, well, if they don't, João Mau-Tempo soon will when they ask, Now, Mau-Tempo, have you enough money to get home, and he replies, I have a little, comrades, but I'll be all right, and they start collecting money, five escudos here, ten there, and they manage to scrape together enough for the journey with a little left over, and then, when he sees that a little money can also be great love, João Mau-Tempo will no longer be able to hold back his tears, and he will say, Thank you, comrades, and goodbye, I wish you all the best, and thank you again for everything you've done for me. This party atmosphere is repeated each time someone is released, ah, the joys of prison life.

It was dark when the van dropped João Mau-Tempo at the door of Aljube prison, it seems that this devilish Black Maria knows no other roads, and when João Mau-Tempo steps out, a free man this time, the policeman says to him, Go on, get lost, he seems almost sorry to see him leave, but that's what they're like, they grow fond of the prisoners and find it hard to lose them. João Mau-Tempo runs down the road as if the devil were after him, so much so that he glances over his shoulder to see if anyone is following him, perhaps the police indulge in such amusements, pretending to set a prisoner free and then mounting a hunt for him, and however hard the poor man runs, there'll be a net waiting for him down some passageway, and he'll be caught again, shoved into the police car, with all the policemen laughing and clutching their bellies, God, it was funny, oh, I haven't laughed so much in ages, not even at the circus. They're perfectly capable of such tricks.

The street is completely deserted, it's black night, it's not raining, which is fortunate, but the wind whips in between these tall buildings like the blunt razor of a barber in a hurry, it keeps cutting through João Mau-Tempo's thin clothes, the wind is as naked as he is, or so it seems. He has stopped running, his legs feel awkward and he's out of breath, he's forgotten how to walk, he leans against a wall with his bag and a suitcase tied up with string, and although both are quite light, his arms can barely carry them, which is why he puts them down on the ground, who would think it, this same man who once carried such enormous weights couldn't swing a cat by its tail, and if it weren't so cold, he would lie down, he has too much suffering on his shoulders to remain standing, and yet he does. People pass him, there's always someone out and about, but they don't look at him, each thinking about his own life, I've got quite enough problems of my own, thank you, they have no idea that the man standing at the corner has just been let out of Caxias prison, where he has spent the past six months, and where he was beaten and made to play the statue for seventy-two hours, they wouldn't believe that such things could happen in our lovely country, such stories are doubtless greatly exaggerated. What will João Mau-Tempo do in a city he doesn't know, there is no door he can knock on, Comrades, give me shelter for the night, I've just got out of prison, that would be an unusual conversation, and he has no idea whose houses these are, he was arrested in Monte Lavre by the guard José Calmedo, and that is where he must return, not now, because it's dark, but tomorrow, with the money given him by men who needed it themselves, he knows he has comrades there, but he can hardly go to Caxias now, knock on the door of room six, assuming he would be allowed back into the prison, and, when they opened, say, Comrades, give me shelter for the night, he is clearly mad, or perhaps he fell asleep despite the cold, yes, he must have fallen asleep, for he's no longer standing up as he thought, but sitting on his suitcase, and now it occurs to him, well, it had occurred to him before but now it occurs to him again, to go and knock on the door of the house where his sister works as a maid and say, Maria da Conceição, do you think your employers would let me sleep here tonight, but he won't do this, although in other circumstances he might have, they would have told Maria da Conceição to put a mattress down in the kitchen, you can't leave a fellow Christian to sleep out in the street like a stray dog, but given that he has just come out of prison, out of that prison and for those particular reasons, even if they agreed, they might view his sister differently afterward, poor thing, she never married and has always worked for the same boss, it's as if that's what she was born for, who knows what they will have told her already, it's not hard to imagine, The ungrateful wretches, they would starve to death if it wasn't for us, your brother will pay dearly for those ideas of his, they're against us, you see, they're all against us, but we're your friends and we won't punish you for his crazy ideas, but from now on, it would be best if he didn't come to the house, so you be careful now, you've been warned.

This is the domestic litany repeated by the mistress of the house, the master of the house is more categorical and more to the point, He's never to set foot in this house again, and I'm going to tell our estates in Monte Lavre that he is to be given no more work, let him go to Moscow. It seems that João Mau-Tempo went back to sleep, he must be very tired indeed to be able to sleep in this bitter cold, he stamps his feet on the ground, and the noise echoes and re-echoes in the icy air, a policeman might come along and arrest him for disturbing the peace, then João Mau-Tempo picks up his bag and his suitcase and heads back down the road, he can barely walk, he's limping, he seems to recall that the station is off to the left, but he's afraid he might get lost, that's why he asks a passerby, who tells him, Yes, you're going in the right direction, and adds a few more details, João Mau-Tempo, holding his suitcase and his bag in numb hands, is about to carry on, but the passerby asks, Do you want some help, here we all tremble, what if this man is a thief and has decided to rob this poor farm laborer, what could be easier, even in the dark it's clear he can barely walk, No, sir, thank you, says João Mau-Tempo politely, and the man does not insist, he isn't a ruffian after all, he says only, You look like you've been in prison, and we, who know João Mau-Tempo and how sensitive he is to kind words, can hear him telling his whole story, how he was in Caxias for six months and has just arrived in Lisbon, how they dumped him there, and how he has to get back to his village, to Monte Lavre, in the parish of Montemor, yes, I'm from the Alentejo, he doesn't know if there's a boat at this hour or a train, I'm going to the station to see, no, he has nowhere to sleep, although a sister of his works as a housemaid, But I don't want to bother her, her employers might not like it, and the other man asks, he's a very inquisitive fellow, And what if there isn't a boat and a train, and João Mau-Tempo says simply, Then I'll spend the night in the station, there's sure to be a bench there, it's a shame it's so cold, but I'm used to that, thanks very much for your help, and having said this, he moves off, but the other man says, I'll come with you, let me carry that bag for you, and João Mau-Tempo hesitates, but having spent six months with humane and generous men, who looked after him, taught him, gave him tobacco and money for the journey, it seems churlish to distrust this man, so he hands him the bag, the city can be full of surprises, and off they go, down the remaining streets, as far as the big square, under the arcade and into the station, João Mau-Tempo has difficulty reading the timetable, all those tiny figures, and the man helps him, running his finger down the columns, No, there's no train, the earliest one is tomorrow morning, and when he hears this, João Mau-Tempo immediately starts looking for a place where he can curl up, but the man says, You're tired, and you're obviously hungry too, come and sleep at my house, have a bowl of soup and rest, you'll die of cold if you stay here, that's what he said, no one believes such things can happen, and yet it's true, João Mau-Tempo can only answer, Thank you very much, it's a real act of charity, Father Agamedes would cry hosanna were he here, he would praise the kindness of man to man, and he's quite right, this man carrying the bag on his back deserves to be praised, though he's not a churchgoer, not that he's said as much, but the narrator knows these things, as well as others that have nothing to do with the story, because this is a story about the latifundio, not about the city. The man is older than João Mau-Tempo, but stronger and quicker on his feet, indeed, he has to slow down to accommodate the painful pace of this man raised from the dead, and to cheer him up, he says, I live near here, in Alfama, and he turns onto Rua da Alfândega, and João Mau-Tempo is already feeling better, and they set off down damp, steep-sided alleyways, well, in this weather it's hardly surprising they're damp, a door, the narrowest of stairways, an attic room, Hi, Ermelinda, this gentleman is sleeping here tonight, he's going home tomorrow and has nowhere to stay, Ermelinda is a plump woman who opens the door to them as if she were opening her arms, Come in, and João Mau-Tempo, and sensitive readers, forgive me, and those who only appreciate large, dramatic events, but the first thing he notices is the smell of food, a bean and vegetable soup bubbling on the stove, and the man says, Make yourself at home, and then, What's your name, and João Mau-Tempo, who is already sitting down, overcome by a sudden weariness, tells him his name, Well, I'm Ricardo Reis,* and this is my wife Ermelinda, these are ordinary enough names, and that's pretty much all we know about them, that and these bowls of soup on the kitchen table, Eat up, the cold is easing now, Lisbon has turned out to be a kindly place, this window at the back looks out over the river, there are a few small lights on boats, but fewer on the farther shore, who would have thought that one day, seen from here, they would be a feast for the eyes.

---

* One of the heteronyms of the Portuguese writer Fernando Pessoa and the main character in Saramago's later novel *The Year of the Death of Ricardo Reis.*

Have another glass of wine, and perhaps that's why, after a second glass of strong wine, João Mau-Tempo is smiling so broadly, even when he tells them what happened to him in prison, by the time he's finished it's getting late, and he can barely keep his eyes open, Ricardo Reis is looking serious, and Ermelinda is drying her tears, and then they say, It's time you went to bed, you need to rest, and João Mau-Tempo doesn't notice that it's a double bed they've given him, he hears footsteps in the corridor, but they're not the guard's footsteps, not the guard, not the guard, and, free at last, he falls asleep.

THERE HAVE BEEN six months of changes, which sometimes seem too few and sometimes too many. They are barely noticeable in the landscape, apart from the usual seasonal variations, but it's frightening to see how people have aged, both the men just let out of prison and those who never left Monte Lavre, and how the children have grown, only João Mau-Tempo and Sigismundo Canastro seem unchanged in each other's eyes. Sigismundo Canastro arrived yesterday and has already said that they must meet and talk, he's as stubborn and determined as ever, you see, but that's the way he is. Some people, however, are a pleasure to look at, as is the case with Gracinda Mau-Tempo, who has grown into a beautiful young woman, marriage clearly suits her, or so say the gossips, both the kindly and the cruel, but that's as far as the latter will go, and there are other changes too, for example, Father Agamedes has gone from being tall and thin to being short and fat, and the amount of money owed at the shop has grown enormously, as is to be expected when the man of the house has been away. That's why, when the time came, João Mau-Tempo set off with his daughter Amélia for the ricefields near Elvas, and to give you an idea of the geographical sensibilities of these rustic inhabitants, it's said in

Monte Lavre that beyond Elvas lies Spanish Extremadura, heaven knows how they stumbled upon this knowledge of a larger universe, which pays no heed to frontiers or borders, and if we want to know what lies behind João Mau-Tempo's excursion to Évora, it's largely to do with the latifundio's suspicions about the ways and wiles of João Mau-Tempo, political prisoner. It's true that he was never tried, but that's the fault of the police, who are not as efficient as they ought to be. After a few months, things will get back to normal, but meanwhile, it's best if he keeps his distance, then he won't contaminate our beloved land, and as for Sigismundo Canastro, they tell him there's no work and that he'll have to find it elsewhere.

So off João Mau-Tempo went to Elvas, taking with him his daughter Amélia, the one with the bad teeth, although if she had good teeth, she would easily be a match for her sister. Let it be said now that hell is not far away. There are one hundred and fifty men and women, divided into five groups, and this torment will last sixteen weeks, it's a veritable harvest of scabies and fevers, a labor not of love but of pain, weeding and planting from before the sun rises until after it has set, and when night falls, one hundred and fifty ghosts trudge up to the place where they have their lodgings, the men to one side, the women to the other, all of them scratching at the scabies caught in the flooded fields, all suffering from the fevers picked up from the rice paddies. You need sugar, milk, rice and a few eggs to make that delicacy rice pudding, how often do I have to tell you, Maria, it should be fluffy, not this stodgy pap, you should be able to taste every grain. All through the night in the dormitories, you can hear these poor people sighing and moaning, the anxious scratching of hard, black nails on skin that is already bleeding, while others lie, teeth chattering and staring up at the roof with eyes glassy with fever. There is little difference between this and the death camps, except that fewer people actually die, doubtless due to the Christian charity and concomitant self-interest with which the bosses, almost every day, load up the trucks with all that mangy, feverish misery and transport it to the hospital in Elvas, some today, others tomorrow, an endless coming and going, the poor things set off close to death, but are saved by the miraculous medicine, which, in a matter of days, has them as good as new, with very weak, tremulous legs, it's true, but who cares about such trivia, you can go back to work, the doctors say, addressing us contemptuously as *tu*, and the truck disgorges its load of broken-backed laborers, there's work to be done, there's no time to waste, Are you better, father, asked Amélia, and he answered, Yes, daughter, what could be simpler.

There haven't been that many changes. Weeding and planting the ricefields is done exactly as it was in my grandfather's day, the creepy-crawlies in the water haven't changed their stings or their slime since the Lord God made them, and if a hidden sliver of glass cuts a finger, the blood that flows is still the same color. You would need a lot of imagination to invent any extraordinary incidents. This way of life is made up of repeated words and repeated gestures, the arc made by the sickle is precisely adjusted to the length of the arm, and the sawing of the blade through the dry stems of wheat produces the same sound, always the same sound, how is it that the ears of these men and women do not grow weary, it's the same with that hoarse-voiced bird that some say lives in the cork oak, between the bark and the trunk, and that screams whenever they tear off its skin or perhaps pluck out its feathers, and what is left is painful, goosepimpled flesh, but this idea that trees cry out and feel pain comes purely from the narrator's private imaginings. We would do far better to notice Manuel Espada perched, barefoot, at the top of this cork oak, for he is a serious, barefoot bird, hopping from branch to branch, not that he sings, he doesn't feel like singing, the real boss here is the cork ax, chop, chop, chop, making circular incisions around the larger boughs and vertical ones on the trunk, then the handle of the ax serves as a lever, go on, push, there, can't you hear the hoarse-voiced bird that lives in the cork oak, it's screaming, not that anyone feels any pity. The cylinders of bark rain down, falling on the cork already cut from the trunks, there is no poetry in this, we'd like to see someone make a sonnet out of one man losing his grip on his ax and watching it skitter down the branch, catching the bark as it falls, and impaling itself in a bare foot, coarse and grubby but so fragile, because when it comes to skin and the blade of an ax, there is little difference between the delicate, rosy foot of some cultivated maiden and the calloused hoof of a cork cutter, it takes the same time for the blood to spurt out.

But here we are talking about work and the working day, and we nearly forgot to describe the night when João Mau-Tempo arrived back in Monte Lavre, when his house was filled almost to bursting with his closest friends and their wives, those who had them, as well as a cacophony of young lads, some of them intruders, unrelated to any of those present, not that anyone cared, and António Mau-Tempo, who had finished his national service and was now working on the cork plantations, and his sisters Gracinda and Amélia, and his brother-in-law Manuel Espada, a whole crowd of people. Faustina cried all the time, out of joy and grief, she had only to recall the day on which her husband was arrested, who knows why, and taken to Vendas Novas and to Lisbon, with no idea when, if ever, he would come back. She didn't talk about the sad case of her stockings ruined by the tarmac, not a word, that would remain forever a secret between the couple, both of whom felt slightly ashamed, knowing that, even in Monte Lavre, someone might make fun of them, the poor woman with her stockings stuck fast to the tarmac road, dreadful, who wouldn't do their best to avoid such mockery. João Mau-Tempo described his misfortunes and spared no detail, so that they would know just what he had suffered at the hands of the dragons of the PIDE and the national guard. All of this would be confirmed and repeated later by Sigismundo Canastro, but although he wasn't so insensitive as to treat the matter lightly, he did tell the most alarming stories as if they were perfectly natural, and recounted everything with such an air of simplicity that not even the women wept for pity, and the young boys moved away, disappointed, he might as well have been talking about the state of the wheatfields, and perhaps, who knows, they were, indeed, one and the same thing. Maybe that is why, one day, Manuel Espada approached Sigismundo Canastro, with all the respect that their difference in age required, and said, Senhor Sigismundo, if I'm needed, I can help. We would be much deceived if we were to think that this impulse came from Sigismundo Canastro's quiet way of describing his experiences, which, in temperaments like Manuel Espada's, might well have provoked such an important decision, the proof of this is that Manuel Espada went on to say, No one should treat a man the way they treated my father-in-law, and Sigismundo Canastro answered, No one should treat men the way we were treated, but let's talk later, these arrests and imprisonments have muddied the waters, best to let a little time pass to allow the mud to settle, because these things, like fishing nets, take longer to mend than to break, and Manuel Espada responded, I'll wait as long as is necessary.

Sometimes, when you sit down to read the history of this Portuguese land, you come across such silly things they make you smile, although in this case, outright laughter seems to be called for, and I mean no offense, each person does what he can or as the hierarchy orders him to do, and if it was a fine and praiseworthy thing for Dona Filipa de Vilhena* to arm her sons so that they could go and fight for the restoration of the fatherland, what can one make of Manuel Espada, who, with no cavalry to back him up, says sim-

---

* Filipa de Vilhena was a Portuguese noblewoman who became a symbol of patriotism in Portugal when, in 1640, she urged her sons to fight for the restoration of the country's independence from Spain. Almeida Garrett wrote a play about her, which further contributed to her heroic image.

ply, Here I am, he has no mother to urge him on, she, of course, is dead, only his own will. Dona Filipa did not lack for people to sing her praises and describe her heroism, there was João Pinto Ribeiro, the Count of Ericeira, Vicente Gusmão Soares, Almeida Garrett, and Vieira Portuense painted her portrait, but Manuel Espada and Sigismundo Canastro have no one to take their part, it's simply a conversation between two men, they have said what they have to say and now each goes his own way, there is no call for oratory or paintbrushes, this narrator is all they need.

Indeed, as an aid to our understanding of these events, let us take another slow walk about the latifundio, with no particular goal in mind apart from picking up a stone or a branch and giving it a proper name, seeing what animals live there and why, and since we can hear guns firing over there, although what that's about we have no idea, let us begin right here, well, what a coincidence, this is the same road that José Calmedo took when he went to arrest João Mau-Tempo, indeed, given how easy it is to find oneself back where one was before, the latifundio seems more like a minifundio, not a large estate but a very small one. True, the last time we came this way it wasn't quite as noisy, but there's the ruined water wheel and, beyond, invisible, the brick kiln, don't worry about the shooting, it's probably just target practice or something, with proper bullets, mind, none of those lead pellets fit only for a little light hunting, quite a different kettle of fish.

The firing has stopped and we can walk on quite happily now, but look, there's a man coming from the same direction as the shooting, by his looks we would say he's one of us, and he crosses the valley, that smooth expanse of dark earth, goes over a small bridge with a low handrail, it's only a tiny stream, and starts to climb up this side of the valley, through thick, thorny undergrowth marked by the faintest of trails, Why is he going over there, with no hoe and no mattock, with no ax and no pruning hook, let's sit here and rest awhile, he'll have to go back down again and then we'll know, you were saying that this is a wilderness, Well, it is, and don't go thinking that the track through the brambles will be much use to the lackey who just passed, You mean he's a lackey, He certainly is, But he's not wearing livery, No, livery's a thing of the past, from the days when the countess armed her own sons, if you know who I mean, no, nowadays lackeys dress like you and me, well, not like you, you're from the city, even we can tell them apart by the way they behave, But why do you say that the track through the brambles won't be much use to him, Because what he's looking for lies off the beaten track, and he can't turn around, he has to go straight ahead, those are his orders, using his crook to beat a path through the undergrowth, that's worse than useless, But why is he doing it, Because he's a lackey, and the more scratches he has on him when he goes back, the better, So that old rule applies here as well, does it, It does, but to go back to our conversation, I was saying what a wilderness it is here, but it wasn't always like this, believe you me, there was a time when this whole area was cultivated right down to the bottom of the valley, it's good soil, and there are springs aplenty, not to mention the stream, So how did it become like this, Let's see now, the father of the present owners, the ones who were doing the shooting, eventually took over this whole area, it was the usual thing, a few small farmers got into financial difficulties, and he, I can't remember what his name was now, Gilberto or Adalberto or Norberto, something like that, lent them money, which they couldn't pay back, well, times were hard, and he ended up owning the lot, That doesn't seem possible, It's perfectly possible, it's what's happened all the time on the latifundio, the latifundio is like one of those mules that's always biting the mule next to it, You amaze me, Oh, if I told you everything I know, we'd be here for the rest of our days, and the story would have to be passed on to our grandchildren, if you have any, but here's the lackey, let's follow him.

The sound was that of slithering feet and of some heavy object being dragged along. Once, he fell and went rolling back down to the bottom, he could have been killed, What's that he's carrying on his back, It's a barrel, the owners of both barrel and lackey use the barrel as their target, But I thought slavery had been abolished, That's what you think, How can a man submit to such a thing, Ask him, Oh, I will, excuse me, friend, what is that you're carrying on your back, It's a barrel, But it's full of holes, you couldn't use it to store water or other liquids, or are you going to fill it up with stones, It serves as a target for my masters Alberto and Angilberto, they shoot at the barrel and I go and find it to check the number of hits, and then I put it back in the same place until it's so full of holes, it's like a sieve, at which point I fetch a new one, And you submit to their orders. The world suddenly becomes unfit for conversation, with Alberto and Angilberto on the far side of the valley shouting, impatient at the lackey's delay, it's getting late, they're saying, and we've still got two boxes of bullets left, and the poor slave trots across the valley and over the bridge, the barrel is like a huge rust-red hump, and now, as he climbs the hill on the far side, he looks more like a beetle than a man, So, do you still believe slavery was abolished, It seems impossible, And what do you know about impossibilities, Oh, I'm beginning to learn, Let me tell you about another impossibility, over there, on the right bank of the stream, beyond the viaduct, are some fields that extend as far as the foot of the hills, do you see, fine, well, those same marksmen sold that land to some small farmers, and if they had been decent, honorable men, as they should have been, they would have included the stream in the sale, but no, they kept back the ten or twenty meters of land that bordered the stream, so if the farmers wanted water, they had to dig wells, what do you say to that, Again, it seems impossible, Yes, it does, doesn't it, it would be like me refusing you a drink of water when you were thirsty, and telling you, if you want water, then dig a well with your bare hands, while I empty my glass and amuse myself watching the water flow, So a dog could go and drink from the stream, but not the farmers, Ah, now you're beginning to understand, look, there's another lackey bringing a new barrel, Your masters are obviously good shots, Yes, sir, but they wanted to know who you are, and when I said I didn't know, they said that if you don't leave right now, they'll call the guards. The two walkers withdrew, the threat had its effect and the argument a certain authority, trespassing on private property, even when it isn't fenced off, would be taken very seriously indeed, especially if the guards happened to be in a bad mood, there would be no point explaining to them that they didn't know the boundaries, in fact, given that there's no right of way here, they were very lucky not to get shot, Just pretend it was a stray bullet, Alberto, those two were asking for it anyway.

But there are times when one would be perfectly justified in roaring with laughter at what happens on the latifundio, if, that is, we were in the mood for some fun, but I'm not sure it would be worthwhile, we're so used to laughter turning into tears or a howl of rage so loud it could be heard in heaven, not that there is any bloody heaven, Father Agamedes is more easily accessible, and he never hears or else pretends that he doesn't, yes, a howl that would be heard throughout the earth, although I wonder if it would be heard and if anyone would come to our aid, unless, of course, the reason they couldn't hear us was because they were shouting so loudly themselves. Let's tell one such story, and laugh if you can, especially since that is what the guards are for, not to be laughed at, heaven forfend, but to be summoned and dispatched, and although it's usually the governor or some other official who does the summoning and dispatching, the latifundio has a great deal of power and authority over them as well, as you will see in this excellent tale involving Adalberto, a shepherd, his two assistants, three dogs, six hundred sheep, a jeep and a patrol of republican guards, rather than a whole squadron, that would be excessive, shoulder arms, quick march.

These sheep have strayed. They are on land belonging to Berto and are heading for more land belonging to Berto, well, that's a generalization and not entirely true, because while the lands do belong to Adalberto, en route the sheep will pass through Norberto's lands, and as they pass, they graze, because sheep aren't like a pack of dogs you can muzzle, and even if this were practicable and the sheep allowed it, the shepherd would never do it, it wouldn't be worth the fuss, but one should perhaps add another hypothesis, in situations where the shepherd has no real excuse for traveling from one man's property to another, he could claim to have become disoriented and to have crossed the boundary accidentally, for the real skill lies in taking advantage of those vague boundaries, making any such incursion seem purely accidental and putting on an air of wounded innocence if suspicions are aroused, Oh, I am sorry, I didn't notice, I was just walking along with my flock and kept going straight, thinking I was still on my master's land, that's all, no offense intended. Those who are quicker on the uptake will be thinking, He's lying, and they're not far wrong, but something more subtle is at work here, and the first thing to ascertain would be this, in carrying out this highly irregular act, was the shepherd thinking more about his sheep's bellies than about the interests of his master Berto. And this being noted, so that all eventualities will be covered, let us return to the story, to the six hundred sheep trotting briskly along, under the protection of the shepherd, his two assistants and his dogs, and let us city dwellers withdraw into the shade, it's wonderful to see the sheep pouring down the hillside or across the plain, so peaceful, far from the insalubrious urban hubbub, from the disorderly tumult of the metropolis, Begin, O muses, begin your bucolic song, and we're in luck, because the flock is coming over here, so we'll be able to savor the episode right from the start, let's just hope the dogs don't bite us.

On that day, as chance would have it, Adalberto had set out in his car to go for a spin in the countryside to view his estate, sometimes a love of nature requires such outings, and although the car cannot plunge in among the foliage, down tracks and over fallow fields, it nonetheless gives him freedom enough to roam along these cart tracks, as long as his car has a good suspension and he keeps a light touch on the steering wheel and doesn't attempt to drive too fast. Adalberto is alone, the better to enjoy the rural solitude and the birdsong, although the car engine does somewhat disturb both the peace and the music, but it's all a matter of knowing how to combine ancient and modern, rather than clinging to past pleasures, the easy gait of the horse pulling the tilbury, and the straw hat in profile beneath the limber length of the whip, which now and then caresses the horse's rump, which is all it takes for the horse to understand what you want. These are delights rarely encountered now, a horse costs a fortune and eats even when it isn't working, the horse, needless to say, is a distinguished beast, with its somewhat feudal echoes, but times inevitably change, and not only is the car much cleaner, it impresses the populace and saves one from unnecessary familiarities, we haven't got time for that.

Today, however, Adalberto is at peace, following the gentle curves of the road, his elbow nonchalantly leaning on the open window, since Lamberto died, all this land is mine, although, in fact, not all of Lamberto's land went to him, because that would make another good story, the divisions and redivisions, the amalgamations and accretions, but we don't have time right now, we should have started earlier, now Adalberto's car appears among the trees, the sun glinting on its polished body and on the chrome, and suddenly he stops. He's probably seen us, we'd better go a little farther down the hill, just to avoid any awkward questions, because I'm a peace-loving man and a respecter of other people's property, and when we look back to see if a furious Adalberto is following hard on our heels, we see, with horror, that he is getting out of his car and staring, enraged, at the languid flock, which takes no notice of him, just as they took no notice of us, not even the dogs see him, intent as they are on sniffing out rabbits, and then, shaking his fist, he gets back in the car, turns around, jolting over the rough ground, and, as they say in novels, disappears in a cloud of dust. We, needless to say, have legged it already, something is about to happen, why did he storm off like that, after all, this is a flock of sheep, not a pride of lions, but only Adalberto knows why as he hurtles back to Monte Lavre in search of reinforcements, namely the guards, who, at this very moment, are dying of boredom at the barracks, but that's what the latifundio is like, it's either man the barricades or complete idleness, such is the fate of those who choose the military life, and the reason why their superiors put on maneuvers and exercises, otherwise, Corporal, it's all or nothing.

Adalberto arrives at the entrance to the barracks in the aforesaid cloud of dust, and although his body is heavy with age and other excesses, he steps lightly in, it's not a large space but it coped easily enough, as I'm sure you'll recall, with all those orchestrated entrances and exits during that business over the thirty-three escudos, and when he leaves, he is not alone, he's joined by Corporal Tacabo and by a private, and all three climb into Adalberto's car, Holy Mother, where are those guards off to in such a hurry, the old ladies standing at their doors do not know, but we do, they are coming here where the flock is grazing, while the shepherd rests beneath a holm oak, and his assistants, with the help of the dogs, watch the sheep, it's not a major operation but it's not without its problems either, keeping such a large flock together, without too many gaps, after all, a sheep, too, needs a little breathing space, And what next, while we wait for Adalberto, there's something I don't quite understand, why this close relationship between the latifundio and the guards, You're either very naïve or you haven't been paying attention, how can you still be asking such questions at this stage in the story, or are you just play-acting, pretending that you don't know, perhaps it's a mere rhetorical device, the effective use of repetition, be that as it may, even a child knows that the guards are here to guard the latifundio, To guard it from what, it's not going anywhere, From the risk of theft, looting and other such wickedness, because the ordinary people we've been talking about until now have bad blood, by which I mean that the wretches and their parents and grandparents and the parents of their grandparents have known nothing but hunger all their lives, how could they not covet another's wealth, And is that wrong, It's the worst sin there is, You're kidding, Of course I am, but there are plenty of people who genuinely believe that this band of rustics want to steal their land, these sacred lands that go way back, and so the guards were posted here to maintain order, to suppress the slightest murmur of discontent, And do the guards like that, Oh, they do, the guards have their reward, a uniform, boots, a rifle, the authority to use and abuse, and the gratitude of the latifundio, let me give you one example, in payment for this extraordinary military operation, Corporal Tacabo will receive a few dozen liters of olive oil and a few cartloads of firewood, and while he may receive seventy of something, the mere guard will receive less because he's lower down the ranks, but he'll nonetheless receive some thirty or forty of whatever is on offer, because the latifundio is very reliable on that score, it always repays a favor, and the national guard is pretty easy to please, just imagine what must go on in Lisbon behind closed doors, How sad, Don't start crying now, imagine coming back from a day spent clearing land and walking miles with a sack of kindling on your back, panting like a beast of burden, and the guards ambush you, rifles cocked, hands up, what have you got in that sack, and you say, I've been working in such-and-such a place, and they'll check to see if you're telling the truth, and if not, you're in trouble, Personally, I'd rather be ambushed by José Gato, for at least he, Yes, José Gato would be preferable, but even worse would be to find, farther on, a whole cartload of six or seven hundred or a thousand kilos of firewood set aside for the guards, a gift from the latifundio in payment for their good and loyal service, They sell people very cheap, Whether they sell them cheap or dear doesn't matter, the problem isn't how much or how little.

This conversation went no further, what would be the point, although the narrator is free to say what he likes, that's his privilege, but now Adalberto has arrived along with his army, he stops the car, the doors open, it's an invasion, a landing, and from high up they wave to the shepherd, but he's a lazybones, a native of these parts, seated he is and seated he remains, then, finally, he gets to his feet, making it quite clear what an effort this entails, and yells, What's the problem, and Corporal Tacabo gives the order to charge, to attack, to release the bombs, take no notice of these warlike exaggerations, what do you expect, they have so few opportunities, by now, the shepherd has understood the situation, the same thing once happened to his father, laughter bubbles up inside him, the lines around his eyes betray him, it's enough to make you split your sides, Do you have permission to be on this land, the question comes from Corporal Tacabo, who, as master of the law and the carbine, thunders, That's a fine of five escudos per sheep, let's see, six hundred sheep at five escudos each, six times five is thirty, add the zeros, why that's three thousand escudos, that's very expensive grazing, and the shepherd says, There must be some mistake, the sheep belong to the boss here and I'm on his land, What did you say, asks Corporal Tacabo foolishly, and the private with them gazes up at the skies, and Adalberto, backtracking, says, You mean this is mine, Yes, sir, I'm in charge of these sheep, and these sheep are yours, Go, beloved muses, my song is ended.

The troops returned to the barracks, the three men on the expedition said not a word, and when Adalberto arrived home, he issued orders about the olive oil, while Corporal Tacabo and the private put away their weapons, totting up how much they would earn and praying to Saint Michael the archangel for more such dangerous but profitable adventures. This is the kind of minor incident that occurs on the latifundio, but many pebbles go to make a wall and many grains make a harvest, What's that noise, It's an owl, any moment now the other owl will respond, Domingos, he's the one nearest the nest.

J UST BECAUSE Sigismundo Canastro told that story about the dog Constante and the partridge doesn't mean he has a monopoly on strange hunting tales. António Mau-Tempo has his own tales to tell, as well as those he has picked up from others, indeed, so many and so various are they that he could easily have told the aforementioned story, with Sigismundo Canastro chipping in to confirm its truth with the irrefutable proof that he had dreamed about it. To those surprised at the freedom with which people add to, subtract from and generally alter stories, we need only remind them of the vastness of the latifundio, of the way in which words are lost and found, whether mere days or centuries later, when you sit beneath a cork oak, for example, and listen in on the conversation between that tree and its neighbor, ancient, albeit somewhat confused stories, because cork oaks do get muddled as they grow older, but whose fault is that, ours perhaps, because we've never bothered to learn their language. Anyone who has ever got lost on the latifundio always ends up being able to distinguish between the landscape and the words it conceals, which is why we sometimes come across a man standing in the middle of the countryside, as if, as he was walking along, someone had suddenly grabbed his hand and said, now listen to this, he is sure to be hearing words, stories and ripostes, simply because he happened to be in the right place at the right time, when the air unleashed its story, whether it was the magnificent tale of Constante the dog or one about the proven curiosity of hares, as explained by António Mau-Tempo and backed up by all of Sigismundo Canastro's dreams, unless there's someone else here eager to tell us about his dreams.

First, find a good, flat stone, about a span high, and wide enough to cover half a sheet of newspaper. You can't do it on a windy day, mind, because the wind will blow away the little pile of pepper that, among the tangle of headlines and the tiny italic and roman type, will form the trigger of this particular rifle. Now the hare, as everyone knows, is a curious creature, What, you mean even more than the cat, Oh, there's no comparison, the cat isn't interested in what's going on in the world, he simply doesn't care, whereas if a hare sees a newspaper lying on a path, he'll immediately go over to find out the latest news, so much so that some hunters have come up with a game plan, they stand behind a hedge and, when the hare approaches to read the news, bang, they shoot him, the trouble is that the newspaper gets completely shredded by the lead shot and you have to buy yourself another one, some hunters have been seen with their cartridge belts stuffed with newspapers, it's not right, But why the pepper, Ah, yes, the pepper, that's the secret ingredient, but it's essential to choose a windless day, because if you were to leave a newspaper on the path, the wind would catch it and send it flying, and the hare wouldn't be interested, because he likes to read the news in peace, You don't say, Oh, I could say much more on the subject if you have the time, anyway, once you've laid the trap, stone, newspaper and pepper, all you have to do is wait, and if you have to wait a long time, that's because it's not a good place for hares, it can happen, but don't go complaining that you didn't kill any hares, that's entirely your fault, because when you know the area, it never fails, anyway, in a little while, up will hop the first hare, a nibble here, another nibble there, and suddenly its ears go up because it's seen the newspaper, And what does he do then, Poor creature, he never learns, he's so keen to get the latest news that he runs over to the newspaper and starts reading, he's a really happy, contented hare, he doesn't miss a line, but then he sniffs the pepper and sneezes, And what happens next, Exactly what would happen to you if you were him, he sneezes, hits his head on the stone and dies, And then, You just have to go and find him, or, if you like, go a few hours later and you'll find a whole line of hares, one after the other, they're so curious that they can't see a newspaper without wanting to read it, Is that true, Ask anyone, even a babe in arms knows about these things.

António Mau-Tempo had no rifle at the time, which was just as well. If he'd had one, he would have been just another ordinary hunter with a ready-made weapon, rather than the inventor of Saint Hubert's pepper, but this doesn't mean that he scorned the art of marksmanship, the proof is the muzzle-loading rifle he bought one day for twenty escudos from a spendthrift tenant farmer and with which he performed miracles. City dwellers are brought up to be suspicious of miracles, they always want proofs and oaths, which is quite wrong, for example, there was the time when António Mau-Tempo, by then the proud owner of said muzzle-loading rifle, found himself with plenty of gunpowder but no lead shot. We should perhaps mention that it was rabbit-hunting season, in case someone should come along and ask why he didn't use the same stone-newspaper-pepper method as he did with hares. Only someone ignorant of the art of hunting could fail to be aware that rabbits have no curiosity at all, seeing a newspaper lying on the ground or a cloud in the sky is all the same to them, except that rain falls from clouds and not from newspapers, which is why the rabbit hunter still needs a rifle, trap or stick, but in this case we're talking rifles.

There is no greater misfortune for a hunter than to be in possession of a good weapon, even if it's only a flintlock, plenty of gunpowder but no lead shot, Why didn't you buy some, No money, that was the problem, So what did you do, At first I didn't do anything, I just thought, And did you come up with an idea, Of course, that's what thinking is for, So tell me how you solved the problem, because I still don't see how you did it, Well, I had a box of tacks for my boots and I loaded them into the rifle, What, you loaded your rifle with tacks, You may not believe me, but I did, Oh, I believe you, it's just that I've never heard of such a thing, At some point, you'll have to start believing in things you've never heard of, Tell me the rest of the story, then, All right, I was heading out into the countryside when I had a thought that almost made me turn back, What was that, It occurred to me that any rabbit I hit would be reduced to a pulp, torn to shreds, inedible, So, So I started thinking again, And you came up with an idea, Of course, like I said, that's what thinking is for, anyway, I positioned myself opposite a big old tree with a really thick trunk and I waited, Did you wait long, As long as I had to, one never waits too long or too little, So you waited until the rabbit appeared, Yes, when he spotted me, he ran away from me and toward the tree, I had studied the lay of the land, you see, and as soon as he passed close by, I shot him, And he wasn't shot to pieces, No, why else did I do all that thinking, the tacks pierced his ears and nailed him to the tree, which was a holm oak, by the way, Amazing, Yes, it was, and all I had to do was give him a quick blow to the back of the head with my stick, and once I'd eaten the rabbit, I still had the tacks to mend my boots with.

Men are made in such a way that even when they're lying, they tell a kind of truth, and if, on the contrary, it's the truth they want to blurt out, it's always accompanied by a kind of lie, however unintentional. That's why if we started debating what was true and what was false in António Mau-Tempo's hunting tales, we would never reach a conclusion, we should simply be man enough to recognize that everything he described could be touched with one's fingers, be it the hare or the rabbit, the muzzle-loading rifle, of a kind that still exists, gunpowder, which is cheap, the tack with which we shoe the poverty of the ill shod, the boot, which is witness to that, the miraculous pile of pepper all the way from India, the stone of course, the newspaper that hares can read better than humans, and António Mau-Tempo, who is right here, the teller of tales, because if there was no one to tell them, there would be no tales.

I've told you one story, I've told you two, and I'll give you a third, because three is the number God made, the Father, the Son and the Holy Ghost of the ear by which the rabbit was caught in the excellent tale I'm about to tell you, You've spoiled it for us now that we know how the story ends, So what, we all die, what matters is the life we've led or will lead, not the end, All right, tell me about the rabbit, Well, I still had the same rifle, in fact, I'd got so used to it that the sight of those double-barreled ones used to make me laugh, let alone the ones with four barrels, like cannons they are, they should be banned, Why, Think how much nicer it is for a man to slowly and quietly prepare his rifle, loading the gunpowder, tamping it down, measuring out the lead shot, when you have it that is, and watching one of the animals you're hoping to hunt pass you by, saying to itself, phew, that was a close shave, and you feel full of friendly feelings for the feathered or furry creature moving off, it's all a question of believing in fate, for their hour had clearly not yet come, That's one way of looking at it, anyway, what happened next, Next, you mean before, well, on that occasion, too, I had no money to buy lead shot, You never seem to have any money, To listen to you, anyone would think you had never lacked for it yourself, Don't change the subject, my finances are my affair, carry on with the story, All right, so I had no money to buy some shot, but I had a steel ball, one of those ball-bearing things, I found it among the rubbish in a workshop, and I used the same method, but without the tree this time, the tree worked only with the tacks, What do you mean, It seemed to me that if I could somehow sharpen the ball bearing, it would be like a bullet, and wouldn't destroy the animal's flesh or skin, it was all a matter of marksmanship, and, if I do say so myself, I'm a pretty good shot, And then, Then I went into the countryside, to a place I knew, a sandy area where I'd seen a rabbit as big as a baby goat, he was obviously the father rabbit, because no one has ever seen the mother rabbit, she never leaves the burrow, which is as deep as the pool at Ponte Cava, she goes underground and no one knows where she is, Fine, but that's another story, That's where you're wrong, it's exactly the same story, but I don't have time to tell it now, So what happened next, This rabbit had given me the slip on other occasions, and had a way of scooting out of sight as soon as I raised my rifle, but that had been when my rifle was loaded with shot, Ah, so you weren't bothered about spoiling its skin, With a rabbit that big, it wouldn't matter, But you just said, Look, if you're going to keep interrupting, All right, carry on, So I waited and waited, one hour passed, then another, and finally it hopped into view, well, leapt really, because, as I said, it was the size of a small goat, and when it was airborne, I pretended to myself that it was a partridge and shot it, Did you kill it, No, it just shook its ears, gave another hop and then another, and of course I had no more ammunition left, anyway, it ran off into some bushes, gave another leap, one of those really long ones, from here to over there, say, and what did I see, What, The rabbit was caught, squirming and wriggling, as if someone were holding it up by one ear, and then I went over and saw what had happened, Don't keep me in suspense, I'm dying of curiosity, Just like the hares, Stop playing around and tell me the rest of the story, Well, it so happened that someone had been cutting back the bushes, and a few twigs the size of a finger had been left sticking up, and, can you believe it, the rabbit had got caught on a twig through the hole the ball bearing had made in its ear,

So presumably you freed him and hit him hard on the back of the neck, No, I freed him and let him go, You don't say, I do, catching him in the ear like that had nothing to do with marksmanship, it was chance, sheer luck, and the father rabbit couldn't be allowed to die by chance, It's a great story, And it's all true, just as it's true that on that same night, the rabbits came out to dance into the small hours, by the light of the full moon, Why, Because they were so pleased that the father rabbit had escaped, You saw them, did you, No, but I dreamed it.

That's how it is. The fish dies by its mouth unless, because it looks too small on the hook or will cut a sad figure in the frying pan, the man throws it back in the water, an act of compassion for its youth, perhaps, or mere self-interest on his part, hoping that it will grow larger and reappear later on, but the father rabbit, who would certainly not grow anymore, was saved partly by the honesty of António Mau-Tempo, who, although he was perfectly capable of inventing good stories, did not need to invent a better one, given that it was far harder to hit a rabbit in the ear than in the body, and in the silence of the latifundio, once the sound of firing had died away in the undergrowth, he knew that he could not have lived with the memory of the rabbit's wide, angry eye as it watched him approach the bush.

The latifundio is a whole field of twigs, and from each one hangs a squirming rabbit with a hole in one ear, not because it has been shot, but because it has been like that since birth, they stay there all their lives, scrabbling at the earth with their claws, fertilizing it with their excrement, and if there's any grass, they eat as much of it as they can, nose pressed to the ground, while all around they hear the footsteps of hunters, I could die at any moment. One day, António Mau-Tempo freed himself from the bush and crossed the frontier, he did so for five years running, going to France once a year, to northern France, to Normandy, but he was being led by the ear, caught by the bullet hole of necessity, it's true he had never married nor had children who needed bread to eat, but his father wasn't at all well, a consequence of his time in prison, they might not have killed him, but they broke him, and there was an employment crisis in Monte Lavre, whereas in France work was guaranteed and well paid, compared with the norm on the latifundio, in a month and a half he could earn fifteen or sixteen thousand escudos, a fortune. Possibly, but as soon as he arrived home in Monte Lavre, most of that disappeared in back payments, and the little that remained was set aside for the future.

And what exactly is France. France is an endless field of sugarbeet in which you work a double shift of sixteen or seventeen hours a day, that is, all the hours of daylight and quite a few of the night. France is a family of Norman French, who see three Iberian creatures come through their door, two Portuguese men and one Spaniard from Andalusia, António Mau-Tempo and Carolino da Avó from Monte Lavre and, from Fuente Palmera, Miguel Hernández,* who knows a few words of French, picked up as an emigrant worker, and with those words he explains that they have been hired to work there. France is a cheerless barn where one sleeps little and dines on a dish of potatoes, it's a land where, mysteriously, there are no Sundays and no public holidays. France is a bent and aching back, like two knives pressing in here and here, an affliction and a martyrdom, a crucifixion on a piece of land. France is to be viewed with one's eyes a few inches from a sugarbeet stem, the forests and the horizons in France are all made of sugarbeet, that's all there is. France is this scornful, mocking way of speaking and looking. France is the gendarme who comes to check our pa-

---

* Miguel Hernández, after whom this character is apparently named, was a self-taught Spanish poet who spent his childhood working as a farm laborer and goatherd. He published his first book of poetry at twenty-three and achieved considerable fame. He was active on the Republican side in the Spanish Civil War, and after the Republicans were defeated, he was arrested several times and finally sent to prison, where he died of tuberculosis.

pers, line by line, comparing and interrogating, keeping three paces away because of the smell we give off. France is an ever-watchful distrust, a tireless vigilance, it's a Norman Frenchman inspecting the work we've done and placing his foot as if he were stepping on our hands and enjoying it. France is being meanly treated as regards food and cleanliness, certainly compared with the horses on the farm, who are fat, large-footed and proud. France is a bush bristling with twigs, each with a rabbit dangling by the ear like a fish on the end of a rod, slowly suffocating, and Carolino da Avó is the least able to take it, bent double and limp as a penknife in which the spring has suddenly snapped, his blade is blunt and his point broken, he will not return next year. France is long train journeys, an immense sadness, a bundle of notes tied up with string and the stupid envy of those who stayed behind and now say of someone who left, He's rich, you know, these are the petty jealousies and selfish malice of the poor.

António Mau-Tempo and Miguel Hernández know about such things, they write to each other in the meantime, Mau-Tempo from Monte Lavre, Hernández from Fuente Palmera, they are simple letters with spelling mistakes in nearly every word, and so what Hernández reads is not quite Portuguese and what Mau-Tempo reads is not quite Spanish, but a language common to them both, the language of little learning and much feeling, and they understand each other, it's as if they were signaling to each other across the frontier, for example, opening and closing their arms, the unmistakable sign for an embrace, or placing one hand on the heart, signifying affection, or merely looking, which indicates a readiness to reveal one's thoughts, and both sign their letters with the same difficulty, the same grotesque way of holding the pen as if it were a hoe, which is why it looks as if a physical effort were needed to form each letter, Miguel Hernández, uh, António Mau-Tempo, uh. One day, Miguel Hernández will stop writing, two of António Mau-Tempo's letters will go unanswered, and however hard you try to explain these things, they still hurt, it's not exactly a great misfortune, I'm not going to lose my appetite over it, but this is merely what one says to console oneself, perhaps Miguel Hernández has died or been arrested, as happened with António Mau-Tempo's father, if only he could go to Fuente Palmera to find out. António Mau-Tempo will remember Miguel Hernández for many years to come, whenever he speaks of his time in France, he will say, My friend Miguel, and his eyes will fill with tears, he'll laugh them off and tell a story about rabbits or partridges, just to amuse people, none of it invented, you understand, until the wave of memory calms and ebbs away. Only then does he feel any nostalgia for France, for the nights spent talking in the barn, the stories told by Andalusians and those who came from the other side of the Tagus river, from Jaén and Évora, stories about José Gato and Pablo de la Carretera, and those other crazy nights when their work contract had ended, and they went whoring, stealing hasty pleasures, allez, allez, their unslaked blood protesting, and the more exhausted they were, the more they wanted. They were driven out into the street by a rapid-fire language they couldn't understand, allez, nègres, that's how it is with dark-skinned races, everyone's a black for those born in Normandy, where even the whores think they're pure-bloods.

Then one year, António Mau-Tempo decided not to return to France, partly because his health was suffering. After that, he went back to being nothing but a latifundio rabbit, caught on a twig, scratching away with his claws, the ox returns to the furrow, the stream to its familiar course, alongside Manuel Espada and the others, cutting cork, scything, pruning, hoeing, weeding, why do they not weary of such monotony, every day the same as the last, at least as regards the scant food and the desire to earn a little money for tomorrow, which hangs over these places like a threat, tomorrow, tomorrow is just another day, like yesterday, rather than being the hope of something new, if that's what life is.

France is everywhere. The Carriça estate is in France, that's not what it says on the map, but it's true, if not in Normandy, then in Provence, it really doesn't matter, António Mau-Tempo no longer has Miguel Hernández by his side, but Manuel Espada, his brother-in-law and his friend, though they are very different in character, they are scything, doing piecework, as we shall see. Gracinda Mau-Tempo is here too, pregnant at last, when it seemed that she would never have children, and the three of them are living, for as long as the harvest lasts, in an abandoned laborer's hut, which Manuel Espada has cleaned up to make comfortable for his wife. No one had lived there for five or six years, and it was a real ruin, full of snakes and lizards and all kinds of creepy-crawlies, and when it was ready, Manuel Espada, having first sprinkled the floor with water, went to fetch a bundle of rushes to lie down on, and it was so cool inside that he almost fell asleep, it was just an adobe wall with a covering of gorse and straw to serve as a roof, then suddenly a snake slithered over him, as thick as my wrist, which is not of the slenderest. He never told Gracinda Mau-Tempo, and who can say what she would have done had she known, perhaps it wouldn't have bothered her, the women in these parts are made of stern stuff, and when she arrived at the hut, she found it all neat and ready, with a truckle bed for the couple, another for António Mau-Tempo and a large sack to share as a blanket, that is how intimately people live on the latifundio. Oh, don't get all hot under the collar, Father Agamedes, where have you been, by the way, these men are not really going to sleep here, if they do lie down on the bed, they will do so simply in order not to die, and now is perhaps the moment to speak about pay and conditions, they're paid so much a day for a week, plus five hundred escudos for the rest of the field, which must all be harvested by Saturday. This may seem complicated, but it couldn't be simpler. For a whole week, Manuel Espada and António Mau-Tempo will scythe all day and all night, and you need to understand exactly what this means, when they are utterly exhausted after a whole day of work, they will go back to the hut for something to eat and then return to the field and spend all night scything, not picking poppies, and when the sun rises, they will again go back to the hut to eat something, lie down for perhaps ten minutes, snoring like bellows, then get up, work all day, eat whatever there is to eat and again work all night, we know no one is going to believe us, these can't be men, but they are, if they were animals they would have dropped down dead, only three days have passed, and the two men are like two ghosts standing alone in the moonlight in the half-harvested field, Do you think we'll make it, We have to, and meanwhile Gracinda Mau-Tempo, heavily pregnant, is weeding in the ricefield, and when she can't weed, she goes to fetch water, and when she can't fetch water, she cooks food for the men, and when she can't cook, she goes back to the weeding, her belly on a level with the water, her son will be born a frog.

The harvest is done, and in the agreed time too, Gilberto came to pay these two ghosts, but he's seen plenty of ghosts in his time, and António Mau-Tempo has now gone to work on the other side of this France, this killing field. Manuel Espada and his wife Gracinda Mau-Tempo stayed on in the hut until it was time for her to give birth. Manuel Espada took his wife home and then went back to the Carriça estate, where, fortunately, there was work. Anyone who remains unsurprised by all this needs to have the scales removed from his eyes or a hole bored in his ear, if he hasn't got one already and sees them only in the ears of others.

GRACINDA MAU-TEMPO gave birth in pain. Her mother Faustina came to help her during labor, along with old Belisária, who had long practiced as a midwife and been responsible for a fair few deaths in childbirth, of both mothers and babies, but to make up for this, she did create the finest navels in Monte Lavre, and while this may sound like a joke, it isn't, rather, it deserves to be the subject of obstetric research into just how Belisária managed to cut and suture umbilical cords in such a way that they resembled goblets straight out of the thousand and one nights, which, opportunity and audacity allowing, one could verify by comparing them with the bare bellybuttons of the Moorish dancers who, on certain mysterious nights, cast off their veils at the fountain in Amieiro. As for the pain suffered by Gracinda Mau-Tempo, it was neither more nor less than that suffered by all women since Eve's fortunate sin, fortunate, we say, because of the earlier pleasure enjoyed, a view that does not sit well with Father Agamedes, who disagrees out of duty and possibly conviction, as the upholder of the most ancient punishment in human history, meted out by Jehovah himself, You will give birth in pain, and so it has been all the days of all women, even those who didn't know

Jehovah's name. The rancor of the gods lasts much longer than that of men. Men are poor wretches, capable of terrible vengeance, but capable, too, of being moved to tears by the slightest thing, and if the time is right and the light propitious, they will fall into their enemy's arms and weep over how strange it is to be a man, a woman, a person. God, Jehovah or whoever, never forgets anything, the sinner must be punished, which is why there is this endless line of gaping vulvas, dilated, volcanic, out of which burst new men and new women, all covered in blood and mucus, all equal in their misery, but so instantly different, depending on the arms that receive them, the breath that warms them, the clothes that cover them, while the mother draws back into her body that tide of suffering, even while the last flower of blood drips from her torn flesh, and while the flabby skin on her now empty belly slowly stirs and hangs in folds, that is when youth begins to die.

Meanwhile, up above, the balconies of heaven are deserted, the angels are taking a nap, of Jehovah and what remains of his wrath there is no news that makes any human sense, and there is no record that the celestial fireworks were summoned to conceive, create and launch some new star to shine for three days and three nights above the ramshackle hut that is home to Gracinda Mau-Tempo, Manuel Espada and their first child, Maria Adelaide, for that is the name she will bear. And we are in a land that does not lack for shepherds, some who were shepherds as children and others who continued to be and will be until the day they die. The flocks are large too, we saw one of six hundred sheep, and there's no shortage of pigs either, although the pig is not really a suitable animal for nativity scenes, it lacks a sheep's elegance, thick coat, soft woolly caress, pass me my ball of yarn, will you, darling, such creatures are made to bend the knee, whereas the pig rapidly loses its sweet look of a pink, newborn bonbon and becomes instead a bulbous-nosed, malodorous lover of mud, sublime only in the meat that it gives us. As for the oxen, they are busy working, nor are there so many of them on the latifundio that they can afford to attend belated scenes of adoration, and as for the donkeys, beneath their saddle cloths there are only sores, around which buzz bluebottles excited by the smell of blood, while in Manuel Espada's house the flies swarm feverishly above Gracinda Mau-Tempo, who smells like a woman who has just given birth, Keep those flies off, will you, says old Belisária, or perhaps she doesn't, so used is she to this accompanying halo of winged, buzzing angels, who appear as soon as summer arrives and she has to go off to help some woman in labor.

Miracles do happen, though. The child is lying on the sheet, they smacked her as soon as she came into the world, not that this was necessary, because her first cry was already forming in her throat, and one day she will shout other things that now seem quite impossible, she cries, although she sheds no tears, merely screws up her eyes, making a face that would frighten any visiting Martian, but which, nonetheless, makes us sob our hearts out, and since it is a bright, warm day and the door is open, there falls onto this side of the sheet a kind of reflected light, where it comes from doesn't really matter, and Faustina Mau-Tempo, so deaf that she cannot even hear her granddaughter crying, is the first to see her eyes, which are blue, as blue as João Mau-Tempo's eyes, two drops of sky-bathed water, two round hydrangea petals, but neither of these vulgar comparisons serves, they merely reveal a lack of imagination, no comparison will serve, however hard future suitors may struggle to come up with one that does justice to these eyes, which are blue, not aquamarine or azure, not some botanical caprice or the product of some subterranean forge, but bright, intense blue, like João Mau-Tempo's eyes, we can compare them when he arrives, and then we will know what kind of blue it is. For now, though, only Faustina Mau-Tempo knows, which is why she can proclaim, She has her grandfather's eyes, and then the other

two women want to see as well, Belisária, much put out at being
deprived of her midwife's privileges, and Gracinda Mau-Tempo, a
jealous she-wolf to her cub, but Belisária takes her time, which is
why Gracinda Mau-Tempo is last, not that it matters, she will have
time enough to be attached by her nipples to that sucking mouth,
she will have time to lose herself in contemplating those blue, blue
eyes while the milk flows from her breast, whether here beneath
these badly laid roof tiles, or beneath a holm oak in the middle
of the countryside, or standing up when there's nowhere to sit, or
hurriedly when she can't dawdle, milk that flows, in small and large
quantities, from that breast, that life, like white blood made out of
the other, red variety.

Then the three kings arrived. The first was João Mau-Tempo,
who came on foot when it was still light, so he needed no star to
guide him, and the only reason he didn't arrive earlier was male
modesty, because, were such things the norm in that time and
place, he could easily have been there at the birth, after all, what's
wrong with seeing your own daughter give birth, but it's simply
not done, people would talk, such ideas belong in the future. He
arrived early because he's currently out of work, and has been
clearing a piece of land he's been given to cultivate, and when he
went into the house, his wife wasn't there, but his neighbor informed him that he was the grandfather of a little girl, and he was
pleased, but not as pleased as you might expect, because he would
have preferred a boy, men do, in general, prefer boys, and then he
left the house, walked at his usual slow, swaying pace, caught between two different pains, one here, the other there, the old pain
acquired carrying logs to the charcoal pit, and the other, a dull
ache, was the result of being forced to stand for hours like a statue,
he looks like a sailor fresh off the boat after a long voyage, dis-
concerted to find that the ground he walks on doesn't move, or as
if he were riding on the back of a camel, the ship of the desert,

a comparison that paints exactly the right picture, for, given that João Mau-Tempo is the first of the magi to arrive, it is only proper that he should travel according to his condition and tradition, the others can choose their own mode of transport, and he brings no gifts to speak of, unless the ark of suffering that João Mau-Tempo carries in his heart could be considered a gift, fifty years of suffering, but no gold, and incense, Father Agamedes, is for the church, and as for myrrh, that's been used up on those who died along the way. It seems rather mean and in somewhat bad taste to give such a gift to a newborn, but these men from the latifundio can only choose from what they, in turn, were given, as much sweat as one could want, enough joy to fill a toothless smile and a plot of land large enough to devour their bones, because the rest of the land is needed for other crops.

João Mau-Tempo, then, arrives empty-handed, but on the way, he remembers that his first grandchild has just been born, and from a garden he plucks a single geranium flower on its knotty stem, with its acrid smell of poor households, but what a pretty sight it is to see one of the magi mounted on his camel with its gold and crimson saddle cloth, humbly bending down to pick a pelargonium, he didn't order a slave to do this, of the many who accompany and serve him, what a fine example he sets. And when João Mau-Tempo reaches the door of his daughter's house, it seems that the camel knows its duty, for it kneels down to let this lord of the latifundios dismount, while the republican guards from the local barracks present arms, although Corporal Tacabo has his doubts about whether a large, exotic beast like a camel should be allowed to travel the public highway. These are fantasies born of the harsh sun, now sinking in the sky but still beating down on the stones along the road, which are as hot as if the earth had just given birth to them. My dear daughter, and it is then that João Mau-Tempo sees that his eyes are immortal, for there they are again after a long peregrination, even he doesn't know where they started out, where they came from and how, he knows only that there are no other such eyes in Monte Lavre, in his own family or elsewhere, my daughter's children are definitely my grandchildren, while those of my son might and might not be, none of us is free of such popular malice, but who can doubt those eyes, look at me, look into my blue eyes, and now look at those of my granddaughter, who is to be called Maria Adelaide and is the image of her ancestor more than five hundred years ago, for those eyes come from that foreigner, that deflowerer of virgins. All families have their myths, some of which they do not know, as is the case with this Mau-Tempo family, who should, therefore, be very grateful to the narrator.

The second of the magi arrived when night had already fallen. He came straight from work to find no light on in the house, the fire out, and so no hope of a full stewpot, then his heart turned over and did so again when he met the same neighbor who told him, Your sister has had a little girl, your father and mother are there, because by now the whole of Monte Lavre knows that it's a baby girl and is vastly amused to know she has blue eyes, but the neighbor says nothing about this last point, she's a kind woman who believes that surprises have their time and place, why tell António Mau-Tempo, Your niece has blue eyes, she would then be denying him the pleasure of seeing this with his own brown eyes. The guards have returned to the barracks, no one is there to present arms to António Mau-Tempo, well, if you thought there would be, more fool you, but he is, nevertheless, a flesh-and-blood king walking down the street, as dirty as befits someone who has come straight from work, he hasn't had time to wash, but he doesn't forget his brotherly obligations and picks a daisy from a whitewashed can-cum-flowerpot beside a door, and so that it doesn't wilt in his fingers, he puts it between his lips to water it with his saliva, and when he finally goes into the hut, he says, For you, sister, and gives her the marguerite, what could be more natural than for a flower to change its name, it happened earlier with the geranium and the pelargonium, and will happen again one day with the carnation.*

It's just as well that António Mau-Tempo wasn't expecting to see those blue eyes. The child is sleeping peacefully, her eyes are closed, her decision, and she will open them again only for the third wise man, but he will arrive much later, in the dead of night, because he is coming from far away and on foot, he's made this same journey for the past three days or three nights, because for those who like to know the facts, Manuel Espada is now on his third night with little sleep, and he's used to that, as all these people are, but perhaps we should explain. Because Manuel Espada works far from home, he usually sleeps there, in a shepherd's hut or a cabin, it doesn't really matter, but as the time of the birth drew nearer, what did Manuel Espada do, he stopped work at sunset, reached home after midnight, where his child was still nothing but a swollen belly, lay down for an hour or so beside Gracinda Mau-Tempo, then got up halfway between night and morning and went back to work, and this is the third such night, but third time lucky, for when he arrives, he will see his wife and his newborn child, isn't that good.

Faustina, João and António Mau-Tempo killed a chicken to celebrate, and Gracinda Espada drank some of the broth, which is good for mothers who have just given birth, and meanwhile, more uncles and aunts and other relatives came and went, Gracinda needs to rest, at least today, bye, see you tomorrow, what a lovely little girl, the image of her grandfather. The church clock chimed midnight, and if no misfortune has befallen the traveler, if he has not slipped down a hill or into a ditch, if no impatient ne'er-do-

---

* The Portuguese revolution in 1974 came to be known as the Carnation Revolution because, despite its being a military coup, no shots were fired and, in the streets, people handed the soldiers red carnations, which they pinned on their uniforms or placed in the barrels of their guns.

well has broken the rule about not attacking someone as poor as himself, then it should not be long before this third wise man arrives, what gifts will he bring with him, we wonder, what cortege, perhaps he'll be mounted on an Arab steed with hooves of gold and a bridle of silver and coral, perhaps, instead of some bearded scoundrel stepping out onto the road, he will meet his fairy godmother, who will say, Your daughter has been born, and because she has blue eyes, I give you this horse so that you can see her all the sooner, before life drains the color from those eyes, but even were that fairy godmother to intervene, which is, after all, pure fantasy, these paths are difficult, and even more so at night, the horse might tire or break a leg, and then Manuel Espada would have to make the journey on foot anyway, through the great, vast, starry night full of terrors and indecipherable murmurings, but the three kings still have the magical powers they learned in Ur and Babylon, how else explain the two fireflies that go ahead of Manuel Espada, he can't get lost, he simply has to follow them as if they were the two sides of the path, how are such things possible, how can such creatures guide a man, they go up hill and down dale, they skirt ricefields and fly across plains, we can see the first houses in Monte Lavre now, and there the fireflies have alighted on top of the door frame, at head height, to light his way, glory be to man on earth, and Manuel Espada passes between them, a suitable guard of honor for someone who has just come from hours of hard labor to which he will have to return before sunrise.

Manuel Espada brings no gifts from near or far. He reaches out his hands, and each hand is a large flower, then he says, Gracinda, and can say no more, but kisses her on the cheek, just once, but what is it about that one kiss that brings a lump to our throat, and we're not even family, if we did have something to say at this juncture, we wouldn't be able to, and just when those gestures are being made and that word is being spoken, Maria Adelaide opens her eyes, as if she had been waiting for that moment, her first childish trick, and she sees a large shape and large open hands, it's her father, she doesn't yet understand what this means, as Manuel Espada well knows, so much so that he feels as if his heart were going to leap out of his chest, his hands are shaking, how can he pick up this child, his daughter, men are so useless, and then Gracinda Espada says, She looks like you, well, it's possible, although at that age, only a few hours old, you can never tell, but João Mau-Tempo is quite right when he proclaims, But she has my eyes, and António Mau-Tempo says nothing, because he is merely the uncle, and poor deaf Faustina can only guess at what is being said, and says in turn, My love, quite why she doesn't know, because, for reasons of modesty and reserve, these are not words normally used on the latifundio and in these situations.

Two hours later, and however much time he had spent there it would have seemed too short, Manuel Espada left the house, he is going to have to walk very fast to get to work before sunrise. The two waiting fireflies set off again, flying close to the ground now and shining so brightly that the ants' sentinels shouted to their fellow ants inside the nest that the sun was coming up.

THE HISTORY OF THE wheatfields is one that repeats itself with remarkable regularity, but it has its variants too. It's not that sometimes the wheat is ready to be harvested later or earlier, that depends on whether there has been too much or too little rain, or on the sun, which can transgress by sending too much heat or not enough, nor is it that the seeds were sown on a steep slope or on low ground, in clayey or in sandy soil. The men of the latifundio have long been accustomed to the perversities of nature and to their own mistakes, and are unlikely to be thrown by such slight and inevitable occurrences. And although it is true that the aforementioned variants, individually and as a whole, deserve to be dealt with at greater length, unhurriedly, with time to go back and discuss perhaps a forgotten lump of soil, without having to worry about our listeners' growing impatience, it is also true, alas, that such considerations are out of place when telling a story, even when it's a story about the latifundio. Let us accept, then, that we must keep quiet about all these subtle differences and let us add to less serious defects the far graver one of pretending that everything remains the same in the wheatfields from one year to the next, and let us merely ask why this delay, why have the harvesters, human and mechanical, not yet entered the fields, when even we ignorant city dwellers can clearly see that the moment is here and is passing us by, that the dry whisper of the wheat in the wind is like the whisper of dragonfly wings, in short, let us ask what damage is being done here and to whom.

The history of the wheatfields repeats itself, with variants. In the present case, it isn't because the men are kicking up their usual ruckus, demanding more money. Well, it's the same cry every year at every season and about every job, It's as if they don't know how to say anything else, Father Agamedes, instead of worrying about the salvation of their immortal soul, if they have one, they care only about bodily comforts, they have learned nothing from the ascetics, no, all they think about is money, they never ask if there is any or if I can afford to pay. The church is a great source of consolation in these situations, it takes a tiny sip of wine from the chalice, just another drop, please, do not remove this cup from me, and raises remorseful eyes to the heavens from which it hopes one day to receive rewards for the latifundio, when the time comes, of course, but the later the better, Tell me, Father Agamedes, what do you make of these idlers going around cheering this general,* it seems that these days one can trust nobody, I mean, a military man of all people, and he seemed so trustworthy, so well loved by the regime that made him, yet here he is, traveling around stirring up the populace, how did the government allow things to get this far. Father Agamedes has no answer to this question, his kingdom is not always of this world, and yet he has been a witness to and a personal

---

* General Humberto da Silva Delgado was initially a staunch supporter of Salazar's right-wing dictatorship and the youngest general in Portuguese history. However, he later became a defender of democratic ideals and decided to run for the Portuguese presidency in 1958. When asked what he would do about Salazar if he won the election, Delgado famously remarked, "Obviously, I'll sack him." As it happened, he won only twenty-six percent of the vote, losing to the government's preferred candidate, Américo Tomás, amid widespread allegations of vote rigging. On February 13, 1965, Delgado and his secretary were murdered after being lured into an ambush by PIDE agents.

victim of this great national terror, this hothead shouting wildly, I'll sack him, I'll sack him, and who was he referring to, why, Professor Salazar, of course, hardly the behavior of a candidate, a candidate should be polite at all times, but his behavior backfired on him in the end, and they say he's on the run, and to think what a quiet life we had until now, before all this fuss, But between you and me, Father Agamedes, because no one's listening, things could have been worse, it took a lot of skill not to let the situation get out of control, nonetheless, we must remain vigilant, and the first thing we should do is teach these idlers a lesson, which is why not a sheaf of wheat will be harvested this year, That'll teach them, Senhor Norberto, Yes, that'll teach them, Father Agamedes.

It's not known where this spirit of didacticism came from, whether from Lisbon, Évora, Beja or Portalegre, or if it was used in a jocular mode at the club in Montemor or after too much cognac, or if Leandro Leandres brought it home with him from the house of dragons, but whatever its origin, it quickly spread throughout the latifundio, passing from Norberto to Gilberto, from Berto to Lamberto, from Alberto to Angilberto, and, once it had found general acceptance, the overseers were summoned and given their orders, Any harvesting already begun must stop, and don't start work on any new fields. Some calamity must have occurred, perhaps the wheatfields have become leprous, and the latifundio has taken pity on its harvester-children and doesn't want to see them disfigured, their fingers mere stubs, their legs stumps, their noses absences, their lives are unfortunate enough as it is. This bread is poisoned, at the end of each field place scarecrows with horrible gaping skulls for heads, that should put the fear of death into even the most resolute souls, and if that doesn't scare them off, then call the guards, they'll sort them out. And the overseer says, That won't be necessary, no one is likely to go to the fields unless he's sure to get paid, and certainly not if he's going to get a bullet between the shoulder blades, but think of the loss of income. And Alberto says,

Better cut the shoe than pinch the foot, it won't ruin us to leave the wheat unharvested for a year. And the overseer says, They want more money, they say the price of food is going up and up and that they're starving. And Sigisberto says, That's nothing to do with me, we pay them what we want to pay them, food is expensive for us as well. And the overseer says, According to them, they're going to get together to talk to the boss. And Norberto says, I don't want any dogs following behind me, barking.

All over the latifundio one hears only the barking of dogs. They barked when, from the Minho to the Algarve, from the coast to the eastern border, the people rose up in the general's name, and they were barking a new bark, which, in the language of ordinary folk, translated as, If you want better pay, vote Delgado on the day, this taste for rhymes goes back a long way, well, we are, after all, a nation of poets, and they barked so much that soon they were barking at people's doors, it won't be long, Father Agamedes, before they start profaning churches, that's always the first thing they do, spitting in the face of the holy mother church, Please, Dona Clemência, don't even talk about it, not that I'm afraid of martyrdom, but Our Lord will not allow a repetition of the kind of outrage that took place in Santiago do Escoural, where, can you imagine, they turned the church into a school, I didn't see it with my own eyes, of course, it was before my time, but that's what I've been told, It's true, Father Agamedes, as true as we're sitting here now, ah, the follies of the republic, which, God willing, will not be repeated, be careful when you leave, mind the dogs don't bite you. When Father Agamedes peers around the door on the way out, he asks in a shrill, tremulous voice, Are the dogs under control, and someone replies dully, These ones are, but put like that, how do we know which dogs are loose and which not, but Father Agamedes feels certain that this information will ensure the safety of his delicate calves and steps out into the courtyard, where he finds, to his relief, that the dogs are indeed safely tethered, but when he goes out through the street

door, he finds a crowd of people, not barking, all we need is for
men to start barking, but if this murmuring doesn't sound like a
dog growling, I'll eat my hat, and Father Agamedes doesn't see the
line of ants marching along the wall of the building, raising their
heads like dogs, they're quiet now, but whatever will become of us
if the whole pack of them were to join forces.

    As mentioned above, this year's harvest has been canceled, as a
punishment for the usual impertinence of asking for more wages
and for the exceptional crime of supporting Delgado, everywhere
and anywhere. I really don't care, said Adalberto, I just need to
be sure that the government is in agreement, Oh, it is, said Leandro Leandres, and so are we, we think it's a magnificent idea. And
what about the losses, sir, what about the losses, you can count on
our good will, but we'll have to be compensated, everything has
its price, a perfectly justifiable remark made in some unnamed
place on the latifundio, it must have been in a town, because what
would the civil governor be doing in a tiny village unless he was
there to attend some inauguration ceremony, but wherever it was,
the remark was made, perhaps on a balcony looking out over the
countryside, Don't worry, Senhor Berto, we're studying how best
to assist agriculture, the nation is aware of farmers' concerns and
will not forget this patriotic gesture. They almost hoist the flag,
but why bother, election day has been and gone, and while Tomás*
may be our brand-new president, he acts the same as the former
resident, well, if the others can rhyme, why shouldn't I, I'm as important as they are, and I can make very pretty rhymes, for example, I'm always hungry year on year, Through winter and through
spring, While down in hell, Death rings his bell: Your scythe awaits
you here, and after this ditty sung in chorus, a great silence falls

---

* Américo de Deus Rodrigues Tomás became minister of the navy in 1944, was elected
president of the Portuguese republic in 1958 and was reelected in 1965 and 1972. As president, he was a mere figurehead and widely lampooned. His one bold act was to dismiss
Salazar after the latter suffered a crippling stroke in 1968.

over the latifundio, what's going on, and while we're thinking this, our eyes fixed on the ground, a shadow passes rapidly overhead, and when we look up, we see the great red kite hovering above, so the moan that emerged from my throat was actually his cry.

That night, Sigismundo Canastro went over to João Mau-Tempo's house to talk to him and António Mau-Tempo, and from there he went to Manuel Espada's house, where he spent some time. He visited another three houses, two of which were far out in the country, he spoke to people in this way and that, used these words and those, because you can't talk to everyone in the same way, if you do, your words might be misconstrued, and his message, in essence, is to meet in Montemor in two days' time to demonstrate outside the town hall, we want as many people to be there as possible, to demand work, because there's plenty of work to be done, but they're refusing to let us do it. En route they will discuss what the men of the latifundio think about the farce of handing the presidency of this wretched republic over to an out-and-out imbecile and yes man, surely one was enough, how many more will there be. These bitter words come not from excessive drinking or eating, neither of which is much practiced on the latifundio, although having said that, there's no shortage of men who bend the elbow rather too much, but that can be excused, for when a man finds himself tethered to a stake all his life, smoking and drinking are ways of escape, especially drinking, though each drink is another step toward death. This bitterness comes from the frustrated hope that they were finally going to be able to speak freely, had freedom come, but it didn't, someone once caught a glimpse of that much-vaunted freedom, but she is not one to be seen out walking the highways, she won't sit on a stone and wait to be invited in to supper or to share our bed for the rest of our life. Groups of men and some women had been out and about, cheering and shouting, and now we are left with a bitter taste in our mouths as if we, too, had been drinking, our eyes see ashes and little more, only wheatfields as yet unharvested, What are we going to do, Sigismundo Canastro, you who are older and more experienced than us, On Monday we'll go to Montemor to demand bread for our children and for the parents who have to bring them up, But that's what we always do, and to what end, We've done it in the past, we must do it now and must continue to do it until things change, It feels like a never-ending struggle, But it will end, When we're dead and buried and our bones are there for all to see, if there are any dogs around to dig them up, There'll still be enough people around when the time comes, your daughter, you know, gets prettier by the day, She has my father's eyes, these words were spoken by Gracinda Mau-Tempo, all the conversation prior to this having been with her husband Manuel Espada, and it is he who says, I'd sell my soul to the devil to see that day come, not tomorrow, but now, and Gracinda Mau-Tempo picks up her three-year-old daughter and scolds her husband, Don't say such things, Manuel, and Sigismundo Canastro, older in years and experience, smiles, The devil doesn't exist and so can't make any deals, and no amount of oaths and promises will change anything, work is the only way to get what we want, and our work now consists in going to Montemor on Monday, people will be coming from all over.

These June nights are beautiful. If there's a moon, you can see the whole world from high up in Monte Lavre, well, let's pretend you can, we're not that ignorant, we know the world is much bigger, I've been to France, António Mau-Tempo would say, and that's a long way away, but in this silence, anyone, even I, would believe it if someone said, There is no other world apart from Montemor, where we're going on Monday to ask for work. And if there is no moon,* then the world is simply this place where I put my feet and all the rest is stars, perhaps there's a latifundio up there too, which

---

* A possible reference to Luís de Sttau Monteiro's 1962 play *Felizmente há luar!* (*Fortunately There's a Moon!*), which was banned because it was deemed to be critical of the Salazar regime and, in particular, of the Delgado-Tomás presidential campaign.

is why our new president is a rear admiral who's never been to sea and who won the election game with four aces and a few more besides, because nothing trumps being an apparent pillar of society and a cheat. Had Sigismundo Canastro thought such wicked, witty thoughts, we would have stood back at the edge of the road, hat in hand, astonished at the worldly wisdom of the latifundio, but what he is really thinking is that he has spoken to everyone he needed to speak to and that he was right to speak to them today rather than leave it until tomorrow, which is why we don't know what to do with our hat, or even if we should be holding it in our hand, Sigismundo Canastro has done his duty, and that's that. However, despite the gravity of the steps to be taken, he also has a spritely, mischievous side, as we have seen before, and so, noticing that the door to the guards' barracks was locked and in darkness, he went over to the wall and peed long and pleasurably as if he were peeing on the whole lot of them. The childish tricks of an old man whose cock no longer serves him for very much except to make this lovely little stream that finds its way among the cobbles, I wish I had liters of urine in me so that I could stay here peeing all night, like the dam at Ponte Cava, perhaps we should all pee at the same time and flood the latifundio, I wonder who would be saved. It's a fine, starry night. Sigismundo Canastro buttons up his fly, the comedy is over, and sets off home, sometimes the blood still stirs, you never know.

In the days when people made pilgrimages, we used to say that all roads lead to Rome, you just had to walk and ask the way as you went, that's how sayings come into being and are then unthinkingly repeated, and it's not true, for here all the many roads and paths lead to Montemor, and although no one is speaking, only a deaf man could fail to hear the lofty speech echoing around the latifundio. Some, if they can find no better mode of transport and regardless of whether they come from near or far, are on foot, others are pedaling along on ancient bicycles that wobble and creak like mule carts, while those who can, have come by bus, and all are converging on Montemor, arriving from all the points of the compass rose, and carried there by a strong wind. The sentinels on the castle ramparts watch the Moorish host approach, the flag of the prophet folded in their bosom, O Holy Mother of God, the infidels are coming, lock up your wives and daughters, gentlemen, close the doors and raise the drawbridge, for in truth I say unto thee, today is the day of judgment. The narrator is, of course, exaggerating, doubtless the result of too much time spent immersed in medieval studies, fancy imagining armies and pennants when there is only this disparate band of rustics, probably not even a thousand of them, and yet the final gathering will be far larger. But one thing at a time, there's another two hours yet, for the moment Montemor is just a town with more people in the streets than usual, they wander about in the main square talking to each other in low voices, and those with a little money to spend buy themselves a drink. Has the party from Escoural arrived, I don't know, we're from Monte Lavre, there aren't many of them, it's true, but at least they're here, and they've brought a woman with them, because Gracinda Mau-Tempo wanted to come too, there's no stopping women nowadays, that's what the older, more old-fashioned men think, although they say nothing, imagine what they would have said if they had overheard the following conversation, Manuel, I'm going with you, and Manuel Espada, despite himself, thought she must be joking and responded, or, rather, all the Manuels in the world answered for him, This isn't women's business. What did you say, a man should be careful when he speaks, it's not just a matter of saying the words, you can end up looking ridiculous and losing all authority, fortunately Gracinda and Manuel really love each other, nevertheless, the discussion continues for the rest of the evening and even when they're lying in bed, The child can stay with my mother and then you and I can go together, we don't just share a bed, you know, and finally Manuel Espada gave in and, glad to give in, put his arm around his wife and drew her to him, the man invites and the woman consents, the little girl is sleeping and hears nothing, Sigismundo Canastro, too, is asleep in his bed, having tried and succeeded, perhaps the next time will be even better, a man can't just give up, damn it.

What went on between man and wife last night or the night before, and what they will do later, are not matters to be discussed in Montemor, or, indeed, when this day is over, for who knows how it will end. The cavalry, as usual, rides forth from the guards' barracks, while inside, Lieutenant Contente and Leandro Leandres are deep in conversation, the order to mobilize has been issued, now they must await events, although others have decided to wait elsewhere, they are the owners of the latifundio who live in Montemor, and there are quite a few of them, so we were not far off when we spoke of sentinels, for there is a stockade along the walls of the castle, with the braver of the infantes perched on the reconstructed ramparts, and a rosary of fathers and mothers, the former dressed as knights and the latter clad in suitably light colors. The more malicious commentators will say that they have taken shelter there because they are afraid of this invasion of farm laborers, a hypothesis that has a certain ring of truth about it, but let us not forget how few distractions there are here, apart from bullfights and the cinema, this time it's rather like a picnic in the country, there's plenty of shade and, if necessary, there is the safe haven of the convent of Our Lady of the Annunciation, pray for us. It is, however, true and verifiable that they left their houses out of a hitherto unknown fear, the servants remained behind on guard, because if you take on servants when they're young, they tend to be loyal, as is doubtless the case with Amélia Mau-Tempo, who also works as a maid in Montemor, these facts are at once contradictory and inevitable, but given the times we live in, one cannot really trust anyone, not because the workers of the latifundio have joined together to make their demands, it's not the first time they've asked for work, but because one can all too easily imagine those hands closing into fists, there's a lot of anger out there, a lot of conspiracies, dear aunt, a lot of conspiracies. From up here, you can see them walking down the narrow lanes and converging on the square outside the town hall. They look like ants, says an imaginative child heir, and his father corrects him, They may look like ants, but they're dogs, now there's the whole situation summed up in one brief, clear phrase, and then silence falls, we don't want to miss anything, look, there's already a squadron of guards in front of the town hall, and there's the sergeant, what's that he is holding, a machine gun, that's what Gracinda Mau-Tempo thought too, and glancing up at the castle, she saw that it was full of people, who can they be.

The square fills up. The people from Monte Lavre are standing in a group. Gracinda, the only woman, her husband Manuel Espada, her brother and father, António and João Mau-Tempo, and Sigismundo Canastro, who says, Stick together, and there are two other men called José, one is the great-grandson of the Picanços, who kept the mill at Ponte Cava, and the other is José Medronho, whom we haven't had occasion to mention until now. They are in a sea of people, the sun beats down on this sea and burns like a nettle poultice, while up in the castle, the ladies open their sunshades, anyone would think it was a party. Those rifles are loaded, you can tell by the look on the guards' faces, a man carrying a loaded weapon immediately takes on a different air, he grows hard and cold, his lips tighten, and he looks at us with real rancor. People who like horses sometimes give them the name of a person, like that colt called Bom-Tempo, but I don't know if the horses at the end of the street have names, perhaps they simply give them numbers, they do everything by numbers in the guards, call out number twenty-seven, and the horse and the man riding it both step forward, how confusing.

The shouting has begun, We want work, we want work, we

want work, that's about all they say, apart from the occasional insult, you thieves, but spoken so quietly that it's as if the person hurling the insult were ashamed, then someone else shouts, Free elections, what's the point of saying that now, but the great clamor of voices rises up and drowns out everything else, We want work, we want work, what kind of world is it that divides into those who make a profession of idleness and those who want work but can't get it. Someone gave the signal, or perhaps it was agreed that the meeting could go on for a certain number of minutes, or perhaps Leandro Leandres or Lieutenant Contente made a telephone call, or maybe the mayor peered out of the window, There they are, the dogs, but whatever the sequence of events, the mounted guards unsheathed their sabers, oh good heavens, such courage, such heroism, it sends a shiver down the spine, I had quite forgotten about the sun until it glinted on those polished blades, a positively divine light, enough to make a man tremble with patriotic fervor, well, doesn't it you.

The horses break into a trot, there's not enough space for anything bolder, and those who try to escape from beneath the hooves and the saber thrusts immediately fall to the ground. A man could perhaps stand such humiliation, but sometimes he chooses not to, or is suddenly blinded with rage, and then the sea rises, arms are raised, hands grab reins or throw stones picked up from the ground or brought with them in their bags, it's the right of those who have no other weapons, and the stones come flying from the back of the crowd, probably without hurting anyone, horse or rider, because a stone hurled at random like that, if it was, simply drops to the ground. It was a battle scene worthy of a painting on the wall of the commander's office or in the officers' mess, the horses rearing up, the imperial guard, sabers unsheathed, striking with either the flat of the sword or the edge, the rebellious workers retreating then advancing like the tide, the wretches. This was the charge of June twenty-third, fix that date in your memory, children, although other dates also adorn the history of the latifundio and are deemed glorious for the same or similar reasons. The infantry also excelled itself, especially Sergeant Armamento, a man with a blind faith and a wrong-headed view of the law, there's the first burst of machine-gun fire, and another, both of them fired into the air as a warning, and when the people in the castle hear these shots, they cheer and clap, the sweet girls of the latifundio, faces scarlet with heat and bloodthirsty thoughts, and their mothers and fathers, and the boyfriends trembling with the desire to get out there themselves, lance in hand, and finish the job just started, Kill them all. The third burst of fire is aimed low, all that target shooting is proving its worth, let the smoke clear, not bad, although it could have been better, there are three men lying on the ground, one of whom is getting up, clutching his arm, he was lucky, another is dragging himself painfully along, one leg incapacitated, and that one over there isn't moving at all, It's José Adelino dos Santos, it's José Adelino, says someone from Montemor, who knows him. José Adelino dos Santos is dead, he got a bullet in the brain and couldn't believe it at first, but shook his head as if he had been bitten by an insect, then he understood, Those bastards have killed me, and he fell helplessly backward, with no wife there to help him, his own blood formed a cushion under his head, a red cushion, if you please. The people in the castle applaud again, they sense that this time it's serious, and the cavalry charges, scattering the crowd, someone should pick up the body, but no one approaches.

The people from Monte Lavre heard the whistle of the bullets, and José Medronho is bleeding from his face, he was lucky, it was just a graze, but he'll be scarred for the rest of his life. Gracinda Mau-Tempo is weeping, clinging to her husband, she heads off with other people down the narrow streets, how terrible, they can hear the triumphant cry of the guards as they make their arrests, and suddenly Leandro Leandres appears along with other dragons from the PIDE, a half dozen of them, João Mau-Tempo saw them and turned pale, and then he did something quite mad, he stood in the path of the enemy, trembling, but not with fear, ladies and gentlemen, let us be quite clear about that, but the other man either did not see him or did not recognize him, though those eyes are not easy to forget, and when the dragons had passed him by, João Mau-Tempo could no longer hold back his tears, tears of rage and deep sadness too, when will our suffering end. José Medronho's wound is no longer bleeding, no one would think that he had been within a millimeter of having the bones in his face shattered, what would he look like now if that had happened. Sigismundo Canastro is breathing hard, but the others are fine, and Gracinda Mau-Tempo is a girl again, sobbing, I saw him, he fell to the ground, dead, that's what she's saying, but some disagree, no, they say, he was taken to the hospital, although how we don't know, whether on a stretcher or in someone's arms, they wouldn't dare just drag him there even if they wanted to, Kill them all, comes the cry from the castle, however, one must respect the formalities, a man is not dead until a doctor says he is, and even then. Dr. Cordo is here, dressed in his white coat, let us hope his soul is of the same color, and as he is about to approach the body, Leandro Leandres blocks his path and says in a voice of urgent authority, Doctor, this man is wounded, he must be taken to Lisbon at once, and you must go with him for his greater safety. Those of us who have been listening to these stories from the latifundio are amazed to see the dragon Leandro Leandres taking pity on a victim and expressing a wish to save him, Take him, Doctor, an ambulance is already on its way, a car, quickly, there's no time to lose, the sooner he leaves here the better, hearing him talk like this, so urgently, so briskly, it's hard to believe what happened to João Mau-Tempo, or what he claims happened, when he was taken prisoner eight years earlier, that's how long ago it was, they obviously couldn't have treated him so very badly, apart from that statue business, the proof being that he came from Monte Lavre to take part in this demonstration, he clearly hasn't learned his lesson, he was lucky a bullet didn't find him.

Dr. Cordo goes over to José Adelino dos Santos and says, This man is dead, there is no denying such words, after all, a doctor studies for many years, and in that time he must have learned how to tell a dead man from a live one, however, Leandro Leandres was taught from a different primer and is, in his own way, a connoisseur of the living and the dead, and based on that knowledge and on his own self-interest, he insists, This man is wounded, Doctor, and must be taken to Lisbon, even a child would understand that these words are intended as a threat, but the doctor's soul clearly is as white as the coat he's wearing, and if it's stained with blood, that's because the soul has blood in it too, and he responds, I take the wounded to Lisbon, but I do not accompany the dead, and Leandro Leandres loses his temper and propels the doctor into an empty room, I'm warning you, if you don't take him, you'll pay for it, and the doctor answers, Do what you like, but I'm not taking a dead man to Lisbon, and having said that, he left the room to deal with the genuinely wounded, of which there were many, and some of whom went straight from there to prison, in fact, more than a hundred men, whether wounded or unscathed, were arrested, and if José Adelino dos Santos did end up being transported to Lisbon, it was simply a drama put on by the PIDE, a way of pretending that they had done everything they could to save him, a form of mockery really, and along with José Adelino dos Santos, they took other men arrested on that same day, and each one suffered as João Mau-Tempo suffered and as we have described.

The party from Monte Lavre escaped the patrols scouring and encircling the town, and all returned save one, António Mau-Tempo, who told his father, I'm going to stay here in Montemor, I'll be back tomorrow, and there was no point arguing with him, he replied to all their arguments with, Don't worry, I'm not in any danger, and though he had no clear idea of what he was going to do, he felt he had to stay, and then the others set off along ancient paths into the countryside, they're going to be tired out by the time they get home, although perhaps, farther on, when they rejoin the road, someone will come along and give them a lift to Monte Lavre, where the news of what happened has already spread, and oddly enough, when they did arrive, Faustina Mau-Tempo immediately heard their knock at the door and understood everything they said as if she had the keenest hearing in the world, even though she's deaf as a post, although some might hint that she sometimes only pretends to be deaf.

That night, which was again starry but moonless, while many women were grieving in Montemor, one woman more than all the others, there was a great uproar at the guards' barracks. More than once, patrols were dispatched to search the surrounding area, they entered houses, woke people up, in an attempt to solve the mystery of the stones or pebbles that kept falling onto the roof, some tiles had been broken and some windows too, constituting damage to public property, perhaps it was revenge on the part of the angels or mere mischief-making born of sheer boredom up there on heaven's balcony, because miracles shouldn't only involve restoring sight to the blind and giving new legs to the lame, a few well-aimed stones have their place in the secrets of the world and of religion, or so thinks António Mau-Tempo, because that's why he stayed behind, in order to perform that miracle, hidden away high up on the hill, in the pitch-black shadow of the castle, hurling the stones with his strong right arm, and whenever a patrol came by, he hid away in a cave from which he would later emerge as if from the dead, and fortunately no one spotted him. At around one in the morning, his arm grown weary, he threw one last stone and felt as sad as if he were about to die. A tired and hungry man, he went around the south side of the castle and down the hill, then spent the rest of the night walking the four leagues to Monte Lavre, following the road but keeping well away from it, like some malefactor afraid of his own conscience, occasionally having to go around the edge of some of the unharvested wheatfields blocking his path, because he couldn't risk walking through them and had to remain hidden from both the latifundio guards with their hunting rifles and the uniformed national guards armed with carbines.

When he was within sight of Monte Lavre, the sky was beginning to grow light, a glow so faint that only expert eyes would notice. He forded the stream, not wanting to be seen by anyone watching from the bridge, and then he followed the course of the stream, keeping close to the willows, until he reached a point where he could climb up the bank and into the village, taking great care in case any insomniac guards should still be out and about. And when he drew near the house, he saw what awaited him, a light, a lantern, like the lantern on a small fishing boat, where the mother of this boy of thirty-one was watching and waiting for him to return home, late from playing at throwing stones. António Mau-Tempo jumped over the fence and into the yard, he was safe now, but this time Faustina Mau-Tempo, absorbed in tears and dark thoughts, did not hear him arrive, but she did notice the sound of the door latch or perhaps felt a vibration that touched her soul, My son, and they embraced as if he had returned from performing great deeds in a war, and knowing herself to be hard of hearing, she did not wait for his questions, but said, as if she were reciting a rosary, Your father got home safe and so did Gracinda and your brother-in-law, and all the others, you were the only one who had me sick with worry, and António Mau-Tempo again embraced his mother, which is the best and most easily understood of answers. From the next room, still in darkness, João Mau-Tempo asks, and not in the voice of someone who has just woken up, You're back safe then, and António Mau-Tempo answers, Yes, Pa. And since it's nearly time to eat, Faustina Mau-Tempo lights the fire and puts the coffeepot on the trivet.

THE LATIFUNDIO IS AN inland sea. It has its shoals of tiny, edible fish, its barracuda and its deadly piranha, its pelagic fish, its leviathans and its gelatinous manta rays, blind creatures that drag their bellies along in the mud and die there too, as well as other great, strangling, serpentine monsters. It's a Mediterranean sea, but it has its tides and undertows, gentle currents that take time to complete the circuit, and occasional sudden churnings that shake the surface, provoked by winds that come from outside or by unexpected inflows of water, while in the dark depths the waves slowly roll, bringing with them nourishing ooze and slime, for how much longer, one wonders. Comparing the latifundio with the sea is as useful as it is useless, but it has the advantage of being easily understood, if we disturb the water here, the water all around will move, sometimes too far away to be seen, that is why we would be wrong to call this sea a swamp, and even if it were, it would still be a great mistake to believe in mere appearances, however dead this sea might seem to be.

Every day, the men get out of their beds, and every night, they lie down in them, and by beds we mean whatever serves them as a bed, every day, they sit down before their food or their desire to have enough food, every day, they light and extinguish a lantern, there is nothing new under the rose of the sun. This is the great sea of the latifundio, with its clouds of fish-sheep and predators, and if it was ever thus, why should it change, even if we accept that some changes are inevitable, all it needs is for the guards to remain vigilant, that's why every day the armed boats put out to sea with their nets intending to catch fishermen, Where did you get that bag of acorns, or that bundle of firewood, or What are you doing here at this hour, where have you come from, where are you going, a man cannot choose to step out of his usual rut, unless he has been employed to do so and is, therefore, being watched. However, each day brings some hope with its sorrow, or is that just laziness on the part of the narrator, who doubtless once read or heard these words somewhere and liked them, because if sorrow and hope come along together, then the sorrow will never end and the hope will only ever be just that and nothing more, this is what Father Agamedes would say, for he lives off sorrow and hope, and anyone who thinks differently is either mad or foolish. It would be nearer the truth to say that each day is the day it is, plus the day just gone, and that the two together make tomorrow, even a child should know such simple things, but there are those who try to divide up the days like someone cutting slices of melon rind to give to the pigs, the smaller the pieces, the greater the illusion of eternity, that's why pigs say, O god of pigs, when will we ever eat our fill.

This sea of the latifundio is subject to undertows, pounded by storms, lashed by waves, enough sometimes to knock down a wall or simply leap over it, as we understand happened in Peniche, and now you can see how right we were to mention the sea, because Peniche is both a fishing port and a prison-fortress, but still they escaped,* and that escape will be much discussed on the latifun-

---

* A reference to the dramatic escape in January 1960 of ten leading members of the Portuguese Communist Party being held in the high-security prison in Peniche.

dio, but what sea are we talking about, this land is usually as dry as dust, that's why men ask, When will we ever slake our thirst and the thirst of our parents, not to mention the thirst waiting under this stone for any children we might have. The news arrived and was impossible to hide, and there was always someone to fill in what the newspapers didn't say, let's sit down beneath this holm oak and I'll tell you what I know. It's time for the red kites to fly still higher, they cry out over the vast earth, anyone who can understand them will have much to tell, but for the moment we must make do with our human language. That's why Dona Clemência can say to Father Agamedes, The peace we never had is over, which may seem like a contradiction and yet this lady never spoke a truer word, these are new times and they're approaching very fast, It's like a stone rolling down a hill, that is what Father Agamedes says, because he prefers to use secondhand words, a habit acquired at the altar, but let us have enough evangelical charity to try and understand him, what he means is that if we don't get out of the way of the stone, God knows what will happen, and let us forgive him this new ruse, because it's quite clear that we don't need to wait for God in order to know what will happen to someone who fails to get out of the way of a rolling stone, which gathers no moss and spares no Lambertos.

And no sooner had this conversation ended, well, that's not quite true, because there were a few anxious months when negligence joined forces with sacrilege, because it was sheer negligence to allow those prisoners to escape and sacrilege to see a ship once named the *Santa Maria* sailing the seas under the new name of *Santa Liberdade*,* Dona Clemência is, of course, praying fervently

---

* A reference to the hijacking of the Portuguese liner *Santa Maria* by the DRIL (Directorio Revolucionário Ibérico de Liberación) in 1961. The "pirates" sailed the ship out into the Atlantic and renamed it the *Santa Liberdade*, gaining the attention of the world's press and hoping to undermine the Salazar and Franco dictatorships.

and passionately for the salvation of the church and the nation, at the same time demanding punishment for the ruffians, We wouldn't be in this situation if they had better examples to follow, you can't play with other people's lives, still less with my wealth. However, this is merely what the lady of the house says while safe within her four walls, always assuming Norberto is willing to listen to her, she would have no one to talk to if it wasn't for Father Agamedes, for she barely leaves the house now, or only rarely for a trip to Lisbon to see the latest fashions, or to Figueira for the traditional family holiday by the sea, and to be honest, her mind seems to be wandering, it must be her age, talking about her wealth and some ship sailing the sea, it's certainly not sailing on the inland sea of the latifundio, she must be going soft in the head, but there you'd be quite wrong, because she inherited shares in the colonial navigation company from her father, Alberto, God rest his soul, and that's what bothers her.

This bitter cold isn't just because it's January on the latifundio. All the windows are shut, and if this were Lamberto's castle rather than Norberto's palatial mansion, we would see armed men on the ramparts, just as, not so long ago, we saw fearful, bloodthirsty people filling the ruins of Montemor, the times are changing, platoons of guards patrol the latifundio, in their boots and on a war footing, while Norberto reads the newspapers and listens to the radio and shouts at the maids, that's what men do when they get upset. What really angers him is the air of sly contentment he sees on the faces of ordinary people, as if spring had arrived early for them, they don't seem to feel the cold, at least their contentment proved short-lived, for two days later they had to change their tune, God does not sleep and they will be punished, the *Santa Maria* has risen from the deep, pray for us, and let us not think too badly of Father Agamedes, who succumbed to the sin of envy, it was a long time coming in such a holy creature, and all because he couldn't hold a solemn Te Deum Laudamus as an act of thanksgiving, but that would not have gone down well in this wretched village of Monte Lavre with its godless inhabitants.

This is a bad year for the latifundio. There goes the maiden out for a ride on her fine steed, her skirt and saddle cloth flapping, her veil fashionably loose in the wind, the picture of composure, when suddenly the beast stumbles, for these are medieval roads, sir, and she falls flat on the ground, revealing all her most private penumbras, she doesn't seem too seriously hurt, poor love, the worst thing was the way the animal reared up and kicked as it scrambled to its feet. They say that pride goeth before a fall, which is a horsey version of the more melancholy dictum, Misfortunes never come singly, why, only yesterday those prisoners escaped from Peniche, bloody communists, baby eaters, have you seen my children, neighbor, only yesterday souls and seas were all stirred up by that new tale of pirates, we should shoot the lot of them, such a lovely ship too, all dressed in white, *Santa Maria* walking on the water like her divine son, and now there's news from Africa as well, about the blacks, Well, I always said we were too lenient with them, I said as much, but no one would believe me, you have to live there to know how to deal with them, they don't like work, you see, they're shirkers, they'll always go to the bad, and now you see the result, we treated them too kindly, as if they were Christians, but all is not lost, we won't lose Africa if we send in the army and have a proper war, remember Gugunhana,* brave words from the mayor, spoken quickly and boldly, he could have been a general if he'd had the military training, but at least he spoke out. The imperial dream soon faded, best to run away from the mess we made, the black man is now a Portuguese citizen, long live the black man who comes bear-

* Gugunhana, or Ngungunyane, was a tribal king of a territory in Mozambique. He rebelled against the Portuguese and was defeated by General Joaquim Mouzinho de Albuquerque in 1895. He lived the rest of his life in exile, first in Lisbon and then in the Azores, where he died in 1906.

ing no weapon, but keep your eye on him nonetheless, and down with the other sort, and one day, if we happen to wake up in a good mood, we'll declare that these overseas provinces, our former colonies, are now independent states, well, what's in a name, what matters is that the shit stays the same and that those who have eaten nothing else should continue to eat shit, whites and blacks, and anyone who can spot the difference wins a prize.

It would seem, Father Agamedes, that God and the Virgin have turned their benign eyes away from Portugal, look how discontented and restless people are, the devil has clearly taken hold of the gentle hearts of the Lusitanians, perhaps we didn't pray enough, the priests told us as much, and I've done what I can, and I've always been ready with good advice, both in the pulpit and in the confessional, this is, in fact, a dialogue, in which two people take turns to speak, but when Father Agamedes returns to his house, he is thinking something quite different, something more suited to a man of this time or of that other time when souls were conquered with the sword and with fire, What they need is a sound beating, that's telling them.

One really doesn't know where to turn, now it's the fortresses in India, weep, O souls of da Gama, Albuquerque, Almeida and Noronha,* no, that's all we need, for grown men to weep, we must hold out to the last man, we will show the world what we Portuguese are worth, anyone who retreats is betraying the nation, better cut the shoe than pinch the foot, the government calls on everyone to do his duty. It's a sad Christmas in Alberto's house, not that there is any shortage of food or of the Lord's blessings, at least it was a good year for cork, so that's something, but there are black clouds with thunder in their bellies gathering over the country and over the latifundio, what will become of Portugal and of us, true, we have someone to protect us, for a start, there are the guards, to

---

* All are names of Portuguese viceroys of India in the fifteenth and sixteenth centuries.

each of whom we give a gift, to the captain, lieutenant, sergeant and corporal, poor things, it's only right, they earn so little and are always so ready to defend our property, imagine if we had to pay them out of our own pockets, it would cost us a fortune. It's just as well, now that the last vestiges of a Portuguese presence in the East are being removed, along with our soldiers and sailors, that we never really took much interest in Goa, Daman and Diu anyway, a gift, you say, what an idea, I don't mean that kind of gift, we've already mentioned the ones we gave to the captain, the lieutenant, the sergeant and the corporal, each of whom either came to fetch his own or, out of discretion and a desire to avoid prattling tongues, had it brought to him, no, this is a different kind of gift, that given by the soldiers and sailors who, on the point of death, raise themselves up on their elbow and, dying, cry out in response to the roll call, absent, an ancient practice, for when necessary even the dead can vote. The other good thing is that all this is happening a long way off, India and Africa are not exactly close, the fires are burning far from my borders, the sea, lots of sea, separates us from them, they won't come over here, and Portugal won't lack for sons to defend the latifundio from afar, don't bite the hand that feeds you, you've been warned.

Tomorrow, said Dona Clemência to her children, and her nieces and nephews, is New Year's Day, or so she had gleaned from the calendar, placing her hopes in the brand-new year and sending her best wishes to all the Portuguese people, well, that isn't quite what she said, Dona Clemência has always spoken rather differently, but she's learning, we all choose our own teachers, and while these words are still hanging in the air, news comes that there has been an attack on the barracks of the third infantry regiment in Beja, now Beja is not in India or Angola or Guinea-Bissau, it's right next door, it's on the latifundio, and the dogs are outside barking, though the coup was put down, they will speak of little else over the next weeks and months, so how was it possible for a barracks to be attacked, all it took was a little luck, that's all it ever takes, perhaps that's what was lacking the first time around, and no one noticed, that's our fate, if the horse carrying the messenger bearing orders to commence battle loses a shoe, the whole course of history is turned upside down in favor of our enemies, who will triumph, what bad luck. And in saying this we are not being disrespectful to those who left the peace and safety of their homes and set off to try and pull down the pillars of the latifundio, though Samson and everyone else might die in the attempt, and when the dust had settled and we went and looked, we found that it was Samson who had died and not the pillars, perhaps we should have sat down under this holm oak and taken turns telling each other the thoughts we had in our head and heart, because there is nothing worse than distrust, it was good that they hijacked the *Santa Maria*, and the attack in Beja was good too, but no one came to ask us latifundio dogs and ants if either the ship or the attack had anything to do with us, We really value what you're doing, though we don't know who you are, but since we are just dogs and ants, what will we say tomorrow when we all bark together and you pay as little heed to us as did the owners of this latifundio you want to surround, sink and destroy. It's time we all barked together and bit deep, captain general, and meanwhile check to see that your horse doesn't have a shoe missing or that you have only three bullets when you should have four.

THESE MEN AND WOMEN were born to work, like good to average livestock, they leave or are dragged out of their mother's womb, left to grow up one way or another, it doesn't really matter, what matters is that they should be strong and good with their hands, even if they can make only one gesture, so what if, within a few years, they become stiff and heavy, they are walking logs who, when they arrive at work, give themselves a shake and produce from their rigid bodies two arms and two legs that move back and forth, you see how kind and competent the Creator was in making such perfect instruments for digging, scything, hoeing and generally making themselves useful.

Since they were born to work, it would be a contradiction in terms for them to have too much rest. The best machine is the one most capable of continuous work, properly lubricated so that it doesn't jam up, frugally fed and, if possible, given only as much fuel as mere maintenance requires, and, in case of breakdown or old age, it must, above all, be easily replaceable, that's what those human scrap yards, cemeteries, are for, or else the machine simply sits, rusting and creaking at its front door, watching nothing at all pass by or gazing down at its own sad hands, who would have thought it would come to this. On the latifundio, generally speaking, men and women have short lives, it's astonishing that any of them ever reach old age, but when we happen to pass some apparently old man, we learn that he is only forty, and that the shrunken woman with the leathery face is not yet thirty, so living in the country doesn't exactly extend your life, that's an urban myth, as is that most sensible of sayings, Early to bed and early to rise makes a man healthy, wealthy and wise, it would be amusing to see those same urbanites standing with one hand on the handle of their hoe, staring at the horizon, waiting for the sun to come up and, utterly exhausted, longing for a dusk that never comes, because the sun is an awkward so-and-so, always in such a hurry to rise and always so reluctant to set. Just like us.

However, the days of acceptance and resignation are coming to an end. A voice is traveling the roads of the latifundio, it goes into towns and villages, it talks on the hillsides and on cork plantations, a voice that consists of two essential words and many others that serve to explain those two words, eight hours, this may not appear to mean very much, but if we say eight hours of work, then the meaning becomes clearer, there are sure to be those who protest at this scandalous idea, what is it these workers want, if they sleep eight hours and work another eight, what will they do with the remaining eight hours, it's an invitation to idleness, they clearly don't want to work, these are modern ideas, it's all the fault of the war, customs have changed out of all recognition, first they stole India from us, now they want to take Africa away, then there was that ship that sailed the seas causing an international scandal, and the general who rose up against those who gave him his stars, who can one trust, tell me that, and now there's this disastrous business of the eight-hour day, they should have stuck to the law of God, give or take an hour, twelve hours of daylight and twelve hours of night, depending on when the sun rises and sets, of course, and if that isn't God's law, then let's say it's the law of nature, which must be obeyed.

The voice roaming the latifundio may not hear these mutterings, and if it does, it ignores them, these are old-fashioned ideas from the days of Lamberto, Work keeps them busy, if they weren't working, they'd be getting drunk in bars and then going home to beat their wives, poor things. Don't go thinking these are easy paths to follow. This voice has been pounding roads and streets for a whole year now, eight hours, eight hours of work, and some don't believe it, some believe that this will happen only when the world is about to end and the latifundio wants to save its soul and be able to appear at the final judgment and say to the angels and archangels, I took pity on my serfs, they were working far too many hours, and for the love of God, I ordered them to work only eight hours a day, with a rest on Sunday, and because I did this, I expect nothing less than a place in paradise at God's right hand. That is what some skeptics think, afraid that it will be a change for the worse. But the carriers of the voice did not rest all year, they traveled the whole latifundio proclaiming those words, while the guards and the PIDE agents twitched their ears uneasily, the way donkeys do when tormented by flies. Then they unleash furious, martial patrols, all that's missing are the bugles and drums, and they would have loved that, but it didn't fit in with the battle plan, imagine if the conspirators were gathered together on some lonely hillside or deep in the woods and they heard the trumpets blaring in the distance, tantarararatantan, we'd never catch anyone. The guards were given reinforcements, so were the PIDE agents, and any village without a doctor was given the medicine of twenty or thirty guards and accompanying weapons, and these guards were, of course, in permanent communication with the dragons defending the State and who don't like me at all, pity the real dragons, they're as ugly as toads and lizards, but they don't do any real harm, the proof of which is that paradise is full to bursting with fire-breathing dragons.* And given that guards tend to be astute rascals, they invented the subtle art of placing a pamphlet beneath a stone, yet visible enough for a blind man to see, the kind of pamphlet left by those commies who travel around the latifundio saying subversive things about eight-hour days and so forth, they might as well hand over the country to Moscow right now. Anyway, having laid this trap, they hide behind a hedge or in a hollow or behind an innocent tree or boulder, and when some unsuspecting man comes along, he perhaps picks up the pamphlet and puts it in his pocket or inside his hat or between skin and shirt, it's one of those white sheets covered in small black lettering, not only does he not read very well, his eyesight is poor too, anyway, he hasn't gone ten steps when the guards ambush him on the path, Halt, show us what you've got in your pockets, if this doesn't strike you as a show of great astuteness, then all we can say is that there is clearly a lot of ill feeling against the guards, who deserve only praise for their expert application of the principles of hypocrisy and petty mendacity, rammed into them at the same time as they were being taught how to use a gun and organize an ambush.

Surrounded by carbines, the finder of the pamphlet has no choice but to empty his pockets of a gypsy knife, half an ounce of tobacco, a book of cigarette papers, a piece of string, a gnawed crust of bread and ten tostões, but this doesn't satisfy the guards, who have other ambitions, Take another look, it's for your own good, you might get hurt if we were to frisk you, and then, from between skin and shirt, he produces the pamphlet, already damp

---

* Presumably a reference to Salazar's entirely cynical view of rural life as some kind of idyll or paradise (for example, there were often competitions to find the most Portuguese village in Portugal). This paradise may not have a doctor, but there will always be a dragon or two in the form of a PIDE agent.

with sweat, not that it's so very hot, but the poor man isn't made of steel, marooned as he is amid these guffawing guards, things are getting serious, Corporal Tacabo, or some private temporarily promoted to lead the patrol, knows very well what the pamphlet is, but he pretends to be surprised and examines it carefully, before saying slyly, Now you're in for it, we've caught you carrying communist propaganda, we're taking you to the barracks, it's Montemor or Lisbon for you, my lad, I certainly wouldn't want to be in your shoes. And when the man tries to explain that he has just found the pamphlet a moment ago, that he hasn't had time to read it, that he doesn't know how to read, that he happened to be passing by, saw the pamphlet and, out of natural curiosity, picked it up as anyone would, but he doesn't finish what he has to say, because he receives a blow to the chest or the back with the butt of a rifle, or else a kick, get a move on or I'll shoot you, arms are my theme and these matchless heroes.*

Talking is like eating cherries from a bowl, you take hold of one word and others immediately follow, or perhaps they're like ticks, which are equally hard to disentangle if they're attached one to the other, because words never come singly, even the word loneliness needs the person who's feeling lonely, which is just as well, I suppose. These guards are so steadfast and loyal that they go wherever the latifundio sends them, they never question, never argue, they are mere minions, you only have to consider what happened on May Day, when men and women duly celebrated the day of the worker, but when they returned to their labors the following day, the guards were waiting for them, Only those who didn't miss work yesterday can work today, those are our orders, although there was little point in saying this, since everyone had missed

---

* An ironic reference to the first line of Luís Vaz de Camões's poem *The Lusiads*, Portugal's great epic, published in 1572. It glorifies the great Portuguese navigators, who set sail to discover new worlds. It is, of course, also an echo of the opening line of *The Aeneid*.

work. What's going to happen now, the workers draw back, how are they going to resolve this, and because the guards had occupied the terrain, and the overseer was hiding behind them rather than taking his due part in the negotiations, the workers decided to go back to their houses, it was still early in the morning, you see, and enjoy another day's holiday, and the guards stayed behind to keep an eye on the ants, who were going about their business and raising their heads in surprise like dogs. But before the workers left, the sergeant, standing next to the overseer or foreman or manager or whatever, made intelligent use of his interrogation methods, Why didn't you come to work yesterday, Because it was the first of May, the day of the worker, and we're workers. It was an innocent enough reply, there they were, standing before me, Corporal, looking at me with grave eyes, thinking they could deceive me, as if I would be so easily taken in, that's what these shameless wretches do, they look at you gravely like that and you can't tell what they're really thinking, but I gave it to them straight, I know how to deal with them, I said, you'd better tell me the truth, you can't fool me, the reason you didn't come to work was political, but they said, No, sir, it wasn't political, the first of May is the day of the worker, and when they said that, I gave a little mocking laugh, And what would you know about that, and someone at the back, unfortunately I couldn't see his face, said, It's the same all over the world, and that, as you can imagine, really got my goat, This isn't the world, this is Portugal and the Alentejo, we have our own laws, and at this point, the foreman whispered a secret to me, well, it wasn't a secret exactly, it was simply what we'd already agreed I would say, and I declared, with all the authority with which I had been invested, Only those who didn't miss work yesterday can work today, and as soon as I said this, they all moved away, all together as they usually do, it's the same when they sing, and off they went back home, their hoes on their shoulders, because it was hoeing they had come to do, and I couldn't help but feel a certain respect for them really, although I'm not sure why. Words are like ticks, or like the cherries that ripen in May, and if respect is not the final word, it is at least the right one.

April is the month of a thousand words.* Meetings are held at night in the fields, the men can barely see each other's faces, but they can hear each other's voices, slightly muffled if the place isn't deemed particularly safe, or louder and clearer if they're in the middle of nowhere, but they always keep sentinels posted, in accordance with the strategic art of prevention, as if they were defending an encampment. On their side, they are waging a peaceful war. The guards don't come in pairs anymore, but in dozens or half dozens, and when the roads allow, they arrive in jeeps or trucks, or they advance in a line, like beaters, so if in the dark of night the guards are heard approaching, the workers' sentinels draw back to give the alarm, and either the guards pass right by, in which case silence is the best defense, with every man seated or standing, holding both breath and thoughts, turned suddenly to stone like ancient megaliths, or the guards head straight for them, and the order then is to scatter along the beaten tracks, fortunately the guards don't yet have dogs.

The following night, they will pick up the conversation where they left off, in that same place or somewhere else, their patience is infinite. And when they can, they meet by day as well, in smaller groups, or go to someone's house and talk by the fire while the women silently wash the dishes and the children sleep in the corner of the room. And if one man happens to be standing next to another on the threshing floor, each word spoken and heard is like a mallet striking a stake, driving it a little further in, and when, in the fields, it's time to eat, they sit on the ground with their lunch

---

* The expression in Portuguese is "em Abril aguas mil"—literally, "in April a thousand waters"—because April is traditionally a rainy month. This is Saramago's version of that familiar expression.

pails between their legs, and while the spoon rises and falls and the cool breeze chills their body, their words return to the same theme, and they say slowly, Let's demand an eight-hour day, enough of working from dawn to dusk, and the more prudent among them speak fearfully of the future, What will happen if the bosses refuse to give us work, and the women washing the dishes after supper, while the fire burns, feel ashamed of their husbands' caution and agree with the friend who knocked on the door to say, Let's demand an eight-hour day, enough of working from dawn to dusk, because that is how long the women work too, except they often do so when in pain or menstruating or heavily pregnant, or with their breasts overflowing with the milk that should have been suckled, they're lucky it hasn't dried up, so those who believe that all one has to do is raise a banner and say, Right, let's go, are much mistaken. Yes, April has to be the month of a thousand words, because even those who are certain and convinced have their moments of doubt, of soul-searching and despair, there are the guards, the dragons of the PIDE and the black shadow that spreads over the latifundio and never leaves, there is no work, and are we, with our own hands, going to shake the sleeping beast awake and say, Tomorrow we will only work for eight hours, this is not the first of May, the first of May is the least of it, no one can force me to go to work, but if I were to say, Eight hours and no more, it would be like baiting a rabid dog. And the friend says, sitting here on the cork plantation or by my side on the threshing floor or in the night so dark I can't see his face, he says, It's not just about working eight hours, we're going to demand a minimum wage of forty escudos too, if we don't want to die of exhaustion and hunger, these are fine things to ask for and to do, but difficult to achieve. It's good that there are a lot of conversations and a lot of voices, but out of the meeting comes one voice, and this isn't just a manner of speaking, it's true, some voices stand up on their own two feet, What kind of life have we led, tell me that, in the last couple of years, two of my children have died of hunger, and the one child I have left will be brought up to be a beast of burden, and I don't want to carry on being the beast of burden I am, these are words that might wound delicate ears, but there are no such ears here, although no one present at this meeting likes to look in the mirror and see himself stuck between the shafts of a cart or wearing a saddle and a yoke, That's how it's been ever since we were born.

Then another voice emerges, and on the shadow of the night falls another shadow come from who knows where, what can he be thinking of, he's not talking about the eight-hour day or about the forty-escudo minimum wage, that's what we came here to discuss, but no one has the heart to interrupt him, They have always done their best to strip us of our dignity, and everyone knows who he means by they, they are the guards, the PIDE, the latifundio and its owners Alberto or Dagoberto, the dragon and the captain, gnawing hunger and broken bones, anxiety and hernias, They have always done their best to strip us of our dignity, but it can't go on, it must stop, listen to what happened to me and to my father, now dead, it was a secret between us, but I can stay silent no longer, if my story doesn't convince you, then we are lost, there's nothing more to be done, once, many years ago, it was a dark night just like tonight, my father went with me and I with him to pick acorns, because there was nothing to eat at home, and I was already a young man and thinking about getting married, we had a bag with us, just an ordinary bag, and we went together to keep each other company, not because of the heavy load, and when the bag was nearly full, the guards appeared, I'm sure the same thing has happened to many of you here tonight, it's nothing to be ashamed of, picking up acorns from the ground isn't stealing, and even if it was, hunger is a good enough reason to steal, he who steals out of hunger will find forgiveness in heaven, I know that isn't quite how the saying goes, but it should, and if I'm a thief because I stole some acorns, then so is the owner of the acorns, who neither made the

earth nor planted the tree nor tended it, anyway, the guards arrived and said, well, there's no point repeating what they said, I
can't even remember, but they called us every name under the sun,
how have we put up all these years with being called such names,
and when my father begged them for the love of God to let us take
the acorns we had picked, they started laughing and said we could
keep the acorns, but on one condition, and do you know what that
was, they wanted us to fight each other and to let them watch, and
my father said he wasn't going to fight with his own son, and I said
the same, that I wouldn't fight with my father, but they said, in that
case, we would be taken to the barracks, where we would have to
pay a fine and possibly get a beating too, just to teach us some manners, and then my father said, all right, we would fight, but please,
comrades, don't think ill of that poor old man, now dead, and God
forgive me if, in telling you this story, I'm dragging him from his
grave, but we were starving, you see, anyway, my father pretended
to give me a shove, and I pretended he had pushed me over, we
wanted to see if we could fool them, but they said that if we didn't
fight properly, with a real intent to hurt each other, they would arrest us, I don't have words to describe what happened next, my
father became desperate, I saw it in his eyes, and he hit me and
really hurt me, but not because he had hit me that hard, and I responded in kind, and a minute later, we were rolling around on the
ground, and the guards were laughing like mad things, and, once,
I touched my father's face and it felt wet, but not with sweat, and I
was filled with rage, and I grabbed him by the shoulders and shook
him as if he were my worst enemy, and he, underneath me, kept
punching me on the chest, God, what a state to be in, and still the
guards were laughing, it was a dark night like tonight and so cold
that it ate into your bones, all around lay the countryside, and yet
the stones did not rise up, is this what men were born to do, and
when finally we stopped fighting, we were alone, the guards had
left, doubtless in sheer disgust, which was what we deserved, and

then my father started crying and I rocked him in my arms as if he were a child and swore I would never tell anyone, but I can no longer remain silent, it's not just a matter of eight hours or forty escudos, we must do something now if we are not to lose ourselves, because that isn't a life, two men fighting each other, father and son or whoever, purely to amuse the guards, it's not enough that they have weapons and we have none, we are not men if we do not now raise ourselves up from the ground, and I say this not for my own sake but for the sake of my dead father, who won't ever have another life, poor man, only the memory of me beating him and the guards laughing, as if they were drunk, if there was a God, surely he would have intervened then. When the voice stopped speaking, everyone stood up, there was no need to say anything more, each man set off to follow his own destiny, determined to be there on the first of May, determined to hold out for the eight-hour day and the wage of forty escudos, and even today, after all these years, no one knows which of them it was who fought with his own father, our eyes cannot bear the sight of too much suffering.

From hillside to woodland, these and other words did the rounds of the latifundio, although no one ever mentioned that father-son fight, because no one would believe it, and yet it was true, and meetings were arranged in Monte Lavre too, some people were afraid, but others were not, and so when the first of May arrived, everyone was ready, and those who felt afraid stuck fast to those who showed no fear, that's how it is even in time of war, said someone who had been in the war, although whether as one of the brave or of the timorous we don't know. A lot of gasoline and diesel was consumed that day, the spring air was full of fumes from the endless stream of jeeps and trucks laden with rifles and masked guards, they wear masks so as not to feel ashamed, and when they reached some town or village where there was a barracks, they would stop for a conference with the general staff, exchange orders and discuss the situation, how are things over in Setúbal, and in Baixo Alentejo and in Alto Alentejo, and in Ribatejo, which, don't forget, is also the latifundio. Armed patrols roamed the main streets and side streets, hoping to sniff out subversion, and from high vantage points they surveyed the inland sea like fish eagles, to see if they could spot the black or red flag of a pirate ship, as if anyone were going to run up such a flag, but the guards are obsessed, they can think of nothing else, and what they saw was perfectly innocuous, men strolling up and down in the squares, talking, all dressed in their skillfully darned and patched Sunday best, because the women of the latifundio are experts at patching the seats and knees of trousers, you should see them rooting around in the rag basket in search of just the right scrap of fabric, then placing it on the offending trouser leg before carefully cutting the fabric to size and sewing it on, it's a job requiring great precision, I'm sitting on the step outside my front door patching my husband's trousers, well, he can't go to work naked, it's enough that he's naked between the sheets.

Some will think this has nothing to do with the first of May and the eight-hour day and the forty escudos, but they are people who pay little attention to what goes on in the world, they think the world is this sphere rolling through space, pure astronomy, they might as well be blind, for there is nothing more closely connected to the first of May than this needle and this thread in the hand of this woman called Gracinda Mau-Tempo, who is patching these trousers so that her husband Manuel Espada can celebrate the first of May, the day of the worker. The guards pass right by the front door in a military-looking jeep, and Gracinda Mau-Tempo draws her only daughter, Maria Adelaide, closer to her, and the girl, who is seven and has the bluest eyes in the world, watches the jeep pass, these children seem singularly unimpressed by the sight of a uniform, there she is with her stern gaze, she has seen enough of life already to know who these guards are and what that uniform means.

After dark, the men return home. They will spend a restless night, like soldiers on the eve of battle, who knows who will return alive, strikes and demonstrations are one thing, they're used to that and know how bosses and guards usually respond, whereas this is more of a challenge, denying the latifundio a power that has been passed down to them from their great-great-great-grandparents, You will work for me from dawn to dusk all the days of your life, in accordance with my wishes and my needs, on the other days you can do as you please. From now on, Sigismundo Canastro won't need to get up so early, nor will João Mau-Tempo or António Mau-Tempo or Manuel Espada, nor any of the other men and women, who are still awake, thinking about what will happen tomorrow, it's a revolution, an eight-hour day on the latifundio, It's a gamble, win or lose, in Montargil they won, and we can't be seen to be less than them, in the middle of the night, they hear the guards' jeep prowling the streets of Monte Lavre, they want to frighten us, but they'll see.

These words are spoken by other mouths as well, those of Gilberto and Alberto, They'll see, and it was a great moment in the history of the latifundio, for even the owners of the land got up early to be present at the dawning of the day, if you don't look after what's yours, the devil will take it, the sun is up and not a single devil has turned up for work, overseer, foreman and manager are nervous, but the countryside is a balm to the eyes, May, glorious May, and Norberto consults his watch, half past seven, still no one, This has all the look of a strike, says a lackey, but Adalberto responds angrily, Shut up, he is furious, he knows what he intends to do, they all know, it's just a matter of waiting. And then the men begin to arrive, all together at the agreed hour, they politely say Good morning, why be bitter, and when it's eight o'clock, they start work, this is what they had decided to do, but Dagoberto bawls, Stop, and they all stop and look at him with innocent eyes, What is it, sir, such sang-froid is enough to drive a man mad. Who told

you to come to work at this hour, Norberto asks, and it is Manuel
Espada who speaks for the other workers, We did, on some estates they're already working an eight-hour day, and we are no less
than our comrades on those other estates, and Berto strides over
to him as if he were about to hit him, but he doesn't, he wouldn't
go that far, On my land, the timetable is the same as it has always
been, from dawn to dusk, it's up to you, you either stay and tomorrow make up for the time lost this morning, or you leave, because
I don't want you here, That's telling them, Dona Clemência will
say later, when her husband boasts of his deeds, and then what
happened, Then, Manuel Espada, who is married to Mau-Tempo's
daughter, he was the group's spokesman, said, Fine, we'll leave, and
they all left, and when they were walking back up to Monte Lavre,
António Mau-Tempo asked, What next, what do we do now, not
because he was worried or afraid, his question was intended to
help his brother-in-law, Now we do as we agreed, we gather together in the square, and if the guards turn up looking for trouble,
we go home, and tomorrow we go back to work, we start scything at eight o'clock, like today, that, more or less, was what João
Mau-Tempo said to another group of laborers, and Sigismundo
Canastro to his group, and so they all gathered in the square, and
the guards turned up, and Corporal Tacabo came over to them,
So you don't want to work, then, We do, but only for eight hours,
and the boss doesn't want to give us those eight hours of work,
Sigismundo Canastro is speaking the honest truth, but the corporal wants to know more, So this isn't a strike, No, we want to
work, but the boss sent us away, he says we can't work for just eight
hours, and that clear response will cause Corporal Tacabo to say
later on, I don't know what to do with them, Senhor Dagoberto,
the men say they want to work, and that it's you who, but before
he can finish his sentence, Dagoberto roars, They're idlers, that's
what they are, either they work from dawn to dusk or they can die
of hunger, there's no work for them here, as far as I know the gov-

ernment has issued no edict regarding an eight-hour day, and even if they have, I'm in charge here, I own the land, and that was the end of his conversation with Corporal Tacabo, and so the day concluded, with each man going home to his house, and the women wanting to know what had happened, as we saw with Dona Clemência, and as is the right of the other women too.

The men do their calculations, they have earned no money today, and how many more days like this will there be, it depends on the place, elsewhere, the latifundio gave in after two days, in others three, in others four, and in some places they spent weeks embroiled in this tug of war, to see whose strength or patience would win out, in the end, the men didn't bother turning up for work to find out if their conditions would be accepted, they stayed in the towns and villages, on strike, and this was all that was needed for the guards to return to their old ways, beating the workers and patrolling the latifundio on a war footing, but why repeat what everyone knows. Dagoberto and Alberto, Humberto and another Berto held out in their castles, however, the sacred alliance was beginning to unravel, and from other places came news of surrender, What should we do, Oh, leave them to it, they'll pay for it in the end, Yes, I know, Father Agamedes, such vengeful thoughts are most unchristian, and I'll do penance for it later, Well, it's not quite that clear-cut, Senhor Alberto, in Deuteronomy the Lord says, Vengeance is mine, and I will repay, Father Agamedes is a real fount of knowledge, how is it that from a book as big as the bible he managed to glean that one vital passage, what further justification do we need.

Here in Monte Lavre, though, they were fortunate in that the shopkeepers were willing to extend their credit, and in other places too, but this story is of particular interest to us, because João Mau-Tempo has had to walk these streets filled with the shame of owing money he could not pay back, with his wife Faustina weeping in misery and grief, and now he is going from shop to shop to pass on the message, and when he is received rudely, he pretends to feel nothing, suffering has given him a thick skin, he is not dealing here only with his own needs, Senhora Graniza, we are engaged in a struggle to gain the right to work an eight-hour day and the bosses refuse to agree to this, which is why we're on strike, I've come to ask if you could wait another three or four weeks, and as soon as we return to work, we'll start repaying what we owe, no one will be left owing you anything, it's a very big favor we're asking you, and the owner of that shop, a tall woman with pale eyes and a dark gaze, places her hands on the counter and says, respectfully, as a younger person to an older one, Senhor João Mau-Tempo, as surely as I hope that you will one day remember me, my house stands open, and these sibylline words are characteristic of the woman, who holds long mystical and political conversations with her customers and recounts tales and instances of miraculous cures and intercessions, well, all kinds of things happen on the latifundio, not just in the cities. João Mau-Tempo left with this good news, and Maria Graniza prepared a new slate, let's hope they all repay their debts, for they owe her twice over.

The birds of dawn wake up and see no one working. The lark says, How the world has changed. But the red kite, soaring high above, cries out that the world has changed far more than the lark suspects, and not just because the men are working only eight hours now, as the ants know, for they have seen many things and have good memories, which is hardly surprising, since they're always together. What do you say to this, Father Agamedes, I really don't know what to say, Senhora Dona Clemência, apart from farewell to a world that's going from bad to worse.

J OÃO MAU-TEMPO IS in bed. Today will be the day of his
death. The illnesses that poor people die from are almost always indefinable, so much so that doctors find it extremely hard to
fill in the death certificate unless they drastically simplify things,
generally people die of some obscure pain or in childbirth, but
how to translate this into clear nosological terms, all those years
of studying count for nothing. João Mau-Tempo was in the Montemor hospital for two months, although this did him little good,
not that this was the fault of the care he received, some cases are
beyond salvation, and in the end, he was brought back home to
die, and while his death here will be much the same, it will, at least,
be quieter, there'll be the smell of his own bed, the voices of people
passing by in the street, the sounds made by the poultry at dusk,
when the chickens go to their roosting places and the cockerel vigorously shakes its wings, who knows, he might miss these things
in the next world. During the time that João Mau-Tempo lan-
guished in the hospital, he lay awake all night listening to the sighs
and moans and sufferings of the ward, and fell asleep only toward
dawn. He doesn't sleep much better at home, but at least he has
just his own pain to worry about now, and that is something to be

resolved as a matter of confidence between his body and the spirit that still sustains it, with only his family as witness, and although one day their time will come, for they will not be left unharvested, even they will not be able to understand what it means to be a man alone with his own death, knowing, without anyone having to tell him, that today is the day. These are certainties that come into the mind when one wakes very early in the morning to hear the rain falling and dripping from the eaves like the threads of water from a spring, as children we used to perch on the lintel and, leaning against the door frame, hold out our hand to catch the drips, that's what João used to do and others who are not João. Faustina sleeps on top of the chest, at her insistence, so that her husband can have the double bed to himself, and there is no danger that she will forget her duties, you can see her eyes shining in the night, catching either the gleam of the dying fire or the glow from the oil lamp, perhaps her eyes shine so brightly as a compensation for being deaf. But if she falls asleep and João Mau-Tempo's pain becomes such that he cannot bear it alone, there is a piece of string linking his right wrist to his wife's left wrist, having reached a certain age, they are not going to be separated now, he only has to give the string a tug and Faustina will wake from her lightest of sleeps, get up fully dressed, go over to the bed and in the great silence of her deafness take her husband's hand in hers and, unable to do anything more, say a few comforting words to him, not everyone can boast of being able to do so much.

It isn't Sunday today, but in this rain, with the fields waterlogged, no one can go to work. João Mau-Tempo will have all of his small family around him, apart from those who live far away and cannot come, his sister Maria da Conceição, who still works as a maid in Lisbon, still with the same employers, for such examples of loyalty do exist, give them some gold dust and, when you come back, you'll find it all still there and possibly more besides, and his brother Anselmo, who went to live up north and was never heard of again, perhaps he's dead, perhaps he's gone on ahead, like Domingos in whatever year it was he died, who remembers now and who cares. Some lives are erased more completely than others, but that's because we have so many things to think about, we end up not noticing those lives until there comes a day when we regret our neglect, I was wrong, we say, I should have paid more attention, exactly, if only we'd had those feelings earlier, but these are merely twinges of remorse that arise and, fortunately, are almost immediately forgotten. His daughter Amélia will not be there either, as we know, she has worked as a maid in a house in Montemor ever since she was a girl, she was lucky, though, to have been able to visit him in the hospital and keep him company, and she has been able to save enough money to buy false teeth, her one little luxury, alas, her smile came too late to save her. Some friends will be missing too, Tomás Espada, who long withstood the absence of his wife Flor Martinha, no one ever saw their wrists bound together by a piece of string, but then some things that are invisible nevertheless exist, perhaps the people themselves would be unable to explain how, but Sigismundo Canastro, the oldest friend of all, will come, and Joana Canastra will help as much as she can, if only to console Faustina, for they have known each other so long they do not even need to speak, but will simply exchange a look, with no tears shed, because Faustina won't be able to cry and Joana never has, these are mysteries of nature, who can say why it is that this woman can't weep and the other doesn't know how.

António Mau-Tempo, my son, will be here too, he has just got up and is still barefoot, How are you feeling, Father, and I, who know that today is the day of my death, answer, Fine, perhaps he'll believe me, he's leaning on the frame at the foot of the bed, looking at me, he obviously doesn't believe me, you can't convince someone of something if you don't believe it yourself, he's still a long way from fifty, but France really finished him off, as everything does in the end, this pain, this pang, or perhaps it isn't the pang of pain itself but some underlying ache, even I don't know. And my son-in-law Manuel Espada will come, and my daughter Gracinda, they will both be here at my bedside, beside this bed from which I will be carried out, probably by Manuel and António, because they have more strength, but the women will wash me, that's usually women's work, to wash the corpse, ah, the things women have to do, at least I won't hear them crying. And there'll be my granddaughter Maria Adelaide, who has the same blue eyes as me, well, not quite, why am I boasting, my eyes are like dull ashes compared to hers, perhaps when I was younger, when I used to go to dances and was courting Faustina, when I stole her from her parents' house, then my eyes must have been as blue as those that have just walked into the room, Your blessing, Grandfather, how are you feeling, better, I hope, and I make a gesture with my hand, that's all that remains of blessings, none of us believes in them, but it's the custom, and I answer that I'm feeling fine and turn my head toward her so as to see her better, Ah, Maria Adelaide, my granddaughter, although I don't say those words, I think them, it does me good to see her, she's wearing a scarf on her head and a little knitted jacket, her skirt is wet, the umbrella didn't protect her entirely from the rain, and suddenly I feel a terrible urge to weep, because Maria Adelaide took my hand in hers, it was as if we had exchanged eyes, what a daft idea, but a man who is about to die can have whatever ideas he likes, that's his prerogative, he's not going to have many more opportunities to have new ideas or repeat old ones, I wonder what time I will die. And now Faustina is coming over with my bowl of milk, she's going to spoon-feed it to me, I might as well stay hungry today, I would leave the world more lightly, and someone else could drink the milk, what I would really like is for my granddaughter to feed me, but I can't ask that, I can't upset Faustina on my last day, who would console her afterward, when she said, Ah, my dear husband, I didn't give him his milk to drink on the day he died, the grandmother might resent the granddaughter for the rest of her days, perhaps in a little while Maria Adelaide can give me my medicine, according to the doctor's instructions, half an hour after eating, but these are impossible desires. Maria Adelaide is leaving, she just looked in to see how I am, and I'm fine, her father and mother will be here soon, but she's gone already, she's still too young to be a witness to such spectacles, she's only seventeen and has the same blue eyes as me, or have I said that already.

When João Mau-Tempo wakes from the torpor into which he slipped after taking his medicine, which was a real boon, affording him a prolonged respite from the pain and allowing him to sink into what seemed like a natural sleep, but now the pain has returned, and he wakes up moaning, it's like a stake piercing his side, when he recovers full consciousness, he finds himself surrounded by people, there isn't room for anyone else, Faustina and Gracinda are bending over him, Amélia too, so she did come after all, it was the moan that summoned them, and Joana Canastra is standing farther back because she's not a family member, and the men keep their distance too, this is not their moment, they are by the door that opens onto the yard and are blocking the light, Sigismundo Canastro, Manuel Espada and António Mau-Tempo.

If João Mau-Tempo had any doubts, they end here, they all know that today is the day of his death, some of them must have guessed and then passed on the word, but in that case they're not going to hear me groaning, so thought João Mau-Tempo and gritted his teeth, well, that again is a manner of speaking, he can't grit the few teeth he has left, above and below, he has to grit his gums, ah, old age, old age, and yet this man is only sixty-seven, all right, he's no stripling, the years haven't passed in vain, but other men who are older than him are in far better health, yes, but they live far from the latifundio. Anyway, it isn't a matter of having or not having teeth, that isn't the point, the point is stopping the moan or groan when it's still in its infancy and allowing the pain to grow, because that is something one cannot avoid, the point is to take away its voice, to silence it, just as he did more than twenty years ago when he was a prisoner and forced to play statues and withstand the pain in his lower back when they hit him without caring where they struck, his face is drenched in sweat, his limbs tensed, well, his arms at any rate, because he can't feel his legs at all, indeed, at first he thinks perhaps he isn't properly awake, but when he realizes that he is, in fact, fully conscious, he tries to move his feet, just his feet, but they don't move either, he tries to bend his knees, but it's useless, no one has any idea what's going on beneath this sheet, this blanket, it's death, death has lain down with me and no one else has noticed, somehow you imagine that death will walk in through the door or the window, but instead it's actually here in bed with me, and how long has it been here, What time is it. This is a question that everyone asks and which always has an answer, asking what time it is distracts people from thinking about the time left or the time that has already passed, and once the question has been answered, no one thinks any more of it, it was simply the need to interrupt something or to set something else in motion again, there isn't time now to find out, the thing we have been waiting for is here. João Mau-Tempo looks vaguely around him, there are his closest relatives and friends, three men and four women, Faustina, with the string wound around her wrist, Gracinda, who saw men killed in Montemor, Amélia, submissive, but for how much longer, Joana, ever the tough nut, Sigismundo, his comrade, Manuel, grave-faced, António, my son, ah, my son, and these are the people I am about to leave, Where's my granddaughter, and Gracinda answers, her voice tearful, João Mau-Tempo really is about to die, She's gone home to fetch some clothes, someone thought it best she shouldn't be here, she's still so young, and João Mau-Tempo feels a great relief, there's no danger then, if they were all here that would be a bad sign, but now that his granddaughter is missing, he can't die, he will die only when they are all here, if they knew that, they would make sure one of them was always out of the room, what could be simpler.

João Mau-Tempo uses his elbows to drag his body into an upright position, the others rush to help him, but he alone knows that this is the one way he will be able to move his legs, he is sure he will feel better sitting up, it will relieve the tightness he suddenly feels in his chest, not that he's frightened, he knows that nothing will happen until his granddaughter returns, and then perhaps one of the others will leave the room to go and see if the rain is clearing up, it's so hot in here, Open that door, it's the door that opens onto the yard, it's still raining, only in novels do the heavens open like this on these occasions, a white light enters, and suddenly João Mau-Tempo can no longer see it, and even he doesn't know how or why.

MARIA ADELAIDE IS WORKING away from home, over toward Pegões. It's too far for her to travel back and forth, a glance at the map will tell you that it's at least thirty kilometers from Monte Lavre, and the work is killing, as anyone who has ever set foot in a vineyard with a hoe in his hand will tell you, Now get hoeing. And this isn't the kind of work you can finish in a week or so, Maria Adelaide has been here for three months now, and however blue her eyes may be, that counts for nothing. She goes home only every two or three weeks, on a Sunday, and while she's there, she rests in the way women on the latifundio have always rested, by doing some other kind of work, then it's back to the vineyard and the hoe, under the watchful eye of some neighbors who are working there too, much to the relief of her parents, well, Manuel Espada was bound to be concerned about what his only daughter might get up to, especially coming as she does from Monte Lavre, a place rife with distrust when it comes to romantic relationships, a boy can't be seen so much as talking to a girl, and if Maria, say, and Aurora turn out to be flighty creatures who chat away quite happily with boys and laugh at their jokes, you can be sure that they're nothing but flibbertigibbets and hussies. And all because a boy and a girl have been seen talking for a couple of minutes in broad daylight and in the middle of the street. Who knows what they might be hatching, mutter the old and the not so old ladies, and when the gossip reaches the maternal and paternal ears, the usual admonitory questions are asked, who was that boy, what did you say, you be careful, young lady, even if the parents have their own charming love story to tell, as is the case with Manuel Espada and Gracinda Mau-Tempo, although we did not perhaps give the story the detailed description it deserved, but that's what parents are like, they forget so quickly and customs change so slowly. Maria Adelaide is only nineteen and, up until now, has given them no cause for concern, her sole concern being the hard work she has to cope with, but what alternative is there, women weren't born to be princesses, as this story has more than demonstrated.

All days are the same and yet none resemble each other. About halfway through the afternoon, troubling news arrived at the vineyard, no one knew quite what had happened, Something about the army in Lisbon, I heard it on the radio, but if that was the case, you would expect them to know all about it, but it's a mistake to think that it would be easy to find out the facts in a forest of vines only a few short meters from hell, people don't have a radio dangling around their neck as if it were a cowbell, or stuck in their pocket like some singing, talking creature, such frivolities are not allowed, the news came from someone who chanced to be passing and mentioned to the foreman what he had heard on the radio, hence the confusion. The rhythm of work immediately slows, the rise and fall of the hoe seems but an embarrassing distraction, and Maria Adelaide is just as curious as the others, she has her nose up, like a hare that has sensed the presence of a newspaper, as her uncle António Mau-Tempo would say, what's happened, what's happened, but the foreman is no town crier, his job is to watch over and guide the workforce. Come on now, back to work, and since there is no more news, the hoes return to their labors, and those who care about such matters recall that, a month before, the troops in Caldas da Rainha came out onto the streets, although with little result. The afternoon continues and ends, and if they did hear further news, they didn't believe it any more than they had the first lot. In the latifundio, so far from the barracks in the Largo do Carmo in Lisbon,* not a shot has been heard and no one is wandering the fields shouting slogans, it's hard to understand what revolution means and what it involves, and if we were to try and explain, someone would probably comment, with the air of someone who doesn't believe a word we're saying, Ah, so that's what a revolution is.

It is true, however, that the government has been overthrown. When the workers gather together in their barracks, their civil rather than military barracks, everyone knows much more than they had imagined, at least they now have a small radio, one that runs on batteries, screeching and whistling so loudly that, from a meter or so away, you can't understand a word, but it doesn't matter, you get the gist, and then the fever spreads, they're all very excited, talking wildly, So what do we do now, these are the hesitations and anxieties of those waiting in the wings to go on stage, and although there are some who feel happy, others feel not sad exactly, rather, they don't know quite what to think, and if that strikes you as odd, imagine yourself in the latifundio with no voices and no certainties, and then think again. A few more hours of the night passed, and things became clearer, well, that's just a manner of speaking, because, put simply, they knew what had ended, but not what had begun. Then the neighbors who were keeping an eye on Maria Adelaide, the Geraldo family, husband, wife and daughter, an older girl, decided to go back to Monte Lavre the next day, you

---

* The Largo do Carmo barracks was where Marcelo Caetano (appointed prime minister after Salazar suffered a stroke) took refuge, only to find himself surrounded by revolutionary troops.

might say this was a whim of theirs were it not for the very sensible reason they give, namely, that they wanted to be at home, they might lose two or three days' work but at least they'd have a better idea of what was going on, rather than being stuck here in the back of beyond, they asked Maria Adelaide if she wanted to go with them, she had, after all, been entrusted to their care, Your father will be glad to have you back, but this was said simply to say something, because all they knew of Manuel Espada was that he was a good man and a good worker, and as for any suspicions they might have about him, these were only of the kind that arise in all small villages, where people are always guessing at what they don't know. Others had also decided to return to their villages, they would go and come straight back, so many of them, in fact, that the foreman had no choice but to let them, what else could he do. Unfortunately, in the midst of what seemed to be the best possible news, the radio suddenly lost its voice and became a catarrhal growl so low that you couldn't make out a single word, why did the stupid thing have to pick today of all days to go wrong. For the rest of the night, the workers' barracks was an island lost in the latifundio sea, surrounded by a country that did not want to go to bed, exchanging news and rumors, rumors and news, as tends to happen in these situations, until finally, having nothing more to hope for from the defunct machine, they went to their respective mats and tried their best to sleep.

Early the next morning, they set off for the nearest road, a good league from where they were working, praying to the celestial powers who rule over such things that the bus would come along with a few empty seats, and when it appeared, they saw that it had, with practice you can tell these things at once, from a quick head-count and from the driver's oddly obliging air. This is the bus that goes to Vendas Novas, and only the Geraldo family and Maria Adelaide get on, the others from Monte Lavre have decided not to go, preferring to err on the side of caution or unwilling to commit themselves, or perhaps it's that they need the money even more than their colleagues do. Those heading for other destinations remain by the side of the road, what happened to them, what fate, good or bad, awaited them, we will never know. There is little traffic, and so the journey passes quickly, and their more urgent anxieties are dissipated right there and then, for driver, conductor and passengers are all of one mind, the government has been overthrown, no more Tomás and no more Marcelo, but who's in charge now, on that point the general harmony founders, nobody quite knows, someone mentions a junta but others weren't so sure, what's a junta, what kind of a name is junta for a government, there must be some mistake. The bus drives into Vendas Novas, and given the number of people in the street, you'd think it was a public holiday, the horn has to really open its lungs to make its way down the narrow street, and when we finally reach the main square, seeing the troops there with their martial air is enough to give a person goosepimples all over, and Maria Adelaide, who is young and has the dreams appropriate to someone of her age and condition, feels as if her legs had been cut from under her as she gazes out the window at the soldiers outside the barracks, at the cannons decorated with sprigs of eucalyptus, and the Geraldo family are saying to her, Aren't you coming, it's as if she had lived her entire life with her eyes closed and has only now opened them, first she has to understand the nature of light, and these are things that take much longer to explain than to feel, the proof being that when she reaches Monte Lavre and embraces her father, she will discover that she knows everything about his life, even though those things had only ever been spoken of obliquely, Where's Pa gone, Oh, he had some business to deal with some way away, he won't be back tonight, and when he did come home, there was no point asking him what that business was, first because daughters don't interrogate their fathers, and second because when mysteries belong in the outside world, it's best to leave them there. The narrator would like to recount events as they happened, but he can't, for example, just a moment ago, Maria Adelaide was sitting glued to her seat on the bus, apparently feeling quite faint, and suddenly here she is standing in the square, having been the first to get off the bus, well, that's youth for you. And although she is with the Geraldo family, she doesn't live under their wing, she is free to cross the road and take a closer look at the soldiers and wave to them, and the soldiers see her, struggle briefly with the awkwardness of being men trained to respond with weapons and possibly answer for that response, then, having won that battle and thrown discipline to the winds, wave back, well, it isn't every day you see such a pair of blue eyes.

Meanwhile, Geraldo Senior had found some transport to take them to Monte Lavre, a normally difficult enterprise, but today, ah, if only it was always like this, everyone is our friend, it's only a small truck and a bit of a squeeze, but we can cope with a little discomfort, these people are accustomed to sleeping on a board, with a plow handle for a pillow, the driver will charge them only the price of the gas, if that, At least let us buy you a drink, All right, but only because I don't want to be rude, and no one is surprised when Maria Adelaide bursts into tears, she will weep tonight as well when she hears a voice say over the radio, Viva Portugal, either then, or perhaps it was yesterday, when they first heard the news, or when she crossed the street to take a closer look at the soldiers, or when they waved to her, or when she embraced her father, she doesn't know herself, but at that point she realizes that life has changed and says, I just wish Grandpa, but she can't finish her sentence, gripped by the despair of knowing that she cannot bring him back.

We mustn't think, though, that the whole of the latifundio is singing the praises of the revolution. Let us remember what the narrator said about this Mediterranean sea with its barracudas and other perils, as well as the occasional unctuous monkfish.

The whole Lamberto Horques dynasty is gathered together, sitting at their respective round tables, with glum, scowling faces, the less furious members speak hesitantly, cautiously, if, nevertheless, yet, however, perhaps, this is what passes for the great unanimity of the latifundio, What do you think, Father Agamedes, this is a question that would normally never lack for an appropriate answer, but the prudence of the church is infinite, and Father Agamedes, though he is God's humble servant sent to evangelize souls, knows a lot about the church and about prudence, Our kingdom is not of this world, render unto Caesar the things which are Caesar's and unto God the things that are God's, a sower went out to sow his seed, pay no attention, when confronted by such tricky questions, Father Agamedes does tend to go off on a tangent and speak in parables, to gain time until he receives his instructions from the bishop, still, you can always count on him to say something. One cannot, alas, count on Leandro Leandres, who died last year in his bed, having received the sacraments as he deserved, meanwhile, all over the country, his many successors, associates, brothers or superiors have, we learn, been arrested, those, that is, who did not flee, and in Lisbon, we hear, shots were exchanged before they surrendered, people died,* what, I wonder, will happen to them now. There is little news of the national guard, except that it is keeping a low profile and awaiting orders, Corporal Tacabo went, shamefaced, to Norberto's house to say just this, cringing as he did so, as if he were naked, and he left as he had arrived, with eyes downcast, struggling to find an appropriate face to wear as he walked through Monte Lavre, past these men who look at him and watch him from afar, not that he's afraid, a corporal in the national guard

---

* Presumably a reference to an incident that took place during the Carnation Revolution in 1974 near the PIDE headquarters in Rua António Maria Cardoso, where a few desperate PIDE agents opened fire on the troops and the crowds surrounding the building. Four people in the crowd were killed. These were the only casualties in an otherwise bloodless coup.

is never afraid, but the air of the latifundio seems suddenly to have become unbreathable, as if a storm were brewing.

And then the talk turns to the first of May, a conversation that is repeated every year, but now it's a vociferous public debate, with people recalling how only last year the celebrations had to be organized in secret, with the organizers constantly having to regroup, getting in touch with those in the know, encouraging the undecided, reassuring the fearful, and there are those who still can't believe that the first of May will be celebrated as freely as the newspapers claim, the poor distrust charity. It's not charity, declare Sigismundo Canastro and Manuel Espada, opening a newspaper from Lisbon, It says here that the first of May is to be openly celebrated as a national holiday, And what about the guards, insist those with good memories, They'll have to watch us go strolling past them, who would think such a thing would ever happen, the guards standing silently by while we shout hooray for the first of May.

And since we always have to overlay what we are allowed with what we imagine, if not, we do not deserve the bread that we eat, people started saying that we should hang bedspreads out the windows and deck everything with flowers, as we do for religious processions, any moment now they'll be sweeping the streets and whitewashing the houses, that's how easy it is to climb the steps of contentment. This, however, is also how human dramas are created, well, it's an exaggeration to call them dramas, but they are genuine quandaries, what if I have no bedspreads in my house and no garden full of carnations and roses, whose idea was that. Maria Adelaide partly shares this anxiety, but being young and optimistic, she tells her mother that they must do something, if they don't have a bedspread, then a large white tablecloth will do, draped over the door, a flag of peace in the latifundio, any civilian passing by should, out of respect, doff his hat, and any guard or soldier stand at attention and salute in homage outside the door of Manuel Espada, a good worker and a good man. And don't worry about flowers, Mother, I'll go to the spring at Amieiro and pick some of the wild flowers that cover the valleys and hills in May, and I'll bring back some orange blossoms too, that way our front door will be as finely decked out as any castle balcony, we won't be seen to be inferior to anyone, because we are the equal of everyone.

Then Maria Adelaide went down to the spring, although why she chose that particular place she herself doesn't know, after all, as she said, the hills and valleys are covered in flowers, she takes the path that leads between two hedges, and even there she had only to reach out her hand, but she doesn't, these are ancient decisions that run in the blood, she wants flowers picked in this cool place, with its abundant bracken, and farther on, in an especially sunny spot, there are daisies, the very daisies whose name changed when António Mau-Tempo picked one for his niece, Maria Adelaide, on the day she was born. She has her arms full of greenery now, a constellation of suns with yellow hearts, now she will go back up the path, she will cut some orange blossoms from the branches overhanging the wall, but she feels a sudden strange pang, I don't know quite what I feel, I'm not ill, I've never felt so well, so happy, perhaps it's the smell of the ferns clasped to my chest, I do sweet violence to them and they to me. Maria Adelaide sat down on the low wall by the spring, as if she were waiting for someone. Her lap was full of flowers, but no one came.

They're interesting, these stories of enchanted springs, with Moorish girls dancing in the moonlight and Christian girls left raped and weeping on the bracken, and all I can say is that anyone who doesn't think so has clearly lost the key to his own heart. However, only a short time after April and May, the same harsh measures returned to the latifundio, not as applied by the guards or the PIDE, for the latter has been abolished and the former live shut up in their barracks, peering at the street through closed windows, or, if they must go out, they keep close to the houses, hoping not to be seen. The harsh measures are the usual ones, it makes one feel like turning back the pages and repeating the words we said previously, The wheat was ripe but no one was harvesting it, they weren't allowed to, the fields have been abandoned, and when the men go to ask for work, they are told, There is no work, what kind of liberation is this, people are saying that the war in Africa is nearly over, and yet the war on the latifundio rages on. All that talk of change and hope, the soldiers leaving their barracks, the cannons decked with eucalyptus and scarlet carnations, call them red, madam, say red, because we can now, on the radio and the television they preach democracy and equality, and yet when I want work, there is none, tell me, what kind of revolution is this. The guards are lolling in the sun now, the way cats do when they're sharpening their claws, the same people continue to dictate the laws of the latifundio so that the same people obey them, I, Manuel Espada, I, António Mau-Tempo, I, Sigismundo Canastro, I, José Medronho of the scarred face, I, Gracinda Espada and my daughter Maria Adelaide, who wept when she heard them say Viva Portugal, I, the man and the woman of this latifundio, heir to only the tools of my trade, if they're not as spent and broken as I am, desolation has returned to the fields of the Alentejo, there will be more blood spilled.

Don't give them any work and then we'll see who's strongest, says Norberto to Clariberto, it's simply a matter of letting time pass, and the day will come when once again they'll be eating out of our hand, these are the scornful, rancorous words of someone who has just had a nasty fright and who, for some time, remained meekly closeted in his own little domestic shell, whispering with his wife and relatives about the dreadful news of revolution emanating from Lisbon, the rabble in the streets, the demonstrations about everything and nothing, the flags and banners, about how, on the very first day, the police were forced to hand over their weapons, poor things, a grave insult to a fine body of men, who had rendered them so many services and could still do so, but it's like a wave, you see, you mustn't confront it full on, because while that might look like courage, it is, in fact, rank foolishness, no, crouch down as low as you can and it will pass right over, almost without noticing you, having found no obstacle to strike, and now you're safe, out of reach of the break line, the foam and the current, these are fishermen's terms, but how often must we repeat that the latifundio is an inland sea, with its barracuda, its piranha, its giant squid, and if you have workers, dismiss them, keep only the man in charge of the pigs and the sheep, and the estate guard in case the herdsman gets uppity.

The fate of the wheatfields is clear, the crops are lying here on the ground, and it won't be long before it's time to start sowing, what will Gilberto do, let's go to his house and ask him, after all, it's a free country and we all have to give an account of ourselves, Tell your master there are some people here who want to know what he's doing, the first rains have fallen and it's time for sowing to begin, and while the maid goes off to get an answer, we stand at the door, because we haven't been asked inside, and the maid returns and declares rudely, I hope she isn't the Amélia Mau-Tempo mentioned in this story, The master says it's none of your business, the land is his, and if you come here again, he'll call the guards, and with that she slams the door in our face, they wouldn't even do that to a vagrant, because the masters are scared stiff of such wanderers, fearing that they might have a knife. There's no point asking again, Gilberto isn't sowing, Norberto isn't sowing, and if someone of another name is sowing, that's because he's still afraid that the soldiers might come and start asking questions, What's going on here, but there are other ways of swatting these flies, by smiling and pretending to oblige, yes, of course, and then doing exactly the opposite, encouraging intrigue, withdrawing money from the bank and sending it abroad, there's always someone happy to do this in exchange for a reasonable commission, or stashing it away in the car somewhere, the border guards will close their eyes, poor things, they don't want to waste their time crawling underneath the chassis or removing the mudguards, they're not young lads anymore, they're worthy public servants, they have to keep their uniforms clean, and thus five or ten or twenty million escudos or the family jewels, the family silver and gold or whatever, slip out of the country, no problem. What hopeless fools they were, these workers, who, seeing the olive trees laden with fruit, ripe and black and glossy, as if the oil were already oozing out, finally, after much thought and discussion, what's the best way to go about this, picked and sold the olives, then took the money they would have earned, charging the going rate, and gave the rest to the latifundio owner. Who gave them permission, it's a shame the estate guard didn't catch them, they should have been shot, that would teach them to meddle in other people's business, Sir, the olives were ready to be picked, if we had waited any longer, they would have all gone to waste, here's the money left over after we've taken our day's pay, it's more than the amount we set aside for ourselves, the sums are easy enough to do, But I didn't give you permission, and wouldn't have even if you'd asked, We gave ourselves permission. This was one case, a sign that the wind had changed direction, but how could we save the fruits of the earth if Adalberto cut the corn down with machines, if Angilberto let the cattle into the fields, if Ansberto set fire to the wheat, so much bread lost, so much hunger.

Standing at the top of the tower, resting his warrior's hands on the ramparts, his conquistador's hands, grown calloused from gripping his sword, Norberto looked on everything he had made and saw that it was good, and then, as if he had lost track of the number of days, he did not rest, Those devils in Lisbon may be willing to ruin the legacy our grandparents left us, but here on the latifundio we respect the sacred fatherland and the sacred faith, send in Sergeant Armamento, Things are going much better, sir, send in

Father Agamedes, You're looking very well, Father Agamedes, you look younger, That must be because I have been praying for your excellency's health and the preservation of our land, Of my land, Father Agamedes, Yes, sir, of your land, that's what the sergeant here says too, Yes, those were the orders I received from Dom João the First, and I have passed them on to generation upon generation of sergeants, but while these three have been talking in the warmth and shelter of the house, winter has arrived and bitten the workers, and just because they're used to it doesn't mean they feel it any less keenly, The bosses are the owners of the land and of those who work it, We are even less important than the dogs that live in the big house and in all the big houses, they eat every day and from a full bowl, no one would let an animal die of hunger, Well, if you don't know how to look after an animal, you shouldn't keep one, But with men and women it's different, I'm not a dog and I haven't eaten in two days, and these men who have come here to make their demands are a pack of dogs who have been barking for a long time, any day now we'll stop barking and we'll bite, just like those red ants, the ones that raise their heads like dogs, yes, we'll learn from them, see those pincers, if my skin wasn't so tough and calloused from wielding a scythe, I'd be bleeding.

This is empty talk, which relieves one's frustrations but changes nothing, for the moment, it makes no difference whether I'm unemployed or not, I mean what is the point of working, the overseer arrives with the cynical air of one who doesn't care, who knows how deep his cynicism goes, and says, There's no money this week, you'll have to be patient, maybe next week, meanwhile, in his pocket, Dona Maria the First and Dom João the Second* are singing a duet, and a week later, he says exactly the same thing, and one or two or three or four or six weeks later, there's still not so much as a whiff of money. The boss has no cash, the government

---

* These figures appeared on the bank notes of the time.

won't allow the banks to release it, no one believes the overseer, of course, he's been lying for so many centuries now that he doesn't need to use his imagination, but the government should come here and explain the situation, there's no point setting it down in newspapers that we can't read, and they talk so quickly on the television that by the time we've understood one word, they've gabbled another hundred more, what did they say, and on the radio we can't see people's faces, and how can I believe anything you say if I can't see your face.

And somewhere on the latifundio, history will record the exact spot, the workers occupied a piece of land. Just so as to have some work, that's all, may my right hand wither away if I'm lying. And then other workers turned up on another estate and said, We've come to work. And this happened first here and then there, and as in the spring, when a solitary daisy blooms in a field, always assuming there's no Maria Adelaide to come along and pick it, thousands more are born on a single day, where's the first one gone, and all of them are white, their faces turned to the sun, it's like the earth's bridal day.

However, these people are not white but swarthy, a colony of ants spreading over the latifundio as if the land were covered in sugar, you've never seen so many ants, all with their heads raised, I've received bad news from my cousins and from other relatives, Father Agamedes, God did not listen to your prayers, to think the day would come when I would witness such misfortunes, that I should be put to the test like this, seeing the land of my ancestors in the hands of these thieves, it's the end of the world when people start attacking property, the divine and profane foundation of our material and spiritual civilization, You mean secular, my lady, not profane, and forgive me for correcting you, No, profane is the word, for what they are doing is profanation, they'll do the same as they did in Santiago do Escoural, mark my words, but they'll pay for it, in fact, we were talking about that just the other day, what

will become of us, We must be patient, Senhora Dona Clemência, infinitely patient, for who are we to question the Lord's plans
and his wayward paths, for only he knows how to write straight on
crooked lines, perhaps he is casting us down in order to raise us up
tomorrow, perhaps this punishment will be followed by our terrestrial and celestial reward, each in its appointed time and place,
Amen.

This, albeit using different words, is what Lamberto is saying
to Corporal Tacabo, who is a shadow of his former martial self,
It doesn't seem possible, the national guard simply standing by
to witness such apocalyptic events, allowing the invasion of lands
that it is their duty to defend on my behalf, without so much as
lifting a finger, not a shot do they fire, not even a well-aimed kick
or punch or blow with the butt of a rifle, they don't set the dogs on
these idlers' backsides, what's the point of having such expensive,
imported dogs, is this what we pay our taxes for, taxes I have long
since ceased paying, by the way, oh, we're on the slippery slope all
right, I'm moving abroad, to Brazil, to Spain, to Switzerland, so
reassuringly neutral, far from this shameful country, You're quite
right, Senhor Lamberto, but the national guard of which I am a
corporal has its hands tied, with no orders what can we do, we
were used to taking orders and they no longer come from the people who used to issue them, and just between you and me, sir, the
commander of the guards has gone over to the enemy, I know I'm
breaking all the rules by saying this, but perhaps one day they'll
promote me to sergeant, and then, I swear, I'll pay them back in
spades. These are empty threats, they relieve one's frustration but
change nothing, meanwhile, let us not forget the morning round of
gymnastics and weapons instruction, How's my heart, Doctor, De-
fective, Just as well.

IN THE INLAND SEA of the latifundio the waves continue to roll in. One day, Manuel Espada went to see Sigismundo Canastro, the two of them then sought out António Mau-Tempo, and these three then went to find Damião Canelas, We need to have a talk, before calling on José Medronho and Pedro Calção, who made a sixth, and that was their first meeting. At the second meeting, another four voices joined them, two male, Joaquim Caroço and Manuel Martelo, and two female, Emília Profeta and Maria Adelaide Espada, which is her preferred name, and all spoke in secret, and since they needed a spokesperson, they chose Manuel Espada. In the following two weeks, the men went for seemingly casual walks about the estate and, using the old familiar methods, left a word here, another there, discussed and agreed to a plan, for we each have our own war to fight, but let's forgive them this belligerent vocabulary, then they moved on to the second phase, which, one hot midsummer's night, involved summoning the foremen on the estates still being worked and saying, Tomorrow at eight o'clock, all the workers, wherever they are, should get into trailers and head for the Mantas estate, which we're going to occupy, and having gained the agreement of the foremen, who had been spoken to individually beforehand, and having warned many of those who would be the principal combatants in the battle, they all went off to sleep their last night in prison.

This is a just sun. It burns and sears the dry stubble, which is the yellow of washed-clean bones or like the tanned hide of old wheatfields scorched by excessive heat and immoderate rains. The machines flow forth from every workplace, the advance guard of armored vehicles, oh, dear, this bellicose language, it creeps in everywhere, they're not tanks but very slow-moving tractors, intending to meet up with more tractors coming from other places, those that have already met call to each other, and the column grows in size, it's even larger up ahead, the trailers are laden with people, some, the younger ones, are walking, for them it's like a party, and then they reach the Mantas estate, where one hundred and fifty men are cutting cork, they all join forces, and on each parcel of land that they occupy, they appoint a group of workers to be in charge, the column is more than five hundred strong, men and women alike, now there are six hundred, soon there will be a thousand, it's a pilgrimage retracing the paths of martyrdom, following the stations of this particular cross.

After Mantas, they go to Vale da Canseira, to Relvas, to Monte da Areia, to Fonte Pouca, to Serralha, to Pedra Grande, and at each farm they take the keys and draw up an inventory, we are workers, not thieves, not that there is anyone there to contradict them, because in each place they occupy, in each house, room, cellar, barn, stable, hayloft, pen, run, corral, pigsty, chicken coop, cistern and irrigation tank, there are no Norbertos or Gilbertos to be seen, whether talking or singing, silent or weeping, who knows where they have gone. The guards stay in their barracks, the angels are busy sweeping heaven, it's a day of revolution, how many of these workers are there.

Overhead, the red kite is counting, one million, not to mention those we can't see, for the blindness of the living always overlooks those who went before, one thousand living and one hundred thousand dead, or two million sighs rising up from the ground, pick any number and it will always be too small if we do the sums from too great a distance, the dead cling to the sides of the trailers, peering in to see if they recognize anyone, someone close to their body and heart, and if they fail to find the person they're looking for, they join those traveling on foot, my brother, my mother, my wife and my husband, which is why we can see Sara da Conceição over there, carrying a bottle of wine and a rag, and Domingos Mau-Tempo with the noose still around his neck, and here's Joaquim Carranca, who died sitting at the door of his house, and Tomás Espada, hand in hand with his wife Flor Martinha, what kept you so long, how is it that the living notice nothing, they think they're alone, that they're carrying on their task as living people, the dead are dead and buried, that's what they think, but the dead often visit, usually in dribs and drabs, but there are days, rare, it's true, when they all come out, and who could keep them in their graves on a day like this, when the tractors are thundering across the latifundio and there are no words that need go unspoken, Mantas and Pedra Grande, Vale da Canseira, Monte da Areia, Fonte Pouca, little water and much hunger, Serralha, home of the sow thistle, and so on over hill and vale, and here, at this turn in the road, stands João Mau-Tempo, smiling, he's probably waiting for someone, or he can't stir from the spot, perhaps because when he died he couldn't move his legs, we take with us to our death all our ills, including the final ones, but no, we're quite wrong, João Mau-Tempo has had his youthful legs restored to him, and he's leaping about, he's a dancer in full flight, and he's going to sit down beside a very old deaf lady, Faustina, my wife, you and I ate bread and sausage one winter's night and you got your skirt wet, ah, those were the days.

João Mau-Tempo puts his arm of invisible smoke about Faustina's shoulders, and although she hears and feels nothing, she begins, hesitantly at first, to sing the chorus of an old song, she remembers the days when she used to dance with her husband João, who died three years ago, may he rest in peace, an unnecessary wish on Faustina's part, but how is she to know. And when we look farther off, higher up, as high up as a red kite, we can see Augusto Pintéu, the one who died along with his mules on a stormy night, and behind him, almost hanging on to him, his wife Cipriana, and the guard José Calmedo, coming from other parts and dressed in civilian clothes, and others whose names we may not know, although we know about their lives. Here they all are, the living and the dead. And ahead of them, bounding along as a hunting dog should, goes Constante, how could he not be here, on this unique and new-risen day.

Translator's Acknowledgments

The translator would like to thank Tânia Ganho, João Magueijo, Rhian Atkin, David Frier, and Ben Sherriff for all their help and advice.